Resounding acclaim for
SARAH LANGAN's
chilling and extraordinary debut novel
THE KEEPER

"A beautiful, suspenseful novel . . . that sets out
to do exactly what it should: scare the reader
with a combination of well-crafted prose
and page-turning velocity."
Baltimore Sun

"Sarah Langan's debut novel *THE KEEPER* kept
me up, late into the night . . . I'm hoping for a
whole shelf of novels by Langan,
and many other sleepless nights."
Kelly Link, author of *Magic for Beginners*

"Deft and disturbing, *THE KEEPER* twists
expectations into surreal surprises.
Sarah Langan's tale of haunted lives
and landscapes is hypnotic reading."
Douglas E. Winter

"Richly populated with small-town characters at
varying stages of emotional crisis, from numb
puzzlement to unshakable bitterness to abject
despair . . . it's the only horror story I've read
recently that finds adequate metaphors for the
self-destructive properties of anger."
New York Times Book Review

Books by Sarah Langan

THE MISSING
THE KEEPER

THE MISSING

SARAH LANGAN

HARPER

An Imprint of HarperCollins*Publishers*

AUG 17 2009 *M T P*

P B

This is a work of fiction. Names, characters, places, and incidents are products of the author's imagination or are used fictitiously and are not to be construed as real. Any resemblance to actual events, locales, organizations, or persons, living or dead, is entirely coincidental.

HARPER
An Imprint of HarperCollins*Publishers*
10 East 53rd Street
New York, New York 10022-5299

Copyright © 2007 by Sarah Langan
ISBN: 978-0-06-087291-5
ISBN-10: 0-06-087291-8

First Harper paperback printing: October 2007

Printed in the United States of America

Visit Harper paperbacks on the World Wide Web at
www.harpercollins.com

10 9 8 7 6 5 4 3 2 1

For J. T. Petty

Acknowledgments

Thanks to my agents, Joe Veltre and Sarah Self. For their unflagging support they deserve medals. Thanks also to my editors, Sarah Durand and Piers Blofeld, for their advice, honesty, and, ahem, patience. Thanks, finally, to Pam Spengler-Jaffee, for her diligence.

I'm indebted (probably literally) to the folks at the NYU Environmental Health Science Program, particularly Becky Gluskin for her good cheer, Judy Zelikoff for her Organ System Toxicology class, George Thurston, whose weather class inspired Maddie, and Gerry Solomon for letting me into his program.

Thanks also to my writing group Who Wants Cake and its members: Dan Braum, K. Z. Perry, Stefan Petruca, Lee Thomas, and the captain, Nicholas Kaufmann. For their generosity, I'm also grateful to Ramsey Campbell, Ray Garton, Jack Ketchum, Tim Lebbon, Kelly Link, Peter Straub, and Douglas E. Winter.

Finally, a few people who've been there along the way: Milda Devoe, Jon Evans, Michelle and Erik Gustavson, Marybeth Brennan Magee and her family, Brennans and Magees, alike, Debbie Marcus, Laura and James Masterson, Marianna McGillicuddy, Kate

Quinn, my personal hero Artie Schupbach, Lori and Ryan Stattenfield, Arlaina Tibensky, J. T. Petty, Mom and Dad, who let me use their house as a writing colony, Chris, Michael, and the Virginia, Massachusetts, D.C., Syracuse, and Amityville Langans. I'm very grateful that none of you requested, upon reading my work, that I go to a shrink. Please refrain from doing so at Thanksgiving.

Crises, precipitate change.
—*Virus, Deltron 3030*

PROLOGUE

WINTER

In winter the dark creeps up on you. I've hardly finished my dinner and the sky right now is black. There is no electricity anymore, so I navigate at night with candles. The flames throw shadows that assume peculiar and familiar shapes. All the animals are dead, even the squirrels and rabbits. Come to think of it, I have not even heard a cricket. Through the cracks in my windows and chimney flue, there is only the howling wind, and underneath that, barely discernible screams.

But let me begin at the beginning: once upon a time.

Once upon a time Corpus Christi was a sleepy, contented place. Early mornings were silent affairs, disturbed only by the sounds of spoons stirring coffee and alarms set to talk radio with the volume turned low. We were a tightly knit community, and during the summers our children roamed free. At night the younger ones played manhunt on front lawns while the older sneaked beer by the river. They each thought they were getting away with something, as if the rest of us did not remember with fondness those same rites of passage.

Unlike the rest of Mid-Maine, where the only queues to be found were at the unemployment offices, Corpus Christi thrived. Our hospital had the best cancer research facilities on the East Coast, and lured doctors from as far south as New York. We were scientists and bankers, artists and teachers, and our stores were all family owned. Each year Wal-Mart tried to plant its roots along the side of our highway, but in a unanimous vote every spring, we salted the earth.

But even before the bad business with James Walker, there were signs. That spring, a fire at the Clott Paper Mill in nearby Bedford fanned sulfurous clouds into our skies that burned our eyes for days. The chemistry of the woods changed after that, and our trees began to die. While there was no unemployment line, state funding cuts and rampant lawsuits year after year took their toll, and we watched our hospital decline. Fresh coats of paint, new slate roofs, dents in cars that needed to be hammered right again, were all postponed for one year, and then another, and sometimes another. As if we'd been infected by Maine's economic disease, we knew that layoffs and closed shops were soon to follow. But back then, our welcome signs were bright and cheerful, and our streets paved, and our lawns neat and green. We took pride in where we came from, and we expected good things from our futures.

Still, there were signs. The summer before James Walker, my husband and I stopped sleeping through the night. I used to sit in my kitchen with a cup of milky Lipton tea until chirping birds signaled the coming dawn. I could feel something expectant waiting to open its eyes inside me, as if my body knew what my mind could not guess. If I look hard enough, I can find all kinds of signs. On a family vacation, I can remember seeing my daughter swim out past the breaking waves. It was not her hands, but her hair that sank last. I hesitated before I jumped in after her and pulled her out.

Perhaps a part of me knew what my mind could not guess, and had wanted to save myself a broken heart.

But I digress.

I have a story for you. Forgive me if it seems I'm telling you things that I could not possibly know. This is a small town, and you hear gossip. Besides, the dead do speak.

So gather round, as I used to tell the children during story hour. Gather round.

PART ONE

CONTAMINATION

ONE

Where Are You Going,
Where Have You Been?

"George?" Lois Larkin called out to her fourth-grade class. Her voice was muffled, and she held the attendance book close to her nose. It was a sunny Tuesday morning in September, and the clock tower had not yet chimed nine A.M.

"Uh huh," George answered. He was chewing on a red Crayola.

Lois raised her wet eyes from the book. "George, don't eat that. It'll make you thick." Then she took a deep breath, just like she'd learned in speech therapy, and corrected herself: "Sick."

George pulled the crayon out of his mouth. Its entire top half was missing, and his teeth were coated in red wax. Lois shook her head. George Sanford: not the brightest of God's children.

Lois Larkin was twenty-nine years old, and had been teaching fourth grade since she'd moved back to Corpus Christi seven years ago. Her figure was slender but curvy—what the barflies at the Dew Drop Inn called "slammin'." When the boys and even the girls in her class daydreamed out the window, they were usually fantasizing about the feel of her long, black hair, and the scent of her NILLA Wafer–flavored breath.

Kids loved Lois. Parents loved her. Drunks hooted happily at her. Even animals flocked to her. Lois was lovely save for one flaw. The space between her two front teeth was so wide she could cram a pencil through the gap. She'd submitted to six years of braces through middle and high school to close it, but nary a month after the metal cage in her mouth was clipped, her teeth migrated to their nascent terra firma, and the gap returned. When she was excited she lisped, and spit sprayed through the fissure, landing like an indifferent plague on the faces of friends and foes alike. Today, for example, the open page of her attendance book was damp.

"Jameth Walker?" Lois asked.

"Here," James called.

"No kicking, James. Feet thraight ahead . . . straight ahead."

"Yeth, Mith Loith," James sang. His smug grin spread from ear to ear. Lois's first instinct was to crack the boy on the head with her soft book, but instead she continued.

"Caroline?"

"Here, Miss Lois!" Caroline waved both hands in the air and squirmed in her chair like she had to take a piss. It occurred to Lois that maybe she didn't like kids so much.

Lois blotted her eyes with a snot-covered tissue. Took a deep breath. Said the words slowly. "Boys and girls, I have thomething called an allergy. Do you know what that is? Ith when you sneeze a lot and your eyes get all watery. For some people, like Johnnie, dogs make them sneeze. For me, ith mold and ragweed. I'm not crying. Do you understand?"

They nodded. Caroline raised her hand and moaned: "*Oh! Oh!*"

"Yeth, Caroline."

"I have an allergy to penicillin. That's an antibiotic, for, like, if you get AIDS."

Lois nodded. "That's very serious, Caroline, and good to know. Now, ith Kerry here today?"

"Yes."

"Alex Fullbright? . . . Michael Fullbright?"

The list went on.

In fact, Lois was lying. She wasn't suffering from allergies. She was crying. But today was the big class trip, and though she'd wanted to stay home, there hadn't been time to call in a substitute. So here she was, lisping her way through attendance and praying that some snot-nose like James Walker didn't raise his hand and finally point out the obvious—she wasn't wearing her engagement ring.

In hindsight, what happened wasn't surprising. A part of her had always known that Ronnie and Noreen were no good. When they used to tell her about some heart-breakingly stupid decision they'd made, like spending their paychecks on lottery tickets instead of rent, the evidence had been as plain as the gap between her teeth; these people were useless. But then she'd forget, because Ronnie's house was a sty that smelled like stale milk, and who else would remember to open the windows so he didn't get a headache? Because sure, Noreen was mean as Joan Crawford on diet pills, but deep down, she had a huge heart, right? You just had to look with a magnifying glass. Besides, Lois wasn't perfect, either. She lisped, collected bugs, and snacked on raw hamburger meat when she was premenstrual, for Christ's sake.

Besides, it wasn't their fault her life turned out so

crappy. She should never have moved back to Corpus Christi after college. At the University of New Hampshire, she'd been happy. Unlike in high school, where she'd felt like a big-boned giant, college men had asked her on dates. She found friends who shared her love for the Science and Nature category of the Genus edition of Trivial Pursuit. She stopped covering her mouth when she talked, because it turned out that so long as she apologized, people were okay with an occasional ocean spray.

But during the winter of her senior year, her father had been driving down the road that connected Corpus Christi to Bedford. His Nissan hatchback skidded on black ice and flipped once before it landed in the woods. The dashboard crumbled, shattering both his legs. It happened late at night, and his frozen body wasn't found until the morning. No one could explain why he'd left a warm bed and his slumbering wife, Jodi Larkin. He had no secret girlfriend, and he didn't smoke or drink. He'd still been belted into the driver's side of the car when the snowplow driver found him. Even with a set of broken legs, most people would have crawled out the open passenger door and searched for help, but not Russell Larkin. They found his cell phone in his pocket, reception clear as a bell, but he never made a single call. Probably, it wasn't a suicide. He'd just wanted to go out for a drive, feel the night air, and look at the stars. Yes, she'd reassured herself; it probably wasn't a suicide.

After the funeral her grades sank like granite quarry stones. She only barely graduated college. Didn't bother with the applications for PhD programs she'd intended to send out, or make plans for a job that summer. "Don't you love me anymore?" Roddy Chase, her boyfriend of two years, had asked the night before they marched in caps and gowns down College Square's Dimond Hill. They were sitting on the brick stoop outside her dorm, and she knew she was supposed to tell him that his deep voice turned her knees to putty, but there hadn't been room in her heart for love right then. There'd only been room for her dad's gravity-stricken face at the open-casket funeral. Roddy's shoulders had drooped as he'd walked away, like the top of his spine had turned to Jell-O, and that had reminded her of her dad, too. The next thing she knew, she was living at home again, substitute teaching at the elementary school, and hiding her mother's empty bottles of Gordon's Gin in the recycling bin under liters of the Poland Spring they'd started using after the fire.

Corpus Christi was a pretty place, and great for kids, but if you wanted to do something other than work at the hospital or spend your parents' money, you moved to a big city. Lois got bored after a few months, so one night on her way home from work she ducked into the Dew Drop Inn. She'd planned to sit in a corner and sip an apple cosmo for an hour, and then go home. If things had gone according to that plan, her life might have turned out differently. She might have gone back to school, or at least applied for a job teaching high school biology. But life never happens the way it should.

At the Dew Drop Inn, she'd spotted her old high school friend Noreen Castillo. Noreen nursed geriatric patients at the Corpus Christi Medical Center. She was smart and funny and mean. In high school Noreen used to say things like: "Your ass looks fat in that," or "The stories you tell: They're funny but they take too long. People stop listening and then you look stupid. I'm only telling you because we're friends." So there Noreen was, perched over the bar at the Dew Drop

Inn, and Lois knew she should have smiled and kept
walking, because the girl was a nuclear reactor full of
trouble. But Lois was lonely, and Noreen was company. They had a few drinks together that night, and
the night after that. Pretty soon, it became a regular
thing.

Ronnie Koehler and his friends went to the Dew Drop
Inn, too. Ronnie's 1996 season record of twenty-one
home runs still stood at Corpus Christi, and because of
it TJ Wainright poured him every third Budweiser draft
for free. Ronnie wasn't a jerk about how popular he'd
been back in school. He wasn't bitter about it, either,
which Lois thought was pretty admirable since people
had expected him to go pro. When Ronnie's high school
sweetheart went loco and left him for an ashram in
Woodstock, Noreen chased after him like a horny mon-
key. She got drunk and draped herself over his shoulders
like the only way she'd let go was if he carried her home.
But it was Lois that Ronnie eventually asked on a movie
date.

She should have turned Ronnie down. He was Noreen's claim. Besides, he'd dropped out of Thermos Community College to work as a cashier at the Citibank. He
and Andrew Lynack shared the top floor of a house, and
every night before bed they smoked a bowl of Maine's
finest, and every morning before twisting those pin-
striped polyester ties into Windsor knots, they waked
and baked.

But when he asked her out, Ronnie put his hand on
her shoulder. His fingers were meaty, all knuckles and
calluses. Not since Roddy Chase had a man touched
her like he meant it. A warmth ran through her sweater,
under her turtleneck, all the way to her skin. Everything inside her jumped and settled in a way that had

felt exactly right. Before thinking about it, before an-
ticipating Noreen's wicked ire, she'd agreed to go see
Tom Green's *Freddy Got Fingered* at the multiplex
with him.

Within a week Ronnie gave her crabs. Took seven
weeks to get rid of the little devils. Tiny red pinpricks of
blood permanently stained her bedsheets from where
they'd clenched their sharp jaws along her pubis. He
caught them from his ex, and had thought he'd exter-
minated them, but a few determined eggs had clung to
the fibers of his bath towels, waiting to hatch. When
she told him what he'd done, he turned beet red and let
her pick every Netflix they rented for a month (French
films with subtitles that she didn't even like, just to
punish him). If she hadn't been a bug person, fascinated
by every aspect of their tiny bodies, she probably would
have dumped him.

"Ronnie's a total loser," Noreen screeched while sucking so hard on her Camel Ultra Light that its tip sizzled.
They were at the Dew Drop Inn, and over the weeks
they'd been dating, Noreen's jealousy had quietly con-
densed under a flame of hot rage until it became a thick,
black soup. "Also, I'm pretty sure he's gay. He and his
roommate want you to be their beard." Lois knew she
should have defended Ronnie. But instead she'd nodded
like maybe Noreen was right, and then changed the subject. Noreen wasn't worth fighting with. Half the things
she said when she'd been drinking she didn't remember,
and the other half she didn't mean. Life went on like
that for a while. Every Thursday the two of them threw
back a few apple cosmos at the Dew Drop Inn, and
Noreen crapped all over her, and Lois ate it all up like it
tasted good.

Lois and Ronnie kept dating. They got to know each

other, to depend on each other. They fell into it out of boredom, she guessed. But sometimes boredom can turn into love. A lot of times, probably.

Three years later she was accepted into the PhD program in entomology at the University of Massachusetts, a full ride. When she told Ronnie, he asked her to stay in Corpus Christi, so she did. Not smart. When she mailed the letter declining her admission and the twenty-two-thousand-dollar annual stipend that added up to more than her teaching salary, her gut instincts had shrieked inside her at pitches so high that she hadn't heard them, she'd only felt them as they'd ruptured her organs. For three days she didn't eat or sleep, and she knew she'd made a mistake.

But after a while she got used to the mistake, and things went back to normal, which meant they were okay, but not great. Ronnie's roommate, Andrew, took up with Noreen, which made Noreen happy. So better late than never, Noreen calmed down and played nice. The four of them started doing things together; seeing movies, going bowling, plunking quarters into the jukebox at the Dew Drop Inn and listening to Johnny Cash, getting high. Turned out Lois liked getting high a whole lot. Pot made everything as easy as swimming the dead man's float in a heated pool.

And then two months ago, after six years of dating, Ronnie proposed.

They'd just finished their Friday night pasta dinner at Monteleone's Italian Restaurant, and he plopped a brown garnet ring laced with diamond dust onto her greasy plate. It swiveled a few times before it landed flat. A bubble of joy had filled her stomach, and then got caught like a burp in her throat. This was the moment she'd been waiting for. Yup. This was it.

She'd expected him to get down on one knee, but he didn't. Instead he shrugged his shoulders, like he couldn't figure out how they'd gotten there, either. Her mind's eye had telescoped to a view ten years into the future, and in it she'd seen a dingy plaid couch, a couple of kids, and a guy who couldn't hold down a job. A nice guy with a lot of good qualities. He had a winning smile. He could make perfect grilled cheese and tomato sandwiches. He was kind, if spineless. Just like her father. At least she'd always be the boss . . . just like her mother. Did she want to be the boss? *Say no,* an urgent voice inside her had whispered. *Run like he just opened a bag of candied anthrax, and don't you dare look back.*

She lifted the ring and turned it between her fingers. It was soft, like she could flatten it if she squeezed. "Yeth!" she cried, "I will marry you, Ronnie Koehler."

The next day Noreen agreed to be Lois's maid of honor. Then she put the screws to her boyfriend, Andrew. She told him that since Ronnie and Lois were getting married, they ought to get hitched, too. Andrew didn't bother dumping her. He just stopped returning her phone calls. Drunk and crying at the Dew Drop a few days later, Noreen had shouted at Lois. Her cheeks were so red from booze that she looked like she'd started using lye on her face instead of sunscreen. "I'm not going to your wedding," she'd said. "As your friend I have to tell you, you're making a mistake. He doesn't love you, and I happen to know the only reason you ever liked him is because I wanted him first, and you can't ever let me be happy."

Lois should have been relieved to be rid of her, but mostly she was hurt. For the first few weeks without her best friend, she'd felt like a rotten egg had hatched in her stomach, and its poison yolk was circulating through her blood. Still, there was a wedding to plan, and only Lois to plan it. She auditioned the DJs and reserved the Corpus Christi Motor Lodge Meeting Hall. Ronnie was Episcopalian, and she was Catholic. His parents didn't want a priest, and her mother didn't want a minister. *No problem!* She'd told them even though she'd always wanted a church wedding: "Justice of the peace!" Ronnie didn't have a red cent, and her mother had invested Lois's $163,000 inheritance from Russell Larkin's life insurance policy in high-risk technology stocks that bottomed out in 2002 at four grand. *No problem!* Lois had announced: "I'll use those Discover card checks with the twenty percent interest." Why bother working hard for perfect credit, when they'd never be able to afford the down payment on a house, anyway?

And then last week Ronnie parked his red Camaro in her driveway and honked the horn. Somehow, from the quick, polite sound of his single beep, she knew. She'd been waiting for it, like she'd been walking around all month with the taste of copper on her tongue.

For the sake of her pride, she should have been the one to say something as they sat in his parked car that had smelled like pot and stale donuts. Instead she'd said a prayer to him in her mind, and hoped he would hear it: *Oh, please, Ronnie, change your mind. I love you, I really do. I love you more than anybody else in the world. Change your mind, Ronnie. I can't live with my mother another day. I can't sleep one more night in my old bedroom with its eyelet sheets that my mother bought when I was nine. Without you I'm useless, Ronnie. I'm nothing, and everybody knows it.*

Ronnie couldn't look her in the eye when he told her, "I can't do it."

"Why?" It was all she could think to ask.

"I'm not sure I love you. I don't know if I ever did."

She started crying, but then a funny thing happened. A monster stirred in her stomach and opened its eyes. Suddenly, she wanted to do harm. She imagined tearing him to pieces with her hands like his skin was rotten fruit. Running her fingers through the gore and squeezing it. Eating it while the juice ran down her chin. No kidding. Because what kind of crappy thing is that to say? You date a woman for six years, and you tell her you never loved her? Sure, you might not want to marry her, but *you don't love her?*

He asked for his ring back, and she gave it to him. It wasn't his nature to take back a gift. Shiftless, yes. Mean-spirited, no. She should have guessed that he'd been coached. Instead she'd been wondering: *Why me? When everyone else gets being a grown-up exactly right, how have I done it so wrong?*

Sobbing, she walked back into her mother's house. The land of velour couches, Formica kitchen tables, and fading salmon-colored walls. State-of-the-art in the 1980s, sure. But not exactly modern anymore. The den smelled distinctly human with its windows sealed tight, and her mother reclining under a wool blanket since the sun had peeked through the holes in the brown Levolor blinds that morning.

A *Who Wants to Be a Millionaire* rerun was playing on the television. Lois walked into the den, sniffling. In response, Jodi Larkin turned up the volume. Regis was asking how many floors combined used to make up the two towers of the World Trade Center, which even in her sorry state she'd recognized as tasteless. The answer, for eighty thousand dollars, was 220. A buxom young contestant guessed correctly, and her breasts jiggled like she wasn't wearing a bra when she jumped up and down with manic joy. At the commercial break Lois said, "Mom, Ronnie and I had a fight."

Jodi Larkin hesitated for less than a second before her eyes glazed over, and she flipped the channel to a TBS *Law & Order: Special Victims Unit* marathon. Lois knew what that silence meant. She'd heard the actual words behind it twice. Once when she asked for help making a car insurance payment, and then again when she confided to Jodi that she thought she might be pregnant. The gesture meant: *You're a grown woman. This is my time. Don't come to me with no problems, 'cause I got 'em, too.*

For the next week, like a record skipping over and over again in her mind, Lois kept wondering: What had she done wrong? Was there someone else in his life? And what the hell was she going to do with her life *now*?

The field trip to Bedford wasn't the best solution. The school board approved of it, mostly because Portland was too far for fourth graders to travel. She'd promised that they'd stay on the bus until they reached the woods, which for the most part hadn't been affected by the accident. They'd examine some of the indigenous flora, get a mini-lesson on the history of paper mills, have lunch, and head back to Corpus Christi. A cultural expedition. A nature walk.

Mostly, the reason Lois picked Bedford was that she'd been dying to see the place since the fire. After the Clott Corporation closed down last spring, some of the locals had vandalized the building. Out of anger or desperation or just plain stupidity, they'd set fire to the chemicals there, and half the town had gone up in a cloud of smoke. About twenty people died from the fumes, and plenty of others got sick in the aftermath. Some of the wildlife and vegetation died, too. The animals lost their instincts. Deer stopped feeding milk to their young. Birds forgot how to fly and fell out of the sky. House cats died by starvation in a strange kind of suicide. Even the spiders, the *Environmental Scientist* noted, began spinning broken webs.

She'd studied this stuff at UNH, so she knew that the symptoms closely matched methyl mercury poisoning. Mercury targeted the part of the gray matter that regulated survival instincts. In humans it also compromised speech, and caused Tourette's. But the EPA tested the air and the ashes of Bedford for neurotoxins along with everything else they could have tested for. They didn't find anything. They said that the sulfur in the ground from the explosion didn't reach high enough levels to cause alarm. It was acidic, and might kill some trees, but otherwise benign. They declared Bedford safe. Still, no one could explain the birds that crashed to their deaths in mid-flight, or the trees along the town's sidewalks that had shriveled up like Shrinky Dinks in an oven. The whole thing was a mystery.

Despite the EPA's reassurances, everybody left Bedford after the fire. People like the Fullbrights who could afford it moved to Corpus Christi. Others just scattered. Lois had heard that clothes were still strewn across bedroom floors, sunken pies gathered mold in ovens, and clocks ticked the hour for no one to hear. A real, live ghost town—the kids would love it!

Only last night had it occurred to her that Bedford might be dangerous. The *Sentinel*'s photos of scientists collecting samples of the water in the river there had shown them in full space suits and respirators, even after the area was declared clean. But that was months ago. By now, surely, the woods were safe. The rain would have washed any remaining chemicals away. The EPA would never lie about something so important, would they? Besides, everything in life was *a little* risky.

She was living proof that if you spend your whole life avoiding recklessness, your whole life can turn out a wreck.

When she woke up this morning, a week had gone by since Ronnie had chucked her, and the bright sun had shone across her face just a little less insultingly. She hadn't died or anything, and the trip to Bedford might be fun. These years in Corpus Christi, she'd forgotten that she liked new places. She liked learning things. Adventures were a blast!

She'd bounced her way down the stairs, thinking: *Okay, I had a failure. A pretty big one. But I'll get over it. Ronnie was a prick. Mr. Time Waster. Mr. Pothead Black Hole Loser. Mr. Stay-in-Corpus-Christi-Instead-of-Going-to-School-So-Both-Our-Lives-Can-Suck. Mr. I-Never-Loved-You. He can shit up a tree with that garbage. And while I'm on the subject, Noreen can drop dead, too.*

She poured herself some coffee. Her mother was still awake from the night before, watching *Regis and Kelly*, who were bantering, and she couldn't tell if it was their shtick or they hated each other. Maybe hating each other *was* the shtick. Her mother sipped a Gordon's Gin and orange juice. A final nightcap before sleep. Lois warmed her hands against her coffee mug. She thought about grad school applications. She thought about leaving this house one day; acting like she was going out for a roll of Tums or a stick of Trident, and never coming back. Only she'd get farther than Dad. She chuckled at the thought of their faces when Ronnie, or Noreen, or her mother came knocking on her bedroom door looking for a loan or a punching bag, and nobody was home.

Then she opened the morning edition of the *Corpus*

Christi Sentinel and turned pale. She closed her eyes, and in her mind said a hasty Hail Mary (when God closes the door, Mary opens a window). She peered again at the paper. Ronnie and Noreen smiled back at her.

The photo was black and white. Ronnie's arms were wrapped around Noreen's thick waist, and they were both smiling. Matching stars were painted on their cheeks. The photo had been taken at the Memorial Day fair. She knew because she was the person who'd taken it.

Underneath the photo was a wedding announcement.

A misprint! It had to be. But the article said otherwise. Over the years, the author reported, Ronnie and Noreen's friendship had blossomed (blossomed like what, a case of herpes?). This last month, they'd discovered their "eternal and undying love." Lois glared at that article for so long, holding her breath even though she didn't know it, that she got dizzy and fell out of her chair.

She'd felt like somebody had emptied a bottle of Drano into her stomach, and it was burning its way out. It seeped into her throat, her heart, her groin. She could feel it behind her eyes like tears; she could feel it under her fingernails. She could feel it shrinking inside her, taking her organs with it, making her small. Making her bitter. Making her so angry that the only color she could see was red. She wanted blood, suddenly. She wanted to eat Ronnie, or Noreen, or even herself, alive.

Her mother turned from the Folgers Crystals commercial and glanced at the article. She didn't flinch or grimace or even smile. "Weird," she said. Then she plopped her empty glass of gin in the sink and wobbled up the stairs.

Lois sat there for a few seconds. Then she raced to

the bathroom, and threw up. To her credit, it wasn't until she leaned against the cool porcelain, and realized that her period was six weeks late, that she started bawling.

There wasn't time to get a substitute. No time to call in sick. So here Lois was, sniffling in front of her class, trying to figure out how it was that her life got so screwed up when everybody around her with half the brains and twice the meanness was sitting pretty. When she finished roll call, she clapped her hands together and tried her best to smile, because the class mother, Janice Fischer, looked worried, like she thought Lois was about to drown in her own spit-covered attendance book. "Did everyone bring a lunch?" she asked.

The children nodded.

"Doeth everyone remember their partnerth?"

They did not, and so she paired them up by height and told them to stand next to each other as they boarded the bus. Her trouble kid James Walker announced: "I'm too old for a buddy." It was true; he'd been left back twice.

James grinned at her. She didn't like thinking this about an eleven year-old, but he was a bad seed. His wiring wasn't right, and when the other children fell or got hurt, his eyes lit up like it was Christmas morning and he'd found a puppy under the tree. A dead puppy. Keeping James Walker from having a partner was a public service.

"Fine," Lois said. "Don't have a partner. George, you can ride next to me."

They got on the bus and headed for the road that connected Bedford and Corpus Christi. In bad weather it was closed, but on this autumn day without a snowflake on the ground, it was open. She saw the bend in the road where her father's Nissan had crashed, and blinked until the scenery changed, like she did every time she passed it. The trip was only a few miles, but after they crossed the Messalonski River and entered the town of Bedford, they might as well have entered another country.

Bedford was a desolate place. There were no cars on the road, no lit-up houses, no mail trucks. Not even a local sheriff's office. Out her window she saw the heap of rubble and concrete that had once been the Clott Corporation's paper mill. Heavy black ashes surrounded the charred skeletal frame of the building. There hadn't been enough state funds for a serious cleanup, and no one lived in Bedford to complain to the feds, so there the pile remained.

The bus rumbled through Main Street. The ramshackle houses were literally falling apart, and all the front lawns were dead. Signs across abandoned stores were hung askew, or not at all. The sidewalk was broken into pebbles, and front doors were black with soot. The kids got quiet and pressed their noses against the windows. They'd never seen anything like this. They pointed at the old barbershop whose windows were broken, the sickly fawn foraging for food in a dumpster, and the mountain bike without wheels in the middle of the street. The place was an open-air graveyard.

As they neared the woods they saw a trailer by the side of the road. What Lois saw obliterated Ronnie from her mind. Attached to the trailer were crude effigies of people. Nylon-covered wads of cotton shaped like pioneer men and women were hung on nooses affixed to the top of the trailer. They wore jeans and work shirts or frumpy dresses. The cotton had lost its edges, so their arms and legs looked like they were unraveling into squids' appendages. A word in large print was attached to each life-sized doll. All together the words read: "She is always hungry. She is never satisfied."

Lois's stomach sank. Who would do such a thing? A squatter? A local? A lunatic? Maybe this field trip wasn't the best of her bright ideas. Right up there with, say, giving Ronnie money for pot or buying wine for her mother because she wrote "sparkling pink Zinfandel" on the chalkboard in red capital letters like a scream.

"What is that?" George asked, and even at the age of nine, he knew it wasn't a funny thing; it was a bad thing.

"Modern art," Lois said, "for crazy people."

"*Oh! Oh!* My dad says only cousins used to live in Bedford. That's why they burned the mill down. They're all retarded," Caroline called out.

Lois looked back at the girl, and couldn't think of anything to say.

The bus let them off at the cemetery, which led to the woods. She taught them how to rub headstone inscriptions on paper. There were about twenty new graves upon which flowers had been left: April Willow, Susan Marley, Paul Martin, Andrea Jorgenson, Donovan McCormack. At the sight of them, Lois's Catholic upbringing insisted she bend her head and say the Lord's Prayer for their collective souls.

Then they went into the woods, which she was startled to discover weren't woods anymore. Since the EPA last visited, the trees had died. Desiccated husks and branches lay like fallen soldiers along the forest floor. There was less moss, and she didn't see any squirrels or birds.

She looked at Janice Fischer's worried expression, and she knew she should take the children and get back on the bus, but she didn't. She was going to teach them something important today. Something they'd carry with them long after they forgot her name. A lesson about what happens to places left unattended. Places guided by all the wrong instincts.

She stopped them at the foot of the woods and made a speech. "Boyth and girlth . . . do you know what happened here? When the paper mill closed the people who worked for it got mad. They burned it down. They burned down their own town, because they were mad. Now does that make any thense? If you were mad, would you hurt yourselves?" she asked.

In unison the children shook their heads. Caroline Fischer was the most vocal: *"No, Miss Lois!"*

Lois nodded. "Good. I'm proud of you. Now, everyone thay—stay—with their partner. Don't wander farther that that oak tree right there." Then she opened her arms, signaling that they could go, and they tumbled into the woods.

For an hour the children searched under rocks and beneath moss for signs of life. The boys threw bugs at the girls and the girls screamed, not, it seemed to Lois, because they were afraid, but because it was just more fun to scream.

For lunch, they ate at the wooden picnic benches on the edge of the woods. She'd forgotten to pack her own sandwich, and her stomach rumbled. Janice Fischer walked behind the bus to smoke one of her hippie American Spirit cigarettes, and Lois found herself thinking about Ronnie.

Maybe the article in the paper was a hoax. Noreen had submitted it as a mean joke, and right now Ronnie was on his way to find her. Any minute he'd come driving up to the edge of the woods at eighty miles an hour. He'd get out of that cheap heap of bolts he thought was such a chick magnet, and in front of the kids, the bus driver, Janice Fischer, and the whole world he'd shout, "Noreen's a hog. I love you, Lois. I'll always love you."

Lois blew her nose so hard that her tissue broke and her hand got slimy. This trip right now wasn't fun. This trip really sucked. She noticed the children watching her. They seemed sad, and a few were hugging themselves. Only James Walker was not paying attention. "My eyeth," she told them. "They're irritated, do you underthand?"

They looked at her.

"I'm very allergic." These kids, she really did care for them. She loved them as if they were her own, even James. She was so upset she'd forgotten that, but it was true.

Caroline Fischer slid her package of Crackers 'n Cheez along the table until it reached Lois. "I have extra," she said.

Then crayon-eating George Sanford rolled a Granny Smith in her direction. Michael and Alex Fullbright gave her their oranges. Donna Dubois handed her the half-eaten segment of a Kit Kat bar. Lois sighed. It became a competition among them, until all the children donated their snacks or half sandwiches, and a mound of food rose in front of her. The gesture was too much to endure. She drew a ragged breath, terrified that it would end in a sob right in front of these wonderful children, but it did not. "Thank you, boys and girls," she said, biting into a tart Granny Smith.

After she admonished them all to empty their pockets full of sticks and rocks, they boarded the bus. She started roll call, but noticed Caroline waving an empty

Rough Rider condom wrapper at the boys sitting behind her. She'd probably found it in the woods, though Lois doubted she understood its use.

"Thath garbage," she said to Caroline, taking it out of her hand. Then she held it up for the class to see. "Don't touch garbage, boyth and girlth, you never know where it's been." This reminded her of Ronnie. Was he with Noreen right now? Were they working on a family at this very moment? And what about her own period, six weeks late?

She headed for the front of the bus and looked out the window. No red Camaro in sight. There would not be a red Camaro. These people, her friends, they'd betrayed her. They hadn't even called to say: *Uh, look, Lois, you'll hear about this anyway, but we went and did something nutty.* And there was one simple explanation: She'd effed up. She'd surrounded herself with the wrong people, because Ronnie, Noreen, and even her mother were no good.

Worst of all, she knew she was better off without them, but in the end that didn't matter. After school today, she'd stop by Ronnie's house and beg him to take her back, but he'd never do it because Noreen was too damn scary to cross. After a month or so of a broken heart, she'd swallow it all down and stop by the Dew Drop Inn, where Noreen would say something mean, and Ronnie would smile like a milksop, and she'd pretend like nothing was wrong. She'd forgive them even though they hadn't asked for it, because being their friend was better than watching Regis Philbin with her drunk mother. She'd eat shit like always, because she was Lois Larkin, and she didn't have any goddamn sense.

"Drive," Lois said, while Janice Fischer slathered her daughter's condom-tainted hands with gobs of green antibacterial gel. They pulled away from the woods, and Lois started crying all over again.

It was only after they got back to school that she realized that the lump in the seat across from her was not a little boy, but a book bag and jacket. James Walker was missing.

TWO
The Monster in the Woods

The ground under James Walker's feet went crunch, crunch, crunch, like the bamboo xylophone from music appreciation. There were leaves and sticks and rocks, all dried up and hollow. Overhead, leafless branches poked the bright blue sky. He jumped up and down, and listened to things break. It was dead as a rabbit in here!

Instead of boarding the bus when Miss Lois called, he'd pretended his big brother, Danny, was chasing him. He ran until he was panting and sweaty and couldn't see his way out. He knew he wasn't supposed to wander off, but he hated Miss Lois. When she said his name her upper lip curled like somebody was trying to feed her yellow snow. He figured if he ran away today, maybe his dad would get mad enough to have her fired.

It wasn't Miss Lois's fault he was a left-back, though. First his mother started him a year late for kindergarten because he was small for his age, and then Mr. Crozzier flunked him, and wrote in his *Permanent Record* that he was "emotionally and mentally stunted." That's why he was the only eleven-year-old in the fourth grade. Once a month during recess he had to meet with a social worker and talk about his feelings. He didn't usually have any, so mostly they played Iron Man on the Xbox.

James's parents wanted him to be more like his big brother, Danny, who got straight A's and played lacrosse. Danny and Dad shot eighteen holes at the Corpus Christi Golf Club once a month. They wore matching polo shirts and khakis like they were members of Team Jerk America.

Danny liked to take James's hands and hit him in the face with them. *Why are you hitting yourself, James? Why are you hitting yourself?* he'd ask. One time he stuffed James's mouth and nose with salty yellow snow and even after James cried, "Mercy, Master Daniel," Danny had held his lips and nose closed tight until he swallowed. When stuff like that happened, James imagined poking Danny's eyes out with a fork and then eating them like a couple of meatballs so nobody could sew them back into his empty sockets.

James walked deeper. Crunch, crunch, crunch. The fallen trees were hollow inside, like corn husks. An idea came to him, and it made him jump with delight. The Incredible Hulk pretended to be strong, but he probably threw *hollow* trees. In the movie on HBO the trees had looked real but the camera had played a trick. James grinned, because he'd thought of something smart all by himself, which meant he wasn't totally retarded.

To test his theory he lifted a hollow log, which was light as a cardboard box. Underneath he found a slug, so he took out the matches he'd swiped from his mom's kitchen and set it on fire. The slug's skin glowed, and then got wrinkly. A plume of smoke that smelled like burnt tires whirled over its long body. Then the slug's skin split open and white crud oozed out. Even though he'd killed it, he didn't want it to suffer, so he stepped on it to make sure it was dead.

When he was a kid, only eight years old, he'd sneaked into Mr. McGuffin's backyard to play with the newborn baby rabbits in the hutch. They'd been gobs of fuzz with red eyes that were smaller than his fists. His favorite was Gimpy, who'd been born with shriveled hind legs. Gimpy couldn't run like the others, which meant he never left James's lap. Mr. McGuffin said James could adopt Gimpy as soon as he grew big enough.

So one day he was holding Gimpy. The silly rabbit licked his fingers, and he wondered if he loved it, even though it was just a dumb animal. He couldn't remember the last time he'd loved something. Maybe never. Gimpy kept licking. His big red eyes were all innocent-looking, and James decided that Gimpy was a liar. He was like Danny, who was nice on the outside but bad on the inside. So he squeezed Gimpy just a little.

Gimpy didn't screech. He didn't shout for James to stop (now that James was eleven, he knew rabbits couldn't talk, but back then he'd thought maybe they secretly could; they just didn't want to). Gimpy's eyes got all big like they were going to pop out, which was kind of funny. James had wanted to let go, but instead he held on tighter. Squeezed harder. The reaction was all wrong, even though he'd wanted it to be right. He couldn't help it! Sometimes he forgot the right thing.

Gimpy's eyes looked like they were going to fall out. Something popped, and one of his sockets was bleeding. It was just a hole, drippy and red. Not funny like a meatball. Bad. So bad he gagged, only nothing but spit came out. Still, even while Gimpy bled, James squeezed tighter. He didn't know what else to do. He wanted to make it *un-happen*, but he didn't know how.

Gimpy tried one last time to get away, and James knew he should let go, but he got scared. The rabbit was broken like a toy he couldn't fix. What if Mr. McGuffin found his missing eye, and figured out what James had done? His hands were like a metal vise that wouldn't open. The rabbit started kicking—not real kicks. Spazzy, jerky shivers. Then Gimpy screamed this low-pitched, terrible scream. A mix between a grunt and a cry. It lasted for a long time, and it was the kind of sound that hurt to hear. It didn't hurt his ears; it hurt his insides. It hurt his heart, hearing Gimpy cry like that.

After Gimpy screamed everything inside James got quiet, like he wasn't there anymore. Like he was sleeping. Everything went black. His body kept going, but he wasn't in charge of it. He was someplace safe where he didn't have to think about Gimpy. If he tried, he could see what was happening, but he didn't have to feel it. He didn't have to feel anything. It was like falling asleep.

When he woke up Gimpy wasn't moving. The bunny was floppy and cold in his lap, which made him wonder how long he'd been sleeping. The funny thing was, he knew it was bad to hurt an animal, knew that he'd loved Gimpy, but still, a part of him liked it. Even if he wasn't smart, killing Gimpy had been brave. Most people wouldn't have had the guts.

He dug a hole for Gimpy behind the hutch and buried him there. He was so sad about cold Gimpy that he couldn't remember his prayers, so instead he asked God to let him into heaven, even if it turned out that pets aren't normally allowed. Unless Gimpy was going to haunt him, and then he wished Gimpy permanently dead. He covered the filled-in hole with leaves so Mr. McGuffin wouldn't notice the fresh dirt, and then ran home, took the phone off the hook, and told his mom he had to go to bed because he felt sick.

When the front bell rang, James prayed to God it wasn't Mr. McGuffin. He prayed he could undo what he'd done. But it *was* Mr. McGuffin at the door, and James heard him talking to his mother in the front hall. Their voices were soft, and then his mother was shouting, and Mr. McGuffin started shouting, too. He listened, even though he didn't like what he heard. "That's maniac's gonna kill a man one day," Mr. McGuffin yelled.

He pulled the covers tight over his body and wished he was asleep. He was so scared he couldn't even cry. How had this happened? Because he was bad. Those teachers at school, and the kids who didn't invite him to sleepovers because he was too rough, and Danny, and even his parents, who didn't touch him unless he asked, they all knew what he'd just figured out. He was bad inside. He'd killed his own rabbit.

Mr. McGuffin didn't come storming up the stairs and into his room like he'd expected. The front door slammed, and then there was silence. A little while later his mother arrived, carrying a tray of orange juice and cinnamon toast. She laid it across his bed and pulled up a chair. (She never sat on his bed when she wanted to talk. Only Danny's.) "Feeling better?" she asked.

She was fugly. Once he'd punched her in the stomach and told her so. He hadn't counted on her crying about it the way she did. "I feel bad, Felice," he told her, because for as long as he could remember, she'd never answered to "Mom."

She didn't pet his hair or hold him or anything. "Mr. McGuffin was over here," she said. He got scared. But instead of feeling scared, a fire made of ice spread in his stomach. It burned so blue and aching that his skin shivered. It froze his insides and then broke them into little pieces until he didn't feel bad anymore. Like the deep sleep, he didn't feel anything anymore.

"He said he found your favorite rabbit. Someone killed and buried it. He thinks it was you, but I told him that was impossible. I told him you were in the yard practicing the T-ball. That's what you were doing all morning, isn't it?"

He didn't know what to say. Her eyes were narrow, like she was looking at him, but doing her best not to see him. Why was she pretending he'd been in the yard?

"I'm sick," he said.

"You've got a virus, probably," she told him. Then she patted the side of his leg, but her hand didn't linger. "I'll leave you to sleep." She shut the door, and he heard a lock turn. Ever since that day, she didn't look at him the same. Even when her mouth smiled at him, her eyes never did.

James overheard his dad on the phone that night with Mr. McGuffin. He said that if Mr. McGuffin started telling stories about the rabbits in his yard, he'd get sued for slander, and then he wouldn't be able to afford his mortgage, let alone vermin for pets. And by the way, what was a single man doing inviting children to his house to play with rabbits?

Hurting Gimpy was the worst thing James had ever done. It had been wrong, and he didn't want to do anything like it again. But then again, sometimes he did.

James stopped walking. It was dark out here. He'd been thinking about Gimpy coming back from the dead and haunting him in these woods, which had made him forget where he was going. He couldn't see the blue sky overhead anymore. Just dead branches and dry leaves so thick that everything was sort of shadowy, even though it was daytime.

The kids in his class said this place was full of ghosts, which was why the trip to Bedford had sounded like so much fun. But nobody had seen anything special out here, except for Miss Sad Sack Larkin, crying.

He sat on a rock that hung high over a shallow stream, and suddenly felt bad. He didn't like being alone all the time. These woods were too quiet. Sometimes he thought about sneaking into Danny's room and putting a pillow over his face, and then doing the same to his parents. Then he could have a new family that didn't frown when they looked at him.

James climbed out on the overhang and laid across the rock. In the water he saw his reflection. A boy with blond hair and blue eyes. A good-looking boy with a mean streak. He threw a stone, and the water rippled. When it got clear again, his reflection was different. His skin was pale, and his eyes were black. It looked familiar, and James thought for a second that it was the bad thing that lived inside him. The thing that liked to do harm.

It is always hungry; it is never satisfied, he thought, even though he didn't know what that meant. His reflection winked at him, and he jumped. It was alive, even though it was just a reflection.

"Who are you?" he asked. "Do you want to play?"

The woods got darker suddenly, like it was going to rain. The reflection went dark, too. *James,* a voice whispered. The sound echoed through the dead trees.

He looked around, but he couldn't see anyone. In his pants, he got what his brother called a stiffie. You were supposed to get them when you looked at girls, but

James only got them when he was scared or doing something wrong. If he tried to wish them away they got worse, so mostly he just ignored them.

I'll play with you, James. The voice was watery, like it had slithered up from the bottom of the river and wasn't used to being on the surface. He didn't know if it belonged to a man or a woman, which was doubly bad, because that meant he was getting stiffies from men's voices, too. But he couldn't help it!

He jumped off the rock and peered in the direction of the voice. Another breeze blew, and he saw a trail. Birch tree branches jingled as they opened before him. The branches were pointed like fingers showing him the way. It reminded him of a cartoon he'd seen on television when he was little—the enchanted woods leading Little Red Riding Hood to Grandma's house.

He followed the sound of the voice down the path. It opened into a clearing, and when he reached it, the path closed behind him with that same jingling sound. His heart pounded: There was no way he'd find his way back.

James, the thing gurgled.

The chiggers had stopped biting all of a sudden. The animals were missing, too. Even the worms and moss and mushroom fungi were gone. Maybe the thing in the woods had hurt them. He could understand that.

The dirt was as black as squid ink, and the hot ground warmed his toes even though he was wearing rubber-soled Nikes. It was the same kind of warm as the fire that had been in his stomach when Gimpy died. So cold it was hot, and it burned in all the wrong ways.

He knew what he needed to do. The voice told him so. He picked up a sharp rock and broke the black dirt.

The wind picked up a little at first, and then a lot.
Branches jingled like music appreciation on caffeine;
out of tune and heedless. *That's right, James*, the voice
said, only the voice wasn't outside him anymore. It was
crawling inside him. Slithering between his ears. Peer-
ing at the woods from behind his eyes. He blubbered a
little and slapped his face. "Get out!" he shouted, even
though a part of him liked it, too.

Don't hide from me, James, it said. *I know you.* The
voice was like Gimpy's tongue, soothing and ticklish.
He missed Gimpy. He missed being touched. The thing
moved inside him, and nestled in the space between his
ears. How long had it been since a friend had come over
to play? A month? No, longer. Not since last year. In
school they called him the pee eater.

I know you, James, and I like you anyway, it said.
James smiled, because in his mind the thing showed
him a picture of Gimpy, twitching, and he knew it was
true.

He stopped slapping and started digging. The dirt
was hot and inky between his fingers. It felt wrong, like
it had been cooked. He lifted a fistful, and then another. The hole got bigger. He dug for a long time. He
dug until everything hurt, and then he dug past that
until there were new, worse hurts. In his mind the thing
showed him pictures. They were bad pictures, but he
liked them.

He dug past the pain in his back, his aching legs, and
his bleeding fingers. Dug past his own heavy breathing,
past when he remembered what he was doing, or why.
The voice lulled him, like being tucked into a warm
bed. It didn't talk anymore, but he could feel it inside
him. He thought about Gimpy, and his family, and
Miss Lois, whom he wished on that first day of school

hadn't asked him in front of the whole class: "I see you're older than the others, James. Does that mean you require special attention?" And then, after a while, he thought about nothing. Everything went dark. He fell asleep even though he was awake, just like that time with Gimpy. Still, he kept digging.

He woke up in the dark, to someone shouting his name. He was standing in a deep hole, digging. How had it gotten so late so fast? Just five minutes ago the sun had been high in the sky. Now there were stars. His hands were bloody, and his back and legs hurt so bad he couldn't bend without moaning. For how long had be been digging?

"*James!*" a voice cried from far away. Was it his new friend? The voice sounded angry, and too loud. "*Can you hear me, James?*" it shouted again, and it was terrifying because he recognized it. Miss Lois had come back looking for him. Only this time, she'd brought his father. Miller Walker was calling to him on a megaphone. "*Come here right now!*"

James took a deep breath. His chest was so sore that his lungs ached. A vise of muscles in spasm clamped tightly around his back until he hunched over. His bleeding fingers hurt the worst, and he blew on them to take his mind off the pain.

An eye opened inside him, and winked. *Keep digging, James*, it told him. *I know what you want. I'll give it to you.* Yes, James thought. It knew the truth. He was bad. He was that boy from the water, pale skin and black eyes. He'd killed his own rabbit.

He lifted another handful of dirt. And another. Maybe Gimpy was down here, waiting for the bad thing to be undone. If James worked hard enough, maybe he could undo it. Sure, he knew it was impossible. But then again, this place was supposed to be magic.

Something smelled bad in the dirt all the sudden. It was like rotten eggs. It came out in a spray of fog from the hole, and filled the woods. Still, he kept digging. After another handful, he touched something hard and hot. He scraped the dirt from its sides until he could pull it free. *Smart boy!* the voice said to him, and he smiled, because the voice sounded proud. He *was* smart, wasn't he? He'd guessed about the Hulk without anyone's help.

The thing was brown and hard. Lighter than a rock. Longer than a ruler. He dropped it on the ground above because it made his hands hurt like frostbite. A bone, he realized. The bone from an animal's arm. No, not Gimpy. Too big to be Gimpy. It smelled so bad his eyes watered. *It's everything you want, James,* the voice said, and James knew he didn't care about Gimpy anymore. He wanted the thing that was buried. He wanted to see the face behind the voice.

His dad was still shouting into the megaphone, but it was too late to turn back. Miss Lois would never forgive him, and since he'd become a left-back, Miller Walker stopped looking him in the eye, or calling him "good buddy." He kept digging, and pulled out another bone.

His fingers were cramped into loose fists. He was so thirsty that his mouth had dried out and he couldn't move his tongue. He'd lost a fingernail. It had torn from his pointer finger, and he hadn't even noticed. There were more bones. He traced their edges until they were free. His bloody fingers dripped as he eased the bones onto the inky soil outside the hole. There was a skull, and toes. He smiled. The skull was human.

He piled the bones in a red heap. He was bleeding a

lot now. There were cuts all over his hands and arms that he didn't remember having gotten. The wind picked up. Dead trees gnashed against each other until the sound wasn't music; it was screaming.

Sweat dripped from his brow, and his face was set as still as a plaster cast. His blood laced the bones. Marked them with color. It didn't hurt. A part of him, most of him, was sleeping. Something hot was in James's trousers. Another stiffie? No, not a stiffie; he'd wet his pants.

He saw, he didn't know how he'd missed this before, that along the edges of the clearing were dead animals; skunk, squirrels, birds, and deer. Their husks piled the rim of the expanse like stacks of wood. The buried thing had done this. It had gotten inside their minds and told them to attack each other so it could taste their spilled blood from under the ground. It wasn't ink that had made this dirt black.

James felt the wrong emotion. He couldn't help it. He clapped his hands together and laughed.

Everything you want, the thing promised, and James knew it was true. In his mind's eye he saw his parents gored bodies. In his mind's eye his brother, Danny, was the mental cripple, and James sat on the Walker family throne.

A raccoon from the woods approached. Its teeth were bared, and its eyes were black. More came. Their fattened bodies wobbled toward him. They swayed on small legs like they were sick, and they smelled so bad that he cupped his raw hands over his mouth and stopped breathing.

They've gone mad, he thought, *just like me*.

He knew what was going to happen. The thing whispered it in his ear. If he'd been a sane little boy he might have run. The swerving raccoons gnashed their teeth. His blood spilled, and laced the bones, and he thought about Gimpy. He knew then, during the last moments, how his rabbit had felt.

PART TWO

INCUBATION

THREE
Splitting Atoms

On the Tuesday morning that James Walker went missing, Meg Wintrob was crawling underneath the foundation of her house. The paper boy had missed his mark with the *Corpus Christi Sentinel* again, and she got on her hands and knees to retrieve it. Her hips shrieked in protest, and she bit down on her lower lip through the pain. Bursitis. Sure, she kept in shape and dyed her hair jet black with the help of Miss Clairol, but stuff like this made it hard to forget that she was middle-aged.

The crawl space was about two feet high and ran the width and length of the entire house. The *Sentinel* wasn't far out of reach, but as her eyes adjusted to the dark, she could also make out her son David's lost Sit 'n Spin from fifteen years ago, a cluster of three-leafed plants that looked suspiciously like poison ivy, and a collection of aging *Sentinel*s from days, months, and years past. Jack Frost had peed on this morning's paper, and its pages adhered to one another in a soggy clump. She shook her head full of tight black curls and thought: *For once, just one frickin' year, could the town hire a paper boy who didn't throw like a sissy?*

She'd only been in this crawl space a handful of times.

Spiders were down here, she was sure. At this very moment she could feel one of their thick webs flossing her cheek. The wooden beams down here looked sturdy, and there wasn't a single crack in the concrete base. Everything was in order, which was reassuring, she guessed. But disappointing, too. She wanted a reason for the way she felt.

Soggy paper in hand, Meg turned onto her stomach and crawled out. As she shimmied toward the steps, poison ivy brushed against her faded terry-cloth robe. Their leaves shone like plastic. She wasn't allergic, but she knew she should avoid the stuff. Still, it was one of those instincts, like waiting until the last minute before swerving around a beer bottle in the road, that came from a place deep down. She wanted to feel the ivy, rub it on her fingers, taste it on her tongue. Eat the white poison berries, just to see what happened. So she picked a few, and put them in the pocket of her robe.

Then she climbed out and sat on the stoop. The town, along with her family, was still sleeping. Red-orange rays of the coming dawn filtered through the dense pine trees in her yard. Not a single car or neighbor was outside yet. Back in the house, coarsely ground coffee was percolating over a gas flame. Eggs needed to be poached. Appointments had to be scheduled. Theoretically, the day was full of promise.

She'd been feeling blue since her son, David, had left for his sophomore year at UCLA two weeks ago. He bleached his hair and eyebrows now, and wore sparkly coral necklaces that made him look . . . *pretty*. He was either going for the surfer look or working up the courage to tell them he was gay. She suspected the latter. Though he'd never said so, she knew Fenstad blamed her. She'd been too affectionate, made her son a mama's boy. He alluded to it every time she and David went for a long walk, had a tickle fight, or baked cookies together. He'd walk into the kitchen with his eyes open wide like David was her lover and he'd caught them in an affair. Then he'd say something ridiculous like, "A man should stand on his own two feet," and neither she nor David would have any idea how to respond. Fenstad could be a real dipshit.

She missed David more than she'd expected, which probably explained why she got involved with Graham Nero last year. Maddie and Fenstad expected hot meals and paid bills, a clean house and smart advice. They appreciated the things she did, certainly; she was no long-suffering martyr. But still, they expected it.

Take Maddie. Over the summer she'd pierced her belly with a steel ring, using only a swab of alcohol and an ice cube for anesthetic. "*I am so hardcore!*" she'd shouted as she burst into the kitchen with her thumbs, index fingers, and pinkies saluting the ceiling like a heavy metal vixen. Only the blood never stopped gushing down her blue polka dot bathing-suit bottoms. To get the ring to puncture her skin more smoothly, she'd coated its point with Crisco, unwitting of the fact that grease is an anticoagulant. When it's applied, blood won't clot. They almost had to make a trip to the emergency room before Meg's common sense got the better of her, and she pulled the damn ring out herself so the wound could heal. But that was Maddie. The girl acted first, reasoned later. She didn't look both ways when she crossed the street, smiled at strangers, and recently had dyed her hair purple before reading the label and realizing that the color was permanent.

Then there was Fenstad. If left to his own devices he'd limit his diet to beef jerky and wear the laundry from his hamper that smelled least like armpit. Twenty years of marriage, and the man had never learned to

cook pasta. Once in a while she'd look at these two
rubes sitting across from her at the dinner table and
wonder: *Where the hell am I?*

Meg swiveled on the stoop now. Her crossed legs
were numb. Pins and needles pricked through her feet
all the way up to her bottom. Oh, God, she was getting
old. Somebody should give her a tube of Ben-Gay and a
pair of orthopedic shoes and call it a day.

Temperatures today were supposed to spike at sixty
degrees. Perfect sweater weather. Hooky weather, really. She and Fenstad could call in sick, take a drive to
Baxter State Park, hike Katahdin, and gorge themselves
on the last of summer's blueberries along the trail. They
always *meant* to do things like that: take trips, rent
rooms in cheap motels and have aerobic sex, go bowling in the afternoon. They talked about these things all
the time, but they never did them. Somehow, after all
these years, they'd never found the time.

Funny how that can happen. But no, let's not be glib.
It wasn't funny at all.

After the fire in Bedford, Fenstad had suggested that
they sell the house and move to Boston. He'd worried
that the hazmat signs on Exit 117 spelled disaster. But
soon enough the signs came down, and talk of moving
was forgotten. Still, it had gotten her thinking. In another year after Maddie finished school, they could sell
the house if they wanted. Go their separate ways. Move
on while they were both young-ish. Make that middle-
aged. Such thoughts felt like hot metal coursing through
her blood and turning hard. They were too painful to
think, and yet they persisted.

Not the type for sighing, Meg pursed her lips. A nest
of birds that lived in the second-story gutter began to
chirp. Bluebirds? Blackbirds? Sparrows? She didn't know.
Hummingbirds were her favorite. They flapped their

wings so fast they looked like one big blur, just so they could stand still. Now that's dedication.

Meg put her hands in her pockets, and the poison ivy berries squished. Fenstad was probably awake by now. He and Maddie didn't talk lately. Growing pains—he missed that she wasn't his little girl anymore, and so did she. So now they ignored each other because they couldn't figure out how else to act. Unlike Maddie, whose moods swung in a pendulum depending on what she'd eaten, whether she was getting along with her boyfriend, and the time of the month, Fenstad was the voice of reason. Quiet, considered, logical. He rarely laughed and never cried. Cold, really. Her husband was cold.

Meg dropped the berries down the walk, where they rolled. Goose bumps rose on her arms and legs. She shaved practically every place on her body that grew hair except the top of her head, so her skin was smooth as a waxed peach. Her grandparents on both sides came from northern Italy and most of her family was light-skinned, but she was the dark and swarthy throwback from another generation. Adolescence hit when she was only eleven, and during the summer before she began the seventh grade, she started menstruating. As an added, awkward bonus, a furry black mustache appeared like a lost caterpillar across her upper lip. The teasing in school that fall was relentless. More mean-spirited twelve-year-olds than she cared to count fake-asked her out. (*Will you marry me, Dogface?* Phil Payne had begged with tears of laughter streaming down his face. *I love you, Dogface!*) A rumor spread by bathroom wall graffiti and her former friends insisted that she was a hermaphrodite. One girl even claimed to have seen her penis in the girls' locker room.

That Christmas break she bought a home wax kit. In

no time, she learned to pluck, wax, shave, and diet herself into a polished and shiny version of the former Meg Bonelli. Despite the persistent rumors about the appendage between her legs, by the eighth grade she was dating the captain of the junior varsity wrestling team, and at the end of her senior year in high school she was the third runner-up for prom queen, a position she campaigned bitterly for. After the winner was announced, she'd hidden her tears by squatting in a locked bathroom stall for twenty minutes. Still, when she met Fenstad three years later, he would never have guessed that her nickname had once been Dogface, or that if she skipped waxing her lip and chin for a week, she grew a formidable five o'clock shadow. She took some feminine pride in the fact that he *still* didn't know.

To this day, the threat of those short-lived tauntings remained. She took great pains to iron the creases in her trousers into crisp lines, to dry her hair into a straight, blunt edge that framed her small, angular face. She'd learned to value the cleanness of unbroken lines, the order of a bleached-white smile, the silhouette of her own slender waist in a fitted pleated skirt. She regretted that she had bequeathed this perfectionism onto Maddie, who at breakfast sucked on grapefruit slices, one sliver at a time.

Meg squinted. The sun was shining higher in the sky now, and the town was beginning to wake. Her house on River Street overlooked downtown Corpus Christi, and in the distance she could see its squat hospital and abutting four-tiered parking lot. Farther down was the Episcopalian church adorned with a plain copper cross that had turned green. Along River Street were two-level shops that lined up in a row. On the road, a slow procession of cars carrying doctors, nurses, anesthesiologists, and administrators headed for the hospital.

All the lawns in this town were neat and green. Her gardening team came once a week and like magic seeded the earth and clipped the hedges. A legion of domestics rode the bus to Corpus Christi from parts west. They worked off the books, cleaning houses, mopping store floors, and sweating bare-chested in the hot sun. She never spoke to her gardener, or her Wednesday afternoon cleaning lady. Instead she left envelopes full of money for them, across which she scripted their first names. It was the way things were done here in Corpus Christi, which didn't necessarily mean she approved of it.

Meg's empty stomach growled, and she thought about coffee, eggs. The paper in her hand was a clump of heavy mush. But still, she watched. Something about this morning, this town in front of her, this house on which she was perched, made her sad. She missed it, even though it was not yet gone. She loved it the way you love something you are about to lose.

Since the whole Graham Nero disaster, the word was on her mind all the time. It kept her up at night, surfacing as ominously as the unidentifiably bloated Bedford floaters that had risen from the Messalonski River all summer long. She thought about it when fighting with Maddie, while paying bills, while watching late-night television, while kissing her husband good-night. No matter how hard she tried to bury it, the word would not sink. Divorce, she thought at least once during every waking hour of her day. Divorce. Divorce. Divorce.

The birds flew from their nest and pecked their way along the walk. Their heads were black, and their chests white. Their song was a giddy warble, and their name finally came to her: chickadees. Meg took off her slippers and stood. Why not? What was stopping her? With

Maddie leaving next year, and a son already gone, what did she have to lose?

The wet grass drove nails of cold through the soles of her feet. Her goose bumps transformed into eggs, and the paper in her hand was so heavy she dropped it. She was forty-five years old and she'd never been skinny-dipping, never sneaked into a movie, smoked a joint, broken a dish on purpose. She wanted her feet to sink. She wanted to roll across the lawn like a kid. She wanted to take the week off from work and play with her husband, actually play, so that when they went to bed at night their stomachs hurt from laughter.

She wanted to call up to his window like a liberated Juliet, and tell him they were better than this. Fenstad, David, Maddie—every one of them. They were blowing this Popsicle stand. She turned, and seriously considered doing just that, but something stopped her. Something about the birds. She couldn't place it. They were pecking at the ground. Little chickadees. Pretty things. One of them swallowed a berry. Her berry. And then she remembered.

Meg Wintrob's heart beat a little faster. Couldn't birds sense poison? What were they doing? But then again, they ate the dry rice thrown at weddings and then drank water until their stomachs exploded. Or was that a myth? Her heart raced, pumping blood to her face so that it flushed Valentine's Day red. *What were they doing?*

All the berries were gone. There must have been five or six of them. *Oh, no.* She massaged her forehead. On the ground, one of the birds stopped pecking. It flapped its wings, but not fast enough to fly. It hopped along the walk, weaving in a dizzy zigzag. The thing looked drunk, and it would have been funny, would have reminded her of a rummied-up Woody Woodpecker, had she not known what was happening. Its wings stopped flapping, and it began to drag its body by its small feet. She touched its soft feathers, and then cupped it in her palms and felt its slow breath.

She shouldn't be upset. This bird was a moron. It deserved to die rather than reproduce, and bequeath its fool genes to another generation. Its instincts were all wrong. Birds should know not to eat poison. Then why was she crying?

The bird didn't try to wriggle free from her hands. Its hollow-boned chest expanded and contracted very slowly. Without knowing it, she matched its breath in a show of sympathy. She'd killed it. She'd killed the retarded bird.

Meg bent down until the tip of her nose touched its beak. It didn't fight. Her breath hitched. They'd been through two dogs, four or five rabbits, and countless goldfish. Except for the dogs, she'd never shed a tear. But this bird, it was getting cold. It was getting stiff. She wanted to put it back where she'd found it. Pretend she'd never seen it. But she couldn't do that. Couldn't let it die alone. She held on for another couple of minutes, until it stopped breathing. Then she eased it onto the ground.

She wiped her hands against her robe. She was crying in the middle of her front lawn. Neighbors driving by slowed their cars to look. She covered her face with her hands and pretended to be shielding her eyes from the sun. She was wearing a ten-year-old terry-cloth robe with frayed sleeves because her good robe was in the laundry pile. Her hair was a mess. Her feet were cold. Why were they so cold? Oh, right, she wasn't wearing slippers. The bird, the pretty bird. A chickadee.

On the street a car slowed. Fenstad's boss and the CEO of the hospital rolled down his window. "How

are ya, Meggie?" Miller Walker called. He was one of
those jerks who invented nicknames for people like "my
main man at arms," and "Fennie-boy," and "Meggie."
At the annual Christmas Ball he always made a big
show of pinching her ass, and then pretending it was a
huge joke. She grinned a fake grin and waved gaudily,
hoping he was too far away to see her tears. Then Meg
Wintrob pivoted so fast her hips throbbed, and hurried
back inside.

Fenstad Wintrob peered through the foggy window.
His muscles ached like he'd been sparring a few
rounds with Mike Tyson instead of dreaming. He was
a restless sleeper. He kicked and moaned and babbled,
but never remembered it in the morning. Poor Meg.
Every once in a while she showed him some bruise he'd
left on her arm, or woke him during the night because
he'd hogged all the blankets. He hadn't heard her get
out of bed this morning, which was unusual. They were
both light sleepers. But then again, he knew from recent experience that when she wanted, Meg could be
sneaky.

He watched as she climbed out from underneath the
porch. She did it in a single, fluid motion. Her legs un-
folded and slipped out, and her body followed. Then she
slapped the wet newspaper against the wooden steps.
Three quick, hard strikes from which drops of water
spun in small arcs. He felt like less of a man watching
her, his own wife.

Fenstad was lean, wiry, and of medium height. Except for his dark green eyes, he was average-looking
in every way. But he was an attentive listener, and he
never broke eye contact. For this reason the memory
of his face lingered in peoples' minds, even when they'd

met him only once. They could recall, for example, the laugh lines cut into the sides of his cheeks and his large hands that made him appear far stronger than his stature implied.

He was a calm man. Meg, on the other hand, was restless. Even when happy, her fingers tap-tap-tapped against wooden surfaces, steering wheels, her own thighs. Unexpected things soothed her. Frozen Snickers bars, for instance, or rainy days, because she didn't feel bad about not getting outside. Right now, though, she seemed relaxed. Her hair was a frizzy mess around her shoulders, the way he liked it. She was looking out at the road, daydreaming. Her posture was loose, as if the morning dew was a solvent for the glue that lately had locked all her joints in fixed positions. She looked approachable. Sexy, even.

He was startled suddenly by the sound of a loud buzzer, which was quickly followed by a moan, and a slap, and then silence. Maddie's alarm. When she was young he used to wake her. "Rise and shine," he'd say, and then he'd open her blinds so that the sun shone across her bed. Now only Meg entered her room because she slept in the nude. She spent at least an hour in the bathroom every morning, spraying herself with womanly scents and dabbing her eyes with blue shadow. She had a boyfriend, too. Enrique Vargas ate dinner at the house once a week, and Fenstad had to smile and make small talk with the kid who was probably screwing his daughter.

Fenstad shook his head. And then there was David. How had he managed to raise two kids who both dyed their hair like circus clowns?

Down below, Meg tossed something onto the walk. It sprayed out like pebbles. He thought about joining her on the steps. He could surprise her with a kiss on the back of her neck. But she was snappish in the mornings. It was best to keep a distance.

He remembered now that he'd had a nightmare last night. In his dream the house had been cavernously huge. Scores of rooms had led to more rooms, all converging, mazelike, onto the front hall. The rules of Euclidean geometry had not been obeyed: Floors had been slanted, corners were greater or less than ninety degrees, and ceilings were high and occasionally rounded. The rooms had converged on the front door, which a large, growling dog had guarded. It had looked like his neighbor's German shepherd, only its eyes had been wild. He'd seen them clearly; green irises that had dilated in wavelike motions irrespective of the light. He'd known just by sight that the wretch was either rabid or insane. A sign on the front door had read "Hazmat," and outside, men in white plastic suits had loaded his neighbors into black sedans. That's when Meg and his daughter, in mid-conversation, had entered the room. He'd shouted for them to stop, but he was a phantom in his own house, and the women didn't hear.

The dog went after Meg first. It was about 180 pounds, and its open jaws had looked like a steel-toothed bear trap. Before she had the chance to run, it sank its teeth into her calf. She fell, and blood pooled all over the Persian rug. Maddie pulled her mother's arms to free her. Fenstad flinched at the memory, even now. Flinched that his mind had produced such a thing. Maddie had pulled, and the dog had pulled back, like two animals fighting over a bone.

That's all he remembered. But it wasn't so surprising to him now that he felt lousy this morning. The dream lingered in his mind. He felt guilty for having dreamed it, and frightened for her, too.

Just then, the bedroom door flew open, and Meg burst into the room like something was chasing her. Immediately he thought about the dog. Her eyes were red like she'd been crying, and her feet were bare.

He furrowed his brows. "What?"

She put her head on his shoulder. He led her to the bed, where they sat.

"What is it?"

She shrugged. There were dark circles under her eyes. The belt on her robe had come loose, and he could see her small, pert breasts. She'd left the house without underwear or pajamas, and he wondered, with a snap of fury, if any of the neighbors had spied her shaven crotch.

"Graham Nero? Has he been bothering you again?" Fenstad asked.

She sniffled and shook her head. "A bird," she said.

Did she want a bird? Had a bird attacked her out there? Was this the first sign of a brain tumor? He waited for her to say more, but she didn't. Instead she leaned over his hips and peeled back his wet towel. He should have guessed, but the gesture was so unexpected that even after he felt her tongue, her lips, it took him a moment to be sure.

He closed his eyes and moaned. It had been years since she'd done this. He'd forgotten how much he liked it. He decided that if he looked at her or petted the back of her head, he would ruin the moment. She'd feel exposed. So he smiled, and thought how wonderful it was that after all these years she could still surprise him. A woman who hated mornings. In their entire married life he could count on two hands the number of times they'd made love before breakfast.

She smelled like sweat and salt, scents she would bury after her shower with two spritzes of White Linen perfume. Her robe was open. She never believed him when he told her he liked her best in shorts and T-shirts. The things she didn't understand about him. He loved her because she was comfortable in her own skin, because she let him watch when she pleasured herself, which she'd only learned to do after Maddie was born. Because she'd carried his children in her womb.

She worked faster, and a bubble of pleasure caught in his throat. He wanted to cry out but did not. He tried to still his lips, to keep quiet, to watch her. She worked, faster and faster. When he reached his limit, he pushed her back against the bed. They made love. He didn't hold out for as long as he wanted. He was too close. There were sparks, and release. Maddie was just down the hall, and neither of them made a sound.

Afterward, they lay down next to each other.

"Not bad," he said, and by that he meant *fantastic*. Her breath was heavy. The exertion had made the dark green vein along her forehead visible. He thought about the dog in his dream, and put his arm around her as if to protect her from it. Tonight, there would be flowers. Tonight, he'd take her to dinner.

She wiped her mouth and leaned on his chest. She was a small woman, but the joints of her elbows were sharp against his ribs. "A bird died outside. It died in my hands."

He waited for her to say more. What was she talking about? He hadn't seen any birds.

"There's poison ivy under the house and I picked the berries and threw them on the walk. A bird ate them. It died in my hands."

Her normally unflappable voice cracked. He thought she was trying to tell him something. Was this about Graham Nero? Some elaborate way of explaining what she'd done? Birds didn't die from eating berries.

"Don't you have anything to say?" she asked. The rankle in her tone surprised him.

He blinked and tried to think. "Sounds like a dumb bird."

Her eyes narrowed into slits of fury. Should he have said, *Thank you* or *Great blow job, babe! You're aces with me*? This was ridiculous. She was his wife. Why did he need to say the right thing?

"So cold, Fenstad," she said, and at first he thought she was talking about the temperature, and then, from the look on her face, he knew, and he felt himself sink. So disappointing. "You should have been born a trout," she said. Then she turned and started into the bathroom. "You'd have been happier as a fish. We both would."

The water started running, and he did not get up for some time. The sheets were wet, and he was suddenly ashamed, like he was a dog that had pissed the bed. Down the hall Maddie clopped across the hard wood floor. Skinny like her mother, but loud and graceless as an ox. "Nobody woke me up!" she hollered into the ether. "Why didn't anybody wake me up?" Then she was off, down the stairs and in the kitchen, where she would suck the juice out of a sliver of grapefruit, toss the pulp, and declare herself full. Then she and Meg would fight until he left for work, and neither would notice that he was gone.

Don't you know there are people out there with real problems? he wanted to yell. *Don't you understand how lucky we've been?* But the human psyche is the same as its immune system. When it has no enemies to fight, it invents them.

Fenstad waited for Meg to come out of the shower. The door opened in a cloud of steam. Her skin was bright red, like she'd been trying to scald his touch from her body. She shrank from his hand as she passed him, as if his touch was repulsive.

He entered the bathroom and shut the door. It was so hazy with perfume that he sneezed. He closed his eyes and thought about how she had looked on the front lawn. So uncertain. Like she hadn't known if she would go to work today, or how she'd found herself in Corpus Christi, or whether she'd go back inside at all. A pause, as if her person was a mask she wore every morning, but she'd left the house without it, and for an instant been free. He thought about that, and then he thought about the black German shepherd in his dream, and the satisfying sound its teeth had made when they'd crunched on her bones.

FOUR
The War Between the States

At the same time that Lois Larkin discovered she'd accidentally abandoned her least favorite pupil to the desolate Bedford woods, Meg Wintrob was flipping through the pages of the double September issue of *Publishers Weekly*. She circled in red marker the young adult books she planned to acquire. So far she'd picked JT Petty's *Scrivener Bees*, and Stefan Petrucha and Thomas Pendleton's *Wicked Dead*.

Corpus Christi's library had been built in the 1970s, which explained why it was such a god-ugly heap of cinder blocks. Her office was a Plexiglas enclosure in the center of the main floor. One door opened onto the reference section, and the other led to the children's library. She had all the privacy of a goldfish.

The cheese and tomato sandwich she'd packed for lunch was wilting on her desk, but she didn't feel like eating it. The Great Chickadee Fiasco had soured her stomach. It was less about the bird now than about Fenstad. There are certain things you don't insult, and a man's performance in the sack is one of them. It had been cruel. *She* had been cruel. That was the problem: When it came to Fenstad, sometimes she couldn't help herself. He was so cold that she got tired of hugging him and started pinching him, just to be sure he still felt.

"Aheem. Aheem!" Albert Sanguine ticked at a library-volume whisper. Albert was sitting at the Internet terminal that faced Meg's desk. She watched his head twitter, and then become still as he focused on the screen. He was wearing a strange getup, even for Albert. Wingtips, a black turtleneck, and camouflage army pants with pockets full of what looked like junked L. L. Bean catalogs.

Meg picked up her sandwich. She'd had the bright idea of going gourmet, and adding balsamic vinaigrette, which had made the bread soggy. Right now Fenstad and Maddie were probably cursing her.

"Aaaheem! Aaaheem!" Albert ticked again. She wasn't sure if he was clearing his throat or having a spasm, but his voice was getting louder, so she struck her pen against the Plexiglas. He waved his acknowledgment with a shaking hand while his eyes remained focused on the screen.

Years of booze had rotted out Albert's nervous system, and he now had alcohol-induced Tourette's. After state cutbacks, the mental institution in Bangor had booted all its nonviolent patients, no matter how severe their conditions. Four of them were Corpus Christi natives, and when they returned home Fenstad set up a mental health clinic at the hospital for them. When they weren't at his group meetings, they were hanging out at the only other public place that would have them: the library. A few of them lived in subsidized housing near the Motel 6, the only part of Corpus Christi that wasn't solidly upper middle class. They survived on disability benefits and charity. At the library they spent their time reading books, surfing the Internet, and napping on the leather reading chairs that the Walker family had donated. People complained, but the way Meg saw it, the library existed for the public good. So long as they didn't bother anybody, they had a right to be here, too.

Albert was her favorite. Like a connoisseur savoring a 2001 Burgundy, he smelled new books before opening them. More importantly, he returned them on time. He was a voracious reader, and over the years he'd researched subjects that ranged from thermodynamics, to hematology, to his current obsession, Civil War camps. This last month he'd been stuck on the blight in American history that was Andersonville, Georgia. Thirteen thousand Union soldiers died there during its two years of operation. Nearby farmers had remained silent, even while mass graves began appearing like potholes along the camp's periphery.

Meg wasn't keen on supporting Albert's more macabre interests, but when he got ideas in his head he was adamant, and there wasn't much she could do to dissuade him. "Why the Civil War?" she'd asked last week. Without looking up from *The Trials of an Andersonville Prison Guard*, his head and hands shaking, he'd told her, "It's like an organism with immune disease. Aheem. AHEEM. It's a body that attacks itself."

That was the tragedy. Albert was no dope. He was thirty-three years old, but his breakdown happened when he left for college at the Massachusetts Institute of Technology to become a city planning engineer. He was eerily quick with numbers, but the separation from his family, and the pressure of classes and making new friends, had overwhelmed him. He became delusional and insisted that something was calling him back to Maine. He dropped out of MIT and moved home with his parents. Fifteen years later he still hadn't recovered. He refused to medicate the problem with antipsychotics, and instead drank booze until he passed out practically every night. Years of hard living had turned him into an old man. He was missing his eye-teeth, and the sparse tufts of hair on his head were white. He couldn't afford real booze, so he made home brew instead. He filtered Scope through white bread, and kept it in jars under his bed while it continued to ferment. Then he drank the juice, which he called bread pudding. She knew this because the smell was noxious and his landlord had cited him for six sanitation viola-tions, which his aging parents who lived across town, at a loss, had paid.

She'd always thought of him as a gentle and tragic giant, but during a recent fit of delirium tremens at the hospital, he punched a fourteen-year-old candy striper in the throat. The candy striper happened to be a bulimic, so the muscles in her throat were paper-thin. Albert tore a hole in her esophagus. After three hours of surgery, she recovered, though her interest in medicine was, under-standably, dampened. The act was Albert's first display of violence, but for Fenstad once was enough. He told Meg not to let Albert visit the library anymore. *Told* as in *ordered*.

Her husband was right, of course. Albert was worse with every passing day. A few weeks ago he'd confessed to her that he'd trapped a rat in his apartment, and af-ter skinning and then roasting its body over the flame of a Bic cigarette lighter, he'd eaten it. Years of bread pudding had taken their toll. His Tourette's-like erup-tions were intensifying, and he certainly didn't belong near children. But Meg *liked* Albert, and she *didn't like* being ordered around. So for now, until he proved him-self dangerous, he stayed. With mental hospitals closing their doors all over the country, where else were people like Albert supposed to go?

"Aaaheeem!" Albert suddenly ticked loud enough to clear a gorilla out of his throat.

Meg tapped her plastic pen against the Plexiglas a few times, but Albert didn't notice. He took a deep breath that looked like it was going to erupt into a howl. *Not now, Albert,* she thought. *I'm in no damn mood for somebody else's crazy.* She banged her fist until the office wall shivered. From the other side, Albert stopped mid-breath. Now they were both standing, the Plexiglas between them.

He was six-foot-five, and about 180 pounds. She was five-foot-nothing in three-inch heels. She knit her brows and slowly shook her head. On the other side of the plastic wall, Albert blushed. "Sorry, Ms. Wintrob," he mouthed, and sulked back into his chair.

Meg sat back down. Usually she shared her office with the business officer and deputy librarian, but they quit when the city cut their salaries last month. The town was still trying to hire their replacements. The rest of her staff was all volunteer, and they tended to gather at the reception desk, where they could drink coffee and read books in peace without Meg Wintrob's probing eye.

Meg lifted her *Publishers Weekly* and took a bite out of her soggy sandwich. Fenstad, she was thinking. There was a time that she'd loved him, but she couldn't remember it right now. These days when she saw him, she wanted to kick him. This made her think of the bird this morning, which in turn made her eyes watery. The brainless bird.

Five minutes later she looked at the clock. It was edging toward two P.M., and she had to get ready for story hour. She tossed her mostly untouched sandwich into the trash, and stood. Outside, Albert was quiet. All she could hear was the clickety-clack of his fingers typing against the keyboard, searching, no doubt, for photos of Andersonville. She tapped on the Plexiglas and nodded at him, hoping he'd behave while she was gone. Then she opened the door to the children's library.

The walls of the children's library were painted like a cloudy sky, and at the room's center was a circle of interconnected orange plastic chairs designed to look like the Barbapapas. This children's room was Meg's pride. All day it hummed with life. Right now toddlers were wobbling across the rainbow-patterned carpet while seven mothers and two fathers jabbered about their part-time jobs, the *Farmer's Almanac* predictions for the coming winter, and the good old days before babies, when six P.M. had meant cocktail hour.

Meg opened Sarah Shey's picture book about Iowa called *Sky All Around,* and began to read. Every time the book mentioned the sky, Meg pointed at the white cumulus clouds painted against the blue ceiling. All except Isabelle Nero pointed, too. Isabelle contentedly gummed her index finger like it was a chew toy.

Isabelle's mother, Caitlin, was young, blond, and button-cute. She sewed Isabelle's pretty dresses, worked mornings selling advertising space for the *Corpus Christi Sentinel*, and gave her husband nightly back rubs. Meg knew this because Caitlin's husband was Graham Nero.

Graham brokered long distance for a Boston-based investment firm, and in his spare time ogled cocktail waitresses. As their rendezvous he'd chosen room 69 at the Motel 6. Meg had done it partly for the thrill, but mostly for a reaction from Fenstad. Sex the first few times had been fantastic, most likely because she hadn't liked the guy enough to hold back. Still, if you're sleeping with a man, eventually you have to look him in the eye, and respect him. With Graham, that hadn't been possible. She'd looked at him, and cringed.

Fenstad found out within a month of their first visit to room 69. He never confronted her, or even explained how he found out. One night, instead of turning on the tube and watching the evening news, he sat at the kitchen table after she cleared it. Immediately she'd known that something was wrong. "I think you have a new friend," he'd said.

"Yes," she'd said. "I'm sorry." She'd waited for him to shout, to hit a counter, to cry, to announce that one of them had to move out. She'd been looking forward to it. But he didn't say anything. He just nodded, like he'd weather this storm of her temporary insanity, because even if she didn't know it herself, he trusted that she'd return to her senses.

What galled her most was that he was right. She called Graham that very night. Fenstad was listening at the table when she told him, "I can't see you anymore. My husband knows."

"Tough break, babe," Graham had said, which pretty much summed up Graham Nero. And Fenstad, sitting at that table, kept reading the paper, which pretty much summed up Fenstad Wintrob.

When Meg finished reading *Sky All Around*, she directed parents and children alike to the stack of books she'd selected on the subjects of Iowa and clouds. "Thank you, Meg. You're so good at story hour," Caitlin said with a blushing smile when it was over, and Meg nodded: "Anytime."

Meg pitied Caitlin. Graham wasn't inherently bad, but he was selfish. He'd ride her until her health gave out and her looks were gone. Caitlin was such a chump, she'd let it happen. Then Meg felt guilty, because she could quibble with the man's bedside manner, but at least Fenstad was a decent person.

Just then, someone started shouting in the reference

department: "Hey. Hey-o! *Heyoooh!!!*" The voice, un-mistakably, was Albert's. She frowned. He was never this loud.

"I'll be right back," Meg announced. She found Albert slapping his hands against either side of the used iMac he'd been working on, while the Plexiglas partition quivered. "*Heyoooh!*" he shouted, which meant, what, hello? Beads of spit hung in gooey strands between his mouth and the keyboard. Not surprisingly, but nevertheless infuriatingly, the three old ladies that made up the volunteer staff were hiding behind the reception desk. From a distance, Meg could see the top inch of Molly Popek's white bird's nest of hair.

"Albert?" she asked.

"*Heyoooh—Stoopit!*" he said. He was slamming so hard against the machine that for once his tremors weren't noticeable. She translated his babble: *Hey, you! Stop it.*

"Shut up!" Sheila Haggerty, the local bag lady, shrilled. On the table in front of her was the steel chain-link lock that she brought with her to the library every day, but never remembered to use to attach her grocery cart to the library's bike rack. "I hate a whiny whiner! My husband could shoot you!" she hollered.

"He's digging," Albert cried. "Oh, God. He's digging up my pretty bones." Drool flung in wild reams across his cheeks: "*Heyooostooopit!*" he shouted again as he slammed his hands against the monitor. Then she heard a loud click. He kept pounding, and as he did, his left wrist flexed parallel to his hand in a way that could only mean it was broken. What scared her most was that the break didn't slow him down.

"Molly!" she shouted, "Call the police." Molly was standing now. She looked at Meg for a second or two, and then turned her attention back to Albert without picking up the phone. Time was short, but Meg had just enough of it to mentally curse the friggin' coffee-sucking volunteers. Then she summoned the courage to come closer. On Albert's computer screen was a photo of an Andersonville burial. In it, Union soldiers were stacked ten men deep in an open grave. Their gaunt, naked bodies were pressed together like fitted puzzle pieces, inhuman and mundane.

"Albert!" she shouted. His back was to her, and he continued to slam his hands against the plastic machine.

"Albert!" Sheila mimicked in hysterical singsong: "Al-bert! Al-bert!" Then Bram and Joseph, the other two locals that made up the mental illness quartet she'd been abetting at the Corpus Christi Library, started shouting, too. The reference department was a sudden chorus, and she felt like queen of the loonies.

Across the library, parents quietly exited with toddlers in their arms. None of them, sadly, would be checking out or returning any books today. "I'm sorry," she murmured to Christen Fowler, who shook her head while walking out with her son, like it was Meg who was causing the ruckus.

After a while, Albert got tired and stopped banging. Sheila kept screaming his name until Meg shot her the scariest look she could muster: a knit-eyebrow, pruned-lip combo. Then she turned back to Albert, but was careful to keep her distance. "What's eating you?" she asked.

Albert was panting from fright, or exertion, or both. "So itchy. On the inside!" he hissed. "*Hey-ohhhh, stop digging!*"

"Let's go outside, Albert. We'll take a walk." She tried to keep her voice calm, but it wavered, and she could hear her own fright. He was, literally, twice her size.

Albert's eyes were bloodshot from booze. "In my bones it itches. All my places that count. How could that little boy do something so bad?" He came toward her. She thought of the candy striper and covered her throat.

"Molly!" she yelled. "Now. Nine-one-one. Now." Molly blinked but didn't move. In her peripheral vision she saw Lina Varvaran's father, Rich, pull a cell phone out of his pocket. He stood in the doorway of the building with his daughter to get better reception.

There were cuts along the tips of Albert's fingers. Blood had gathered there with such force that his skin had burst open. He was panting and wet with sweat. Slowly his body eased back into the chair, and she hoped he'd spent himself into exhaustion. She decided it was safe and felt his forehead for a temperature. His skin was clammy and cold, but her touch calmed him, and he visibly relaxed. "Does the itch feel like bugs on your skin?" she asked.

Albert shook his head. There were tears in his eyes. She felt very sorry for him just then. As if in some other dimension there was a clean-cut Albert Sanguine who was building bridges and raising a family, but in this one, all the cards he'd been dealt were unlucky.

His pupils got big, so that his eyes looked black instead of brown. "Let me go. Please, Ms. Wintrob," he muttered so quickly that it could have been one long tick.

"Have you had a drink today? Some of that bread?" she asked. "Do you need one?"

He shook his head. "Itches so bad. Like when your foot is rotting, and the moss grows inside where it doesn't belong. Hurts so bad." He was crying.

Meg pulled Albert's chin between her fingers and looked into his eyes. Even though he was sitting, her body was dwarfed next to his. "Pull yourself together," she said. "I mean it."

"It's awake," he whispered, and a chill ran down her spine. What was awake? The demon inside him that drove him to drink? For one frenzied moment she wondered: *What if this voice he's been raving about these fifteen years is real?*

His pupils got even bigger, until no white was left. A seizure? She didn't know. But suddenly his breath came easy. His posture stiffened. Even his tremors were gone. He was different. She couldn't explain how she knew this, but it was true. Albert Sanguine had left the building. At first she was too sad to be frightened. The booze had finally gobbled the remains of Albert's soul, and the last spark of his personality was gone.

"Albert?" she asked.

It happened fast. He squeezed her upper arms with bloody hands. She struggled to get away, but he was strong. As he pulled her between his legs, he flexed his thighs. The gesture was sexual. She gasped. Albert. Her Albert: *How could he do this?*

She was inside his lap. His arms and legs held her in place like a vise. "Stop!" she shouted. His lips were drawn high over the blackness of missing eyeteeth, and his face was a snarl.

He lurched forward and pressed his wet mouth against her ear. She wriggled, and decided that if necessary, she'd bite off his nose while trying her best not to swallow anything. She could smell the bread alcohol. The smell of vinegar and shit. "Where did I go wrong, Meg?" he whispered, and she stopped struggling. She went still. His voice was low. Reasonable, but not at all kind.

Impossible. There was no way. And yet, she knew to whom that voice belonged. "Where did I go wrong?" he asked again, and suddenly she was a young woman, dropping out of law school to marry a Jew her father didn't approve of, and on the morning of the wedding, instead of telling her that he'd always love his little girl, he'd asked: *Where did I go wrong?*

"Daddy?" Meg's voice was halting and childlike.

He pulled back and she looked at him, this man. A black gap in his mouth, a ruined face, white hair. His bleary eyes were full of resentful affection. The only kind of affection, she realized, that she'd ever understood. But her father was dead, wasn't he? Long ago she'd made her peace and let go of him, the man for whom nothing she'd ever done was good enough.

In a quick move he was standing, and she was in his arms. She saw it coming, but there wasn't time to fight. He tossed her against the Plexiglas like a hollow-boned bird. She heard the whistle of air as she flew, and then a smack, and wiggling plastic like techno music. When she looked up from the ground, it took her a second before she figured out how she'd gotten there, or what that snapping sound had been.

To her own dismay (wasn't she supposed to be a fighter?), she didn't get up off the floor, but instead curled into a ball and played dead. When nothing happened she peeked out and saw Albert opening the door to the children's room. Then came the sounds around her that she hadn't noticed before. "Shut up! Shut up!" Sheila was singing. Bram tore his *Corpus Christi Sentinel* into pieces and flung them in Albert's direction, as if trying to confetti him to death. The children's section was ominously quiet.

Her left ankle hurt like fire, but she hobbled toward her office. She stopped when she realized that the only reason she wanted to get there was to call Fenstad. She wanted to hear his steady, calm voice. She wanted, ridiculously, to tell him that she might not like him, but she definitely loved him.

Across the way something smashed. Had Albert pushed over a bookcase? Then a small voice cried, "Help," and adrenaline coursed through her blood so fast she could feel the rush: A kid was in there with Albert. A little kid.

On a hobbled foot, she started to charge. But then she stopped. She needed a plan or he'd swat her like a fly. Her ankle hurt so bad that she was biting on her lip to keep from fainting. She scanned the reference room. There was something she was looking for. Something she could use. She looked at the bookcases, the too-big couches, the computers (electrocution?), the Bic pens not nearly sharp enough to poke out an eye, and then she saw it near the newspapers: Sheila's two-foot chain-link lock. "Shut up!" Sheila sprayed with spit as Meg lifted it off the table and limped into the children's library.

Albert was standing on the rainbow carpet with his back to her. He'd cornered Caitlin Nero and her daughter, Isabelle, behind a Barbapapa chair. Everyone else was gone.

Meg sneaked up behind him. She saw sparks and her peripheral vision went hazy. This pain in her ankle was no sprain: Her leg was turning blue. She bit down harder, until she tasted blood, and it kept her focused. Then she loosened the chain in her hands so that the heavy part hung slack enough to swing.

A second passed, and then another. She waited. Maybe this wasn't necessary. Maybe she was the real nut in the room, swinging a bike lock like some kind of modern-day Bernie Goetz. This was how people got killed. Hotheads overreacted. Her grip started to loosen, but then Isabelle coughed, and Albert charged.

Meg dragged her broken foot behind the good one.

She cocked her arms and swung just before he got hold of Caitlin Nero, who'd inserted herself between Albert and little Isabelle. Meg swung so hard that she spun, and then, off balance, fell.

The lock curved around Albert's back and struck his pelvis. The sound it made was a soft thud, and at first she thought she hadn't swung hard enough, but then his upper body teetered over his still feet, and he collapsed. He fell down next to her so that they lay facing each other. The L. L. Bean catalogs from his pocket scattered across the rainbow carpet.

He didn't look like Albert. His mouth was drawn into a scowl, and the rotten booze on his breath was rancid. Like star-crossed lovers, their lips were inches apart. "Where did I go wrong?" he mouthed. Then his eyes fluttered shut.

Caitlin and crying Isabelle stood over the two of them. She noticed, though she hadn't before, that they were wearing matching pink floral dresses, which even in the moment struck her as asinine.

Caitlin's brow was furrowed in a look of pure hatred. It was shocking in its intensity. In its secrecy, because she did not know that Meg was awake. Her eyes rolled across Meg's small body, and it wasn't Albert, Meg realized, that she hated. *She knows what I did with her husband*, Meg thought with the kind of shame that feels like an open wound. *So why does she keep coming to the library every week?*

Something warm trickled across her fingers, and she guessed, but didn't want to know for sure, that it was Albert's blood. At first she thought Caitlin had begun screaming at her, could have sworn she heard the word "whore!" but then, in the distance, she recognized the sirens.

FIVE

Robitussin for What Ails You!

On the afternoon that his wife swung a steel chain into her good friend's back, Fenstad Wintrob was listening to Lila Schiffer babble. Her voice was Chinese water torture. Duller than a dinner with Andre, more superficial than a "Free Tibet" rally, more painful than the eyeball-bleeding stage of hemorrhagic fever.

Lila had been talking nonstop for twenty minutes. Her current topic was the changing of the seasons, and the fact that autumn always seemed like the end of something. "Like you'll never get it back, because even when next summer comes, it won't be the same. It'll be a different summer," she said.

Her dazed smile gave her the semblance of someone who'd recently undergone an ice-pick lobotomy. She didn't know how to talk to men, even her own psychiatrist, without flirting. But despite her late-night calls, low-cut tube tops, and the lingering smears of bright red lipstick that she left on his cheek when she kissed him good-bye, Fenstad wasn't tempted. Well, that wasn't true. Her body was round and taut as a 1940s pinup girl's. But he'd never seriously considered her. First, she was his patient. Second, infidelity was not something Meg would forgive.

He winced just thinking about this morning. *Cold,* she'd called him. Then she'd shaken her head like a martyr, and he'd wondered whether all women were fickle, because did she think at forty-eight years of age he was going to change?

Besides, cold wasn't so bad. It meant he was practical, dependable. People trusted him. That's why he was a psychiatrist. He didn't chew on problems: He solved them.

His whole life, people had confided in him. Kids on the track team who still wet their bed (well, just the one), teachers who couldn't get dates, fellow med school students with drug problems—you name it. They had always come to him first.

Even his mother used to chew his ear. Back in Wilton, Connecticut, her voice had cut through the air like ammonia. "Fennie!" she'd hollered whenever she heard the patter of his little feet along the wooden hallway. Some of his sharpest childhood memories were of standing vigil at her bedside while she itemized her complaints. From underneath her finely woven Egyptian cotton sheets, she'd weep for her long-dead grandfather and the imaginary cancer that she was convinced was scooping the marrow from her bones. For reasons he still didn't understand, her room had smelled like fermenting cabbage and musky sweat. To this day he associated that scent with her undiagnosed manic depression.

When Fenstad was old enough to stay away from home, he did. He joined the cross country and track teams, and long after meets were over he'd sit on the gym bleachers and study until a janitor turned out the lights. At night he'd sneak through the back door of his parents' house, gobble whatever leftovers in sealed Tupperware he could find, and then collapse into bed without taking off his shoes while his stereo headphones hummed the lullabies of Warren Zevon and Lynyrd Skynyrd.

Still, encounters with Sara Wintrob were unavoidable. "Fennie," she'd call when she heard him tiptoeing down the stairs in rubber-soled sneakers weekend mornings. He'd dutifully visit her room, where she'd tell him, "You're father doesn't love me anymore. He'll leave me, and we'll be all alone," or better yet: "I think I'm dying, Fennie. My heart keeps stopping and starting again."

Despite her endless complaints, she managed to get a lot done while Fenstad and his father were out of the house. The meals got cooked, the groceries bought, and the clothing washed. Even the *Hustler* collection Fenstad hoarded under his mattress got tossed into the garbage bin every month like clockwork.

The incident Fenstad would nominate as most worthy of forgetting took place when he was a sophomore in high school. He'd just come home from track practice after racing three sets of eight hundred-meter time trials. His legs had been weak as wet noodles when Sara called him into her room, and he'd had to hold on to the banister as he'd mounted the stairs. When he got to her bedside, Sara was breathing fast and heavy. *Hypochondria,* he'd immediately thought, and then, deep down, even though he knew it wasn't true, *heart attack.*

"Mom?" he'd asked. Her white cotton nightgown had been tangled around her waist, and he'd noticed that her legs were still firm despite the apparent disuse. Her dark hair had hung in wet, sweaty rings. She took his hand and placed it over her breast: "Do you think it's a lump?"

In those days he'd thought about girls constantly,

though he hadn't touched one yet. In school he got so
horny just looking at them that he had to fill his mind
with images of Cambodian refugees and his grandfather's fungus-filled toenails just to keep from exploding. He'd started to wonder whether he was a pervert,
because even when his fifty-year-old fat-assed biology
teacher stood from behind her desk or even smiled at
him, his body had saluted her, and he'd imagined throwing her down against her steel-backed chair and getting
it on.

And so there he had been with his hand on his mother's breast. Something moved beneath his fingers, and
at first he'd thought it was a slithering insect. It wasn't
a bug. It was her hardening nipple. To his shame, he felt
himself go hard, too. "Feel that, Fennie? Do you think
it's a lump?" she asked. He looked her in the eye and
she winced; they both understood that there was no
tumor.

Sara and Ben still lived in Wilton, Connecticut. Ben
never left, and Sara never died. They called once a
week, and if Fenstad answered the phone he handed it
to Meg, explaining that Meg was better at small talk.
Most of the time, Fenstad believed he'd forgiven Sara
for that small act of madness. Other times, when he
woke from restless dreams and the lingering smell of
fermented cabbage, he knew he hadn't. To this day,
whenever someone called him "Fennie," shivers coursed
along his spine like fallen power lines jigging across
blacktop.

Shortly after the episode with Sara and her thin
nightgown, something inside Fenstad broke. He'd been
wet with his own emotions as a kid, practically leaving
puddles of the stuff like slugs' trails wherever he walked.
People were starving in Africa, he cried. His dad raised
his voice, he quivered. A kid at school asked him why

he didn't celebrate Christmas, he didn't come out of his room all weekend. And then something broke, and he got so depressed that he had a hard time getting out of bed. He couldn't read, sleep, or tie his shoes without choking back tears. Most alarmingly, he started to imagine that the carpeted floor in his parents' bedroom was wet with blood. Every time he walked across it, in his mind the thick fibers squished under his feet and sucked on his shoes.

He never recovered from that break. Instead, after a while, a switch flipped inside him, and the depression ended. In its place he turned cold. Life got a lot easier after that. The burning in his stomach that he would later self-diagnose as juvenile ulcers healed. He was one of three Jews in a WASP town, but he stopped worrying that the kids who called him "kosher" meant something worse, like kike. Instead he put his arm around them, shined 'em a toothy grin, and said things like *Fuck, yeah. Proud of it.* He asked the prettiest girl in American History to the winter formal junior year. Her name was Joanne Streibler, and after the dance she let him lick his index finger and explore her soft, velvety places.

Sure, he didn't feel things with the same intensity that he used to. He wasn't elated the first time he and Joanne made love in his cousin's Chevy G20 van. He didn't jump for joy when he was accepted at Harvard, or when Meg promised to love, honor, and respect him at the Massachusetts State Justice of the Peace. But he was pleased, and that was just fine. Besides, Meg felt things deeply enough for the both of them.

He knew he exhibited symptoms of an antisocial personality disorder. He never cried for people like Lila, or stayed up nights worrying about them. Under different circumstances he might have become a criminal, a thief, or even a sadist. When he learned of Meg's affair he'd wanted to murder her, and he suspected that this instinct had lasted longer in him than in a normal person. He'd imagined burying her alive in the crawl space below the house, trapping her in the sixteen-hundred-degree waste incinerator at the hospital, strangling her with her own pearls while she begged for mercy, you name it. But the point was: He didn't kill her. He forgave her.

It was trite and a little infantile that he blamed his mother for the way he'd turned out, had become a doctor in order to save her, save himself from the nightmares so vivid that in his dreams even now he could smell the fermenting cabbage, feel the bloody rug on his feet, but so be it. You can't help where you come from, and you certainly can't help the direction that place points you.

So he had his complaints, and maybe he was cold, but he was doing his best with what nature had given him. And fortunately, nature had given him a good deal more than it had bequeathed to Lila Schiffer.

"On TV yesterday," Lila said, "Dr. Phil's guest was this guy who was talking about low carbohydrate diets. He said you should only eat red meat. It doesn't make much sense to me, but if they say it on *Dr. Phil* it must be true." With her fingers she traced the folds along the legs of her jeans. Then she continued. "Fall makes me gain weight . . ." He inwardly moaned. She was back on the changing seasons again. He wondered how she'd been able to rant about this for so many sessions without ever knowing that she was really lamenting her own fading beauty. "The houseflies come in fall. I hate bugs. Sometimes I want them to go away so badly I'm tempted to eat them."

Fenstad drooled a little, and then wiped it from the

corner of his mouth with his shirt sleeve. He thought about Meg calling him cold. The bitch had spread her legs for the sleaziest sonofabitch in Corpus Christi, and you'd think he was the one who'd done something wrong. He thought about Chinese torture, the water dripping, dripping, dripping until a man went mad. He thought about a sickroom with plush blue carpet soaked in blood, and the sound his shoes might make as he walked across it.

Lila grinned. He wondered if she was like this at home with her children, a whining hag who woke them from peaceful dreams. Just like Sara Wintrob. For a moment he hated Lila, and his wife, and his mother, and especially Freud.

He looked up and noticed that Lila had stopped talking. He waited for her to begin again, but she didn't. It occurred to him that she'd tired herself out.

Fenstad cleared his throat. It was time to cut the crap. "You're avoiding something. Tell me what happened this week," he said.

She cocked her head, and there was another silence. She was wearing an unprecedented amount of clothing. Usually her dress code was strictly roadhouse fare: tube tops and miniskirts. But today her long-sleeved blouse was buttoned above her bra line, and her jeans were high enough to conceal the butterfly tattoo on her hip.

The clock ticked. He knew he should be paying attention, but instead he was thinking about Meg. This last year had been going great until now. Sure, she had her bad moods once in a while, but mostly he'd been thinking that their life together was on the mend. And then the fish comment. He *hated* when she called him a trout. And what was that supposed to mean, anyway: He was bad in the sack? She'd been faking it for, say, twenty years?

"So," Lila said, "I goofed, but only a little." She shrugged her shoulders and grinned, like she'd been caught filling out a questionnaire in pen rather than pencil. "I was brushing my teeth, and I thought I'd just *taste* it but, well . . ." she said.

"You drank Robitussin again?" he asked.

She nodded. "Chest and cold. Sugar-free, at least. "

"How much?"

"Half the bottle. But then I threw it up again." Robitussin is about 15% alcohol by volume. It's mostly harmless, although a stiff scotch tastes a lot better.

"Can you describe what triggered the drinking?" he asked.

She chewed on her lip like she was thinking about it. Lila was newly divorced from a man who had never let her lift a finger, pay a bill, or even pick out a gown for the Corpus Christi Golf Club cotillion without his say-so. She was a ping-pong ball in an ocean, trying to gain purchase. Her kids snickered at her and called her useless. Her contemporaries had never accepted her, this woman of lesser education and trashy good looks whom they viewed as competition. Her husband had remarried a younger trophy. And now she'd taken to drinking cough syrup because she was afraid that the neighbors would gossip if she bought the real stuff at the local liquor store.

In a year or so she'd meet another man just like the one who'd left her, only older, and with luck she'd marry him. With more luck he'd die of old age or a heart attack before he replaced her, too. And the thing was, Fenstad could try to show her that this was no way to live, but she'd never believe him. In the end the best he could do was channel her cough-syrup drinking into a rigorous jogging program until a new man came around and told her she was pretty again.

Lila grinned winningly, and he wondered: *Who is the woman you're hiding underneath that grin?* It was the question that kept him coming to work every morning. The mystery of people. It was the thing underneath the layers of invention that sloughed away over weeks and months and years of therapy until their hypochondria, their neuroses, their self-flagellation all looked the same. *What are you?* he wondered when he saw these people. It was a question, quite frankly, that he often asked himself.

"The news set me off," she said.

"The news?"

"Yes. I was watching *Entertainment Tonight* and they ran this story about a blind man."

He nodded.

"Aran and Alice were supposed to be doing their homework but they weren't. I knew I should have scolded them, but I was watching the show about the blind man. He lived in Seattle, and the only way he got around was his golden retriever. I like hounds better, but you know where I'm going."

He remembered his dream for a moment, a barking dog, and then promptly forgot it. "You've caught me. I don't know where this is going."

"The seeing-eye dog. They had to retire him because he got too old to take care of the man. He got fired, just like that, you know? That made me think of my first dog, and how he got put to sleep on account he bit my brother Tom. We grew up in Bedford, did you know that? A trailer park—I don't usually tell people that. I only moved away when I married Aran Senior.

"So I was thinking about the dog, and the rain, how it gets all wet in Seattle. And my brother and how much I miss him. He died in the fire in Bedford. He was asthmatic. Anyway, I told the kids I was going to take a bath and they said, 'Fine, Lila,' because they only call me by my first name even though I hate that.

"And I was looking at the razor, you know? The straight one I got for Aran Senior as a gag present because it was an antique and he likes that kind of thing, or he used to. He left everything when he moved out. I guess he only pretended to like the presents I gave him. I guess they weren't any good, those pretty crystal geodes and that Underwood typewriter from 1917. He treated them like they were nothing. And then I remembered you're supposed to slice with the grain, like wood. So I did."

She rolled back the left sleeve of her white cotton blouse. Her wrist was crudely bandaged with brown masking tape and gauze. The exposed skin surrounding the area was red and inflamed.

Fenstad's stomach dropped. For the first time in a long while he was disappointed in himself. He'd failed her. He'd sat in judgment of her, this redundant woman whose husband had thrown her away like a used condom. He'd forgotten that he was supposed to be her advocate. Screw the wall, he was supposed to be her friend.

"Just the one arm." She smiled. "I'm not a fanatic or anything . . ."

"Go on," he said.

"Anyway, the water got all pink, and I was thinking about what would happen when they found me. The kids, they probably wouldn't notice until they had to brush their teeth. They'd call him rather than breaking down the door. They're closer to me, but they trust him. So it would have been a few hours before he found me. The blood would have settled to the bottom of the tub by then. It would have been all sticky like grout. In my hair, too. It would have clotted there. But then again, his new wife's a redhead . . ." Her eyes were dull specks of coal, and her voice was without emotion. This was the real Lila, the one he'd been waiting this last year to meet. A breakthrough, at last.

"I thought he'd find me and I'd look like Grace Kelly or something." She laughed. The sound echoed eerily. "But you know, my skin would have gotten all pruned and thin. And I've packed on about six pounds. It would have scared the devil out of him, seeing me like that. He deserves it, too! The rest of his life he'd feel sorry for what he did to me.

"I don't know. I decided not to cut the other wrist. So I tried to stop the blood." She lifted up her arm, "One of those cotton gauze jobs from a ten-year-old first aid kit. Probably dirtier than toilet paper, but you know me, I don't know how to take care of myself." Her fingers were pale, and each long nail was perfectly shellacked with red paint. "And then I saw the Robitussin and I thought, well, at least it's not permanent, and nobody'll know. So there was that."

"Can I see your arm?" he asked.

She clenched her hand into a fist and rolled down her sleeve so the wound was out of view.

"I'm a doctor. If there's anything to do, I can do it." She didn't move, and it occurred to him that she didn't trust him nearly as much as he'd assumed. "Lila, be reasonable. It might be infected."

She shrugged and, after some time, handed him her arm. He lifted her sleeve while she turned her head, and it made him feel as if he was doing something shameful and too intimate.

The corners of the wound were crusted with yellow pus, and probably full of bacteria. He found a scissors and cut away the loose edges. Then he dabbed it with the peroxide from the hospital stock first aid kit in his bottom desk drawer. Bit by bit he eased the cotton away from the clot. The wound reopened and started to ooze, but only superficially. The cut was a deep fissure, like a sideways mouth, and the skin surrounding it had not closed together. She'd sliced just right, splitting open about three inches of artery. If she'd fallen asleep in that tub, she would not have woken up.

He rebandaged the wound with more gauze, then wrapped it in surgical tape. It would leave a long scar and should have been stitched together by a surgeon, but it was too late for that now. He handed her a tube of antibiotic ointment to take home. "You should have called me," he said.

She nodded. "I didn't want to bother you. I know I talk too much." There was a flicker of comprehension between them, and he understood that he represented her absent husband, father, brother, son. She was trying to punish them. She was trying to punish him, too.

"Do you think you should stay at the hospital for a while?"

She shook her head, "No. I won't do it again."

"Lila, this is big," he said. "I'm glad you told me, but I'm concerned for your safety, and the safety of your children."

She smiled broadly, and her flirtatious manner returned. The rapidity of the transition alarmed him. She cocked her head like a young girl at a debutante ball talking to the best marriage prospect in the room. "Oh, Dr. Wintrob. I promise, I'll never do it again. Really. It was just the news. I won't watch the news anymore."

Fenstad considered. He knew he should check her into the hospital for the night. But she didn't have family or friends, so she'd have to call her ex-husband to take the children. Aran Senior was waiting for an excuse to sue for full custody. This would qualify. Lila would crumble under the pressure and cede the rights to her children. The downward spiral he was trying very hard to prevent would begin. He made his decision.

"I want you to keep up your journal. Try to write down what you're feeling when you find the urge to drink or hurt yourself. Would you do that? And bring it in to me next week?"

She nodded.

The hour had ended five minutes ago, so he opened his desk and wrote her a prescription for a week's supply of the mood stabilizer Stelazine. "This should calm your nerves."

She folded the paper and discreetly slid it into her purse like it was his phone number. "I want you to call me if you feel anything like this coming on again," he said.

"Of course, Dr. Wintrob," she said. Her grin was wide and vacant. She didn't seem to notice that the ointment had made a wet spot on the sleeve of her white silk blouse. She was exposed, and she didn't even know it. He was surprised and a little discomfited by the pity he felt for her. It made him rethink his decision: She needed to be hospitalized.

He was about to tell her so when his secretary burst through the door and announced that his wife had been attacked.

SIX
The Melancholy Choir

By seven o'clock that Tuesday in Corpus Christi, the day was coming to an end. The sun was sinking below the horizon, and street lamps cast a jaundiced glow. Shops lit up their "Open" signs, and people leaving day shifts at the hospital rolled down their windows on their way home to enjoy the temperate night. At the high school track, scrawny and muscle-bound adolescents ran laps. The days had gotten shorter since August. With early dark came a melancholy that made people regret the summer they were leaving behind, and the inevitable winter to come. It was a chill that ran along the backs of their necks; they traded pleasure for purpose. Backyard Stoli and tonics for work that had yet to be done.

Lois Larkin was the exception. She wasn't thinking about the lesson plans she needed to prepare, the graduate school applications that would soon be due, or how she'd intended to grovel at Ronnie's door tonight and beg him to take her back. She was thinking about the little boy she'd lost. The boy without a coat or scarf, who was surely shivering by now. Worse things might be happening to James Walker than just a chill along the back of his neck.

She was curled in a fetal position in the back of the chief of police's blue Dodge. She wanted to close her eyes and make this go away. She wanted a miracle. She wanted, just a little bit, to die.

When she got back to the school this afternoon, a quick head count gave her twenty-five instead of twenty-six. It took her a few seconds, she just couldn't believe how stupid she'd been, didn't *want* to believe it, but she counted again, and remembered the little pain in the butt who'd refused a partner, and before she even called his name and got no answer, she knew that James Walker was missing.

She sent the kids back to class with Janice Fischer and told the bus driver to head to the Bedford woods. Her gut told her that James was playing a prank. She hadn't been upset yet, just galled that he'd outsmarted her.

Her next stop was the principal, Carl Fritz. Carl was forty, unmarried, and his socks always matched the brightly patterned dress shirts he ordered from Bluefly.com. She'd pegged him as gay until the day he told her that he didn't think she knew her own worth. His eyes had lingered on her breasts, and she'd understood that his interest was not brotherly.

When she told Carl what happened, he took a slow and dramatic face dive into his desk, where he moaned like a dying bullfrog. When he surfaced, he started rearranging the yellow, green, and orange Beanie Babies that lined the front of his desk. He'd never cut their tags because he was sure that one day he could sell them on eBay for a lot of money. "You *lost* him?" he repeated, like there was an off-chance Lois would say she'd misspoken, and really, she just wanted another week's vacation.

"Yeah, Carl," she said, even though before this day she'd always called him Mr. Fritz, just to keep their relationship clear. "I did."

He didn't look at her. He surveyed the annual debate team photos dating back to 1972, his vintage *Singin' in the Rain* poster, and finally his shaking hands whose fingernails he got buffed weekly at Lee's Salon.

"I thent—sent—the bus driver back for him, but to cover our beth we should call the police and his family. He'th a clown, only in a mean way. He'll hide until he'th ready to come out."

Carl didn't make a move, and the seconds ticked away. She picked up the phone and hit button two on the speed dial, which he'd made a big deal about adding to his phone after Columbine. "You talk. They should hear it from you," she said, then handed him the receiver. After a dramatic pause, he put it to his ear.

That call was easy one. Once the Walker family name was mentioned, Carl was connected to Tim Carroll, the chief of police. Tim instructed them to meet him at the edge of the woods immediately. The next call was the tricky one. To his credit, Carl didn't dicker around once he got Miller Walker on the line. Instead he blurted: "Your son wasn't on the bus home from his field trip. We're on our way back to Bedford to get him. I'm sure he'll be fine—just wanted to let you know."

Walker's reply, which Lois was close enough to hear, was without hesitation. "I want that teacher's resignation by the end of the day," he said. Probably he'd said *that teacher* because he didn't know her name.

"Of course," Carl replied while simultaneously shrugging his shoulders at Lois as if to say: *Sorry, sweetheart, but my neck's on the line, too.*

They took Carl's green Audi to the Bedford woods. When they got there James wasn't waiting at the crumb-spotted picnic table, where the Granny Smith apple core she'd left behind was now brown. Her stomach sank, but she didn't allow herself to worry: There was a boy to be found.

All seven full-time members of the police department arrived soon after she and Carl. Together they searched the woods. She touched the fresh tracks the school bus had made, looking for clues. After about two hours, Miller Walker and his wife pulled up in a red diesel Mercedes. Felice stayed in the car while Miller took a moment to straighten his tie, sneer at Lois, and join the search.

Even then, it hadn't truly hit her. She'd been thinking about Ronnie, Noreen, and the engagement announcement in the morning paper. She'd been thinking about how she needed to get a pregnancy test from CVS on her way home. She'd been thinking about her mother, probably drunk by now, and how this thing with James was just more proof that the world was against her.

By hour three, the temperature dropped below forty degrees. The worry in her stomach got bigger. It spread like an itch she couldn't scratch. No little boy would hide for this long, not even a cretin like James. He had to be lost. But what if he wasn't lost? What if a wild animal had attacked him, or some pedophile had locked him in the trunk of a car and was now speeding across the border to Canada?

She'd lost a kid. On her watch, a kid might have been hurt or kidnapped or worse. By six that evening more than twenty searchers were combing the woods. Volunteer firemen, members of the PTA, and Miller Walker's neighbors and friends trampled the grounds surrounding the woods, so that stray pine needles and strands of grass were impressed like fossils in hardened boot treads.

As dusk fell, Tim organized a wider search. Like an elaborate game of Marco Polo with gaps no greater than ten feet apart, they formed a line and called to one another as they marched through the woods. The arcs of their flashlights shone against dead trees. Lois searched feverishly. The itch in her stomach spread into her chest and legs, and even her throat. The woods were trampled, the boy was missing: a mess, her mess. She had to find James Walker. She had to clean it up. But as darkness settled, and six inched its way to seven, there was no James to be found.

She was tempted to get down on her hands and knees and pray, but she didn't. If people hadn't guessed how serious this was, seeing her prostrate in prayer would give them a pretty good hint. Who cared what the EPA said, these trees looked like empty corn husks. Nothing lived here anymore! No birds. No deer. Nothing. What if James got thirsty and drank the polluted river water, or ate the leaves full of God knew what? There were crazies in these woods. Genuine Bedford locals. The kind who let their cars turn to rust in their front yards and hung effigies of dead men on the sides of their RVs. The kind who stayed in toxic ghost towns, long after the sane had fled.

She started to lose it. A mess. Her life was a mess. Being a loser was one thing, screwing up a kid's life was a whole different story. James had been missing for six hours, and they'd found nothing. Not a piece of clothing. Not a lock of hair or even a juice box. Nothing.

A tear rolled down the side of her face, but she didn't wipe it away. She knew if she did, more would follow. She'd start bawling right in front of Miller Walker, Tim Carroll, Carl Fritz, and the whole dang PTA. So she asked Tim for the keys to his Dodge and curled up in a ball in his backseat.

As soon as she got there, her mind started spinning. There was Ronnie, and her mom, and Noreen, and now

James Walker, whom she'd never given a chance or gone out of her way to help with his long division. The kid might have turned out okay despite the boy he was now. He might have cured cancer or invented painless braces. Only now they might never find out.

She was thinking about this, and the itch in her stomach kept growing until she could feel it in her heart and kidneys and bladder. An itching, like everything inside her was red and inflamed. And then, suddenly, a squawk burst out of her mouth. A braying explosion that sounded like crying without tears. Its vibrations rippled through her chest. It lasted about five seconds, and then stopped just as suddenly as it had started. She ran her hands along the tops of her breasts and pressed, as if searching for a hidden animal in there. It was unnerving that she'd been able to produce such a noise. Like something in her lungs had woken up, and decided to bark.

Out the window, a haze settled over the woods. It looked like a dirty fog. She watched it drift down the hill and through the vents of the car. It stank like skunk. Particulate sulfur pollution and ash from the old mill. Another reason she should never have planned a class trip here. Right now every one of those searchers had to be thinking: *That Lois Larkin, what an imbecile!*

Suddenly, from outside the car, she heard a child's voice; high-pitched but not girlish. It was muffled, and she couldn't tell what it said. *James?* she wondered. Was he out there? Had they found him?

She got out of the car. The base of the woods was full of parked SUVs, Audis, Saabs, and Hondas. She could hear the searchers calling to one another, but it didn't sound like they'd found him. The voice was coming from the woods, too. It was muffled, but it definitely belonged to a child. A boy. She sighed with relief. Thank God. Oh, thank the dear, sweet Lord.

She jogged into the woods, and now she could hear what the boy said. "Lois," he called. *James,* she thought with relief so sweet that her saliva could have been Necco wafers: Only a terror like James would use her first name.

She jogged through the search party's net. Her brow was sweating, and she was beginning to pant. "That you, Miss Larkin?" a volunteer fireman asked. He shone a white sphere of light across her face. She shielded her eyes with her hands.

"Yeah, ith me."

"Okay. Take it easy. We'll find him."

"Sure."

Deeper in the woods, the voice called again: "Lois!" The sound reverberated through the air. An idea occurred to her, but she didn't want to think about it. A part of the voice came from the woods, but if she was going to be honest, really honest, it came from a closer place, too. It was soft and barely discernible. A whisper. It came from inside her own head.

Did she want to find this kid so badly she was inventing him? Probably. Still, he might be out there. He might be alive, and if she found him, she could fix this mess she'd made. She lifted her shirt and began to scratch her belly: The itch had spread from her organs all the way out to her skin.

She reached the river where the searchers had turned around, and crossed it. Beyond the rocks was a clearing. The voice wasn't calling her anymore, but she could feel it. She could feel it inside her. Was she going crazy? Maybe. It didn't matter. One way or another, she was going to find James Walker.

The haze and the river water reflected the moonlight so that the clearing was bright. The sulfur was strong here. The place stank so bad that her eyes teared. Ashes from the mill fire, probably. As she neared the clearing, she saw something red against the soot-blackened earth. A piece of clothing. She picked it up. The hood from a child's sweatshirt. The tears were jagged and full of threads, as if pulled from a shirt with bare hands. Strong hands. Sweet relief turned bitter on her tongue.

Then she saw the hole in the ground. About three feet deep. Had James dug it? Was James *in* it? She looked inside, but save for some rocks, the hole was empty.

Lois, the voice said. It came from two places. It licked her ears and sated the itch like rain on a thirsty flower. A trick, she realized with a moan. The voice was a trick. James had gotten her good . . . But no boy knew how to play this kind of trick. Ronnie? Noreen? Were they doing this?

The voice answered her, only now it didn't sound like it belonged to a child. It was deep, and throaty. *He's down here with me, Lois.*

She uttered that sound again, that bark of pain too fresh to be accompanied by tears. She got dizzy and had to kneel on top of the rocks over the empty hole to keep from falling. Dead, she realized. The boy was dead.

Something moved inside her, and she jumped back and scrambled a few feet from the hole while sliding on her butt so that the legs of her trousers turned dark with soot. The thing peered out from her eyes. She could feel it. An enemy slithering between her ears. *Lois,* it whispered. Her heart pounded, and for a moment she was tempted to gouge her eyes in order to pull the thing out.

And then, from down the hole, she heard a child's voice. "Here Miss Lois!" it called, as if she was taking attendance. She bit her lip and wanted to cry, with hope or with dread, she did not know which. Was he alive? Was he somehow down that empty hole? Or was he . . . something else. She cupped her hands around her mouth to call for help, but the voice stopped her. *If you tell I'll kill him. They'll blame you. Then where will you be? Watching* Millionaire *on TV?*

Lois clutched the frayed red hood in her hands and squeezed. "Please," she begged. "Where is he?"

It didn't answer, and she began to hear the shouts of the searchers. She dropped the hood. Her instincts told her something, and she tried to listen to them. Something she should guess, if she thought hard enough. The voice was familiar. She knew this voice. But the air here was thick with sulfur, and it was making her dizzy.

He'll die without you, unless you clean up your mess, Lois. Clean it up good.

Leave me alone, she wanted to say, but she couldn't. What if she yelled, and it hurt James to get even?

Sweet Lois, the thing said. *Stop hiding behind that broken smile. Clean up your mess.*

"Please, where is he?" she asked.

In reply it slithered like ice between her ears. It soothed her itch. It touched her in places no one had touched her for a long time. It occurred to her that she'd never thought very highly of Ronnie, Noreen, or even her parents. They'd held her back. She hated them a little. She wanted them dead, just a little. They deserved it for what they'd done.

What was she thinking?

Clean up your mess, Lois, and I promise you'll have everything you want, even James. Especially James.

"Help me!" a child cried from down the hole, and it sounded just like James Walker, only its tone was flat. Lifeless. Lois crawled toward the sound, but then stopped. She should run now. She knew she should run, because this thing was inside her, and she wasn't the captain of her own ship. "Is he really hurt?" she asked.

He's bleeding all over, the voice answered, and Lois knew that even if this was a trick, she had to look. She was his teacher. This was her job. She knelt by the side of the hole. The stones clicked together, but the sound they made was more hollow than she'd expected. She looked closer, and with a gasp saw that they weren't rocks, but bones. Then she saw what she hadn't noticed before. The sound came out of her, the bark. A gasp of air pushed out so fast that her windpipes became a horn.

Animals lined the clearing. In her mind, she saw what they'd done. A deer lay on its side not twenty feet away. On its stomach lay the dying moose that had chewed out half of its underside. They'd gored each other.

This place had no respect for the living or the dead.

They held you down. They made you weak. They don't know what you are. They don't know what you could be, but I do. Clean up your last mess, Lois, it told her, and she hated it for saying that. She hated it for speaking to her . . . Then why did it feel so good?

The soil smelled rich as copper (blood?). It slithered inside her. A balm for the itch. She thought about Noreen and Ronnie. Her mom. Her dad, who'd lived his life like an apology. She thought about the little shit James Walker, who right now was calling her name: *"Miss Lois, help me!"* But it wasn't really his voice, she knew that. It was a trick someone was playing. Maybe even a trick she was playing on herself. She thought about the path she could walk out of the woods that would lead to lead to misery, and the Dew Drop Inn.

You know what you have to do, Lois. Clean up the mess, and I'll give you everything you want.

In her mind's eye she saw her fourth-grade class grinning at her with red smiles. She saw herself walking out of these woods with James in hand, a queen. Mostly she saw the spilled blood of those who had wronged her, and she liked that, too.

Clean it up, the voice told her, and she knew what to do.

Ronnie. School. A wedding. A kitchen with real parquet tiles. Three dogs, so none of them ever got lonely. They slipped away. All the things she'd wanted but never got. All the hopes she'd had. They ran out of her like water until she was empty. A vacant thing that wanted filling.

Clean it up, it told her, and she licked her lips.

The ground was damp, and she ran her fingers through it. She bent her face close to the earth and smelled it. The itch in her stomach came back. It spread to her blood. It crawled across her skin. It lived behind her eyes. She wanted this so bad.

Clean it up.

Her stomach roared. She was so hungry. Hungrier than she'd been in her whole life. Her instincts were screaming. They were telling her to run, because in this dirt she could see James's blood. But her whole life she'd made the wrong decisions. Cared for people, and gotten nothing back. Maybe it was time to listen to another voice. A better voice.

Clean up your last mess, lovely Lois.

Still on her knees, she pressed her face against the dirt and opened wide. Clay and sand, iron and granite. It tasted so good, and she knew that every mistake she'd ever made, every wrong path she'd ever taken would be proven right, because it had led her here.

She licked the bones. The taste warmed her stomach, her fingers, sent heat through her toes. James's blood.

It filled her with that freshly fucked feeling Ronnie had never given her, but she'd pretended, she'd always pretended.

Clean it up, Lois. It said her name like a caress, like a kiss. She felt herself go hot between the legs. *You know you want it.* She lost herself, and she didn't even feel it happen, because she'd been lost for a long time. She ate the dirt, fistfuls of it. She ate the blood until it was gone.

Far away, the search party called James's name, but he was gone. The voice had gotten him. The voice that lived inside her now. The voice she'd given a home.

Ronnie, Noreen, her mother. Tim Carroll. Carl Fritz. Miller Walker. Fenstad Wintrob. The bitch at the salon who always looked her up and down like her clothes weren't good enough. That asshole bartender TJ Wainright at the Dew Drop who watered down her apple cosmos. They'd be sorry now.

Lois swallowed another handful of dirt. It didn't go down this time, but stuck in her throat. Her stomach clenched and then rolled. She retched. Tears came to her eyes. It had been such long a time since she'd thrown up (New Year's Eve, 2000?) that she wasn't sure what was happening. Her whole body spasmed. Dirt and small rocks heaved from her mouth. Mud ran down her chin and splattered against the collar of her pink jersey, and James's sweatshirt, too. It trickled down the small incline on the ground and pooled around her knees.

Along the periphery she saw the carcasses of animals. Possum, birds, the fawn she'd seen eating out of a Dumpster that morning. Its lone glassy eye watched her, unblinking. She remembered then where she was, what she was doing, what she had done. An earthworm squirmed between the gap in her teeth, and she gagged, crushing it there. She spit it into her hand, along with another mouthful of mud. Then she stopped.

Into her palm, she'd spit something solid. She flexed her fingers, and it rolled. Her face burned red, and more than any other time in her life, she hoped that right now was not happening. The thing was round and small. Soft, but substantial. Its skin was peeling back from its bone, and its nail was missing, but its shape was unmistakable. It was a child's pinkie toe.

She opened her mouth into another dry sob, only this time she screamed.

SEVEN
Do Not Forsake Me, Oh My Darlin'

"**Y**our wife's in the ICU. She came in with the ambulance," Fenstad's secretary, Val Pliner, announced. He blinked, and ran the words over in his mind a few times to make sure he understood them. His wife never got sick, and if she did she kept the evidence of her frailty (tissues and Tylenol Cold) hidden in purse like a secret drinking habit. This had to be a mistake.

"You're sure it was Meg?"

Val's thick gray hair was gathered by a rubber band into a functional, if unappealing, ponytail. She nodded. There was a blue thumb-shaped smudge of ink on her forehead, and he focused on it while he tried to steady himself. "Admitting called me as soon as they read her last name," she said. Since they were one of ten Jewish families in town, people tended to take note at the name Wintrob.

"She's here or she's hurt?"

"Hurt. She was attacked. I don't know by who."

Fenstad saw the color red. It washed over his eyes and dripped onto the floor. It puddled around his shoes and sucked at them like thirsty mouths. He was that kid in Wilton, Connecticut, all over again. Squish, squish, along a carpet of blood. He took a breath. She was fine. He took another breath, there was no blood. He took a final breath, and willed himself not to feel it, this pounding in his chest. "What happened?" he asked when he trusted his voice not to break.

Lila hovered in the doorway. "Dr. Wintrob?" she asked. Her blouse was wet with antibiotic ointment, and he knew there was something he'd wanted to tell her, but he couldn't remember now, what it was. "I'll see you next week," he said.

Lila's delicate features tightened. "But—" she said.

He shook his head. "Not now."

Lila pushed past Val and started down the hall. Her heels clacked unevenly, as if her shoes were too big for her feet. Fenstad knew he should go after her, but he couldn't. A weight was pressing hard on his chest like he was going to suffocate, and in his mind the floor was wet with blood. "How bad is it?"

Val shrugged helplessly. "That's all I know. She was rushed in. I'll call back, find out more."

This last part he hardly heard. He didn't bother to tell her he couldn't wait for a phone call. He was already walking away. ICU was six hallways, three colored tape changes, and one floor down. He didn't know it, but he was running. His leather shoes squeaked against the tile like basketball players shooting hoops in a gym.

It was that fuck Graham Nero. It had to be. He'd been meaning to pay Graham a visit for a long time now, let the sonofabitch know where things stood. But time had passed, and his rage had settled into cold reason, and he'd let things stand, which turned out to be the worst decision he could have made.

That smug prick. He'd probably been planning this for months. Staking out the house, watching. Biding his time. And then this morning, he'd spied Meg's open legs on the front lawn, seen that she wasn't wearing panties.

After Fenstad left for work and Maddie for school, he'd strolled up the driveway. Opened the back door like he paid the mortgage on it, like master of the fucking universe. She'd probably been washing dishes when he'd sneaked up behind her. The morning news on the radio would have drowned out his footsteps. Graham was too smart for a gun. Most likely, he'd lifted the serrated knife over the bread bin that Fenstad had used to slice his morning roll, and pressed it against her neck.

Fenstad raced from the blue line to the red one. Skidded past a fat orderly wearing light pink scrubs, and two patients in gurneys pushed against a wall. His breath was fast and wheezing. Louder than his own thoughts. Graham Nero. He pictured the guy tearing his wife's robe. Graham Nero. He pictured the guy pounding her against the kitchen floor. Graham Nero. He pictured them in bed at the Motel 6, room 69.

He was wet with sweat when he got to the ICU. Cyril Patrikakos, the body-building receptionist, didn't bother talking when Fenstad came racing by. He pointed at room 132. Fenstad rushed in. A bloody pulp attached to an IV drip lay in the bed. Fenstad couldn't make out the patient's face. Too many white coats clogged the room. His breath rushed out like a deflating balloon, and his knees buckled as he leaned against the wall. He slid down along his back until he was squatting. Fucking Graham Nero. In his mind, a neighbor's German shepherd was barking and the floor was wet with blood.

He startled when someone touched his shoulder. Meg. He sputtered. Meg! She was leaning on a set of aluminum crutches, and her left leg was set in a still-damp fiberglass cast.

"That was fast. I was just about to call you." Her normally pin-straight hair had given way to messy curls, and her blouse was missing a button. He circled his arms around her crutches and hugged her tight. Breathed her salty sweat deep into his chest until he owned a part of it. Then he led her into the bright hall. Once there he asked, "What happened?"

She shook her head. "I'm sorry. Were you worried? I planned to call you."

He knew this wasn't true. Meg didn't like leaning on people, especially Fenstad. More likely, she'd planned to go straight home from the hospital, cook dinner like always, and tonight when he pointed out that her leg was broken she'd say something like, *This old thing? I hardly noticed it.*

"You've got nine lives. I knew you were okay," he said. "What happened to your leg?"

She shrugged. "I got beat up is what happened."

Fenstad clenched his jaw tightly enough to give him an instant headache. Still, he kept his tone light. "Who?"

"Albert Sanguine went berserk," she told him. "So I hit him with a bike lock."

"Albert?"

She nodded. "The library's a mess. I'll be lucky if the town doesn't fire me."

Fenstad peered into the hospital room, where the cardiac monitor beat unevenly, and then back at his wife. "That's Albert?"

She nodded. The two of them looked at each other for a few long seconds. Albert was skinny, but tall. When he panhandled outside Citibank, he got more money than anybody else because the sucker was *big*. Fenstad and his wife bent their heads together until they touched noses. "You took him out with a bike lock?" he whispered.

She shrugged. "A bike lock was all I could find." Her expression was deadpan, and after a beat they were both grinning. As often happened, he was awed by her beauty. Meg Wintrob got better, and more sure of herself, with age. She leaned on his chest, and he gathered her crutches in one hand.

"What happened?" he asked.

She told him about Albert's nervous fit and subsequent violence. When she finished she said, "Your friend, the internist Mike Yunes, told me that Albert's liver is, what's the word?"

"Cirrhotic," he said.

She nodded. "When I swung the chain, I ruptured it. He started bleeding out his mouth. Mike says he was dying anyway. Now it'll happen a little sooner."

"But you're okay?"

She nodded. "Embarrassed, mostly. This wouldn't have happened if I'd listened to you about Albert. He'd be okay, too."

"True," he said, and her smile disappeared. Then he quickly amended, "But it doesn't matter. What about your leg?"

She looked down at it. The cast extended from the bottom of her foot to right below her knee, which was bruised and purple. "My ankle. Mike said the break was clean but it's going to heal slow."

He shook his head, truly impressed. His wife, she was tough as nails. "It's broken?"

"That's why there's a cast, Fenstad."

"Meg, I thought it was sprained. Walking on that the way you did, most people would have passed out from the pain."

She smiled, pleased with herself. "Not bad."

He had to agree. "Not bad at all."

After Meg gave her statement to the deputy police officer on duty (Tim Carroll was busy with the search for James Walker, so it was Gabe Simpson who returned from the woods to fill out a report), she left for the ladies' room to wash her face, and Fenstad returned to room 132.

The room was now empty, save for slumbering Albert Sanguine. The chart clipped to his bed reported that the trauma of surgery to repair his hemorrhaging liver would only hasten his death. Fenstad leaned over the bed. Albert's slow breath caught in his throat like a snore. He smelled like home brew and the bile that was clogging his GI tract. His white hair was combed to one side, and his yellow skin sagged over his face like dough. He looked sixty years old.

Fenstad sighed. He'd become unmoored for a while back there. Since that nonsense with Graham Nero last year, he wasn't nearly as steady as he used to be. At times he was even unreasonable. He knew he had a problem, but it was pointless to go confessing such things to some staff shrink who might give him a bad psych evaluation. When his name got mentioned for promotion to department head, a bad evaluation was the kind of thing that would hold him back. The salary was half a million a year. Meg wanted that. She'd been counting on it. He took a deep breath. He'd overreacted; that was all. But now he had everything under control: Physician, heal thyself.

In the bed, Albert's breath caught, but he didn't wake. He'd punched a candy striper a few months ago, but Fenstad had never imagined he was capable of attacking two small women and a little girl. As with Lila earlier today, he felt a measure of shame that he had not guessed this might happen, and acted to prevent it.

He'd been Albert's doctor for six years, and over that time they'd weathered his delusions, his annual effort to kick the Scope habit, and one suicide attempt. In group therapy he didn't jabber endlessly about himself like the rest of them; he listened. When sessions ended, no matter how sick the booze the evening before had made him, he shook everybody's hand and wished them a good week. He was a class act, which made his refusal to stay on the meds all the more tragic.

This violence was not in his nature. But then again, everyone has a dark side. Fenstad looked at the man who'd tossed his wife against a Plexiglas wall like a ceramic doll. A part of him wanted to pull the morphine drip from his arm, so that he knew the kind of pain Meg was smiling through right now.

Albert opened his eyes. They took a second to focus, but when he recognized Fenstad, his face tightened into a mask of pain. "The library," he rasped. He tried to lift his head from the pillow, but couldn't.

"Easy," Fenstad said. Looking at Albert's deep-socketed eyes and ashen, toothless gums, he didn't give him a couple of days to live: He gave him a couple of hours.

"Mrs. Wintrob, is she . . . dead?" he asked.

"You broke her ankle."

His mouth pruned into a look of pain, and he squinted. "I didn't mean to hurt her," Albert whispered. Then he added. "She's always so nice to me. I love her."

Fenstad's throat went dry. "Lots of people love Meg."

Albert nodded. His hair was as white as the pillow, and the few teeth he still had were brown. "Can't you smell it?"

"You're safe here, Albert."

Albert shook his head. "No, I'm not," he whispered. "I hear it calling in the woods, Don't you?" Then he opened his fist flat along the side of his leg, and he wiggled his fingers. Fenstad took his hand, and held it. He didn't usually cross this physical barrier with patients, particularly the ones who beat up his wife, but then again, his patients weren't usually dying.

Great things had once been expected of Albert. He'd planned to organize new mass transit trains in Los Angeles and design waterfront parks off ribbons of highway in Florida. And now he would die young, and in disgrace.

"It's not fair, is it?" Fenstad asked.

Albert blinked, and they were both quiet. Then he whispered so softly that it might have been a tick, "Put a pillow over my face. I'll be dead, and it won't like my taste."

Fenstad pulled his hand free. "Get some rest. I'll come back tomorrow."

"Tick-tock! In a week you'll all drop!" Albert sputtered. Spit flew out from the gap of his missing teeth.

"It doesn't live in the woods, Albert. It's you. It lives in you."

Another tear rolled down Albert's cheek. "It's real. You'll see. The pillow, please."

Fenstad paused for a moment. Something in the sound of Albert's voice. Something ominous, like déjà vu, and a dog barking. He shook his head, turned his back, and started out of the room. "Rest well," he called as he walked out.

Fenstad met Meg at reception. Her hair was straight again, and she'd replaced the button missing from her blouse with a safety pin. Together they left the hospital. He walked slowly while she labored across the blacktop. "I'll bring the car around," he said, but she nodded her head at the crutches.

"I should learn how to use these. I'll be living with them for the next six months."

Night had descended, and the parking lot was dark. Meg grunted with each step, but he knew better than to offer to carry her. When they got to the Cadillac Escalade, she climbed the two steps, grimacing through the pain, and he realized that the bursitis in her hips had to be excruciating. Vanity, he thought, thy name is Meg Wintrob.

As they drove down the lit-up stores along River Street, he asked, "You take any codeine?"

She looked straight ahead. "I had to. It really hurt."

"Well, yes. I should think from the way you're sweating that it *still* hurts."

She didn't answer, and he didn't say anything more. When they got to the house, she didn't make a move to get out of the car. Maddie's bike was not in the garage, which meant that she was visiting with her boyfriend at the Puffin Stop, which in theory she was supposed to ask permission for. "I know what you're thinking," Meg said.

"You do?" Could she guess what he'd imagined about Graham Nero?

Her tone was matter-of-fact, and a little bit angry. "It's my fault. I shouldn't have let Albert come around. I hate to imagine what those parents must think of me."

He sighed. "A madman threw you against a wall. Nobody blames you for that."

"But you knew it would happen. You warned me."

"I'm just glad it wasn't you on that IV drip."

She wiped her eyes, and at first he thought they itched, but then he realized she was crying. This he knew how to respond to with some competence. He slid across the leather seat and held her. At first she stiffened, but then she let go. She wiped her nose with the back of her hand. "Here," he said. Trying to be chivalrous, he offered her his shirt sleeve. They smiled at each other, and then she burst into another round of tears.

"I was scared." She spoke with her face pressed

against his chest. It was easier for her to confess this, he surmised, when she didn't have to look at him.

He nodded: *I was scared, too,* he thought, even though he didn't say so. *I still am.*

"I wanted to call you. I wanted to see you. That's all I wanted when it happened. Isn't that silly?"

He felt the tension in him leave. For the first time in a long while, he felt . . . okay. "No," he said, "It's not silly."

"I wanted to tell you I love you," she said, and he squeezed her tighter.

As she cried, he surveyed their Victorian Tudor that he'd loved from the first day they'd moved into it fifteen years ago, and the garden that had only recently lost its bloom, and the beautiful woman in his arms. He wondered if, despite everything that had happened between them, things would work out after all. Maybe, he thought. Just maybe.

EIGHT
The Hunger

Danny Walker was watching his favorite show, *Elimidate*. If you wanted to gawk at a train wreck, forget Jerry Springer; this was where it was at. On tonight's half hour, four skanks were taking turns French kissing a skinny hayseed from Duluth. The hayseed was supposed to bounce the worst kisser from the show. Then he and his remaining slut pack would frolic in a hot tub. With luck, in a bid for the hottest chick with the lowest self-esteem, they'd all take off their tops. Right now they were sloppy drunk, which he guessed explained why they didn't care that they were acting like degenerates on national television. Or maybe in the land of white trash, this was what passed for famous.

To keep things interesting, Danny started imagining the kinds of things he'd do to the girls, if he was the hayseed. Three of them were blond with inhumanly massive knockers, which he guessed were implants. He knew silicone was supposed to gross him out, but those six perky tits were pretty hot.

The cordless phone was in his lap, and any minute his parents might call with news about James, which was why he'd jerked off only once tonight. Also, he'd never have guessed it, but he was worried about the crazy fuck.

On TV, the really hot girl with long red hair had a pot belly, so after the French kiss round robin, the blondes called her a heifer. In reply, she stuck out her tongue, lifted her tube top, and flicked the diamond in her belly ring, which she seemed to think was a flaming comeback. Then the other girls tried to slap her gut flab, and all of them came close to throwing hands. Then the hayseed announced, "Ladies, don't fight! There's more than enough of me to go around," which convinced Danny that the hayseed was high, because when in his sorry life would four girls fight over him again? Cat-fights were Danny's favorite part of *Elimidate*. Girls ripped one another to shreds over losers they wouldn't ordinarily let buy them dinner.

In the end, the hayseed gave the hot girl the boot because he said she had too much junk in her trunk. "Shithead," Danny called, and threw a ruffled Lay's potato chip at the screen. As he let it fly, he acciden-tally leaned against the talk button on the cordless, so the dial tone resounded, which for a nanosecond he mistook for ringing. He had a moment of real hope that his dad might be on the line with news about James. But nope. Danny pressed off and sank down in the couch. The kid had to be lost, right? James was too fruity to abduct. Christ's sake, he'd killed a rabbit once, even though nobody wanted to admit it. The kid was a total psycho.

But then again, James was small, and he didn't have much common sense. Last month he'd put orange juice in his cereal because they were out of milk. He'd been shocked when he'd swallowed a spoonful and realized it tasted like piss. And *he* would know . . .

On *Elimidate,* four fake boobs rose above the water line in the hot tub like the soldiers in *Apocalypse Now.*

He should have been nicer to James. Miller and Felice thought he was a psycho, so the kid was starting with two strikes against him. He shouldn't have picked on him so badly when they'd shared a bus stop. He should have given him some advice once in a while, like letting him know that Mr. Crozzier, the teacher who left him back, had a thing for extra credit. If you wanted your report card filled with "outstandings!" all you had to do was write a two-paragraph report on the history of the Iroquois Indians, or Balto the Wonder Dog. But Danny never gave that advice, and now James was a two-time left-back.

Danny shoved a greasy chip in his mouth. What if James had been hurt, or even killed? It was possible. He didn't like to think it, but the kid had been missing now for nine hours. If the worst happened, Miller would handle it okay. He'd drink an extra quart of scotch at the club for a while and get a few people over at the school fired, but he'd handle it. Felice, on the other hand, would have another breakdown. Her first one came right after James was born. She got taken away in a padded wagon and everything, which maybe explained why no one had been all that keen on James's entrance into the world. His colicky crying had been the final straw to drive Felice Walker from permanently nervous to stark-raving-bananas. The day the orderlies had taken her away, she hadn't recognized her three-month-old baby, or Miller, or even Danny. Danny never forgot how bad it had hurt when he'd waved good-bye, and she hadn't waved back. A part of him still hated her for it.

When people wanted to piss Danny off at school, all they had to do was say, "Your mom's a psycho," and he went ape-shit. But most knew better than to mess with him. Last time it happened two years ago, he broke Pete O'Donnell's nose. Felice was still on a bunch of drugs, and at dinner or while watching late-night reruns she usually spaced out even though she wasn't drunk.

James wasn't much help around the house, so everything pretty much fell on Danny's shoulders. He had to be his dad's friend, even though Miller was a jackass. At the country club, Miller liked to collect the Irish waitresses' phone numbers and then wink at Danny, like screwing around was a cute little joke he was playing on Mom. It was Danny who cleaned the dishes and asked Felice about her day because nobody else ever bothered.

Danny groaned. James. Where was he? He'd never been nice to the kid, so it was unnerving how much he wanted him to be okay. But then again, James was his brother, and it didn't matter that they weren't alike, or that the kid was slow. Danny still loved him.

Just then Danny heard a rap on the door. James? No, he wouldn't knock. The cops? Maybe they'd found James's body near the river, or in some gay guy's torture chamber basement. Or maybe the little shit was eating stale donuts at the Puffin Stop with the druggies and the spic housecleaners waiting for the late bus out of Corpus Christi. God, he hoped it was the donuts. He really did.

Danny opened the door, but no one was there. He walked out into the dark night. Street lamps shone their yellow sickness in every direction. A few cars drove down the road. It was brisk tonight, and Danny wasn't wearing a sweater. He started to shiver, and thought about going back inside, but James might be out here. Maybe he was afraid to come home because in those woods today, he'd done something worse than kill a rabbit. And then what would they do? Get a lawyer? Pay off a judge so that James would grow up thinking he could get away with murder? For the first time in a while, he wondered if they were lucky or cursed by Miller's money.

Danny circled the house. It was the biggest in town, but there wasn't much land surrounding it. In the mornings he could hear the Wintrobs next door arguing with Maddie. He didn't usually use the word "freak," but man, when you looked it up in the dictionary, you saw purple-haired Maddie Wintrob's picture.

Danny cupped his hands about his mouth. "James!" he hollered, but nobody answered. Then he smiled, because one of the hemlocks in front of the house was shaking, like someone was hiding inside it. "James. It's okay," he called as he headed for the bush. "I'm not mad. I promise. Everybody's too worried to be mad."

He talked at a lower and lower volume as he approached, so that he could sneak up on the kid. It reminded him of the way he used to pretend he was Michael Myers from *Halloween* back when they were little. He'd walked slowly through the house, not speaking, while James ran. Inevitably James lost his cool and trapped himself in a corner. There Danny would stroll, calm as the bogeyman, to give him a pounding.

"Mom and Dad are really worried," Danny said. "Mom'll probably buy you a rabbit, she'll be so happy you're back."

The bush that had been shaking went still. Danny

was close enough. He pushed the branches aside with
one quick stroke and—*yes!*—there was James, hunched
down. Fuck, yeah, he'd found him! He'd throttle the
mutant for scaring him this bad.

James knelt on all fours in the dirt. He raised his
eyes. They weren't the right color, though. Instead of
blue, they were big and black. Danny stepped back. His
stomach got queasy. James was holding something between his teeth.

Despite the darkness, Danny could see the blood that
ran in a line down James's chin and against the front of
his torn Iron Man sweatshirt. His jaw was clamped
tight around a lump of fur with paws.

Danny tried to say something—to make a joke, even,
like: *Hey, fuckface, need a napkin?* but instead he only
gurgled. His throat was full of bubbles. There was acid
there, too, and it rose until it burned his tongue.

James dropped the lump of fur and leaped out from
the bushes. An instinct told him to get ready for a fight,
but he forced his fists to unclench. *This* was his brother?

"James, you okay?" he asked.

James bared his teeth. He leaped in Danny's direction, just as a car pulled into the driveway. Its headlights shone blindingly into James's black eyes. He fell.
They were close enough now that Danny could see the
bib of blood on his shirt, and his bare, gored feet.

He looked at Danny, but on his face there was no
sign of recognition. Light poured over the lawn, and he
started to run. Still on all fours, he charged across the
yard, and through the Wintrobs' morning glories. Like
an animal, his hind legs pushed him in the air, and his
arms caught him when he came down. The bottoms of
his feet and the toes he still had were black.

Danny took a few breaths, in and out. Fast. From

what felt like a thousand miles away, he could hear his dad slam the Mercedes's heavy door. On the ground was the husk of a rabbit. All that was left was its skin, a few slivers of meat along its spine, and the imprint of James's small teeth.

PART THREE

INFECTION

NINE
The Human Trick

The search for James Walker continued long after the sun had set on Tuesday evening. Cops and volunteers combed the Bedford woods. At a clearing two miles in, Tim Carroll stumbled. He shone his flashlight along the edges of the glade, and saw that it was scattered with animal carcasses. He'd caught his foot on an antelope's horns, and he focused his light on its unblinking eyes. It clutched a mouthful of a possum's snout between its teeth. The ground was inky with their blood. He whistled out his breath. Then he shone his light along the circle, and saw that all the animals' teeth were bared. He took a step back, and he knew that James Walker hadn't been abducted by a pedophile. The boy had found this terrible place, where the animals had learned a human trick. They'd learned murder.

That's when he heard the scream. It sounded like another animal, but by his flashlight, he found Lois Larkin kneeling over a hole in the center of the clearing. Her mouth was ringed with dirt. Like the antelope, her eyes were black. "Lois!" he shouted. She didn't stop screaming until he took off his standard-issue wool peacoat and draped it over her shoulders.

"I saw James," Danny Walker told his parents late Tuesday night. "He killed another rabbit."

Miller Walker stabbed his index finger into the middle of Danny's chest hard enough to leave a bruise. "Shut up about that fucking rabbit," he said.

Wednesday morning, the search expanded, and state troopers from Augusta, along with volunteers, called James's name. The search area widened through the town of Bedford to the edges of Corpus Christi. Still, he was not found.

Lois Larkin woke Wednesday morning with a chest cold and a wide-open window, even though, the night before, she'd left it closed. The morning light hurt her eyes, so she rolled over and hid her face under the sheets. Depression, she guessed. Her life had gone south fast. It wasn't until late afternoon that she noticed the pile of feathers on her windowsill. She kept a feeder for hummingbirds out there. Had a dog gotten to one of them, and left the feathers for her as a gift? She ran her tongue along the inside of her mouth, and between her teeth. She pulled a string of feathery gristle from the gap. Before she realized what she was doing, she sucked out the last of its blood.

Meg Wintrob didn't go to work Wednesday morning. Fenstad told her to stay home, and that was all the permission to bum around that she needed. She read the *Boston Globe* in front of *Days of Our Lives*, *Oprah*, and *Dr. Phil*. By three o'clock she was so bored that she'd finished the crossword puzzle and was scrawling items like "Clean the grout under the refrigerator" on her things-to-do list. It occurred to her that she didn't know how to relax.

Fenstad went to work as usual on Wednesday. His first order of business was to call Lila Schiffer. He'd wanted to keep her in the hospital yesterday, but when he'd learned about Meg's attack, he'd forgotten. Lila was passive-aggressive, and it wasn't beneath her to slit her other wrist just to spite him for his negligence. Turned out, he needn't have worried. Wednesday morning Lila answered the phone unharmed and nearly chipper. Her kids were both sick with chest colds, and she was tending to them. They'd been so grateful for her cinnamon toast and back rubs that they'd called her "Mom" for the first time in months. She told him, "Maybe it's the Stelazine, Dr. Wintrob. But suddenly I'm in a super-good mood. See you next week!"

As the sun set Wednesday night, Lois Larkin lay in bed with the taste of salty gristle on her tongue. Her stomach growled, and a hazy memory returned to her, of opening the window the night before, and reaching into the bird feeder. She admitted to herself the thing she'd been trying to deny: Something lived inside her now, and in the darkness, it began to speak.

It was hard for James to understand words now, and he didn't recognize faces. He didn't remember about the hollow trees anymore, or the Incredible Hulk. He'd lost something, parts of him. What was the word? Hands? No, not hands. Something else. Shoes. He'd lost pieces of the things that went inside shoes.

Last night he'd visited half the houses of the children in his fourth-grade class. He'd wanted to show them what he'd become. That he was special. Sometimes he bit them. Other times he just spit. Now he climbed terraces and backyard porches, and returned for the rest of them. As Wednesday rolled into Thursday, the virus continued to spread.

TEN
Babes in the Woods

Thursday afternoon, Madeline Wintrob pedaled her twelve-speed Trek down Silver Street. She didn't drive like the other seniors at Corpus Christi High School. Her brother, David, got the junker Volvo station wagon when he left for college in California, and since nobody thought she was responsible enough to drive, she hadn't bothered suffering through six Saturday morning sessions of driver's education.

She didn't want a car anyway. Because of cars the polar ice caps would dissolve in one hundred years, and winter would be a memory. Currency wouldn't be dollars anymore; it would be grain and livestock. Relentless tropical storms would make the East Coast uninhabitable, and Canada would close its borders so there'd be no place to flee but Mexico—and who wanted to go there? Her ruling class pigs-for-parents were worried about the thread counts of their Egyptian sheets and the fuel efficiency of their SUV death machines, meanwhile the end of the world was on it way. So fine, her whole family thought she was nuts. They were wrong. She wasn't nuts; it was the rest of this world that was off its rocker.

She was cutting school right now to meet Enrique in

the woods. Last class of the day, home ec. Right now everybody else was learning how to pour Cheez Whiz over a two-minute nuked potato, and she was free. She wasn't going to be like all the other robots who put one foot in front of the other their whole lives and burned their time like it was made of wood. She was going to make every second count.

The sky overhead was blue as a deep lake, and the air had to be at least seventy degrees. She frowned: global warming, no doubt. When people got old they stopped caring about stuff like greenhouse gases and melting ice caps. They bought houses on credit so they couldn't quit their jobs, and they got so tired from living lives they hated that their hearts dried up like clotted blood. That would never happen to her. Her heart would always bleed, even if it hurt. Someone's had to.

She couldn't *help* caring about this stuff! Even if she wanted, she'd never be one of those girls with blow-dried hair and pink lip gloss who got perfect grades in lame classes and wrote fashion editorials for the school paper. The world was colliding toward disaster, for crap's sake, so who cared about pencil skirts? Sure, people *acted* like rising estrogen rates in drinking water that would one day make men sterile were a big deal. Her parents always pseudo sympathized when she freaked out about the hormone-infested Omaha Steaks they served every time David visited, like his arrival was the frickin' second coming. They nodded their heads like they cared about eating lower on the food chain, and then they slathered their cow offal with A.1. sauce.

Her mom had really been pissing her off lately. Last night she'd limped around the kitchen like Captain Ahab after Moby Dick bit off his leg. For a while Maddie'd wanted to bitch-slap Albert Sanguine for what he'd done.

Seriously. What kind of guy hits somebody's mom? But then at dinner, Meg made her eat five bites of a cheese lasagna even though she wasn't hungry. All night it sat in her stomach like a tub of lard. She was force fed like one of those caged sows PETA was always trying to free, and she'd started thinking that short of a permanent injury, Meg Wintrob deserved what she got.

Still, this morning had been pretty neat. She'd come down the stairs to find her parents kissing, which she hadn't seen for at least a year. They left for work before she left for school, and when they did they both kissed her good-bye. Each parent got a cheek. It was totally gay. She told them they were complete dipshits even while they did it. Meanwhile, she'd liked it so much she hadn't ever wanted to leave her chair, just so she could wallow in that good feeling.

As soon as they were gone she'd thought: Love is in the air, so why not today?

"Of course," Enrique had said when she'd called this morning to see if he was up for an afternoon in the woods. Then she'd added, *And bring the thing.* "What thing?" he'd asked. She'd wanted him to guess, but it busted out of her like an explosion: *The rubbers!*

"Oh. Right . . . Okay," he'd told her.

Hooray!

Now, she pedaled. She was wearing high-top Converse sneakers and lace thigh-highs, a knee-length felt skirt with a slit up the side, and a red wool cardigan. The outfit was ridiculous, she knew, but it suited her. Plus, if you're gonna have purple hair, you might as well look the part. People had stared at her at school today, and she'd even noticed a couple of full-on pointers, but that was fine. Today was all about whims and loud colors and getting exactly what she wanted. She smiled and pedaled faster. The lines to a song were playing in her mind: "Girl, you'll be a woman, soon." She couldn't frickin' wait!

He was standing at the edge of the woods where they'd agreed to meet. Clenched in his hands were corn-flower blue daisies from the Puffin Stop. She giggled even though she didn't think the flowers were funny; she thought they were romantic.

He was dark-skinned and small, and no matter how much she dieted, she'd probably always outweigh him. His family was from Mexico, so he rolled his Rs and chose his words carefully like he was translating from the Spanish in his mind. When she hopped off her bike, he grabbed the handlebar and steered it into the woods for her. She loved that he did that kind of manly stuff. It was one of the many things that made him perfect.

When they got a few feet inside the woods he leaned the bike next to his moped and turned to her. Some sticks were tangled in her hair, and he pulled them out. She giggled because it reminded her of the way mon-keys groomed each other: They combed their fingers through their mate's pelts, then picked out the lice and ate them. That was the two of them: a pair of monkeys. This made her think of sea monkeys, and those lounge chairs they were supposed to sit on at the bottom of fish tanks, which made her giggle even more.

Enrique kept walking. He'd forgotten to give her the daisies. The branches hit the flowers so that their bright blue petals glided in a trail behind them. At least if they got lost they'd find their way out. He was being really quiet. He hadn't even kissed her hello. She knew it was silly to think, but still she wondered: Was he having second thoughts?

They'd been dating for almost a year. In gym class the girls were always talking about sex and blow jobs. Or-gasms. Jizz. Gross stuff that made her blush, not because it was gross, but because she found herself nodding, even though she'd never done it. She found herself pretending to be a woman, even though she wasn't yet.

But the last couple of months, even after she told him she wanted it, he'd stalled. Every time they got hot and heavy he invented some excuse, like the back of his dad's hatchback wasn't classy enough. He said he wanted to wait for the right time, but she was starting to think he wanted to wait for the right person, who happened *not* to be neurotic Maddie Wintrob. She started to think that he'd rather find a nice Mexican girl with big eyes like Natalie Wood from *West Side Story*, who would never pick fights and who knew how to cook a grilled cheese without burning it. Who could blame him? She knew she was a weirdo. But then again, she did blame him. The world made sense when they were together, and with each day he made her wait because he'd decided to treat her like a flower instead of a girl, she trusted him less, and he killed the thing between them a tiny bit more.

"If you're being all quiet because you're going to dump me, you're in a lot of trouble," she said. "I mean it. I'll beat you up."

Enrique shook his head in mock disappointment. "Madeline," he muttered. "You're so crazy." His accent wrapped around her name like the Mexican flag: "MAD-e-LINE," and she was immediately reassured.

People in Corpus Christi raised their voices around Enrique because they thought he didn't speak English. Meanwhile, he wrote poetry and read T. S. Eliot. But when his father's heart seized up two years ago, he took over the store and delayed college. He had five younger siblings (four girls, one boy), so he'd pretty much been the head of the family ever since.

Now that his dad had started taking shifts at the

store again, Enrique had enlisted in the army. He planned to serve a tour of duty and get his tuition financed when he came home so he could study poetry at any state school in the country. His orders were supposed to arrive within the week. She worried about him a lot. He expected everybody to be like him: decent and honest. That kind of stupid gets a boy shipped home in a bag.

So she'd been thinking about that, too, when she called him this morning. She wanted to have sex with him before he left. That way, even if he got hurt or came back changed or stopped loving her, at least they'd have been each other's first. But really, she didn't want him to go away at all. She sort of hoped the world would blow up instead. It would be easier than life without him.

Enrique's palms were sweating. He walked in front and held the branches back so they didn't slap against Maddie's legs or face. He'd seen a few clearings that might have worked, but he wanted to find a place where the ground was soft and without too many logs or sticks. He was glad he'd skipped lunch, because otherwise he might throw up.

He hoped he wasn't coming down with the cold everyone who stopped by the shop today seemed to have. They'd all coughed themselves red in the face, and some had even sported rashes on their arms, hands, necks, and faces—all over their exposed skin. He'd meant to ask Maddie about it because her father was a doctor, but now wasn't the time. He knew it wasn't allergy season, but he couldn't figure out how a sickness could spread so fast.

He'd known Maddie since before either of them was tall enough to reach the Puffin Stop counter, but it

wasn't until his dad got sick and he took over the shop
that she became a regular customer. She stopped by on
her way home from school a few times a month and
sipped black coffee while flipping through the fashion
magazines under the counter, or else she puffed her
Marlboro Lights on the front curb. She didn't have any
friends. At first he thought it was because she was shy,
but after a while he realized it was because she was a
kook.

She was also spoiled. Her clothes were new and clean,
and the legs of her jeans were always creased in perfectly ironed pleats, which meant either a Mexican
cleaning lady or a mother with too much time on her
hands. She didn't have a job, but she paid for her smokes
and *OK!* magazines with crisp twenty-, fifty-, and even
hundred-dollar bills. She was pushy, too, and expected
things to go her way: "Not the *red* lighter, Enrique. I
want the *blue* lighter." "Hi, Mom. No, I'm at the store
right now. I can start dinner, but I'm not heating up
your fettuccine. It's gross. I'm either ordering cheese-
less pizza or making stir-fry. Dad likes that better anyway."

About a year and a half ago she came into the shop
and he complimented the forest green of her sweater
because it matched her eyes. After that, she wore the
sweater every time she visited. That's when he knew for
sure that she liked him. But he didn't ask her on a date
for two reasons. First, he'd never been very comfortable
around girls. Second, she looked like a lot of work.

That summer, her parents extended her curfew to ten
o'clock, and she started coming to the Puffin Stop at
night. Sometimes her brother, David, would drop her
off like the store was her destination, and then he'd give
Enrique this look, like, *Sorry dude, but she made me do
it.* Once, David even plopped a few banana PowerBars

onto the counter and then leaned over and whispered, "You know what an eight-hundred-pound gorilla gets?" Then he'd nodded at skinny Maddie Wintrob: "Anything it wants."

But Enrique liked the company. Maddie was funny. She clomped when she walked, like she expected people to notice when she entered a room. If she wasn't smoking, she was chewing grape Bubblicious so hard it snapped. When closing time came, she'd read celebrity gossip in OK! without paying for it while he mopped the floor (she never offered to help, he noticed). Since it was on his way, he'd walk her home, and they'd talk about all the things that were important to her, like whether the guests on Jerry Springer were real, and the melting arctic permafrost that had once been a methane sink. "We'll all be dead soon," she'd once said to him without even the hint of a smile. Then she'd skipped a few paces and added, "Thanks for the Fun Dip Sticks. They're frickin' awesome!"

He hadn't known for sure that he cared for her until she stopped visiting. The first week, he hardly noticed. The second week, he decided she'd found a boyfriend. Some other guy got to watch her act like a screwball. Some other guy got to hear all about environmental disaster, and the poor chimps kept in cages for animal testing. Some other guy had found the only girl in the world who had read, and liked, Octavio Paz.

Turned out, she'd been on a family vacation in Gettysburg. When school started again, he resolved to ask her out. But every time he saw her, the words sealed his mouth shut like a lump of dry oatmeal. He had no money, not even for a movie. Where would they go? Besides, she was fair-skinned and tall and smart, and he was the guy behind the convenience store counter with five kid siblings like he came from the third world. And then he got angry at her for making him feel second-rate, and he promised himself that after the army funded his college, he'd win the Nobel Prize in Poetry. In fifteen years he'd come back to Corpus Christi with a wife even whiter and better-looking than Maddie Wintrob, and boy, would she be sorry.

So he was thinking these things one crisp September night, when she leaned over the register and kissed him. Sloppy and untrained, like a pair of nicotine-flavored fish lips. And that was all it took. He was a goner. They'd been dating for almost a year now, and the only thing he regretted was that he hadn't been the one to make the first move.

And now they were in the woods. His armpits were wet even though he'd sprayed them with half a bottle of Right Guard. Behind him, Maddie muttered something. Probably a complaint. They'd been walking for a while. It was quiet out here. The closer they got to Bedford, the less the birds chirped and the gnats swarmed. People said the air was fine here, but he didn't believe them. Since the fire, it smelled like sulfur, and even in Corpus Christi, birds had begun to twitter on the ground before dying, as if they'd forgotten how to fly. James Walker got lost here the other day, and he'd heard from his mother that overnight more kids James's age had gone missing. He was worried it wasn't a safe place to take Madeline, but with no car and no apartment, where else could they go?

Up ahead was a grassy clearing. His heart started to pound, and he thought about turning back before Maddie spotted it, too. This thing they were about to do was irrevocable. But he kept walking until they both stood on its periphery. They were panting a little, but not from exertion. From nerves. She smelled like grape-fruits and rose-scented lotion.

The grass was mostly dead. He could see the remnants of a campfire and some beer cans that had been sitting around for so long that their painted labels had worn away. "What a dump," she said.

She was tall for a woman, and he didn't like to let her see his naked body because he was scrawny by comparison. She nudged him, and he kicked his foot behind her knee and caught her off balance. She fell on her bottom with a thud. The girls he'd dated before her (all two of them), would have sneered right now and feigned some kind of injury, but not Maddie. She started laughing with her hand over her mouth while shouting, "Shhh, shhh," as if it was he, not she, who was making all the noise.

He lowered his hand to help her up. She tugged hard, and pulled him down with her. She was laughing so hard that she was crying, and it occurred to him that she was nervous, too. They sat like that for a little while, and then she took a blanket out of her bag. She opened it in the wind like a sail and set it down.

They sat. She unbuttoned her cotton blouse so that it hung open and he could see her red lace bra. He rubbed his hands on the legs of his jeans and tried to warm them for her. Everyone assumed they were doing it. The people who stopped by the shop, their families, even his brother joked about making sure there were no babies.

But she was his girl, and he wanted to do right by her. Show her that he was good enough. He'd enlisted for the same reason. He was sick of people asking whether he missed his home country when he'd been born in Bangor. No one would be able to take the army away from him. So maybe Maddie didn't know about waiting for the perfect moment, but he did. You only had one chance to get things right.

When his hands were warm, he touched her. Reached under her felt skirt. She'd shaved her hair down below in the shape of a heart. He traced the curve with his fingers. He knew she liked it. He had learned, day by day, the things that made her squirm with delight.

She touched him, too. He closed his eyes. Now, today? Was this right? One of her eyes was bigger than the other, but you had to look very closely to notice. He unbuttoned his jeans.

He tore the foil from the Trojan Ultra Pleasure with his teeth. He knew this part, had practiced in the dark on his way home from work, tossing the evidence away so that his family would not find it. A garbage can on Micmac Street full of expectations. He pulled it out. Unrolled it. Put it on. She arched her back so that her stomach pressed against him. But he'd done it wrong. It wasn't rolling. It was stuck. Hardly covered the tip. The blood rushed from his groin to his face: He'd messed up something really important. He turned to his side so that she couldn't see.

"Wait!" he cried.

Her silence was like a weight on his chest, and his fingers got clumsy. He knew she was looking. Her eyes were burning the skin on his back.

"Don't you want to?" she asked.

"I do," he said. How could he explain this? Men weren't supposed to mess this up; they were supposed to hold a woman close, and promise to be gentle.

"So what is it?" she asked.

"The timing is not right," he answered, before he realized how she would hear his words. He wished he could stop time and draw them back.

Her voice was cold. Furious. "I'm not a fucking flower."

He nodded. "I know. You're Maddie. I know." He fumbled through his pockets, looking for another one. Had he brought two? Why hadn't he brought two? Would this used one still work, if he flipped it to the other side?

He turned around and faced her. Her brow had knitted together into a single black line, and her purple hair was a mess of leaves and knots, like a vengeful Shakespearean wood sprite. "Aren't I pretty enough?" she asked.

"Of course," he said. But already, he was going soft. "So what is it?"

He sighed. Didn't she know? Couldn't she guess from the way he'd been fumbling?

"Fine!" she cried. "I hate you." She pulled on her blouse and ran into the brush.

He lay there. What was wrong with him? He'd gotten through this like a pro when it had been only a table for one. Was he dying of prostrate cancer, and this was the first symptom? He frowned. Wishful thinking. It wasn't cancer. And now he was going to have to explain to Maddie Wintrob that he'd gotten a case of nerves before she convinced herself that he and her brother were having an affair.

Just then he heard a high-pitched, girly scream. His heart pumped fast, because Maddie shouted plenty but she *never* screamed. He charged into the woods. A noxious smell of rotten eggs, strong sulfur, preceded him.

He found Maddie kneeling with her back to him over a beige stone. He bent down next to her, and gasped. It wasn't a stone, but a tiny bone, attached to more tiny bones. Connecting the bones was a thin layer of what looked like corn husk. It took him a while before he figured it out: The husk was dry skin.

Maddie turned to him with wet eyes. Her hands hovered over the corpse, almost touching it, and he knew that she wanted to sweep the thing into her arms, and protect it from whatever had happened long ago. Along its skull was a tuft of black hair. It was the hair that convinced him that this was a human infant.

"Who?" she asked, and he knew she wasn't asking about the child. She was asking: *Who did this terrible thing?*

He shook his head. Then he heard the sounds of twigs breaking in the woods. He stood fast, and pulled her up behind him. Together, they peered into the brush. Then he saw it. The figure knelt on all fours. It was watching them, and Enrique instantly took a step closer, to protect both Maddie, and the child's remains.

"Get out of here!" he yelled. The thing looked at him, and Enrique's breath caught in his throat. It moaned a sorrowful sound, like a loon whose cry has become music. He felt sorry for it, even though he knew he should be frightened. It leaped over a fallen log and scrambled away. Enrique held Maddie tightly as he let himself understand what he'd just seen. The figure wasn't an animal. It was Albert Sanguine in a hospital gown, with a mouth caked in blood.

ELEVEN

It Was So Sad It Was Funny, or Maybe It Was So Funny It Was Sad

"Still," Ronnie Koehler told his second fiancée in four weeks, "I feel pretty bad about this."

Noreen rolled her eyes. She'd been scheduled for an extra shift at the hospital tonight because so many nurses were laid up with the flu. She hadn't bothered putting on street clothes this morning, and was instead wearing dumpy pink scrubs. The two of them were smoking a blunt on his plaid couch. He'd rolled it tight, and they'd been burning it for about ten minutes. When he was high, the air felt thick as pea soup, and everything mattered just a little bit less. Still, he couldn't get Lois Larkin off his mind.

Noreen aimed the remote control at Ronnie's head like she wanted to zap him into oblivion. Maybe she was joking, maybe not. Noreen had a mean sense of humor. On the tube, American Maid, the super-hero cleaning lady, threw her magic stiletto heel into a bank robber's back. Ronnie chuckled. Hands down, *The Tick* was the best cartoon *ever*. Then Noreen fired the remote's beam through his skull, and suddenly *The Tick* was gone. In its place was Noreen's favorite soap opera, *Gilmore Girls*. The camera was focused on a mother and daughter who were laughing and crying at the same time. It was all so sad it was funny, or maybe it was so funny it was sad.

Not for the first time today, Ronnie missed Lois, who used to let him watch whatever he wanted. A realization that he'd been avoiding suddenly struck him like falling bird poop: Now that he was with Noreen, there was a whole lot of bad television in his future. "Aw, shit," he muttered.

Noreen leaned back. She was grinning like she'd just tripped a blue-haired old lady. "Rory's pregnant," she explained, and then gulped noisily on her Puffin Stop root beer Slurpee. "Not in real life. Just on the show."

There was something Ronnie wanted to say, but he couldn't remember what it was. He took another drag off his blunt, which he guessed would solve the problem either way. Then he remembered.

Without his knowledge Noreen had submitted their picture and a wedding announcement to the *Corpus Christi Sentinel*. That's how Lois Larkin had learned that he was marrying her best friend. "I feel bad about Lois," he said.

Noreen's smile fell. "I feel bad, too." She was talking to him, but looking at the television. A clean-cut family so different from him and Noreen that they could have been Martians was exchanging wisecracks in a fancy seafood restaurant. They were eating oysters with tiny forks. Noreen kept talking, but he could tell she was more interested in the fancy people with the fancy forks. "We fell in love, you know? Any way she found out was going to hurt. So she read it in the paper. Probably easier for her—this way she won't have to choke back the tears in front of us."

Ronnie half nodded. Well, that *sounded* true. Noreen set her Slurpee down on the coffee table, where it would form a ring, which would fit in with all the other rings the table had collected over the years. She'd pretty much moved in, and as a result his roommate Andrew had moved to an apartment across town. In one way it was good; he didn't have to put on pants if he wanted to see her. In another way it was bewildering, because one minute he'd been at the Dew Drop Inn, literally blind drunk, and the next thing he knew, his medicine cabinet was filled with tampons and Stri-Dex.

The apartment smelled like foot cheese. Lois used to vacuum once a week and wash the dishes. He'd have married her if Noreen hadn't come along and set him straight. At the Dew Drop Inn last month she'd clinked her apple cosmopolitan against his Jim Beam shooter and said, "You think you're in love but you're not. It's convenience." Then she'd swiveled her plump hips and pointed them at him like a weapon. "Take me and you, for instance. We've got more chemistry between us than anybody in this room. That's what you base love on, not some girl who bosses you and does your laundry."

Ronnie had been shocked—his parents loved Lois. He loved Lois . . . mostly. But after a few seconds, her words had seeped through his skull like lye. Lois *did* boss him, and lately he'd been thinking marriage might be a mistake. He wasn't ready for kids. He didn't want to be somebody's daddy, and no way he was going to quit the sweet air. Besides, the sex wasn't so good anymore. It was below average, so he was staring down a the barrel of a mediocre lay twice a week for the next fifty years, which suddenly sounded more like a prison sentence than a marriage.

"Tell me you haven't imagined being in my panties,

Ronnie. You tell me that and I'll stop talking. I'll take this drink of mine and go over there." Noreen had pointed to a crowd of guys shooting pool. She was a short girl, just about five feet tall, and she had cold gray eyes.

Lois had been at her mom's house that night, arranging seating for the wedding, which had sounded really stupid to him. Why couldn't people just sit wherever they found an empty chair? Ronnie had never considered getting into Noreen's pants, but once she set the idea loose inside his empty head, it bounced around until it found a sticking place. If he took Noreen home, someone at the bar might tell Lois, and she'd dump him, so in a few days he'd be a free man. It was this thought, even though he'd been so drunk that he no longer remembered it, that had made him kiss Noreen Castillo. The kiss was bad, and not quite on target since neither of them had been sober enough to aim their lips. Dimly he remembered getting his hand caught inside her roomy T-shirt, but he didn't know if that had happened before or after they left the bar. The next morning he woke up with a throbbing head and a fatty in his arms. At the time, he hadn't been sure which was worse. Not long after that, he and Lois broke up.

Noreen burped meatily and then rubbed her belly. She was kind of gross, which at first he'd thought was cool, because it meant she'd lay off about his table manners and the mold on half the food he kept in his fridge. But now he wasn't sure it was such a great thing that both of them were slobs. Switching one girl for the other had never been his plan. He'd planned to become a free agent, and instead he was in serious soup: another wedding! This thought set loose a nest of wasps in his stomach, so he took another couple of drags to calm down. Then he grinned, because he remembered something good. With Noreen, he'd never have to give up his grass.

They'd been talking about something, but he couldn't remember what. Oh, right, Lois. "I think I should see her."

Noreen didn't answer. She grabbed his joint and goobered Slurpee juice all over it, then handed it back to him. "Lois had you by the balls, Ronnie. She didn't care about you, and if you go over there she won't be nice. You wouldn't believe the way she used to complain about you. Just stay clear of her and thank God you got out when you did."

Like most of the things Noreen said, it sounded right until he thought about it. Lois didn't have a mean bone in her body. He looked at the television, where a man wearing a black suit was driving an SUV through the arctic to the tune of the Rolling Stones' "Free." It looked fun in the arctic. He thought he'd like to visit one day. Except, did the arctic exist anymore?

"I'm gonna go over to Lois's house," he said, and as soon as he said it, something rare happened: He was certain. He needed to see Lois. He needed to explain. He needed her forgiveness, because what he'd done had been eating him for so long now that even the pot wasn't making him forget.

Noreen frowned like he was the biggest loser on earth, and he knew he'd better get used to that look. "If you're going, I'm going. You can drop me off at work after. I don't trust you as far as I can throw you." She smiled like she was joking, but he knew she wasn't.

When Jodi Larkin swung open the front door, the first thing Ronnie noticed was that she hadn't been drinking. He could see the whites of her eyes. "Mrs.

Larkin . . . er, Jodi," he said, because he'd never been comfortable with either. At least now he'd never have to call her "Mom."

Noreen's greasy hand was inserted firmly into his. Jodi glared, so he tried to make her let go, but she wouldn't. "Is Lois home?" he asked. He couldn't think of anything worth saying, so instead he smiled, like maybe if he pretended to be in a good mood, it would be contagious.

"What do you want with her?" Jodi asked.

"We want to explain," Ronnie said.

Jodi looked at him for a while, but he didn't say anything else. Unhappiness had worn cross-hatched lines above her lips and under her eyes. She didn't look old, just haggard. "You know about James Walker?"

"What about him?" Ronnie asked.

"Good. You don't need to. Don't mention that school or her rivets'll come loose . . ."

Ronnie was confused. *Rivets?* But he didn't like talking to Jodi, so he didn't ask. "Okay. Can we see her?"

Jodi shrugged. "She's not making any sense. Not that she ever did."

"Thanks, Jodi!" Noreen said. She was smiling like life was an all-night Pink Floyd laser light show. "We'd love to see Lois!"

Jodi stepped aside, and the three of them walked into the front hall. It was dark and smelled like gin. The fabric on the rug was so worn that he could see the brown mat holding it together. The place was clean, though, which meant that Lois had been keeping it up.

Jodi led them down the hall to Lois's room. "I'm really sorry about everything," he said. Jodi kept walking. She was a lifeless thing, withered and small. He'd never seen her smile, and maybe she was angry with him now, but maybe she was just generally miserable. She opened Lois's door without knocking, which he thought was pretty obnoxious.

The room was cold. Like a pocket of deep lake water that cramps your toes. It smelled like skunk musk. The sun was setting against the drawn shades, which tinted the white walls red. He couldn't see her face. Just a mop of jet black hair that spilled across her pillow. It reminded him of the Indian room at the Maine Heritage Museum. Warring tribes used to keep each others' scalps as trophies, and the museum had displayed a bunch under glass for people to view. As a kid he'd wondered: Who wants a reminder of something *that* bad?

The lump in the bed stirred, and Ronnie's throat tightened. Right then he wished he could take it all back. He wished he'd never kissed Noreen. He wished he'd married Lois, if only to prevent having to stand here and face what he'd done.

"She's sick," Jodi said. Then she shivered, and wrapped her hands around her waist, "Boiler's broken. Too bad there's not a man around to fix it."

He wasn't sure if she was insulting him or asking for help. Before he had the chance to think it through, she pulled a chair up to Lois's bed and sat.

He and Noreen came closer. Lois's breath was wheezy and wet, and he guessed she had the chest cold that was going around. Jodi pulled down the blanket, and he saw her strikingly pale face. The blood was gone from her lips so they looked blue. He made a sound, even though he didn't mean to. He moaned.

"Lois?" he asked.

Jodi shook her by the shoulders. She tried to be gentle but she didn't know how. She squeezed Lois hard. Lois had a rash of red dots scattered like sand across her skin. Ronnie was tempted to carry her away from this place. But then again, he wasn't. She was a delicate, white-nightgown kind of a girl. Somewhere in this town was a guy who wanted that, but that guy wasn't him.

Lois woke up. Her pupils were dilated and black like she was high on angel dust. She'd lost weight in her face, so by contrast her teeth looked enormous. He wanted to smile at her, because this was his sweetheart, with a kind word for even her worst enemies. But he didn't smile. He was afraid.

"What do you want?" Lois asked. She didn't say, *Hello*, or *How you been, Ronnie?* She was still pretty; it was impossible for Lois Larkin *not* to be pretty. But now she was damaged, too. He wished he's smoked a bowl before ringing her bell. He wished he'd smoked ten.

Noreen came to his side, and he felt a little better. "We're getting married," she blurted. "It was an accident. We never meant to hurt you. But we fell in love." Even Noreen sounded unsure of herself.

"We wanted to say we're sorry about the article in the paper. We should have told you in person," Ronnie said.

Lois's chapped lower lip was bleeding a little. She tucked it into her mouth and sucked. "Ummm," she said, like it tasted really good. The gap between her teeth had narrowed. Was she using night braces again?

"It sleeps during the day, because it's used to being underground. I mostly only hear it at night," she said.

"What?" Noreen asked. She and Ronnie exchanged a look. They'd expected an emotional hug or two, and a round of sorrys, all capped off by a "See ya at the Dew Drop!" They'd expected easy forgiveness, and maybe a slice of Lois's cherry pie. It didn't look like that was going to happen.

"I told you. Girl's outta her gourd. Needs a shot of gin." Jodi scowled.

"What do you hear?" Ronnie asked, but Lois wasn't paying attention. It surprised him, even though he should have guessed that things were different. When they'd been dating, she'd hung on his every word like without his voice she'd drown.

"I fight it but I don't know why. It's not worth it, what I'm fighting for," Lois said. Then she coughed, and a gob of phlegm landed on her chin. No one came closer, or handed her a tissue, not even Jodi, so she wiped it on her nightgown, where it glistened.

She looked up and smiled. "I need a steak and a man. But you're not up to it, are you, Ronnie?" she asked. "Let's face it. You never *were* up to it."

A shelf in Ronnie's stomach dropped like he was riding the Freefall at Six Flags, and God help him, even though this was sweet Lois Larkin (*No, it's not!* Everything inside him was screaming that it wasn't Lois at all), he clenched his right fist like he was about to throw a punch.

"Lois, please," Jodi pleaded. She wrung her hands while she spoke, and left red wrinkles from pressing too hard. It occurred to him that Jodi hadn't kicked booze because her daughter needed her. Nothing scares a drunk sober like terror.

Lois turned to him. Her eyes were like lasers cutting him open. His guts were falling out all over the floor. He didn't look, but he could feel them, out in the open. He felt ashamed, like he was naked. His guts making a mess on the wood. "Do you believe in the soul? I think mine is dying," she said.

He wondered if he'd driven a woman crazy just by

jilting her. His friend Andrew would have been proud of something like that, but Ronnie just felt bad.

"It planted its seed inside me and I'm trying to starve it out. I'm trying to starve your seed, too, Ronnie," Lois said.

Ronnie didn't know what that meant. He didn't *want* to know. He and his friends used to have this joke back in high school. When you drank too much and the spins had you laid up in a corner or kissing a toilet, you didn't hold anybody back. "Save yourself!" you cried, and your friends went to their party, or hooked up with their girls while you fended for yourself. Ronnie thought about that now. He wanted somebody to shout, "Save yourself!" so he could bolt.

"I gotta get to work," Noreen said, and if he didn't love her already, he fell for her right that second. She squeezed his hand, and this time he was glad for it.

The light in the room was almost gone. Lois's eyes were shiny black orbs, and even though he wanted to go, those eyes held him where he stood. They touched his skin until it crawled. For a second he thought he could feel her inside him. It was a bad feeling, like an enemy in your bed, and he wondered if he'd ever really known Lois at all. "Was it worth it, what you did to me?" she asked.

"We're in love," Noreen insisted, only it sounded like a question: *We're in love?*

Lois grinned. She didn't look like the girl he'd dated. She wasn't gentle. She wasn't sweet. She was bitter, just like her mother.

"You could come to the wedding." Noreen mumbled. It was so absurd, probably even to Noreen's own ears, that the room got quiet. Then Lois laughed. Not a quick chuckle. A mean-spirited, monotone bray.

His skin literally crawled.

Noreen started shaking, and he thought maybe she was shivering until he looked at her. She was crying. She wiped her nose with the sleeve of her pink scrub top and said, "I do these things. I can't help myself, Lois, but you were my best friend. For real. I miss you. I'm sorry. I really am." What shocked him was that she sounded sincere.

The shriveled thing in the bed smiled while Noreen cried, and he knew for sure that it wasn't Lois Larkin. Anybody with a beating heart, even his old roommate Andrew, would take pity on Noreen right now. They'd understand she was trying, and with Noreen, trying counted for a lot.

Lois brayed harder, and he realized that the gap in her teeth had gotten smaller. In fact, she hadn't lisped once tonight. He squeezed Noreen hard. This thing, *not Lois*, it meant harm.

Together, he and Noreen backed away. Noreen wasn't crying anymore. She was shaking, and he knew that she was scared, too.

Before he turned for the door, a red glow against her windowpane caught his eye. *Shit! Blood!* he thought at first, but it wasn't blood. It was a reflection. There was a bird feeder out on the ledge, and in the summer Lois liked to watch them gather and sing their songs. Like a pied piper, animals had always been attracted to her. Once during a picnic, a whole slew of ladybugs had landed on her yellow sweater and jeans. They'd moved across it so that her clothes had looked alive, and for a second there he'd thought Lois Larkin was magic.

On the sill was a pile of cardinal red feathers. His eyes focused, and he saw the bird's sticklike bones, too. The pile was far away, but he thought he could make out a skull, and, yeah, a tiny claw.

He turned fast and started for the door.

"Ronnie!" Lois called. Her voice was rasping and wet.

He kept walking, calm as he knew how. *Please,* he thought. *Don't say it. I'm begging you, Lois Larkin. Don't say it.*

"I told you I was hungry," she said.

He gave up the pretense of a dignified exit. Holding Noreen's hand, he ran.

TWELVE
God Only Knows

Fenstad Wintrob was whistling. The tune was the Beach Boys' "God Only Knows," and he smiled as he strode down the hospital corridor. He and Meg had slept curled like spoons for the last few nights, and for the first time in a long while, he hadn't thrashed from bad dreams.

Humbled by the sight of Meg's injury, and by extension the frailty of her parents' health, Maddie had been genuinely pleasant at the breakfast table this morning. She'd eaten her entire grapefruit, and gone so far as to bus the table and run the dishwasher. She'd donned the motley of a court jester (purple hair *and* lace stockings), but neither he nor Meg had objected. In its way it was charming, and so was she.

Before leaving for work he'd kissed Maddie's cheek. She'd grinned so wide that her green eyes had sparkled, and he realized that one day somebody besides Enrique Vargas would see past her thrift-store hand-me-downs and black eyeliner. They'd recognize her for the swan she really was, and that day would break his heart.

The first order of business was outpatient group therapy. Sheila, the heavyset bag lady with the rich son, was the first to arrive. She'd double-wrapped a chain-link bicycle lock around her waist like a belt. As she sat down on the couch, the chain rattled.

"What are you wearing?" Fenstad asked. Likely it was the same lock that Meg had swung at Albert.

She fussily lifted a link and then dropped it again so that it plinked back into place. "My lucky charm!"

Bram and Joseph arrived soon afterward. In Albert's absence the session was dour. Fenstad tried to address their grief, but they weren't ready, so instead he just checked the dosage on their meds. "Coulda been me," Sheila muttered, then drew her linked belt tight around her waist like an autistic's hug. "I saw the look on his face. He'da hit me, too."

"He's very sick," Fenstad said.

Bram interrupted. He was the most functional of the group, and over the last two years had managed to hold down a job editing copy for the *Sentinel*. "He was my friend."

"I'll miss him," Fenstad said, and as soon as he said it, he knew it was true. He was going to miss toothless, Tourette-ticking Albert Sanguine. Something about the guy, despite this bad business, had always seemed genuinely good-natured. Decent, even.

After group therapy, Fenstad's schedule was free. The rest of his appointments, all six of them, had canceled due to a virulent chest cold making the rounds through town. He decided to visit Albert. When he got to Albert's room, his foot collided with the IV tree on the floor and its metal stand swiveled. Wire tubing ran the length of its stand, and the needle attached to it was on the floor. Fenstad spied a small pinprick of dried blood on the white sheets. Other than that, all traces of Albert were gone.

Fenstad poked his head out the open window. The chart hanging from the bed had been updated only an hour ago. There was no way Sanguine could have made the jump. It was a ten-foot drop to the parking lot. Last he'd checked, Albert had been too weak to stand.

Fenstad notified the attending physician. An hour later hospital security had checked every closet, empty room, and gurney in the building, but Albert was nowhere to be found. Fenstad was in the middle of searching the inpatient mental health ward when something occurred to him: Meg. If Albert had beaten all odds and gotten loose, she might be in danger. He called her from Cyril Patrikakos's station straightaway.

"How are you?" he asked when she picked up the phone.

She moaned like she was in pain. "No one showed up for story hour. Molly says it's all my fault: I killed the library." Then she lowered her voice, and in good humor whispered, "Crusty hag!"

"I've got something to tell you," he said.

"Uh oh. What now?"

"Albert Sanguine is missing. Last I checked he had one foot in the grave, but there's a possibility he escaped. I wanted you to know because he might go back to the library, since it's a place he feels comfortable."

Meg didn't say anything, so he filled in the silence. "He was too sick to lift his head Tuesday night. My guess is he crawled off some place looking for booze, and died there."

Meg didn't answer. He tried to think of additional words of comfort, but his mind went blank.

"Fenstad?" she finally asked.

"Yes?"

"I want to come home." Her voice cracked. She was whispering so that Molly didn't hear. It surprised him how quickly she'd turned from cheery to weeping. And then he got it. She was still in shock. Two days ago her friend had beaten her senseless, and in self-defense she'd opened his liver. Recovering from such a trauma would take time. She should never have gone to work today.

"That's a good idea," he told her.

"I don't want to be alone."

For one brief instant, his reason left him. She couldn't be talking about Nero, could she?

"So you'll stay with me?" she asked.

He closed his eyes and squeezed the bridge of his nose between his index finger and thumb. How could he keep misinterpreting her this way? Was it possible that something was seriously wrong with him? "Yeah. My patients all canceled. I'll come right home."

He found Meg propped on the love seat in the television room with her cast lifted awkwardly on the arm of the furniture. She was watching *All My Children,* which meant she was in bad shape. He hadn't seen her watch daytime television since her baby blues with Maddie. For two months she'd refused to brush her hair and had threatened to leave him. And then, just as suddenly as she'd become a stranger, she'd returned to herself and started keeping house again.

The room was dark, and the curtains were all drawn. It was so unlike Meg to take anything this hard that he was thrown by it. "He's not coming for you. And if he does, I'll stop him," he said.

She didn't answer for a long while. On the television, Susan Lucci was telling her husband that she was actually his long lost half sister so they'd have to get divorced, but they could still exchange cards over Christmas. "It's not just that, Fenstad. Something happened."

Room 69 at the Motel 6 flashed into his mind. It was

on the ground floor, and the sweaty blankets had been maroon and gray. "What is it?" he asked.

"I want to pretend I imagined it," she said.

He lifted her injured leg and sat beneath it. With his fingers he reached inside her cast and scratched. "I'm listening," he said. It was a joke between them; the shrink of the house, always listening. It had become less of a joke during the early years, when he'd worked too hard to come home for dinner or help around the house, or even discipline the children. But she smiled again, like the misgivings between them were a river that had run dry.

"Remember how Daddy wouldn't come to our wedding?"

Fenstad nodded. Her father had been the loud, pot-bellied vice-president of a men's loafer company in Philadelphia. He'd never approved of Fenstad, and because of that he'd died without meeting his grandkids. The rest of his children still lived at home. They worked odd jobs like convenience store clerk and door-to-door Mary Kay lady. None of them married. Frank Bonelli hadn't wanted the competition, so he'd crushed every instinct in his children that had smacked of independence or ambition. As the eldest, Meg had been his favorite, which explained why she'd been the only one strong enough to leave.

"Yeah. I remember your dad," Fenstad said.

"Did you tell Albert about him in group therapy?"

He shook his head emphatically. "No personal information. You know that."

She shrugged like she wasn't quite sure she believed him.

He reiterated. "I never said a word, Meg."

She frowned. "Then I must be crazy . . . Do you know what he said to me? He made me sit on his lap—I didn't tell you this part because I knew you'd get upset, but he held me down. I thought he was going to . . . Well, you can guess what I thought he'd do."

Fenstad's hand paused in mid-scratch. *That sneaky bastard.* "Go on," he said.

Meg continued. "He was holding me so hard. And then he said that thing my dad said to me the morning we got married: 'Where did I go wrong?' And the worst part, you won't believe this, Fenstad, but he *sounded* like my dad. He really did."

Any other woman, Fenstad wouldn't have believed it. He would have guessed that she was still hysterical, or in shock, or even delusional. But Meg wasn't prone to fits of fancy. If he didn't know for a fact that such a thing was impossible, he'd believe her simply because she was Meg. "He sounded like your father?"

Her eyes were watery, and he pulled her close. Her mean-spirited father. Things came into focus, and he understood this crisis she'd lately been suffering from. Her father had died ten years ago, but for Meg his memory was still strong. Frank Bonelli was still whispering that nothing she did and no one she loved was good enough. It explained her anger, and the way, every once in a while, she looked at him and Maddie like they were strangers. In a way, it even explained Graham Nero.

She sighed. "Just telling you about it, I know it can't be true. It was probably a coincidence. But at the time, I don't know. I felt like I was looking at my dad, not Albert Sanguine . . ."

He started scratching her leg again. "It's not silly. Albert's sick, but he's smart. People like him can manipulate without even knowing it. He's known you for years. Maybe you once mentioned your dad to him, and he guessed that it was a sore point. So he used it."

She didn't say anything for a while, and then finally

nodded. "That makes sense," she said. It made him feel good, and useful. The way a man *should* feel.

"Let me fix you something to eat," he said.

He started to get up, but she pulled him back onto the edge of the couch, so that he was sitting by her waist. Then she unbuttoned her blouse. "After he said that to me, I thought of you. How you're so much better than most of the men I've known." She was looking at him when she said this, and he knew she meant it.

The diamond pendant he'd given her for their tenth anniversary sparkled between her breasts. He laid his palm flat over it, and watched for a reaction. She arched her back. "Think you can be gentle?" she asked.

"I can try," he said.

THIRTEEN
Make Friends and Solve Crime in Your Spare Time!

*F*ate! Jean Rizzo had decided when she saw the announcement last week. She'd been eating a peanut butter and fluff sandwich in a locked bathroom stall during lunch when she noticed the blue cardboard sign taped to the wall: "*Become a Baker Street Irregular. Make Friends and Solve Crime in Your Spare Time!*— Sponsored by the Sherlock Holmes Admiration Society." She got so excited that she'd dropped her Fluffernutter on the pee-sticky floor right then and there.

Sherlock Holmes was cool under pressure. Smart. Classy. A loner, sure, but people respected him. Even Data from *Star Trek: TNG* wanted to be more like Sherlock. Hooray! She was going to become a Baker Street Irregular! Sophomore year was going to *rock*.

Every September she tried something new. Seventh grade was the year of the disco hot pants and matching feather barrettes. She'd been going for *Xanadu*-era Olivia Newton-John, but achieved transvestite-hooker-with-something-to-prove instead. In the eighth grade she tried smiling all day long. She figured popular people were happy, so if she grinned like a moron they'd mistake her for one of their own. "Whatcha so happy about *Jeannie*?" Justin Ross had mocked relentlessly from the seat in back of her (why did their names have to be so close in the alphabet?). Then there was cheerleading. She didn't even want to *think* about those pretend pom-poms. But seeing that sign for Sherlock Holmes while picking the hunks of Wonder bread from between her teeth, she'd decided that things would change. No one was going to flick spitballs into her hair that she wouldn't find until she got home and her dad shined his shit-eating grin and asked, "Is it snowing loogies out?" Justin Ross wasn't going to pull her chair out from under her so she fell on her ass. Teachers would stop looking at their seat chart to remember her name. Yes, sophomore year was going to be different.

For one, she had a not-so-secret weapon. Over the summer, magic happened, and her boobs had swelled from A cups to full Cs. She'd stolen a $19.99 red gingham strapless dress from Target to show them off. Stowed it in her backpack, and then bought cheap Bonne Bell raspberry lip shimmer at the counter so the security guards didn't get suspicious. She was wearing the dress in honor of club day today, and when she looked in the mirror she knew she was the spitting image of a sexed-up Mary Ann from *Gilligan's Island*.

Right now she was strutting through the gymnasium while her bra-less boobs jiggled (if you've got it, flaunt it!). School was over, and practically everybody was at club day. Well, everybody who showed up. A ton of kids were out sick today.

Ubiquitous table tents advertised things like yearbook committee, computer programming, and theater set design. She scanned the rows for the Sherlock Holmes Society, but didn't see it. "Cheerleaders Are S-E-X-Y!" one sign announced, and around it, girls with perfect figures and dimpled smiles lazed like lizards enjoying the sun. She walked past them as fast as she could, because last year she'd tried out for the JV team. The tryouts were a sham, it turned out. The senior selection committee picked their little sisters for the team. That was how most things worked in Corpus Christi. Everybody told you that you had a fair shot, but they were full of shit.

Anyway, she'd tried out because her dad was always harping on how important it was to be on the winning side of things, and cheerleaders were definitely winners. When her turn came, she shouted her lungs out in front of almost every girl in her ninth grade class: *Every*body in Corpus Christi wanted to be a cheerleader. She'd waved her arms and moved not just with energy, but with real grace. Some of the girls had smiled like they were impressed, and she'd thought: *Three weeks hollering "Rah-Rah-Team" in my dad's moldy basement, and I finally found something I'm good at.*

Suddenly one of the judges in the bleachers snickered. Her teeth were blindingly white, like she gargled with bleach. She covered her mouth to keep from exploding, like the sight of Jean Rizzo holding pretend pom-poms because the stockroom had run out of real ones was just too funny. All the popular girls, Jean realized right then, had magically gotten real pom-poms, and the losers hadn't even gotten batons. The girls with pom-poms were in the running, and all the rest, no matter how hard they worked, no matter how many fake catcalls and spitballs they endured, would never make the cut.

That's when she lost steam. She'd whispered the final "Go-o-o-o Trojans!" before dropping her imaginary pom-poms and wandering off the athletic field. Maybe the lucky girls who'd made the team still remembered that, or even felt bad about it. Maybe they didn't care, so long as they got what they wanted. At home that day, her father was waiting. When he saw the tears in her eyes, he shined his ever reliable shit-eating grin and asked, "Didn't make the cut, Jeannie?"

Now, everywhere she looked at the club sign-up event, kids were laughing and talking like the high school belonged to them. Like they were kings. Even the shaggy-haired, peach fuzz–faced, waiting-for-the-apocalypse-so-I-can-shoot-up-the-school rifle-team kids were yucking it up. She walked down the rows of tables like passing through a gauntlet: auto shop gearheads, red-eyed environmental club potheads, Ivy League–bound young Republicans.

That was the thing about the people at this school. Even the losers had it easy. Sure, some of them acted human. If they teased her too much, they felt bad and apologized later. The dorky ones even invited her to sit with them at lunch, but in the end they were all the same. Their lives were perfect. They worried about luxuries like the prom, boys, homework, and whether they'd go to college out of state. They didn't have to steal their clothes, and nobody ever handed them a jar of fluff and told them it counted as dairy. They came home every night to a home-cooked meal, and she came home to a shit-eating grin.

But passing through that club gauntlet, she decided that today everything would change. She'd find people just like her, who loved Sherlock Holmes. Maybe there was a secret society of them, even, and they ran the school. She'd add her name to the sign-up sheet, and tonight she'd get an anonymous phone call. A deep-throated, mysterious voice would confide: "The invisible hands that elect the class president. Prom queen. Winners of the Battle of the Bands. That's us, the Sherlock Holmes Society. We've been watching you. Sorry we made these last fifteen years so hard, but we needed to be sure you were cool. Welcome aboard. We knew you had it in you. First meeting's in Danny Walker's basement. Wear your red dress. You look like Mary Ann from *Gilligan's Island* in it."

At the very end of the rows of tables, she found the Sherlock Holmes Society. There was no giant crowd. No official-looking sign-up sheet. No gaggle of popular people quietly nodding their approval as she approached. Nope. The twelve-year-old genius freshman who'd skipped two grades was helming the table. Draped over his shoulders was a checked wool cape, and he was chewing on a decorative corn-cob pipe.

He was pale and doughy, like in bed at night he ate Skippy Super Chunk peanut butter out of the jar with his fingers. He looked at her boobs for a long while, so she crossed her arms over them. He didn't stop looking, which made her hate him, because only cool boys were supposed to notice the outline of her nipples, and by seeing them become spellbound and announce that they loved her so much they'd kill for her. They'd die for her, or at least buy a porterhouse for her.

The genius freshman chewed on the fake pipe that his parents had probably bought for him as a souvenir from the Indian reservation on Penobscot Island. "We need three people to form a club or the school won't assign a teacher," he said. Then he flicked the sign-up sheet in her direction like he was doing her a favor. Like he figured she wasn't smart enough to solve a Sherlock Holmes mystery, but hey, he needed a warm body for the head count.

"Screw you, freshman," she thought to say ten minutes later, but in the moment she only mumbled, "This isn't cheering practice," and walked away.

At the racks, she unlocked her rusty red boy's bike that her dad had gotten for her from the dump when she was a kid. It was too short now, and her knees scrunched when she rode it. No one else was out here. Every other kid in Corpus Christi was back at the high school having fun. Even the football team canceled practice for club day. Yeah, right now they were all laughing at the way she'd run out of the auditorium. As soon as she left, the party had started. They were doing keg stands, turning off the lights, hooking up. And the genius freshman, he'd been a test. The Sherlock Holmes Admiration Society really *was* the secret society of popular kids, only to get accepted, you had to shove the freshman's corn-cob pipe up his ass. Literally.

Her dad was right. She was a loser.

She kicked her bike, which sent sparks of pain through her toes, but she didn't care. She kicked it again, and this time her whole foot cramped up. It felt good to hurt. She was glad she hurt. The bike fell over, so she jumped on it until its frame bent and its chain came loose, and the plastic flower broke off its handlebar. She pretended the bike was her school, her dad, the dough-faced genius freshman, her crappy strapless dress from Target. After a few minutes, she was panting. The bike was bent. Some of its paint was ground into the cement, and it sparkled there like red granite dust. A drip of sweat rolled into her eye. The bike lay there, unmoving. The bike was dead.

She started walking. Screw the bike. Screw everything. She wished she had a knife so she could cut herself with it. She wished she'd kicked the bike so hard that it had exploded into metal ash. She wished she could crush the school in the palm of her hands so everybody inside it would die while she laughed. She wanted the blood vessels in her brain to burst so that she'd fall into a coma, and everyone would write cards saying they were sorry for keeping her on the outside all these years; they'd only been kidding. Really, they liked her. *We took the joke too far*, they'd say.

But that wouldn't happen. Sophomore year wasn't going to be any different from freshman year. Sure, her dress fit tighter than a sausage's second skin, but nobody'd asked her out. Except for the dorkiest freshman in the world, nobody had even looked at her. Her grades were bad except in art, where they were mediocre. Even her online friends didn't like her. They'd write long, soul-baring notes to each other at first, but after a while, even if she IM'ed ten or fifteen times a day, they stopped answering, and sometimes even blocked her mail. She didn't have a special talent or a pretty face. Couldn't run fast or dance. To be honest, the genius freshman had been right. She never figured out Sherlock Holmes's cases before the stories ended. Sometimes she couldn't even figure them out *after* the books explained them. This year would be just like last year, which had been like every year before that. She was a nobody. An embarrassment. A sack of shit.

She kept walking. She didn't want to go home, but she didn't have any other place to go. Maybe she'd wander around for a few hours, and after dark she'd walk through the front door and tell her dad that she'd joined the club anyway. Been elected president, in fact. He might believe her. At least it would delay the shit-eating grin, like he was so happy they were both swimming in this loser stew together, and he didn't have to go it alone.

Half a mile down the road, she reached the Puffin Stop. She looked in the window, but Enrique Vargas wasn't there. Instead his little brother was ringing up sales behind the counter. Enrique was nice. He let her hang around the shop even if she didn't buy anything. Twice he'd turned a blind eye when she'd reached inside the revolving spits of the "Frankenator" and stolen two shriveled Ball Park hot dogs. She loved Enrique a little bit. She'd written him three letters, all of which she'd buried under the loose boards in the basement so her dad wouldn't find them. Probably she should have burned them, but if she'd done that, she figured they wouldn't come true. "My love," one of them said, "Even though you're foreign, I'd die for you. You're just like Leo from *Titanic*, so I know you'd die for me, too."

But Enrique's little brother sucked. At school he sneered at her because she wasn't pretty, or maybe because he knew he could get away with it. He probably thought if he teased her, people would like him even though he had an accent. He was right. So even though she was thirsty and wanted a Coke and for once had the dollar fifty-five for all sixteen ounces, she kept walking.

She went up the hill. Past town. Toward the woods. She wished she'd worn a coat or even a sweater. But she'd been too excited about her pretty dress and big boobs. After a while she came to the back road that spanned the distance between Corpus Christi and Bedford. She'd heard a kid was missing and half the town was looking for him. He was the son of the CEO of the hospital, which explained why everybody cared so much. Last year her dad got fired from the morgue for taking too many sick days. His severance package was running out, and he needed to get off the couch and start looking for work again, but she doubted he would. Probably he'd just sit around drinking beer until he lost the house, and then where would she live?

Meanwhile, they didn't ever go out to eat, or buy groceries except at the Puffin Stop. They didn't say grace like they'd done before her sister left to tend bar in Florida. Their lawn was brown even in summer.

They didn't wave to people in town, and no one ever waved to them.

Her dad's beer club was in a shack about a mile down the road. Most of its members were from Bedford, because Corpus Christi people usually belonged to the golf club. The beer club was a place where her dad met his friends and played cards. Since the fire at the mill her dad didn't go there much. Most of the members had moved away.

Cars drove by in either direction every few minutes. Cops and volunteers looking for James Walker, she guessed. They slowed as they passed. When they saw that she wasn't someone they recognized or knew well enough to offer a lift, they sped up again. One of the cars practically came to a dead stop at her side. She turned to give the driver a dirty look, because she was sick of everything right now. Sick of happy cheerleaders, her dad, her crappy dead bike, and Fluffernutter: What the hell? Marshmallow's not dairy, is it? She turned, ready to flip the bird at the driver. Instead of raising her middle finger, she blushed. The car was a used yellow Saturn. She and the driver locked eyes. The driver was her dad.

He was a skinny guy with a full head of curly brown hair, which he was stupid proud of. He dated lots of widows and divorced ladies in their thirties, but none of them ever stuck around. He couldn't hold his tongue. "You're ugly, stupid, lazy, useless," he probably told them after a week or two. She knew because he couldn't hold his tongue with her, either.

He was wearing his favorite gray sweat suit. Favorite and only. In the passenger seat were three Tall Boy Budweisers. Which meant that the other three lay empty on the floor. He'd been driving around, drinking them, while waiting for the club to open. For a second she saw him not as her dad, but as a middle-aged lush trying to pick up jail bait on the side of the road. She was ashamed of him. What was worse, he looked disappointed, like he'd thought he might get lucky tonight, and instead he'd found his least favorite girl. So they were both disappointed.

But it was cold out, and the sun had set. She wasn't wearing a coat. Just a flimsy dress. There were no street lamps along this road. Best to look on the bright side. At least she had a ride. She slumped her shoulders like somebody who's so accustomed to defeat that being sad about it is a formality, and headed for the passenger-side door. Everything felt like it was closing in around her, like life was sucking the air out of her lungs. Home again, home again. Another year with no place to go but the four walls of her room. She shivered as she walked. The shit-eating grin spread across her father's boozy red face. He gunned the accelerator. The door handle tore loose from her fingers, and before she knew what was happening, he was driving away.

She watched the car roll down the road. Smoke wheezed from its tailpipe and its orange lights faded in the distance. She stood shivering in the middle of the street for a while, expecting him to come back. *Only kidding*, he'd say. *I'm sorry. I took the joke too far. You must be freezing*. But he didn't come back. He left her there, all by herself. She held out for about ten minutes before she started crying.

She walked for a long while after that, even though it was getting dark, and her teeth were chattering. After about a mile she passed the beer club where her dad's car was parked. She thought about kicking it, just like her bike, or running a key along its cheap yellow paint, but she kept walking. Another hour passed. After a while she could see flashlights flickering inside the woods. A few people were calling James Walker's name.

She headed for the searchlights. Maybe someone out there had an extra sweater. The woods were dry and brittle. Crack, crack, crack was the sound under her shoes. Her dad would be out late tonight. If she turned around now, she could be sleeping in bed before he got home. But she'd still have to see him tomorrow. The branches scratched her face, and she thought about his shit-eating grin. She started crying again. She'd seen the look in her father's eye, like driving away wasn't the thing he'd really wanted to do. Really, he'd wanted to hurt her. She couldn't go home. Not tonight. Not ever again.

That's when she heard the rustling. It sounded like leaves being raked across dry grass. She stopped. There wasn't any wind, but the branches between two big pine trees were shaking. *An animal?* she wondered. And then her heart beat faster. The branches were high up, and thick. *A big animal.*

She backed away. Slowly. One foot behind the other. You're not supposed to run from bears. You're supposed to shout and jangle bells to scare them away, but right now shouting at a bear sounded pretty brainless. The branches of the trees shook harder until at the top, even their trunks began to sway. The lower branches swung in wide circles, and she thought, strangely, of the oars of a gigantic boat. This thing was strong.

One foot, the next. She backed away. Her heart slowed. She wasn't thinking about her dad, or home, or how much she hated everyone in the whole world. She was backing away, one step at a time.

It came out from between the trees. The man. He was bigger than any man she'd ever seen. At least seven

feet tall. Except for an open hospital gown, he was naked. She tried not to look at his hairiness down below.
Along his belly she could see a line of stitches. Some
were torn open, and inside she saw an unbleeding pink
lesion, like his wound was from the movies, and made
of dye and wax. His sagging skin slid up and down his
ribs as he got closer. She wasn't sure what was happening, but then she understood. His skin was bouncing
because he was running straight for her!

The distance closed. Ten feet. Eight feet. Five feet.
Displaced wind rushed against her as her mind fired off
segmented thoughts like a string of firecrackers. *What
dark eyes you have,* she thought, and then: *The better
to swallow you with, my dear.* And: *Rah-Rah Team!*
And finally: *Run. Run. RUN!*

Before she made the decision to do so, she was sprint-
ing. Her Payless slingbacks went flying. Sticks and sharp
rocks stabbed the soles of her feet. Behind her, the
ground shook as the man in the woods gave chase.

She didn't look back. Her mind was still firing off
thoughts, but they hardly made sense now (*Black-Eyed-
Monster-Shit-Eating-Grin!*).

It was dark suddenly, and she didn't remember if
clouds had rolled in, or it had always been this way. She
leaped over what looked like a log and her feet sank
down (*Mud? Blood? A Tall Boy of Bud?*) into something wet and soft. She fell, and then crawled on her
knees for two strides before getting back on her feet
again.

Behind her the ground shook with each heavy step the
man took. But was he really a man? He was hunched, as
if more suited for crawling on four legs. He closed the
distance between them. Her bouncing breasts ached as
she ran, and she wished she'd worn a bra today. She
tripped again, this time over a rock, and scrambled to

get up, but now someone was in front of her, too. Not
the man, but a group of people. About ten of them. They
were short, or else hunched down. The searchers!

"Help me!" she tried to scream, but it came out a
panting whisper: "Hhhh meee."

They came closer, and she saw the way the moonlight
reflected off their lunatic black eyes. She scrambled
along the leafy ground, but was afraid to stand. The
naked man was behind her, but maybe these things
were worse.

More of them came out from the shadows. She didn't
know how many. She was too scared to count. Their
bare feet were dirty, like they lived out here now. Most
of them were kids. Young, like James Walker's age. A
few were her age, too. The ones who'd been out sick
from school. Though it didn't matter, she couldn't help
but wonder: *Are the cool kids hanging out someplace
new?*

"Hey Jeannie, are ya lost?" Justin Ross asked. He
was crouching so that his fingertips were touching the
ground. For ten years he'd sat behind her in school. For
ten years he'd tormented her. But he was different now.
Leaner. Paler. Meaner.

She stood and crossed her arms around her chest,
like somehow building that barrier would protect her.
It would make her invisible like when she was watching
TV with her dad, and they'd leave her alone.

"Naw, she's just looking for her mom who ran off,"
said Liesa Perry, who spent twenty-three dollars on
blue eye shadow from Chanel. She was wearing it now,
even though the rest of her face was gaunt and pale.

"You steal that dress, Jeannie? I think you did. I
think your daddy's welfare only covers booze," said
Jackie Wyatt, who had written on the chalkboard in

the seventh grade, "Jean Rizzo can't *give* it away!" All of Jackie's pretty black hair was gone, and Jean wondered if she'd stumbled across the real truth in these woods: Popular kids were monsters.

"No," Jean whispered. Liesa's mouth was red, and the color wasn't from lipstick. Jean made a sound. A gasp, sort of. Then she bumped into something warm and firm. She swiveled. The man clapped his hands and smiled, like they were playing a game. His gown was open.

She looked in every direction, but there was no place to run. Could she shout? Would the searchers hear her?

At first she didn't feel it. But then she recognized that familiar pinch. One of the kids behind her was lightly plucking strand after strand of her hair from her scalp. She knew it was Justin, because he'd teased her this way every day for ten years. "I think you stole that cheap dress," she heard him whisper, "I think you should be punished."

Her instincts took over. She took a swing. It connected it with the wet hole in the naked man's gut. Her hand came out red and the man reeled. Blood spilled from his mouth and he dropped to his knees. She used the time. She ran.

She didn't make it far. Justin grabbed her by the shoulders. She fell backward. *Pins and needles, needles and pins, it's a happy girl who always grins,* she was thinking: *Rah-Rah Team!* He dragged her along the dirt while she struggled until all of them, even the man, were holding her down against the ground.

"Shh—" she said, which maybe was going to turn into *shit*, maybe was a plea for them to please, for once, leave her alone.

She looked up from the ground at their black-eyed

faces. They grinned, like this was funny. The man had chased her here on purpose, she understood. A trap. "What did I ever do to you?" she whispered.

Their breath was rotten. She tried to crawl away, but they held down her arms. Someone was sitting on her legs. She saw her reflection in their black eyes: a cheap gingham dress. It was torn at the hem, and her cowlike breasts were poking out from the fabric. She tried to cover herself with her hands, but her arms were pinned. The cold air stung her exposed places. They could see her secret things: her birthmark shaped like a butterfly, and the stray black hairs encircling her nipples. *Why don't you like me?* she wondered. *Am I that bad?*

She saw herself in them; twenty black orbs like spider eyes. Her reflection swam inside them. She lived in the reflection, and the reflection lived in her. They smiled and waved hello at each other: dead Jeannie and living Jeannie. She whimpered as she swam, and then stopped swimming, and sank into the black.

Justin bared his perfectly straight, store-bought teeth, and then so did Liesa, and Jackie, and the rest of them. "Hungry," Justin said, only he was hardly speaking anymore. "Hunnneee," he said, like maybe, if she wanted to badly enough, she could pretend he was calling her sweet.

She tried not to let them see her tears, but her breasts were cold, and exposed, and she was so ashamed. She tried to keep her mind from comprehending the obvious: They'd been feeding in these woods.

Someone, maybe Jackie, took the first bite. She tried to keep it inside, but the pain was too great. She screamed.

FOURTEEN
A House Divided

"It was the *worst!*" Maddie Wintrob announced. "He *ate* that baby." She and her boyfriend had just ridden their bikes from the police department, where they'd reported finding a child's skeleton, along with a spry and very much alive Albert Sanguine.

"It *sounds* bad," Fenstad said.

The four of them were sitting in the den. Maddie and Enrique occupied one couch, and Fenstad and Meg held the other. A year ago Maddie had been slamming across the wood floors in child-sized tap shoes even though she didn't take tap; she just liked being loud. Well, maybe not a year ago. Maybe ten years ago. "*Ta-da!*" she'd shouted with wide-open arms at the end of every leaden-footed routine.

Maddie had just finished explaining her trip to the woods. Her reason for being there instead of at school remained a mystery. Fenstad could guess. He'd done the same things when he was eighteen with a girl named Joanne "Giggles" Streibler. But when he looked at his daughter, a psychedelic gazelle in bright colors and ruffles, and compared her to the convenience store clerk with the black peach-fuzz mustache, he didn't want to guess.

"I'm just glad you're safe," Meg said.

Fenstad nodded, but his jaw was locked in place, and his blood was boiling. He looked out the bay window so they wouldn't see how close he was to bursting. He focused on the lawn, which had recently been mowed, and the dogwood trees in bloom. He focused on the cars driving by with their headlights shining, and his view of the town from the top of the hill. His Victorian was big and impressive. A perfect fit for a family of four. He was proud of what he'd built, even though the world seemed determined, plank by plank, to tear it down.

"Are you sure it was Albert?" Meg asked. Her leg was propped on the coffee table between the two couches. They'd made love this afternoon on the couch where they now sat, and in the bed, too. Her face was still glowing, and the only sign that she was not pleased by the mention of Albert's name was the way she scratched the skin beneath her cast in firm, swift strokes. Her fingernails were long, and the sound was as loud as a chirping cricket.

"I'm sure. But he was strange. He didn't move like a man." Enrique's English was flawless but halting, and clearly foreign. "When he saw us, he ran. He leaped on all fours." Enrique mimicked the motion, curling his hands into claws and bending forward to prove his point: "Like an animal. It was unnatural. They didn't believe us at the police station, but it's true. It was Albert Sanguine."

Meg stiffened next to him, and for a moment he got nervous. Could this be true? He'd jumped out a second-story window, and was now in the woods? Like every other paranoid delusional, Albert's fantasies had always been intricate, but they'd also been something more rare: consistent. In six years he'd never varied from his story: a presence in the Bedford woods had found a home inside him, and would not set him free.

Had something been calling him all this time? Fenstad wondered. Then he shook his head: No. Albert Sanguine was dead. Soon, someone would smell his body in some dark corner of the hospital where he'd been trying to scavenge rubbing alcohol. The kids had seen something, and in their hysteria, attached Albert's face to it. That was the only possible explanation.

"If it really was him, he couldn't have hurt you. What you saw was the adrenaline rush of a dying man," he said. Meg was still scratching, but less frequently. Her skin was red, and he placed his hand over hers to make her still.

Maddie took a hitching breath. "Dad . . . I think he did something to that baby," she said.

"Maddie," Fenstad said. "You said it was a skeleton. It probably came from Bedford before the fire. It was a stillborn that its mother abandoned."

"Bull," Maddie countered. "Its skin was all dried up, and its bones were broken." She took a deep breath, and he could see she was working herself into a froth.

Normally he'd have started comforting her by now, but instead Enrique Vargas was running his thumb in circular motions along the junction of her bony shoulder blades.

Since he'd enlisted, Enrique had started spending more time at the Casa de Wintrob. At night he and Maddie sat on the front porch and whispered to each other. It wasn't fun whispering. It was intense, and without humor, and probably involved heartfelt protestations of undying love. Fenstad got the idea that an engagement ring was on its way. Something cheap that would turn Maddie's finger green.

"Dad, its bones were broken. That's not natural."

"Sweetheart," Meg said. "An animal could have done that."

Maddie pursed her lips. Enrique leaned away from her, like he knew what was coming. Her lips quivered for one second, two seconds. On three she exploded. The veins along her neck thickened into cords and spit went flying. "That guy's lips were bloody! Where do you think that blood came from? He'd been eating, Mom! He's out there, and he went after you. Why won't you believe me? You never listen. He eats babies!"

Meg wiped her face with her hands like she was trying to erase it. Fenstad thought about the aspirin in the medicine cabinet, or maybe Tylenol would work faster. No, aspirin; he could chew it.

Still, watching Maddie, he remembered the way he'd once been. Wet with emotions, a nuclear reactor without a cooling vent. Meg didn't know where Maddie had inherited these histrionics, but *he* did. They were more alike than he wanted to admit, only where he'd learned to contain his feelings within walls upon walls, Maddie wallowed.

Underneath his hand, Meg made a fist. "Madeline Wintrob. You stop your nonsense right now," she said. "Albert Sanguine did not eat that baby. We're glad you're not hurt. We understand it was serious. Don't exaggerate."

Maddie's eyes narrowed. Her brow knit, just like Meg's, into a single line. "So why would somebody leave their baby? Even if it was stillborn, why would they throw it away?"

"The mother was probably a teenager, and unmarried," Meg said.

Maddie looked from Meg, to Fenstad, and back to Meg again. "Oh, lay off."

"So you left school early?" Meg asked.

"I'm sorry. It's my fault," Enrique said. Then he gently pulled a twig from Maddie's purple hair. When he saw Fenstad watching him, he blushed. Instead of tossing the twig onto the coffee table, he shoved it into his denim pocket like a dirty secret. Fenstad knew for certain, then, what his only daughter had been doing in the woods. This dime store clerk had to go. Right now, before Fenstad bloodied his lip.

"It's not Enrique's fault. It was my idea," Maddie said.

Fenstad's blood was boiling. A dog was barking. He wanted to kill this scrawny little shit. Meg took his hand, and squeezed. Hard. "I guessed as much, but it's good of you to say so." Then she added, "You're grounded."

"Mom!" Maddie pouted. "I'm a senior. I don't even have to pass that class. We're learning how to microwave Cheez Whiz. It's completely retarded."

"One week. After school you'll come to the library where you'll do your homework, and then I'll drive you home. I'm doing this for your own good. If what you say is true, Albert might still be out there. Until the police find him I don't want you riding your bike all over creation."

"Are you serious?" Maddie asked. Her mouth hung open in shock.

Fenstad realized that his wife was a genius. Enrique was leaving for basic training soon. By the time Maddie was allowed out again, he'd be gone. No elopement, no green ring.

"No phone. No trips to the woods. No visiting Enrique at the Puffin Stop," Meg said.

"*No way!*" Maddie shouted. "You'd never do this to David. Not in a million years. I never do anything bad, but you always act like I'm crazy. I don't need protection. I can take care of myself."

"Honey," Meg said, "You cut school." Then she elbowed Fenstad.

"This is for your own good," he added.

Maddie glared at Fenstad, and for a second she looked as scary as Meg during her worst rages. "You always take her side. You're so spineless. You think I don't get it, but I know. It's because he's a spic!"

Next to her, Enrique went rigid.

Maddie jumped up from the couch but didn't go anywhere. Normally she'd be halfway to her room by now, but that would mean leaving Enrique behind.

Fenstad's tone was severe. "Maddie Bonelli Wintrob, do not say that word in this house."

"Sorry, Dad." Her face flushed red because it occurred to her that she might have hurt her boyfriend's feelings. Judging by Enrique's wide-eyed silence, she was right. The kid looked crushed.

"Thank you for the hospitality, Mrs. Wintrob," he said as he stood.

"You're leaving?" Maddie asked. Her voice was tiny, and he could tell she was ashamed, and perplexed, too. She didn't know what she'd done wrong, or why Enrique was so hurt.

"Yes. I'm going," Enrique said.

The difference in age and maturity between them wasn't usually noticeable, but right now Fenstad could see it. This man had mouths to feed, and Maddie wanted to educate the masses on the importance of recycling. Enrique hugged Maddie fiercely, and before she was able to object, he walked out the front door. Fenstad felt a pang of something when he saw the tears in Enrique's eyes. Something like regret.

Meg reached across the coffee table and tried to take Maddie's hand. "We just think—"

Maddie whirled. Thick, cordlike veins traced the sides of her neck and she balled her hands into fists. "I hate you!" she shouted. Her lip was curled, and the sight wasn't pretty. It was scary. She was shaking with rage, and Fenstad thought, for a second, that she was going to strike her mother.

"You think you're so smart, but you're just a couple of jerks," she said, and this time her voice was cold. He felt like he'd been punched, and the wind left his body. She watched for their reactions. Whatever she saw made her curl her lip in disgust. She clomped up to her bedroom and slammed the door. A few seconds later music blasted so loud that he could feel the bass vibrations through the soles of his feet.

He and Meg looked at each other and shook their heads. They were both out of breath, like they'd just finished a race. He wanted to follow Maddie up those stairs and take it all back. "Let's start over, from the beginning," he wanted to say.

"When's the last time we grounded her?" he asked.

Meg smiled in a disappointed way: "Never. This is the first time. And she's done worse things than cut home economics."

Fenstad shook his head. "This is different."

They didn't speak for a while. Up the stairs, music throbbed. He put his hand on Meg's firm thigh. She didn't flinch. She moved closer, and he remembered their sex this afternoon, how it had been exactly what they'd needed. This rage in Maddie would pass of course, just like all her moods. Even her feelings for Enrique would pass.

"She's *pissed*," Meg said.

"She'll get over it."

"Yeah. But I wasn't thinking about Albert when I grounded her, were you?"

"A little of Albert. A little of the other."

Meg started to scratch her leg again, and he stilled her hand. He folded a piece of paper, and pushed it inside her cast. When it gained purchase he began to scratch. She made a satisfied purring sound, like a cat, and closed her eyes.

"She never thinks things through," she said sleepily. "She'd marry him in a heartbeat if he asked, and then forget Brown University. Brown's down the toilet. She's so spoiled. She has no idea about working, or money. I mean, he's a nice kid, but he'll ruin her life."

"Well, that's an even better reason to ground her."

"It's just . . . I see all the things that could happen to her, and I want to protect her. She's so sensitive and sweet. I'd hate for that to change. But she's a grown woman, practically. We can't keep treating her like this or we'll turn her into a cripple."

Up above, the music was going strong, and now they could hear objects being hurled against a wall. Books? A lamp? Who knew?

"Let's wait," Fenstad said. "Trust me. She'll calm down."

Meg shrugged. "I'm tired of thinking about it. I need an aspirin."

He nodded. "Me, too."

FIFTEEN
The Fat Kids Kept Coughing

Friday morning marked the third day that James Walker was missing. Fenstad's sleep the night before was not peaceful. Around three, Maddie blasted the Sex Pistols' "God Save the Queen" so loud he'd felt the beat rattling in his bones. "You're kidding me," Meg's voice rasped in the dark next to him. "Now she's a punk?" He started to get up but she stopped him. "That's all we need, you opening the door on her while she's naked. She'll scream incest." Meg hopped out of bed, and limped without her crutches down the hall. Fenstad heard brisk knocking and a door opening: "We get it, young lady. You're mad. Now shut the hell up!"

At the breakfast table all three of them looked like they'd gone through the spin cycle of a washing machine. Meg's curly hair corkscrewed into a nappy frizz, and she was wearing the same dirty terry-cloth robe from Tuesday morning. Maddie's eyes were bloodshot and swollen from hours of crying, and since Meg's injury had gotten her behind on the housework, Fenstad was forced to don the least offensive-smelling pair of jeans he could find in his hamper. These ingredients made a morning argument inevitable.

Meg pointed at the section of string holding up Maddie's oversized plaid trousers. "Put on a belt after you finish your breakfast," she said.

Maddie slammed her fork against her plate so hard that a chip of ceramic cruised like a missile past his nose. "Why can't you ever leave me alone?"

"Because you dress like a clown," Meg sniped.

Maddie's waterworks started fast. "You never care about me. You want me to look nice and be skinny but not anorexic, and date the right people, who aren't Enrique. Meanwhile I'm a person, and you don't care."

And then, of course, came the shouting. Fenstad drifted for a second or two. He started thinking about that black dog from his dream. Which neighbor's German shepherd had it looked like? He couldn't remember, but its jaws had been sharp and relentless as a steel trap.

He was jolted back to the present when Maddie announced, "After I leave for college I'm never coming back! Then you'll have to think about your own stupid life and how bored you are, instead of bossing me around!" Her voice was shrill, passionate, and specifically eighteen.

"Oh, yeah? If you run away who'll pay for all those clown clothes?" Meg spit back.

There was more. Fenstad tried to ignore it. When he got involved tensions escalated, so he'd learned the hard way to keep his mouth shut. He got up from the table. Neither of them disengaged from their three-mile stares long enough to say good-bye as he left for work.

At the hospital his vision was so blurry from lack of sleep that the edges of the fluorescent lights emitted a sickly yellow glow. His secretary, Val, handed him a pile of messages, all written on Post-it notes. "About five from the answering service, and the rest this last hour," she said.

He took a deep breath. In his mind the black German shepherd was barking. Val was wearing her usual rubber band–clasped ponytail. Since last night a cold sore the size of a sprig of cauliflower had sprouted on her upper lip. She was an ugly woman, and right now he hated her for it. Hated her more than Albert in the woods, and his selfish wife, disturbed daughter, and effeminate son. Hated her more than his patients, and Enrique Vargas. The anger burned inside him, and he wondered vaguely if he needed a nap. "What is all this?" he asked.

"This morning everybody went crazy," Val answered, completely innocent of the fact that right now he wanted a train to bust through the wall and mow her down, Anna Karenina style. She tapped her felt tip pen against her temple so that it left a black freckle, then recited: "Lila says her kids are acting up. And then something about cough syrup?" She looked to Fenstad, and he nodded to let her know that he got the reference. "You're free at noon, so I told her she could stop in with the kids. If she can't wait that long I told her to go to the emergency room. You don't have to call her back."

"Next?" he asked.

"Jodi Larkin says her daughter's sick. Wheezing or something. But she thinks it's mental. She wants you to call. Carl Fritz needs more Ritalin." Val smiled wryly. "A pill-eating sink swallowed all his last scrip."

Fenstad shook his head: Fritz had been snorting his stash again. He called at least twice a month, trying to wheedle second and third prescriptions.

Val continued. "Your group therapy is acting up. Their families called mostly. Sheila locked herself in her room and won't let anybody in. She says Albert is the devil and he's after her . . . Devil or Satan, or, I don't know. Is there a difference?" She wasn't being glib. Val could spend her whole life pondering inanities and mistaking them for depth. He cleared his throat, and she continued. "Bram's brother called because Bram's got some kind of chest bug and he thought you could prescribe something. I told him you can't, and he has to go to his medical doctor.

Fenstad took a deep breath. "They really did all go crazy."

Val nodded as if to say: *What did I tell you?*

After two canceled sessions (both patients were sick with chest infections), Lila showed up around noon with her two kids, Alice and Aran. She was wearing a yellow and black nylon exercise suit that hid all her curves. At first he didn't recognize her because he'd only ever seen her in full makeup and high heels. Her surprisingly enormous kids stood behind her, like elephants seeking shelter from a palm tree. He gestured at the couch, where all three sat.

Aran and Alice jiggled when they moved. The girl wore high-heeled plastic jellies, low-rise jeans, and a tube top through which her belly spilled. The boy favored a long T-shirt and jeans. His dark hair shone with grease.

"Well?" Fenstad asked, opening his hands.

The gauze from Lila's slit wrist peeked out from the sleeve of her track jacket, and she tugged on it nervously. She didn't smile or try to allure him. He wasn't sure what that meant. Either he'd broken through to her the other day, or she was breaking down.

"They're not themselves," she said. "I should have known. They were trying to fool me by being nice. They hate me, usually."

The kids' eyes were framed by circles so dark, it looked like they'd rubbed them with charcoal. Despite their heft, their pale skin and lethargy were telltale signs of malnutrition.

"My eyes," Aran said, only it sounded like a demand.

Lila walked over to the window. "The sun bothers them," she said, and pulled the shades so the room got dark.

Fenstad joined her so they could talk privately. Not surprisingly, her breath was cherry-flavored. "You've been drinking Robitussin," he said.

"That's not the point," she answered. Without makeup, she looked younger and prettier. A line of freckles dotted the bridge of her nose. He remembered that she'd married the much older Aran Senior when she was only eighteen. Child bride.

Lila lowered her voice and cupped her hand around his ear. "Something mean got inside them. I don't know how to get it out."

Her breath was overpowering. He was thinking Munchausen by proxy, or Robitussin-induced delirium. He was thinking full-on nervous breakdown, and these poor kids had witnessed it. Sara Wintrob, he was thinking, and her sweaty brunette ringlets in a four-poster bed.

He nodded at Lila, then approached the girl first. She was about 250 pounds, and only thirteen years old. If she stayed this weight she'd have type-two diabetes by the time she was twenty. Lila had neglected to mention that her daughter was a heifer. Somebody in that house, the same person buying the Robitussin, was also buying a lot of Ding Dongs.

"Take a deep breath," he told Alice, and she did. The fluid in her lungs fought against her. She wheezed, and then coughed, getting what looked like only about half a lungful of air. He felt her doughy wrist. It was cold and wet. Her heart rate was about fifty beats per minute. For a girl her size, fifty beats was dangerously low.

"Now you," he said to the boy. Aran was almost as big as his sister, but blessed with enough muscle that he probably didn't get teased at school. He looked about fifteen, and Fenstad remembered hearing that he was second string on the varsity wrestling team. His wheezing was the same as Alice's: loud and tubercular. They also shared identical red rashes along their arms and hands. The rashes had come to a head, and small pinpricks of blood dotted their skin.

"Allergies?" he asked.

"I left the windows open the last few nights for the breeze. I think maybe bugs got in . . ." Lila said.

Aran coughed. He didn't cover his mouth, and a wad of phlegm slapped against Fenstad's cheek. It lingered for a second, and then ran down his chin. Fenstad was a doctor, yes. But this was still gross.

Aran and Alice started chuckling. They were so weak he was surprised they'd waste the energy. Fenstad mopped his face with a tissue.

"Aran!" Lila scolded, "you apologize right now."

The kids made of point of laughing harder, and Fenstad narrowed his eyes. They were old enough to know their mother was fragile, so why were they baiting her? "You should mind your mother," he said.

Lila wrapped her arms around her slender waist. Her nylon suit billowed. He realized he should have hospitalized her long ago. It didn't matter that their father wasn't an acceptable alternative; these kids were wrecks.

"Lila, I'm taking them down to the emergency room. It could be pneumonia."

"No," Lila said. "I thought that too, at first. But they're not sick. They're changed."

"Come on," he said to the kids, and motioned for them to stand. The boy got up, but the girl needed help.

Fenstad pulled her by the arms until she stood. The momentum of her blubber propelled her forward, and Fenstad had to grab her to keep her from falling in the other direction. As he held her, she leaned into his chest and sniffed his shirt. The gesture wasn't cute: It was predatory, and for a moment he forgot she was a little girl. The hairs on the back of his neck stood erect, and her breath filled him with revulsion. It was sulfuric, like rot. Lila was right. Something about these kids was very off. "Let's go," he said, leading them to the emergency room.

Turned out, the ER was filled to capacity. Bram was there, and so was Sheila. In fact, at least half of the forty patients he saw regularly were lying on gurneys. Every bed was taken, and the intensive care unit was standing room only. Fenstad frowned, and then he got nervous: September wasn't even flu season!

Patients coughed in every corner. They mopped the junk from their mouths with whatever they could find: paper towels and tissues; white examining room paper; even the sleeves of their shirts. A cord of worry wove its way through his stomach and down his bowels like a snake. Was this an epidemic? A respiratory irritant in the school or library that had only recently become airborne? A biological weapon? Had Maddie or Meg been exposed?

He wheeled a pair of cots out of the supply closet and had the kids lie down while they waited for a doctor. He didn't like the looks on their faces. Their pupils were dilated. They were still grinning, but he'd bet money that their blood wasn't getting more than seventy percent of the oxygen it needed. So what the hell did they think was so funny?

He looked around the hospital, and was overcome

with dread. The air here had that same sulfuric taint as Alice's breath, which meant this thing was probably airborne.

He turned to Lila. "I'm calling your husband."

He watched her try to marshal her emotions, but her fluttering hands and unfocused eyes betrayed her. "No," she said. The corners of her lips were white with crud. She was drunk on Robitussin. Probably she'd had a bottle this morning because she hadn't known what to do when she'd realized her kids were seriously sick. And then she'd told herself a little story. Told herself it was okay she wasn't taking them to a hospital, because they weren't really her kids.

Fenstad pushed her down into a chair where she sat. "Take a deep breath," he said. She breathed in, but the follow-through was wanting. She burst into tears.

She hid her face from him, and tugged on her gauze. "You don't understand," she said.

"Lila. You made the right decision and you came here. They're sick. You might be right. The infection might have altered their personalities, at least temporarily. But the thing is, you're sick, too. I'm sorry, but you'll have to stay overnight."

She could hardly talk, she was crying so hard. "I . . . I knew," she cried.

"What?"

She wiped her nose with the back of her hand, still hitching her breath. "All . . . along, I knew . . . you . . . were like the rest." Her tears transformed into a scowl. "You think I'm too dumb to have children . . . You pretend to care but you don't, just like Aran Senior. My babies are changed and you want to say it's because I'm a bad mother. He was the one, the bad father. He broke them into pieces and left them to me to glue together. You think it's easy keeping food away from Alice? If I hide the bread and butter she eats sugar with her hands. Last night the two of them ate all the meat in the house. Raw! And when I tried to take it away, Aran Junior tore off my bandage! For Jesus' sake, he tried to lick the blood! Still, I'm trying. But people like you . . . you won't let me." Her voice was low, and not the slightest bit shrill.

Fenstad looked at her for a long time. Her cough syrup breath was strong. His decision was simple, but that didn't make it easy.

He found an orderly and gave his instructions: Under no circumstances were the children permitted to leave the hospital until they were treated by a physician and signed out by their father. Then he ordered Lila into psychiatric lockdown.

He didn't stop to talk to either Lila or her children as he left the emergency room, but as he walked out, Lila shouted after him. It cut through the din in the room, and suddenly everyone got quiet. "I knew you'd do this. You were always so cold. So fucking *cold*!"

He tried not to think about Lila as he walked back to his office. Instead he thought about the black dog from his dream, and Enrique Vargas, and Albert Sanguine. He thought about Graham Nero, and his wife, sweaty and naked, in room 69. Then he looked down at his shoes, just to make certain the carpet wasn't soaked in blood.

SIXTEEN
I Hate You!

Friday morning, Meg's ankle itched. She and her husband had made love on the couch yesterday. Horny and breathless like a couple of kids. Funny how something like that can make everything else a little easier. It had made her remember the way she'd felt about him when they were first married, like there was no problem he couldn't solve, no question for which the brilliant Fenstad Wintrob didn't have an answer. It had always puzzled her that he'd picked psychiatry as his specialty because he was the only man she'd known who hadn't whined endlessly about his feelings. But then again, he was a quiet guy with his gears always spinning. He'd never fit in at school, or even with other doctors. Helping people with their problems turned him from an outsider to a trusted friend.

She was sitting at the breakfast nook table, and her daughter was smack in the middle of a temper tantrum. "*You never listen . . .*" Maddie cried while picking apart a sliver of grapefruit. Her fingers glistened with juice. Meg looked out the window. The sun was bright and the lawn was green, but something was amiss. She couldn't put her finger on it; the town looked more perfect than a Normal Rockwell painting, but still. Something wasn't *right*.

"I wish Albert Sanguine had hit you harder!" Maddie cried, and Meg returned her attention to the girl in front of her.

"*What* did you say?" she asked.

Maddie looked down at her plate. Swallowed. Her purple hair hung moplike over her eyes. "Forget it," she mumbled.

Meg blinked, and waited for her daughter to apologize. The seconds passed. She'd been attacked three days ago, her ankle was broken, and the house was a mess because she wasn't ambulatory enough to clean it, and no one in her family had the sense to pick up after themselves. It was possible that these things were the reason that she was biting her lip to keep from crying, but more likely it was Maddie's words that hurt the most *(Where did I go wrong?)*.

She peered into the kitchen, hoping Fenstad would offer his help, but she hadn't heard him puttering with the coffeepot for the last few minutes. In fact, she vaguely remembered the sound of a car engine pulling out from the driveway. She fumed. He'd sneaked away without even saying good-bye! Always the good cop to her prison warden. Always the parent Maddie loved best. Even yesterday, he'd acted like he'd only been going along with grounding her to keep the peace.

They kept looking at each other. Meg waited for the big *I'm sorry. I shouldn't have said I'm glad you got beat up by a drooling madman, Mom,* but it didn't come.

Maddie pulled the purple hair out of her face, and the two women locked eyes in a battle of wills. *Oh, kid,* Meg thought. *Eighteen years and you still have no idea who you're dealing with.*

"The only person you care about is David. You don't love me or Dad," Maddie said, only this time she didn't mumble.

Meg's eyes watered, but she didn't let Maddie see. She thought about the bird that had died in her hands. She'd felt foolish burying it, so instead she'd thrown it in the trash above a pile of coffee grounds. She regretted that now. She should have dug a hole for it out behind the garage with the rest of the family pets.

And where was Fenstad at a time like this? Gone, like always. At work, and when he wasn't at work, mentally gone. So why not now? Why wait until this little bitch left for college? When she served him those divorce papers, he'd never know what hit him. The vision of his shocked face—*How unexpected! The brilliant Fenstad Wintrob for once caught off-guard!*—comforted her, and she was able to stifle her tears. Then she wondered: *Why do I always think such terrible things?*

"Don't you dare tell me I don't love you, Maddie," she said when she trusted herself to sound calm.

Maddie's green eyes were cold, and her gaunt face was pruned into a collection of angles. Her anger had made her ugly. "I wish you were dead," she said.

Meg acted without thinking. She slapped Maddie hard across the face. The sound was loud, like a cue ball breaking up a rack of billiards.

Maddie reeled, and Meg couldn't see whether she'd done any damage for a good few seconds. But then the imprint of her hand slowly surfaced like bubbles in a lake. Four fingers ran in a diagonal line from Madeline's ear to the corner of her mouth. She didn't yelp or holler. Probably she was too shocked.

"You want to be treated like a woman, you stop acting like a baby," Meg said. Her fury sounded foreign to her own ears. She knew she should be sorry, knew she should apologize, but she didn't want to just yet.

Maddie's chest heaved in what looked like the beginning of an extended crying jag. Meg looked into the kitchen, somehow still hoping that Fenstad might be here. Maybe he'd only been running an errand, and was back. Maybe, for once, he would break this up. But she didn't see him in the kitchen. Instead she saw the clock—ten past nine. Maddie was late for school, and she had a calculus test first period. Meg moaned. "Get in the car. I'll drive you," she said.

The ride was silent. Maddie bit back her tears, which wasn't like her, and probably meant that they were genuine. The welt reddened as the minutes passed. Maddie rubbed the side of her face with exaggerated gentleness, like she was made of porcelain. *Wonderful,* Meg thought. *Now I'll get a call from a guidance counselor accusing me of child abuse.*

This was bad. She and Maddie had just entered a new and grotesque realm of cruelty toward each other. She wanted to take it back. She wanted to make it unhappen. But it *had* happened.

"Maddie . . ." she said, but she wasn't sure what else to say. Should she cave, and let her see Enrique? That's what the fight had been about, hadn't it? Or had it started with the clown belt? She couldn't remember for sure.

The radio was tuned to NPR's morning edition, and the host announced that American deaths in Iraq had officially surpassed four thousand. She let out a sigh. All those boys. She couldn't imagine what she'd do if one of them was David. What a terrible thing, to lose someone you love. Next to her, Maddie sniffled. Then she wiped her nose on the back of her hand. She was looking out the window at the perfect, cloudless day.

A thought occurred to Meg like a bolt of lightning. She could have kicked herself for not having guessed it before. She pulled to the side of the road and turned to her daughter. "Maddie," she said. "He's a sharp boy. He'll be fine."

Maddie let out a ragged breath and pressed her nose against the window. Outside, the sun shone bright. The grass on all the freshly mowed lawns was green. "How do you know?" she whispered. In profile, Meg could see the blood drain from her face, so that the handprint became more prominent. It drove home the point that Meg had been avoiding: She'd hit her own kid.

She often wished for an extra day, or month, or year with Maddie and David as children, because they really do grow up too fast. Even when you're paying attention, there are things you miss, or weren't smart enough to understand the first time around. She loved Maddie, David, and even Fenstad so much she didn't like to think about it, because it frightened her. She would do anything for them, and not because they were her blood. Even if Maddie wasn't hers, even if she was a stranger wandering down Micmac Street in lace garters and purple hair, she knew she'd be charmed. She'd smile and think: *That girl's all right*. So what was it about the two of them that made them tear each other to pieces?

"He won't get hurt," Meg said. "Hardly any of them do. This is good for him. He'll go to college now."

Maddie wiped the hair from the side of her face where Meg could make out the indentation of her wedding rings. The diamond had cut Maddie's skin, and Meg bit her lip to hold back her own tears: She'd made Maddie bleed.

"I'd run away with him but I don't think he wants to," Maddie said. All traces of her pruned ugliness were gone. "I love him more than he loves me," she said, and Meg knew that David wasn't really her favorite. Her girl was so brave to say such things.

"He's a boy. He loves you differently. He wants to provide."

Maddie nodded. "I guess . . . Mom?"

"Yeah?"

Maddie dragged her hand against the closed window so that it left a streak. Cars slowed as they passed, curious as to why the Wintrob family Saab was parked in a tow-away zone near the hospital, with its hazards flashing. "He's never had fun . . . That's why he's going. He wants to drink beer and meet girls on leave. He'll do all the things he couldn't before, when he had to take care of his family." She didn't look at Meg when she said this. Instead she traced the steamy trails she'd left along the window.

Meg frowned. Enrique wasn't the type to run away from anything, and he adored Maddie. But then again, he was only twenty, and his whole life he'd worked the counter of a convenience store. Maybe Maddie was right. Poor kid. As if being dumped for the army wasn't bad enough. "Come here," Meg said.

Maddie didn't comply. Instead she rubbed the mark on her face as if she expected Meg to give her another one. The gesture wasn't for show, and for a brief moment, Meg saw herself through her daughter's eyes: a capricious tyrant whose purpose was not her daughter's well-being, but her obedience. Just like good old Dad.

"I don't want to fight," Meg said, and in response, Maddie sniffled. The sound was shameful, because with it Meg understood that Maddie was frightened.

"I'll tell you what. You're still grounded, but if Enrique gets his leave orders, you can spend the day with him."

Maddie burst into tears.

"What is it? What'd I do now?" Meg asked.

Maddie shook her head. Then she scooted over and flopped into Meg's arms. "Thanks, Mom," she said. Her weight pressed against Meg's bad leg, but she didn't want to ruin the moment so she gritted her teeth through the pain and let her daughter cry. "I'm so mad at him. I'm sorry I said that stuff. He's the one I hate," Maddie's voice was muffled by Meg's blouse. "Daddy never did this to you. Daddy never left you."

She bit back the response on the tip of her tongue (*Sometimes I wish he had*), and said, "Everybody's not like Daddy."

Maddie nodded like she thought Fenstad was perfect, and Meg felt that familiar tinge. But this time she tried to let it go. All girls deserve to think their fathers are divine, even if it makes their mothers that much more human.

"Maddie," Meg said. "I shouldn't have hit you. That was wrong. But what you said hurt me. You can't say those kinds of things."

Maddie cocked her head. "Yeah," she said. "That was totally out of hand."

SEVENTEEN
The Dandy

After dropping Maddie off at the school bus circle (she'd galloped cheerfully to the front entrance, oblivious of the handprint of her face), Meg opened the library. The volunteers had their own keys, but the parking lot was empty. Upon not seeing her at her desk, they'd probably declared a holiday and gone out for coffee. She entered the empty building, flicking overhead lights as she hobbled across the industrial blue carpet. There were no phone messages, and no one had returned a single book to the drop box since she'd left early yesterday afternoon. She wondered if the flu going around had confined her regulars to bed.

The library was a wreck. She'd cleaned as best she could yesterday, which turned out not to be very much. Books and papers were scattered like snow. Albert's bloody fingerprints were perfectly preserved on the iMac keyboard he'd thrashed against. The Plexiglas was scratched, and she couldn't figure out where it came from until she saw the broken face of her three-year-old gold Seiko on the floor. She'd felt weightless as he'd thrown her. She hadn't understood the sensation, but had still known to protect her face from the impact. She'd heard only the wind in her ears as she'd flown.

She lifted the keyboard where Albert's sausage-sized fingerprints had dried. Then butterflies started drowning in her stomach. Was he really out there, in the woods?

She looked out the window, and that same unsettled feeling from breakfast returned. Something about the lawn, and the trees. The breeze was mild, and things were just beginning to dry up and die. A few cars were on the road, but not as many as usual. It was too quiet. Like one of those kid's pictures from *Highlights* magazine that asked: "What's wrong here?" while birds flew backward, and people had been drawn without lips or eyes.

What if Albert was right? What if something really did live in the woods, and it had somehow gotten inside him? In a way it made sense. He hadn't really been Albert at the library on Tuesday. He'd been . . . someone else (*Where did I go wrong?*).

She knew she should feel sorry for him. He was probably dead. But mostly she was frightened of this empty place. She wanted to go home.

The bloody smudge over the shift button was fine enough to show Albert's fingerprint. She'd planned on washing the keyboard off, good as new. Instead she dumped it in the trash. Then she hobbled into the children's room. The rainbow carpet's fabric was gathered in the middle and stained with Albert's blood. Specs of dust drifted against the light coming through the windows. The old clock ticked its seconds, half past ten. What if Albert came here today, looking for her? What if he wanted to finish the job he'd started, and break her neck?

Where did I go wrong?

Her ankle hurt. Weak thing, it had betrayed her to break so easily. She leaned against a wall. The tears came fast. Who was kidding whom? It wasn't Albert's eyes she'd looked into three days ago. Frank Bonelli had reached out from beyond the grave. *Where did I go wrong?* The phrase was haunting her, but then again, it always had.

She wiped her eyes. Another day with the library closed wasn't going to kill the rich Barnes & Noble lovers of Corpus Christi. Nobody borrowed books when they could buy them instead. She was going home. She grabbed her crutches and started turning out the lights just as a red Porsche cruised into the library parking lot. Her pulse raced. *Oh, no.*

She looked fast in every direction. The office was transparent. He'd find her. The women's bathroom? That might work. Then she shook her head. Forget it. He'd probably gotten lost on his way to the country club, and was looking for directions. She doubted he remembered that she worked here.

Just then Graham Nero strode through the library's double glass doors. He didn't stop at checkout, but instead wove his way toward her office. She'd never seen him here before, so it surprised her that he knew where to look. He cupped his hands around his eyes and peered through the Plexiglas, looking for her. Then he coughed a few times. A gob of spit smacked against the plastic. It clung there, unmoving, and he didn't clean it up. The sun shone brightly through the reference section. He turned and drew the blinds.

She swallowed deeply, even though this was just Graham. But he'd made the place dark, and suddenly she didn't like the dark. She limped through the side door and tapped him on the shoulder. "Looking for someone?"

He turned. His breath smelled so strongly of peppermint Altoids that her eyes watered. Then he coughed.

This time he covered his mouth with a monogrammed handkerchief: GUN in big, gold letters. His hair was coiffed with pomade, and she thought it was less receding than when they'd last met. She looked closer: a toupee! She rolled her eyes. The man was such a dandy.

"Caitlin told me what happened. I wanted to come to the hospital but . . ." He spread his hands open, as if the answer was self-evident. Then he smiled warmly, like the thing between them had been love.

"It's fine. Thanks for the thought," Meg told him.

Graham squeezed her waist in his hands. His soft fingers had never raked leaves or washed dishes. Even his chin was soft. Funny that for a while she'd imagined running away with him.

"I was so worried. You saved my family." His voice was flat, like he was reading from a speech.

"Get your hands off me, Graham."

He cocked his head and grinned. "I'm grateful to you, but I shouldn't have expected anything less." His skin was pale, and his eyes were lined with dark blue circles. His business-casual tan trousers were wrinkled, and upon his shirt pocket was a round, red stain. Frumpy attire for a man who primped in front of the mirror for an hour every morning.

She slapped his hands. He held her tighter, like this was all part of their foreplay. Through her blouse, his cold fingers chilled her skin. "Go home to your wife," she said.

Graham frowned. He didn't actually look sad. It was a handsome frown. "I can't go home. Caitlin's gone," he said.

Meg slapped his hands again, hard, and this time he let go. Unfortunately he'd been holding her steady. She lost her balance and fell.

He caught her by the underarms. His fingers touched her breasts as he held her steady. "She figured out about you. And then she was gone. It was the attack that changed her," he said. The Altoids on his breath were beginning to fade. In their place was something rancid.

Meg's face got hot, and everything was spinning. She'd broken up a marriage, or at least helped it fray. Meanwhile, this jerk was copping a feel. She tried to pull away but he held her tighter. "Graham. I'm sorry to hear this."

"Yes." Graham affected a hangdog expression like his heart was broken. "I hate being alone. I keep thinking about you. Caitlin knew that. That's why she's gone."

Meg was flabbergasted. In the month they'd spent together, they'd never gotten past impersonal niceties like *please* and *thank you*. She didn't know whether he believed in God, or just went to church out of habit. She didn't know how he took his coffee. She didn't even know whether he was any good at picking up large objects with his toes. "Graham," she said, "that's nice. But be honest. I'm not the first woman you brought to a sleazy motel."

Graham turned his head and coughed. Spit landed on the carpet. She saw a rash through his open shirt collar. In places, the rash had come to a head, and blood dotted his smooth, hairless neck. "Let's get something to eat, Meg. I'm so hungry."

A chill ran down her spine. She thought about sweet Albert Sanguine, and the monster that lived inside him. What if it was real, and now it was in Graham, too? Soon all the men in her life would turn on her. They'd hold her down and break her spirit like she'd always expected. Like her dad had always wanted to do. Was this her dad, haunting her?

"Graham, I'm at work. This is where I work," she said. "I'm not going out to eat with you."

He tugged on a curl in her hair and she swatted his hand. His eyes narrowed. For a second she thought he was going to strike her. She flinched and he smiled. "You ought to be a good girl, and not make me angry," he said.

Meg backed into the office wall behind her. What the hell was going on? Graham Nero was a vacuous dandy. He wasn't violent. He didn't care about anybody enough to have strong feelings, or even declare his love, unless she was really good-looking and willing to wash his sheets.

"Come on, Meg. A little drink. You and me. I rented the same room. I have the key." He pulled it out. Just looking at the plastic keycard made her blush. What a Jerry Springer thing she'd done.

"You should go," she said. Her tone was forceful, and betrayed nothing but a cool head. If he'd looked at her hands, though, he would have seen that she was shaking.

He squeezed her shoulder. She tried to turn, but her bum leg buckled. This time he didn't catch her. She used the wall for support and slid down the side of it. Sparks radiated from her foot to her groin, all the way into her stomach. Her ankle hurt so much that she wished, for a moment, she could amputate it. "*Ooohhhh.*" She was crying. She couldn't help it. The only thing that kept her from fainting was that it would mean leaving this lunatic alone with her body.

At first she hardly noticed how close he'd gotten. Hardly noticed his hot, rotten breath until a bead of

sweat rolled down the side of his face. It dripped onto
her cheek. His eyes got strange. The pupils dilated so
they looked almost black. They shone, and inside them,
she saw her own terrified reflection. It was getting
closer. Its mouth opened into a silent scream. He was
getting closer, too. "I love you," he whispered.

She clenched her fists, and remembered what every
Italian mother tells her daughter: Go for the balls, then
the eyes. "Get out. Now. Don't come back. I don't love
you. I never did. I don't even like you," she said.

The smell was worse. It wasn't just his breath. His
body was rotting.

"Go!" she shouted, and then she flinched, because
her voice echoed throughout the library, and no one
came running. She was alone here, with this predator,
and now he knew it.

He was almost close enough to kiss her. She scooted in
the opposite direction and her ankle twisted. "Ooooshttt,"
she cried out with closed eyes and gritted teeth. Sparks of
pain ignited anew, and she shivered, as if strapped inside
an electric chair. His breath was strong against her cheek.
Then something wet. It couldn't be, could it? The blood
drained from her face and for a very short instant, her
revulsion outweighed her pain.

Graham Nero ran his sandy tongue along her forehead, and her cheek, and all the way down her chin, to
her neck. *Where did I go wrong?* he asked, only it
didn't sound like him. It sounded like her father.

Then he was standing. He straightened his shirt, put
on his sunglasses, pulled a tin of Altoids from his
pocket, opened it, and emptied its entire contents into
his mouth. "The woods, Meggie. Tonight. It can be
nice or it can hurt. Don't make me do it the hard way,"
he called over his shoulder as he walked out.

As the saliva dried on her skin, she watched him get into his Porsche and pull away. She realized then what was wrong with the view out her window. Not once today had she seen any birds.

EIGHTEEN
Bloody Carpet

It was mid-afternoon, and the sun's rays were turning red. They shone through the newly colored leaves. Fenstad drove, but he didn't notice any of it. Not even the fact that there was no traffic near the hospital, and hardly any of Corpus Christi was out enjoying the pretty day.

He'd just come from Lila Schiffer's hospital room, where he'd convinced her to sign self-commitment papers. First Albert, now Lila. He was starting to take this personally. Lila's blood alcohol had been three times the legal limit. In session she'd told him that she drank Robitussin infrequently, and only late at night. He knew now that wasn't true. She drank all the time, and in front of the kids, and in doing so had damaged herself and everyone around her. He should have tried harder. He shouldn't have been daydreaming about Meg Bonelli while people with real problems had sat across from his desk every week, begging for help. Maybe that was why he'd agreed to drive to Lois Larkin's house even though the last time he'd seen a genuine house call, it had been on an episode of *Dr. Kildare*. He didn't want to lose another patient. Well, that, and the hospital was a Petri dish full of mystery cough.

He'd learned through the grapevine that the feds were in town. This bug had spread fast enough to warrant their notification by the hospital's public health advocate, and since no one had determined whether its source was viral, bacterial, or chemical, the Centers for Disease Control and the Environmental Protection Agency were each conducting investigations. Right now scientists from both teams were interviewing the patients clogging the emergency room halls, and measuring toxicity levels in the water, air, and public buildings. By the time Fenstad left the hospital, ambulances were being redirected to neighboring towns for two reasons: There wasn't room for them in Corpus Christi, and the town might soon be under quarantine.

So far today seven patients had moved from the emergency room to the morgue. It had happened with stunning speed, and Fenstad was still reeling. Every one of them had suffocated—drowned in his own phlegm. He'd seen a boy Maddie's age with black hair and a jaw sharp enough to cut glass coughing one second, and dead the next. He'd gone out smiling, like he'd wanted to reassure everyone that he was fine, please don't worry, Mom and Dad.

Something broke loose inside him when he saw that grinning corpse that somebody had once called "son." He thought of Maddie, and how he'd feel if she was gone. Like a hurricane had smashed the house he'd spent his whole life building. This mystery infection wasn't Meg's long-suffering ennui, or the slight social embarrassment of a gay son and a purple-haired daughter, or even a lost job. This was serious.

He called Meg's cell phone. As soon as she answered he told her, "Pull Maddie out of school, buy a few gallons of bottled water, and a HEPA filter and purifier from Target. I promised I'd stop by Lois Larkin's house—I'm afraid she might be suicidal, but after that I'm coming straight home." Turned out she'd had a bad day at the library and was already at the house watching the soaps. As soon as he told her how many people were sick, she was hobbling into the Saab to get Maddie. "We'll be waiting. Take care of yourself. I love you," she said.

Ten minutes later he was on the road, headed for Lois. Police cars and government sedans were parked at the top of the hill near the woods. They were still searching for James Walker, and rumors had spread at the hospital that a lot of other people were missing, too.

He wasn't sure what it all meant. The bug caused chest congestion, light sensitivity, rash, foul breath, and if Lila was to be believed, it altered the personality. In less than two days, it had spread to at least twenty-five percent of the town, which meant either it was airborne, or it had contaminated the water supply. So far no one had gotten better, and at least seven people had died. It didn't look like a regular infection; it looked like immune response. Something got in their systems that their bodies recognized as an enemy, but couldn't kill. White blood cells and oxidative damage inflamed organs and tissues at an accelerated rate. These caused the rash and lethally wet lungs, while the infection persisted unharmed. The same thing had happened during the 1918 influenza epidemic. Two million people died. In an obscene perversion of the natural order, the young and the women, whose metabolisms and immune responses were the most reactive to foreign invaders, were the first to fall. A dread settled over him, because he remembered that in 1918, people had gone missing, too. Only they weren't missing: Entire families expired overnight in their homes, and no one found them until the epidemic was over.

With luck the CDC would know more tonight. The

hospital or perhaps the government would issue a press release. If the news was bad, he and Meg needed to give some serious consideration to leaving town.

At the end of Micmac Street, he pulled his Escalade in front of the Larkins' wooden ranch house. Its white paint was peeling, and the lawn was brown and short, as if someone had lit it on fire. On the front porch was a dead bluebird. Its head and half its chest were missing, but its wings were still spread, as if captured in mid-flight.

He rang the bell and waited. It chimed the tune of "Michael Row the Boat Ashore, Hallelujah!" He wasn't sure whether to laugh or to shiver. He rang the bell twice more while the chimes continued. To his relief, Jodi Larkin finally opened the door. She stepped aside without speaking, and he entered the house. The place was dark, and all the shades were drawn. Its furniture was frozen in 1980s gold-gilded wallpaper and worn velvet couches like a shrine to better times, or perhaps just younger ones. Jodi was a small, shriveled woman who reminded him of the photos he'd seen of dust bowl survivors from the Great Depression: mean and ugly.

"She hates the sun all the sudden," Jodi whispered, as if Lois might hear. "Don't ask me why. Miss Smarty Pants and all her pie-in-the-sky ideas, she never made any sense to me. And look where she wound up after all that school."

"Where is she?" he asked.

Jodi nodded her head down the hall. "Her room. She's been begging me to call you since the kid went missing, so she should be happy you're here, but who knows. She's not herself most of the time. I was thinking you could give her something to calm her down."

Jodi began walking. She favored her left hip, which

reminded him of Meg. He hoped that she and Maddie were safe at home.

Lois's room was dark and damp. The wooden floorboards groaned as he walked across them. Some of them were loose. The place smelled like the sickly-sweet baby's breath flowers from a funeral. In a few strides he reached the window and pulled open the blinds, which reminded him of Maddie for a second: *Rise and shine, munchkin*. It reminded him of his mother, Sara, too.

"Shut the blinds, Dr. Wintrob," Lois said. Her voice was gravelly, and she held a slender hand over her eyes to protect them from the late-afternoon glare. "The sun . . . It *hurts*."

Tacked to her walls were two Brad Pitt posters. A pile of stuffed animals stood like sentries along her pink desk. The pink wallpaper was peeling, and her blankets were white eyelet that had faded over time into yellow. This was the room of a child, and yet she'd lived here for seven years since graduating from college.

He put his hand on her neck, where her lymph nodes had swollen like goiters. Her temperature was subnormal, and her hands were covered in the telltale rash. She'd been scratching, and her fingers were bleeding. One of her fingernails was missing, and the flesh there was bright pink. "Please, Mother," Lois repeated. "It burns."

Jodi shut the blinds so the room was dark and stagnant. He caught himself holding his breath. This virus would be quite a present to bring home to his family tonight. Then again, if this thing was airborne, precautions wouldn't make much difference. "How long have you been feeling this way?" he asked.

She wheezed her answer. It sounded more like breath with shapes than words. "Since the woods."

"There's a bad bug going around. You've definitely

got it." He sat on the corner of her bed and felt her pulse. It was slow and thick. Her breath smelled like offal, and he thought for some illogical reason of the bird on the stoop. What had she been eating, to smell this bad?

Jodi fluffed the pillow behind Lois's head. Then she felt Lois's forehead with her lips. He'd seen this before. The enabler and the enabled switch places. It confirms their relationship, and binds them more tightly together, like an oath sealed in blood.

After her failed engagement to Ronnie Koehler, Lois had been considering leaving town. Now she spent her time watching afternoon game shows in bed. Albert, Lila, Lois, the kids in the morgue. He was losing them. One after the next, like ducks in a shooting rage. Pling, pling, pling.

"I've got to get my *TV Guide*. Season premieres start this week," Jodi announced. "I'll be right back."

After she left the room Fenstad said, "You've had some bad luck."

"Yeth." she said. Then she started coughing. The phlegm left a trail between her lips and her bedsheets. He handed her the box of Kleenex at her bedside. She breathed out fast when she took it, and her breath almost initiated his gag reflex. He swallowed fast to keep from retching, and thought again about the bird.

"A lot of people have this, so I don't think you should go to the hospital. You won't get any decent attention. But the second your breathing gets worse, don't tell your mother. I don't trust her to make a smart decision. Dial nine-one-one."

She nodded, and he knew she would heed his advice. She was a sensible girl, with the exception of the company she kept. She reached out her hand, and he took it. A small, guilt-filled voice told him that he needed to leave here—she was infected, and now he might get infected, too. He might bring this home to the women. He silenced that voice. They didn't pay him three hundred thousand dollars a year to abandon the people who needed him most.

Lois was cold, so he folded her palm into a fist and rubbed. He liked her a lot. Every time she came in for therapy, he hoped she'd stand up during a session and realize what he'd known all along: She was lovely in every way.

"I need your help," Lois breathed. He saw that her eyes were wet. "In the woods. Tim Carroll found me. Did he tell anyone what he saw?"

Fenstad shrugged. He'd heard she was hysterical, but that was all.

She smiled wryly. He didn't like that smile. It looked like defeat. "Then he didn't tell anyone. He's thuch a gentleman. I wonder how they didn't notice the animals. I guess they didn't want to thee them . . . I ate the dirt out there. The dirt was full of blood. James's blood. And thomething else, too. Something's inthide me now. At night I don't even lisp . . ."

Her tone was flat and her lisp was indeed less pronounced. Autohypnosis, perhaps. It was understandable. Under extreme stress, otherwise ordinary people crumbled. Like buildings, they toppled in unpredictable ways.

"How do you know you ate blood?" he asked.

A tear ran down her face but she didn't break down. "Because it tasted tho good."

Fenstad let out his breath. This was worse than he'd guessed. This was hospitalization bad. Maybe even schizophrenic-break bad.

"I would have eaten the toe, too. Thath why I screamed. Because I was hungry for it."

He tried to conceal his shock. It wasn't easy. "What toe?"

Lois couldn't lift her head from the pillow, but her wide, dark eyes focused on his face. "James Walker. I ate his toe. I eat other things, too. Birdth . . . mostly birds. At night it geth worse. It's something inside me from the woods." She coughed again, and this time wiped the phlegm on her hair so that it shone. Much of her hair was plastered to her scalp in nappy locks, and when he'd first come in he'd mistaken it for grease. Now he realized that she'd been using her head as a handkerchief for days.

"I locked my windows last night. Nailed them shut so I couldn't get out. I'm more myself than I was yesterday. I'm trying to starve it, so it leaves me alone. But I can't last another night without . . . eating. I need you to lock me up."

He noticed now that she'd hammered nails diagonally through the window ledges. They formed a bent and uneven line across the wood. A few were rusty, and most were quite thick. He looked down at the floor, saw the hammer on her desk, and realized she'd gotten the nails by plucking them from the joints in her own floorboards.

"I was wrong," he said. "You belong in a hospital. You're not well."

She nodded. The tears returned, and she squeezed his hand hard. "Ever since the woods, I can feel it looking out from my eyes. The problem is, I *like* it. I'm afraid I'll break the windows tonight unless you lock me up."

Fenstad shook his head. He'd studied cases in which viral infections passed the blood-brain barrier and caused dementia and even schizophrenia. He hoped it wasn't a virus. He hoped it was stress. Stress, at least, was less likely to leave her permanently damaged.

"I wish it was stress, Dr. Wintrob," she said, as if she'd read his mind. Then she laughed that same bitter laugh. "I wish it was cancer."

He shook his head like he was trying to shake something loose from it. "You need to go to the hospital."

She looked at him, a large set of black eyes and gaunt skin. "You know, I don't feel things the thame way I used to. The baby in my stomach is too little to move, but since the woods, it kicks. Maybe it's sick, too. Normally I'd care about my own baby, but I don't, you see."

"You're pregnant?" Fenstad asked, and he wondered whether it was an hysterical pregnancy—she needed a reason to go on living. On the heels of this, he'd solved the mystery. This change in her person wasn't viral; it was psychological. She needed to get away from the people closest to her, but she didn't have the courage to leave them, so instead she'd developed a new personality to do her dirty work for her. It would make enemies of them, and set her free. Smart machine, the subconscious. It insisted on survival, even when good manners would have us all six feet deep.

Lois smiled. "Do you know some women invent pregnancies? They get big and then suddenly, poof, they get small again. They want the attention so bad that their bodies change, just so people will notice them."

"I didn't say you were having an hysterical pregnancy, Lois," Fenstad answered.

She smiled. "No?"

Her brows, what remained of them, were knit together and he thought that he didn't like this new identity she'd created. There was violence lurking beneath this girl's black eyes. There was madness there, too. "I'll help you. We'll go to the hospital. I'll have you confined for the night, and tomorrow we can decide what to do."

"If you hate someone, does it mean you never loved them?" she asked.

Fenstad shrugged. "Depends on why you hate them. Are you talking about your mother, or yourself?"

Lois chuckled. The sun had begun to set, and its red rays were moving slowly out of sight. "I think it means you never loved them . . ."

Just then Jodi came through the door. Out the window, the last of the sun's rays clung to the far wall in slanted red lines that splashed across Lois's dilated pupils, and out of sight. The room went dark. Only her eyes and the phosphorescence of his watch hands illuminated the room.

Lois coughed. She didn't cover her mouth, and the smell was pure sulfur. Then she closed her eyes. Her breath clicked, and wheezed, and finally stopped. Fenstad shook her. "Lois!" he yelled. Behind him, Jodi dropped her *TV Guide* with the show about Mormons and their many wives emblazoned on its cover.

Lois's head rolled. Her nightgown was open to the third button. He felt her heartbeat with his palm. It was weak, but present. After a few seconds, she opened her eyes again. "Fennie," she said.

Fenstad blinked. Looked at his hand on her breast and promptly removed it. "Dr. Wintrob," he corrected.

"Right." She smiled. Her pupils were so massive that the brown of her irises was gone. He wished, suddenly, that he had not come to this sick place. He wanted to be home with his wife, where he belonged. He wanted to be anywhere but here.

"I'm hungry," she said.

Jodi began to shiver like she had late-stage Parkinson's, and he realized that she was terrified. "She ate all the steak Tuesday night while I was sleeping in front of the *Wheel of Fortune* marathon. I don't even think she cooked it. She goes out at night, too, but last night I locked her in her room. Don't want the whole neighborhood seeing her in her skivvies. And there's something . . . New friends of hers from the bar, maybe. They bang on the windows at night. They tease me." Jodi was crying now. She picked up her *TV Guide* and rubbed Bill Paxton's face as if for reassurance.

Fenstad's stomach dropped. Neither woman was making sense. Could the infection have caused some kind of mass hysteria? Did its smell have a neurological effect? He didn't know, but this child's room with its torn-up floors where a grown woman spent her days watching television was dark and cold. "She needs to go to the hospital. Help me get her to my car."

"I don't want to go," Lois said. "I like it here, in my room. Don't I, Mom?"

Jodi looked from Fenstad to Lois, and didn't answer. She cupped her mouth with her hand in an unwitting pantomime of speak no evil.

"Lois. You're going to the hospital," Fenstad said.

Lois laughed. Her wheezing was less pronounced, but still audible. "I changed my mind."

"You're too sick to make decisions," Fenstad said.

Lois nodded. "Exactly right. It's my mother's decision, and you don't want to make me angry, do you? Because I know where you live, Jodi. I've lived with you my whole fucking life." Then she smiled. He noticed with a start that the gap between her teeth was gone.

Jodi covered her face and peeked between her fingers. "But Lois," she said with phony concern. "I want what's best for you."

"Really?" Lois asked. Then she smiled, because all three of them were in on the dark, unbearable joke.

Fenstad looked from one woman to the next, and he thought the worst part of this bedside scene was not

Lois's madness, but the grotesquerie of their relation-ship. For almost thirty years these two had played the roles of loving mother and daughter. Probably neither of them knew right now how much they hated each other.

"I like it here," Lois said. "We've got lots of wonder-ful game shows on the television." Her teeth were as straight as those of a 1950s Hollywood actress. The lisp he could understand: Autohypnosis made men walk on hot coals. But the teeth? What *was* this?

Jodi nodded. She was shaking so hard that even her head was jittering. "You know best, Lois," she said.

Lois's nightgown was white, and for a moment he was back in Wilton, Connecticut, where the carpet was deep blue, and in the sickbed slept a crone. *Fennie? Is it a lump?*

Lois's breath smelled like a fly-infested slaughter-house. Even in textbooks, no one changed this much this fast. He remembered the half-eaten bird on the front lawn, and with a jolt wondered if Lois's alter ego had murdered James Walker in those woods.

"I read in the paper that Ronnie and Noreen set a date," he said, because he wanted to get her talking.

"So?" she asked.

He shrugged. "Miller Walker can't be happy about his missing son. Things won't go over well for you if you stay in town, Lois. A little time at the hospital will be good for you."

Lois shook her head. "You'll see," she said.

"What happened in the woods? Tell me again," he said.

Her voice was deep and watery. "You'll see, Fennie. You'll see."

"Dr. Wintrob to you." He took a shot in the dark: "Is it seeing out from your eyes right now? Can I talk to it?"

"Time's up, Dr, Wintrob," Lois said. "Fifty minutes. Session's over. I noticed that sometimes you cut me off at forty-five, and even forty. Am I that dull?"

Fenstad didn't move. "I'm not leaving. I like you too much."

Lois grinned. "I think my heart stopped beating."

He looked down at the creaking floors. Their nails were missing, but instead he thought he saw the plush blue carpet in Wilton, Connecticut, soaked in blood. "Stop it," he said.

Lois lifted her hand to the middle of her chest. Then she opened another button, so that he could see her exposed breasts. "Feel," she said.

He shook his head. She lunged for his hand and forced it against her bare skin. He thought about girlie magazines, and track practice. He thought about Lois Larkin's nipple under his palm, and her beautiful beating heart. He felt himself go hard.

"You want me, don't you?" she asked.

He pulled his hand back and shook his head. The room was dark, and he could see only shapes, the tiny slivers of white in her eyes, and her perfect grin. "He'll leave us all alone. Daddy doesn't love me anymore. Do you?"

Fenstad's brow was sweating. The sulfuric scent in the room was thick. Why was he wearing jeans? He *never* wore jeans to work. They smelled, too. They smelled dirty like he was in high school again, fishing his school clothes from the hamper because when she was angry with him, Sara Wintrob left his laundry untouched.

"Do you love me?" the woman in the sickbed asked, and he answered her immediately. Answered her the way he'd always answered her.

"Yes, Mother."

The floor was full of blood. It squished, and his leather shoes were soaked. It sucked on his feet like hungry mouths, pulling him down. Deep down. Drowning him. How old was he? Forty-six? Sixteen? He didn't remember for sure.

"I'm not sick," she said.

Her voice. He hated it. His hand made a fist. He would strike her, his mother. He'd beat her senseless and bloody like he'd always meant to do.

"You know I was never sick, don't you?" she asked. She was laughing at him. He'd wipe that grin off her face. He'd wrap his hands around her throat like she deserved. "Speak up, boy. I can't hear you," she said.

"That's enough!" Jodi cried distantly, but her voice was like static. He could hardly hear it over the barking black dog. Whose dog? His dog? Did he own a dog, now?

He didn't hold back because she was a woman. He swung as hard as he could. Her face turned red, and something went flying. A tooth? Her mouth was bleeding. Bitch. He'd shown her. Oh, yeah. Now she knew. Back in Wilton, Connecticut, she was crying her fucking eyes out.

She didn't cry. The look on her black-eyed face wasn't shock. It was satisfaction. She laughed, this woman. Not his mother. God, why had he thought she was his mother? Just his patient, Lois Larkin. He'd struck a woman. His own patient. Her mouth dripped blood all over the dingy yellow sheets. As she watched him, she cupped her hands under her chin and began to drink.

"It tastes so good," she said.

"That's enough!" Jodi howled while Lois cackled. His hand hurt bad. His hand was on the door. He should stay even though he'd done wrong. He should fix what he'd broken, and make it better. That was his job. It had always been his job. He'd better not lose his job, or his wooden house would come tumbling down.

"Fennie? Do you feel it?" the woman in bed whispered, and he was running out the door.

NINETEEN
Leaky Eyes

Fenstad's eyes were leaking. He'd parked his Escalade in the driveway of his house, but he wasn't ready to go inside. He was waiting for the leak to stop dripping.

Maddie was dancing in front of her mirror on the second floor, and down below Meg was reading at the kitchen table. He focused on his daughter's awkward hip thrusts (the girl was no Ginger Rogers), and the light that reflected against Meg's still face, but his eyes kept leaking.

What had happened at Lois Larkin's house? He wasn't sure he remembered correctly. She said she'd eaten a bird, and he'd believed her. He pictured her catching it in her hands, and stabbing those huge, gapless teeth into its chest. Why would he think something so outlandish? There was more. His mother. Sara had been there, too. But how was that possible?

"Feel Flows" was playing on the radio. He tapped his fingers against the dashboard, which comforted him, because at least he was doing something. He wasn't just sitting around, letting his eyes rust. He kept tapping, hoping that soon the world would make sense again. The Beach Boys were playing, after all. How bad could things be if Brian Wilson could still croon?

He'd had a bad day. Not as bad as the day at Motel 6, room 69, where the carpet had been maroon, and the bedspread dirty gray. No, not that bad. But bad enough. Patients dropping like flies, kids cramming the hospital beds and morgue—a bad day. He tapped his fingers. Started humming "Feel Flows." Tried to tune out his thoughts, until all that was left, like the end of the world, was one song.

A voice called out to him from the void, and he remembered Lois's bloody grin: *Fennie, is it a lump?*

The basketball hoop over the garage had rusted, and its net was gone. Once he'd used an entire vacation day to play "horse" in the driveway with his son. He'd bested David at five games straight, and was ready to throw one so the kid would start smiling, when David ran into the house, crying like a girl. He'd hidden behind Meg's skinny trousers and whined that he never wanted to play again, and he never did. Fenstad came walking in a minute later, ready to explain to the kid about winning and losing, how you need to be good at both to be a man, but Meg's furious frown had stopped him.

That's what you got for trying with people. His whole life he'd done for others. Listened to their problems. Analyzed pointless dreams, held hands, filled bank accounts in his children's names. And now his patients were turning on him one after the next: Albert. Lila. Lois. His kids were no better. Maddie and her screaming. David lost for good. Meg had loved the boy too much, squeezed him too tight. Made him a sissy who liked it up the ass. And then there was Meg. That whore. In his mind a dog was barking. In his mind it was tearing her apart while his house made of slate and wood began to smolder, and then blaze.

Brian Wilson sang. He hummed along and wondered

whether, when the end of the world came, anyone would recognize it.

> Encasing all embracing wreath of repose
> Engulfs all the senses
> . . . You know I was never sick, don't you?

And now he wasn't sure: Was that his mother talking to him on the radio?

Suddenly Sara Wintrob was knocking on the window. His heart beat fast and everything started screaming. In the dark, he saw her silhouette. Thin and pale. She grinned with gapless teeth, the bitch.

Fennie, is it a lump? the radio asked.

She was watching him. She wasn't his mother anymore. Lois? Lila? He would throttle her. Pile her into the trunk. No one would guess if he waited until late tonight, and burned her body in the hospital incinerator. And if the other bitch who lived in this house happened to catch him in the act? Well, then he'd throttle her, too.

The woman knocked harder. He'd gut her like a trout. His leaky eyes, they were starting to rust. She kept knocking. Meg. His wife. Lois, Sara. He'd punched them tonight. Which one?

He waited for his eyes to clear. Thought about the Beach Boys even though the song on the radio now was "Wonderful Tonight." *Fennie, is it a lump?* the radio asked. He thought about the track team and fermented cabbage. He thought about his first finger feel inside Joanne Streibler, and a bloody carpet, the missing rivets in Lois's floors, and Lila Schiffer's fat kids. Most of all he thought about how hard he'd worked his whole life, only to find his wife fucking a yuppie in room 69.

Meg was shouting his name. Sure, now she wanted him. Now that Nero had infected her with the virus and she was used goods. "Let me in!" she shouted. He took a breath and waited for his eyes to clear. He made sure not to wipe them, but instead let them dry in the air. Finally he rolled down the window and flashed a jolly grin. "Yeah?"

She was hopping on one foot. He couldn't figure out why until he remembered her broken ankle. "What are you doing out here?" she asked. Her voice was soft, concerned. She poked her head through the window. He could slam her skull against the side of the door if he wanted. A tragic slip of the hand: *Oops, sorry babe! By the way, faux gold trim mirrors all over the walls aren't classy, just Guinea.*

"You look awful. Are you sick?" she asked. She stepped down off the runner and opened the door. He moved over and she climbed in. She smelled like sugary perfume, and her hair was pin-straight. Instead of shoes she was wearing ratty moccasin slippers.

"Say something. You're scaring me," she said.

He looked at her for a long while. Women's faces played through his mind. Lois, Sara, Lila, Maddie, and finally he recognized her: *Meg.* She slipped her hand inside his and squeezed.

She was so small. Her breath was fast, and her brow was sweating, which could only mean that she hadn't taken enough codeine. "Fenstad?" she asked. "Can you hear me?"

In easy listening paradise, Eric Clapton was telling his girl that she looked wonderful while diminutive Meg Bonelli peered up at him, and he thought about smashing her face.

"Fenstad?" she asked. "Can you hear me?" Her voice cracked, and she held his face in her hands.

A lump caught in his throat, and he thought he might
cry again. He'd met her a thousand years ago, a wait-
ress at the diner he liked, who also happened to be first-
year law at Boston University. He'd asked her out when
he ran into her at a bar on Boylston Street because she
was pretty, and at the time he'd had a thing for brunettes. Unexpectedly, she got under his skin. Six months
later, instead of heading to Germany for an internship,
he finished his classes early and got down on one knee.

"What is it?" she asked, and he felt himself crumble.
He was going to leak all over her delicate hands. The
tears built up inside him like a tidal wave ready to crash.
He was going to have to tell her everything. From Lois,
to Sara, to the fact that he might be infected, to the spy-
ing he'd done on her at room 69. Why had he watched
such a thing outside the motel window and never said a
word? Why had he tortured himself like that? It was
time he told her. It would be a relief to tell her. She'd
know now that there was something wrong with him.
Maybe there always had been.

"What is it?" she asked.

"Nothing," he said. His voice was hoarse. He climbed
out of the car. She met him in front of it. He held her by
the waist, and together, they walked to the house.

TWENTY
An Itch in Her Bones

Meg scratched her leg with the wire from an un-
tangled coat hanger while Fenstad sliced into his
porterhouse. His eyes were red like he'd been crying,
but she knew that was impossible; to the best of her
knowledge, Fenstad Wintrob had been born without
tear ducts.

She'd been trying to report Graham Nero to the police when Fenstad had called and told her to retrieve
Maddie from school. At first she'd thought he was
overreacting—really, how often does a woman get an
urgent call from her husband to gather the kids, lock
the doors, and buy an air filter? It was ludicrous. Still,
she'd done it. And then, as she and Maddie had flipped
on the evening news tonight, he'd proved himself right.
As usual. You could set a clock by Fenstad's instincts.
She'd looked at Maddie then, with whom she'd been
sharing a blanket and rubbing toes, and been grateful.
The man was handy in a pinch.

Corpus Christi didn't make just the local news. Even
the networks reported on the illness contracted by half
the population of a small, affluent town in Maine. Ten
people so far were dead, scores more were missing, and
no one yet had recovered. It had chilled her to watch

smiling Katie Couric announce that the state government was advising people in Mid-Maine to stay indoors. The EPA had ruled out chemical exposure, and
while the CDC hadn't isolated the agent of infection,
they suspected a virus. At about eight tonight NBC announced that Maine's governor was declaring a state
of local emergency. To keep infection from spreading,
starting tomorrow morning, all stores and businesses
in Maine were closed.

This explained Graham Nero's visit to the library.
The guy had been sick, half crazy, and maybe even dying. After getting Maddie safely home, she'd tried to
call the police department for the third time, but all she
got for her troubles was sixty minutes of Barry Man-
ilow elevator Muzak. This time, at least, a harried receptionist answered at the end of the hold time. She
told Meg that too many people were calling, and then
accidentally, or maybe intentionally, hung up. In turn,
Meg gave up. Her ankle was hurting pretty badly, and
the back of her turtleneck was wet with sweat. She'd
hardly made it to the high school, and after that had
sent Maddie into Target with a credit card and a list,
rather than joining her. When she got home she took
three 200mg codeine tablets, and was even now still
woozy, but at least her leg didn't hurt. Probably she
should see a doctor, but other than her husband, she
doubted any were available.

Fenstad sipped his V&T while she scratched her leg.
She was having a hard time jettisoning the memory of
Graham Nero. That fool had licked her. She wiped her
face just thinking about it. Then she looked at Fenstad,
who was staring at his quarter-pound steak like a
mountain he'd never be able to summit, and blushed.
What if Graham had given her the virus? What if she'd
brought it home to her family?

Fenstad took a small bite of steak. He chewed, swallowed, looked at his fork, then gave up and gulped down half his vodka tonic. The man was too tired to eat.

"What was the hospital like?" she asked.

He shook his head. "Bad." Then he took another swig. He kept his stress buried so deeply that when he was thirty his gallbladder backed up and he had to have it surgically removed. Yet he still insisted on V&Ts and steak three times a week, like the rules of healthy living didn't apply to doctors. Mr. Cold Fish. Still, she was glad she was here with him. Glad to stay here with him tomorrow, too. It was safe in this house where her husband would protect her. Suddenly, after Albert and Graham and now this virus, that seemed very important.

She scratched again. Her ankle itched so bad that she could feel it, not just on her skin, but in her bones. Fenstad nodded at her leg. "I told you to take the codeine."

She sighed and put the coat hanger on the table. He'd hardly said two words except to make sure that Maddie knew to stay in the house, and that the air purifiers were running. Before he sat down at the table he'd insisted on showering in scalding hot water and diluted bleach, in case he'd been contaminated at the hospital or Lois Larkin's house. "You okay?" she asked.

He didn't look up from his plate. Hardly even paused. "Fine. Thank you."

What was wrong with him? He wasn't even looking at her. Over the years, blue and green veins had crawled across her legs like ivy, and her slender waist had thickened, but Fenstad's admiration of her figure had always remained constant. Even last month when he got food poisoning, she'd caught him checking out her rear as she'd emptied the bucket by his bed. But right now he wasn't looking. He was acting distant. Hostile, even.

Then it came to her. Someone must have told him they'd seen Graham's Porsche at the library, and he'd drawn the wrong conclusion. She'd wanted to spare him this (been ashamed that it had happened at all), but now she'd have to tell him.

"Something happened," she said.

He glared at her from behind his plate, and for a moment she was frightened. The expression was full of hate. But in an instant it was gone. She'd imagined it, surely.

"What is it this time?" he asked.

She wasn't sure how to answer. She looked out the window and into the dark night. The bird was gone now. She'd thrown it away . . . But where were all the other birds? And the squirrels? And . . . the deer? "Graham Nero came to the library today," she said.

Fenstad didn't answer, which was pretty much what she'd expected. She continued. "He made a scene. His wife left him. He was talking nonsense. He was sick with the virus, I think. I told him to leave . . ."

Fenstad looked at his fingernails and began to pick out the dirt. Even for him, the reaction was peculiar. "Did he touch you?" he asked without looking up at her.

"I told you. I made him leave. Nothing happened."

His took a deep breath through his nose so that his nostrils flared. She had the idea that he was smelling her skin for Graham's scent. "Did he touch you?"

She closed her eyes. "Yes . . . He had me pinned, and he licked me. I didn't want him—"

Fenstad stood so fast that his chair fell backward into the floor. It rattled as he spoke, so he yelled to be heard. "Stay away from Maddie. You could have the virus," he said. Then he started out of the room.

"Where are you going?" she called after him.

"Target. I'm buying a deadbolt for the door, and

some more water. In case you didn't notice, we're at the center of an epidemic. We may be camped out at the house for a while."

"Fenstad, that's crazy. It's twenty miles to Target, and you don't even know how to install a lock."

He turned, and she realized that she hadn't imagined the look he'd given her before, because it was back, only this time he was baring his teeth. She said it without hesitation or guile. She said it because it was true. "You know I love you."

He looked at her for a second, and then two seconds, and then three. His scowl softened. "Yeah," he whispered. "I think . . . I know. I should get that lock, though. We'll need it if there's a quarantine and not enough police to patrol the streets. We could leave, but if we're infected we'd be spreading it. I don't want to do that. Besides, the less contact we have with the outside, the better." He turned and headed for the door.

In the next room she heard him stumble, then mutter, "Shit!" She gimped her way to the hall. Fresh pain and a groggy codeine hangover made her bite her lip anew. She found him standing in the doorway. He was holding the husk of a large, dead animal. Its fur was damp with blood. All that was left of its corpse was bones and pelt. Even its eyes were missing.

"What is that?" she asked.

Fenstad's voice was barely a whisper. "Did you do this?"

She didn't know he was talking to her until he turned and glared. "How could you do this?"

She was so shocked that all she could do was shake her head: *I didn't.*

He dropped the pile of gristle to the stoop. "Kaufmann, the Fowlers' German shepherd. I couldn't remember until now, but it's the Fowlers' dog . . . How did you know about my dream?" he asked.

His voice was quivering, furious and full of emotion. Not at all like the man she knew. He walked over the corpse and headed for the car. She hardly noticed the dog, though, because she could have sworn—yes, she could have sworn—that as he'd climbed into the Escalade, Fenstad Wintrob had been crying.

TWENTY-ONE
Romeo and Juliet

The cherry of Maddie's Marlboro Light glowed. She was leaning out her window, and it was late Saturday night. She'd been trapped in her house for an entire thirty hours. As if grounding wasn't enough, starting tonight, the whole freaking town had been put under quarantine. Enrique's phone wasn't working again (his brother sometimes wandered off with it, and forgot to recharge it), so she hadn't been able to call him since he'd left her house in a huff. This was the longest she'd gone without hearing from him since her vacation to Gettysburg. She'd spent yesterday helping her dad drill holes for deadbolts into the front and back doors while Captain Ahab had watched with folded arms. "If someone wants to get in, they will," her mom had scolded, and her dad had answered, "No thanks to you," which Maddie guessed had something to do with Albert. Everything between them was back to normal, which meant they hated each other.

More people were sick with this virus, and she'd heard on the radio tonight that it had spread outside Maine to New Hampshire and Massachusetts. Isolated cases had been found as far south as Hartford, Connecticut.

The government agencies that had come to Corpus Christi earlier in the week had finished collecting their samples and returned to Washington. The CDC declared the infection viral, and the result of the increase in sulfur in the Bedford woods after the fire. The sulfur fed a special bacteria, and the bacteria fed a virus that infected human brains. A statement issued by the governor and read on the local news advised everybody to remain calm, and that a vaccine would be made available as soon as possible. In the meantime, everybody living in Waldo, Kennebec, Knox, Lincoln, Androscoggin, and Sagadahoc counties was supposed to stay indoors. They suspected that the virus spread through blood and saliva, and that only the sick and immune-compromised had any risk of mortality. Well, that's what *they* said. In an internal NIH document leaked to The Smoking Gun, the mortality rate was located at thirty percent, the virus was airborne, there was no vaccine in the pipeline, and not a single patient had recovered from infection.

The state police replaced the CDC Friday night. They transported the sick to hospitals farther south, which sounded pretty stupid if they were really trying to contain the disease, but whatever. They left this afternoon to close I–95 to all nonessential traffic and enforce the quarantine. Army reinforcements were supposed to arrive tonight, but from what she'd heard, no one had seen them yet. For now, Corpus Christi was on its own.

She'd heard from her dad, who'd heard from his boss, that a lot of people had died today, and the hospital morgue was full. They all died the same way—with lymph nodes so swollen that their necks had looked like goiters, and chests full of phlegm. Basically, this town was in the crapper.

She knew she should be hysterical right now. After all, she was the most high-strung girl in all of Corpus Christi. But she wasn't hysterical. Just scared. She'd been screaming about Armageddon for years, and now that it was here, she was all yelled out. So she smoked her cigarette, and watched its light glow and then recede, and thought about Enrique, and all the people who'd died, and the fact that vaccines only work on people who aren't infected to begin with (so who were they kidding? The people who were sick were probably going to die), and wished her big brother was home.

She finished her cigarette, and dropped it into the empty Snapple jar she used as an ashtray. Just then a pebble from the driveway sailed past her face. She flinched. *What the hell?* Then another one went flying. It zinged her square in the nose. Then someone called her name in stage whisper: "Mad-e-line!"

She beamed: *Enrique!*

"Where are you?" she stage-whispered right back. This was like Romeo and Juliet. She'd always wanted a boy to come to her window. It was awesome! Her life was a frickin' movie!

"Over here!" Enrique called, which didn't help. But then she saw him standing on the porch underneath her window. He held a palm full of pebbles in his hand. "You jack-donkey! You hit me!" she scolded, only she was giggling. She raced down the stairs to the door, where, after fighting with the new deadbolt for a few minutes, she got outside and clobbered him with a hug. He rocked back and forth like a willowy tree, but managed not to fall.

She grinned hugely. This was so fun. Thrilling! She squeezed tight through his nylon jacket. She could feel his warm skin, and ribs, and heartbeat. She wanted to cry suddenly, because she loved him so much.

"I tried to call you but you forgot to charge your cell phone again," she said. "My mom said I'm still grounded but we can see each other if you get your orders."

He didn't answer for a second or two. He was smelling her hair, which was weird, but typical Enrique. He was always smelling her. "I got the letter. They sent it before the virus broke out. I'm supposed to ship out to Camp Lejeune in North Carolina tomorrow morning. I can't get hold of anybody on the phone, so I don't know if the quarantine applies. I should at least try, I might get arrested."

She squeezed him harder. Hard enough so that maybe she could burrow inside his chest, and stay there. She'd live inside him, and make him stay with her, where he belonged. This wasn't happening. This couldn't really be happening.

"I had to see you," he said.

She wanted to say something smart. Something girls were supposed to say when their boys left for war. She should tell him he was brave, and that she loved him. But all she could think about was his curly black hair. It was long for a boy, and they'd shave it in North Carolina. They'd snap their steel-jawed scissors until it was all gone.

"You're, like, the only person I even like in this town," she said.

"I'll be back in a year. We'll go to college together," he said, but she knew it wasn't true. He was leaving, and by the time he got back she'd be in her sophomore year at Brown. They were breaking up. She started sobbing then. She didn't want to wake her parents, so she pressed her mouth into his shoulder, where she left a round, wet circle.

"Why did you do this?"

"I had to," he said.

It was warm out, even though it was September. All she needed was a light jacket, but she was wearing only cotton pajamas. Her bare feet smarted against the cold cement. "You did your job. You stayed here while your dad was sick. Why are you doing this? Do you want to get away from me?"

"No," he said. "Never."

"Is it your family?"

"Maybe," he answered.

That made her cry even harder, because it was so stupid. "You ruined everything!" she said.

His shoulders fell, and he opened his hands out wide to her. "Shh. Stop. I didn't come here to fight, Mad-e-line."

"I don't care what you want!" she shouted loud enough to wake the neighbors, but luckily her parents' windows were closed. "I'm not kidding. You ruined it. We could have been happy and then you went and screwed it up. I wish I'd never met you. And now you're leaving and I'm not even special enough for you to pop my cherry."

He shook his head, like he didn't know where to begin with his response. Then he shrugged and gave up trying. "I'm scared," he said. She saw that his eyes were wet, too. It made her want to kick the crap out of him. What a dumb thing to do: enlist in the army because your family won't cut you enough slack. Or maybe because underneath it all you think you're supposed to marry the first girl you have sex with, just like your dad, only you're not ready to trade one responsibility for another, so instead you decide to go to Iraq. Real smart. She punched him in the arm. It was a girly punch, even though she tried with all her might. Her big brother, David, had taught her how to punch, and David was a pussy. Freaking David! She punched him again.

"You *should* be scared. People are gonna shoot at you."

His body was hunched from his shoulders to his knees, like he was carrying a large weight. "It's too late. I can't change my mind. If I don't go, the military police will arrest me." He buried his face in her hair, mostly, she thought, because he was trying to hide his tears.

"I'll miss you," he said. "But I can't explain . . . I *have* to."

"Yeah."

So now they were both crying, which maybe some people thought was romantic, but she thought was stupid. Then a solution occurred to her, and she brightened. "My room," she said. "Tonight. Now."

He didn't answer for a second, and she waited until he understood. Then she nodded, to let him know she wasn't whistling Dixie; she meant it.

"Won't they wake up?" he asked. From his lightning-straight posture, she could tell he liked the idea. She also knew for certain that she was one of the things he was running away from. He wanted to be with her forever, yes. But he didn't want forever to start right now.

"My parents? What are they going to do, send you to Iraq?" Before reason reared its ugly head, she turned back into the house. He had no choice but to follow. He took off his sneakers, and she showed him where to step so that the stairs didn't creak. When they got to her room, they sat without touching on the edge of her bed. She took off her pajama top, a purple tank with matching paisley bottoms. They sat. Goose bumps rose on her arms. He looked around bedroom. Along its walls were framed museum prints. The furniture was teak. Stored in her drawers were her papers, makeup, and old books. But on the surface, the room was as anonymous as a hotel.

"Weird, right?" she asked. He'd probably expected candles, sexy lingerie, a bulletin board covered with old movie stubs and photos, at least. But in this way she was like her mother: Clutter gave her the willies.

He shook his head. "It's how I expected. You didn't pick out the Hoppers and Rockwells, did you?"

"No. I don't care about much except for you and my books."

He kissed her cheeks and mouth. Her tears, she imagined, were salty on his tongue. Soon, they were naked. He climbed on top of her, but held himself up by his elbows. He looked serious, which made her want to giggle, but she didn't. He tore the condom from its wrapper with his teeth and rolled it on. From the relieved expression on his face, she understood what had happened in the woods and smiled. He hadn't thought she was too ugly, after all.

They stayed under the sheets: She didn't want him to see her body. It happened fast, and his hips were sharp. She pulled him close so that he was pressed against her. It felt a little lonely, because it hurt, and he didn't seem to notice, but then she looked at him, and he smiled, and she wasn't lonely anymore. She was surprised when he rolled off her that it was over.

"Did you come?" he asked.

"Maybe?" she said. He was sweating even though he hadn't exercised, and he looked a little drunk.

"Did it hurt?" he asked.

"No, I liked it . . ." Since he was leaving for a year, she figured it didn't matter if she confessed the truth. "I've been practicing with my finger so I think it hurt less. Is that crazy?"

He didn't say anything, and his eyes got wide. She thought maybe she'd finally gone too far and convinced him that she was deranged. But then his face softened and he chuckled. She covered his mouth with her hand to keep him quiet. "For you? For *you* it's not crazy," he said. Then he added, "I love you, Madeline."

"Me, too. About you," she told him. "Are you mad I called you a spic?"

He took a second to answer. "Are you mad that I am one?"

"No."

"Then I'm not mad," he said, which relieved her so much that she started crying all over again. The room was pitch black, and she held on to him tightly.

After a while her tears were dry. Her legs felt strangely sore, and his boy sweat had rubbed off and was drying on her skin. Her eyes adjusted to the dark room, and she could see the framed prints that her mom had brought home from the Portland Museum (a man at a gas station, a pig-tailed girl with a black eye at the principal's office), and her pink elephant slippers that doubled as her Mr.-Lefty-Extinct and Mr.-Righty-Extinct stuffed animals, peeking out from under the bed.

She'd had sex with a boy she wasn't going to marry. She'd fallen in love with him, knowing that it would never work. Right now the pain seemed worth it because she was in his arms. It wasn't true what they said. She felt different now that she wasn't a virgin. She felt sad.

Before long, she was sleeping. A piercing sound awoke her from a dream, in which she was swimming in rough ocean waters. "Help!" a man shouted in the stillness, and it took her a few seconds before she realized that she was awake, and someone out her window had shouted.

She bolted toward the window. Outside, everything was dark, and the screaming was gone. A cop car was parked outside the Walker house, but its lights weren't flashing. Next to it, a group of people whose faces she couldn't make out were crowded together in the street. They were bent over something, and a bad feeling filled her, like swallowing cold ocean water. They moved strangely, and with too much grace. The word that came to mind was *murder*.

Something touched her shoulder and she jumped, but it was only Enrique. He'd pulled on his jeans, and was rubbing his dark, flat belly. She put her hand against it, because she wanted to feel his warmth.

"Who's down there?" he asked. He was still half sleeping.

She pointed at the crowd. "I don't know. It's bad, though."

He shook his head. "I can't see. Everything's dark."

"We'd better call the police. There's a curfew. No one should be out there," she said. And then she added, even though she didn't want to acknowledge this part. "Is that police car empty? Do you think something happened to the cops inside it?"

He wasn't next to her anymore. He was sitting on the bed, lacing his tennis shoes. She followed suit and pulled on her purple pajamas. She tried to hide it from him, but her lower lip quivered. "He cried for help," she said. Then the obvious answer came to her. She reached for her cell phone, and dialed 911. It rang. And rang. And rang.

Finally, the line connected, and a message informed her that due to unusual traffic, the wait time to speak to an operator was thirty minutes. "What if someone's dying out there!" she hissed.

"I'll go check it out," he said.

"No. It's the virus. It makes people crazy. And even if it's not the virus, it's some kind of riot. We need the cops." She banged the phone against her night table in frustration, then dialed again. "Why won't anybody answer!"

He was at the door. "We have to go see," he said.

She nodded, because she knew he was right. Somebody screams for help, and you pretty much have to try to help. But she also knew it was a bad idea. They could get the virus this way, or worse. *Murder*, she thought. Though she had no proof, she could feel it in her bones. Outside her house someone was doing murder. "We should wake my dad. He'll know what to do."

Enrique shook his head. "Let me look first. I have to leave anyway. It might be nothing. If they don't find out I'm here, you can meet me at the bus station in the morning to say good-bye. Otherwise, this is the last time we see each other."

She nodded. She hated what he'd just said. She hated that he'd said it out loud. "Fine," she said.

He crept down the stairs. She followed. Her stomach was queasy like she was going to vomit. He opened the front door. The stoop was lit by a single lamp, and no one was standing on the porch or front walk. The street was empty. No one was inside the cop car, and its lights were out. She squinted into the darkness and listened. She thought she heard something, but maybe it was the wind.

"Where'd they go?" she asked.

He shook his head. "Maybe they were just out for a walk."

The air smelled strange. A little rancid, like rotten eggs. "Do you smell that? Aren't people with the virus supposed to smell bad?"

Enrique rested his hand on her shoulder. "You've been reading The Smoking Gun again."

"So?"

He bent down and kissed her forehead. "So, I have to go."

She tried not to cry. He'd never take her seriously unless she was strong. "Don't go," she said, "please. Wait until it's light out."

"I have to pack, still. And it would be an insult to your father if I stayed."

"I don't care. It's not safe."

He didn't argue with her. Instead he took her in his arms and squeezed. "I'll call you in the morning. If it's running, you can meet me at the bus, and if it's not, then I'm here for a while," he said. Then he was off. She watched him walk across her lawn, where the grass was wet with dew. His body was a shadow that became smaller and smaller. The only indication of his sadness was his hunched shoulders. She stood frozen on the porch, thinking that as long as her eyes were on him, he'd be safe. But then he strode past the street lamp and into the darkness. He was gone. She stood there, marking with her mind the way the wet lawn felt between her toes, and the quiet of the street, and her house behind her that had suddenly become less familiar. Her heart was heavy, and she knew she'd get over this, deep down she was the kind of girl who could get over anything, but right then, she didn't want to get over it.

Finally she turned, and went back into the house.

If she'd carried a flashlight with her and shone it in the street, she might have seen the human bones that lay next to the police car. If she hadn't shut her window when she went back to her room, she might have heard Enrique Vargas scream.

TWENTY-TWO
A House in Ruins

Saturday night, somebody had secretly replaced Danny Walker's regular Lay's potato chips with butane-coated granite. They were clogging his stomach right now, and his body was about to explode. And let's not get started on the smell. Seriously. If he lit a match, his whole friggin' room would explode. On the plus side, a fire would burn off the stink.

His family had done this to him. Turned him into a nervous bag of gas. His blisters from digging the hole at the dump without gloves were raw, and the salty Lay's weren't helping. Under normal circumstances, he wouldn't have smeared salt on his wounds, which led him to the conclusion that his family had made him not only gassy, but stupid. So he started scraping the dirt crammed inside his fingernails, and let out another stinker.

The thing with Lou McGuffin went down fast. At the crack of dawn this morning, Lou started hammering his fists against the front door. Danny'd been awake, thinking about James. He'd wanted to let his parents sleep, so he'd run down the stairs and swung open the door.

"Where's your father?" Lou had snapped.

"What do you want?" Danny had countered, because

what the hell? He was fifteen years old, and he deserved a little respect.

McGuffin was holding a brown paper grocery bag. Its bottom was red and wet, like it was full of butcher meat. The paper broke open all of a sudden, and pink and white lumps of wet fur landed in a heap on the stoop.

Danny could make out multiple sets of ears. Like pelts from the Old West, the animals' insides were gone, and all that remained was their heads and coats. On top of the pile, he saw a mouth partly open to reveal a tiny pink tongue.

"Where's Miller?" he asked again. His voice was hoarse.

Was this guy out of his fucking mind? Danny wanted to close the door and lock it. But a split second later he understood, even though he didn't want to believe it. He'd told his parents about finding James and the rabbit in the bushes the other night, but they hadn't believed him. Hadn't wanted to believe him. And now, looking down at the porch, Danny understood. James, his kid brother, had killed Lou McGuffin's animals. "I'll get my dad," he said, but by then his father was already standing behind him.

Miller shoved Danny aside and faced Lou McGuffin. He pointed at the hill of dead rabbits. "What the hell is this, Lou?"

Lou didn't flinch. "You tell me," he said.

A vein in Miller's neck throbbed. "Get off my property before I kick your ass from here to Florida." He was tired or he would never have lost his cool. *Don't ever let 'em know you're coming*, was one of his favorite aphorisms, like life was one big guerrilla warfare circle jerk.

Louis didn't budge. "Your son," he said, and then he

looked up at Danny. His eyes were full of hate, even though before this he'd always been Danny's friendly next-door neighbor. The guy had taught him how to shuck corn, play cribbage, and tie an anchor hitch, all while his mom had orbited the earth. "Not him," Lou spit out, looking at Danny. "The other one was at my rabbits last night."

Miller arched his brow. "You dumb fuck. My kid got lost in the woods four days ago. He's missing. My wife hasn't slept since."

Lou shook his head. "You're protecting him. I saw him break open the hutch last night." A tear rolled down his face. "I saw him doing this." He pointed at the wet pile, "To the animals. I tried to stop him, but by the time I got there, they were all dead. It was your son, Miller. I wanted to give you the chance to mind this yourself before I went to the police."

Danny felt bad for his dad all of a sudden. Everybody on that stoop knew James was guilty. Down below, the rabbit husks didn't bleed. They were wet, but not runny, like they'd been sucked dry. Looking at them made Danny woozy.

"Mr. McGuffin," Danny said. He was trying to find the words to explain, to apologize, but then Miller clamped his hand around Danny's shoulder, tight as a vise.

"My son is lost. Maybe murdered, or worse. And you show up at my door with this shit. You're lucky I don't shoot you dead." The part that surprised Danny was that Miller sounded earnest, like he'd been up all night worried about James.

"I saw him," Lou said, but suddenly he was uncertain. A shred of doubt grew inside him. It was a truth most people didn't know. If you're loud and angry enough, the weak buy any story you're selling. Especially when *you* believe the lie, too.

Miller stuck his ample gut out like he was going to bowl Lou over with it. "For all I know you're the one who has James, and the other missing kids, too. You never liked him. We all know that."

Danny found himself rooting for Lou, even while his dad's grip tightened. He wanted Lou to yell right back. Lou didn't say anything for a while, and Danny hoped he was gearing up for a real knock-down drag-out. But then his lip quivered, and he started blubbering. At first Danny was awed: His dad was like the fucking Almighty. And then he lowered his eyes, because a pile of rabbits were dead. "It was your son," Lou whispered.

"Get off my property before I kill you where you stand," Miller countered. Lou held his ground for maybe three seconds. Then he turned tail. They watched from the doorway. Lou walked fast, with his head lowered, and then, after a few paces, he broke into a jog. He was a tall, thin man, and his faded khaki pants were too big. They swaddled his ass like a diaper, and Danny imagined the man's life in a different light: a lonely schmuck who ate frozen low-carb dinners to stay trim, but couldn't toss a ball or boss somebody at the office. He was weak, and Danny hated him for it, and he hated himself for thinking it because before this morning he'd always respected Lou McGuffin. The man was everything Miller Walker wasn't: human.

Once Lou was out of sight, Miller pointed at the carcasses. "Clean that up. Put it in a bag," he said. "The whole deal. Scrape the blood off the cement, everything. Do it before I leave for work. Then come get me."

Danny shook his head. "Dad. The other night, when I saw James . . . I think Mr. McGuffin is right—"

Miller cut him off. "Don't tell me. I'll tell you. Now clean this shit up before that pussy figures out he threw away the evidence."

Danny didn't move. Miller grabbed his upper arm and yanked. "Your mother finds out about this, on top of James missing, and she's right back in the loony bin. You know that. She can't take much more. She's already mumbling to herself. You want to be the one who sends her over the edge?"

To his own surprise, Danny started crying, weak as Lou McGuffin.

"I didn't think so," Miller said. "Now clean it up."

Danny got a plastic bag and scooped the bodies into it with a snow shovel. They didn't make any sounds when they landed, not even a thud. Their silence was worse, somehow.

Bleach worked best on the stoop, and he poured about half a gallon, then hosed it down so he didn't have to get on his knees and scrape. He was done an hour later. His father was leaving for work, and his mother was still in bed. He hadn't gone to school since Tuesday. First he'd stayed home to look after Felice, and then the school had closed because of the virus.

His dad tossed him the keys to Felice's Benz. "The dump. Bring the spade from the shed. Make it deep. Don't let anybody see you." Then he left, like that was all the explanation Danny needed. But that was the problem: Danny had never needed much explanation. He and Miller thought the same way. He'd already guessed that the dump was the best place for the bodies, since the woods were lousy with cops.

Danny drove even though he didn't have a license. It was a Saturday morning, so normally the dump would be full of dads unloading all their old crap, but because of the virus the streets were empty. He hoped that meant they'd left town or were home watching the news, because otherwise, a lot of people were sick. Dead, even.

He found a wrecked car that he figured no one would want to move for a while and dug underneath it. He worked fast. The hole was about a foot deep. He thought about emptying the bunnies from the bag. They'd degrade faster, and it would look more natural if someone found them that way, but he didn't want to see their bodies again. So he dropped everything in the hole, bag and all.

He stopped at the hospital before he went home to tell his dad the deed was done. The lot was full of cars that looked like they hadn't been moved for days. Most of the CDC had left for Washington, which Danny suspected was a bad sign. If they thought they could help without getting sick too, they'd still be here. They said they were working on a vaccine, but Danny doubted that part, too. If they'd found it, they'd be using it.

State troopers patrolled the entrances to the hospital. Plastic walls and separate vents partitioned the east wing. He had to explain to three different pale-faced, coughing men who he was before one of them finally let him into the main office.

The halls didn't smell like ammonia. They stank like disease. From every direction Danny could hear people coughing; patients, doctors, nurses, soldiers. All of them were busting a lung. There wasn't much staff. The floors were dirty with mud, and in some places, blood.

He would have turned and gone home if his dad's office hadn't been so close. "Finished," was all he said when he leaned in the doorway. Miller clapped him on the back, really hard, which was as close as the guy ever got to a hug. "Thanks, son. I knew you were a team player," he said. Danny couldn't help it, he was proud.

"Are we safe here, Dad? Mom and me?" he asked. He tried to keep his voice from cracking. It wasn't easy.

Miller shrugged. "Safe from what?"

"The virus. I heard more than half the high school is sick with it, or missing. Are they missing because they left town?"

Miller waved his hand dismissively. "I was just on the phone with the shareholders. I told them the same thing I'm telling you. We don't panic. That's the thing. We panic, we lose our shirts. Right Danny?"

"Right, Dad," he said.

Miller called the chief of police while Danny hovered near the door and listened. "I hate to think this, Tim," he shot into the phone, "but it might have been an abduction. Lou McGuffin lives next door. He's single, you know. He came to my house this morning babbling about James. He's always been a little off, but this time I think it's gone farther than that . . ."

Danny didn't want to listen anymore. He walked away, and his stomach filled with rocks. By the time he got home, three squad cars had beat him to McGuffin's house. Not long after, Tim Carroll was leading Lou McGuffin down the walk in handcuffs. Danny watched from his window. Lou looked at him for a second, and Danny wanted to shout something, or wave, but he didn't. Skinny Lou in his cheap khaki pants big as sails. Danny hated the sight of him so much, he closed his blinds.

About an hour later, Danny's friend John called. He didn't answer the phone, but he listened to the message. "Hey, *D-man*!" John hooted, because John was an idiot. "You hear what happened? That guy that lives next door to you? Cops found kiddie porn on his computer. Plus, like, everybody we know is sick or missing—fucking awesome! *Dude!* Call me *now*!"

Danny didn't call him. He didn't want to believe it, but he knew it was true. His father had framed Lou

McGuffin and paid off a cop to plant the porn, just so he could keep secret the fact that his kid was a psycho.

Danny's stomach churned. This was bad. But what could he do? People liked him for his dad's money. He could drive without a license and drink beer in the woods. He never ran from the cops, because he'd never get arrested so long as his dad covered the bill. With the money Miller made, his mom would never be his burden, and neither would James.

Yeah, that kiddie porn shit made all the sense in the world. Lou deserved it, for accusing James of something so bizarre. Seriously, James was psycho, but could any kid really eat a half-dozen grown rabbits? Maybe Lou McGuffin really *was* into toddlers. If he told the cops, his dad would fuck him. He'd never see it coming. Smiling, his dad would say: *Proud of you son, you told the truth just like your mom and I taught you*, and the next thing he knew he and Lou would have adjoining cells. Best to do nothing. Best to chase some tail and play a little more golf this fall, so long as he didn't get the virus and lived to see next week. Better yet, he should have a beer. Or ten.

So Danny went to the kitchen, and pulled out a Shipyard, and was feeling just fine until he opened it, and smelled what he thought was a future full of beer and bullshit. He dry-heaved in the kitchen sink.

And now it was after midnight, and his room smelled like a stink bomb. Downstairs, he could smell cigarette smoke. After five years' cold turkey, his mom was back in Marlboro country. His dad was shouting on the phone, because a lot of people were dead, and the public health commission wanted the bodies burned, but the lawyers wanted them stored in freezers, so instead nobody was doing anything. Eight different people had left messages on Danny's cell phone over the last two days. His girlfriend Janice. His friends on the lacrosse team. They were talking about leaving town, and the people who'd gotten sick. They were talking about the stuff they'd seen during the night, and the rumors about half-eaten animals, like James wasn't the only kid in town with a thing for vivisection.

And now maybe his brother was dead, and Lou McGuffin was in the slammer, and he was jerking off while four whores talked about whether they'd have sex with a guy on the first date (apparently, if he buys you dinner, the answer is a resounding yes), and he started crying, because even though he'd showered, the dirt from the hole he'd dug was still crammed in his fingernails, and potato chip salt was burning his blisters. He was crying because his room was dark, and his mom's Marlboros were wafting under his door, and instead of feeling sad, he felt mean. He wanted to punch a wall. He wanted to find his mom, and start yelling about how none of this would have happened if she wasn't popping pills all the time. He wanted to hurt somebody weaker than him, just like good old dad.

So he wiped his tears and decided. He wasn't going to be like his dad. He'd go to the police station. He'd tell them about the rabbits. Maybe Miller would kick the shit out of him, or ship him to military school like he was always threatening. Either way, he'd finally be out of this house.

He put on his coat and shoes and grabbed his mom's keys. Tiptoed down the stairs. They wouldn't notice he was leaving until they heard the car. By then he'd be gone. In the kitchen the radio was playing classical crap on low volume—Wagner. It smelled down here, almost as bad as the stink bomb in his room. He could hear the echo of his footsteps, which seemed wrong. Miller wasn't yelling into the phone anymore. His mom wasn't flipping through *Being Your Own Best Friend*.

He knew he should go, but the silence was unnerving. He pressed open the door to the master dining room and peeked inside. A cigarette's plume curled from an ashtray. He opened wider. An arm in a blue sweater dangled from a chair. It moved in slow circles. *Mama*, he thought, even though he hadn't called her that since before the loony bin.

He opened the door all the way. She was leaning back in the Louis XIV chair with her neck exposed, while on the wood floor below, blood pooled. As each drop fell, it splashed.

His heart migrated from his chest and lodged in his esophagus. It kept beating, even though it was in the wrong place. Everything in his body was in the wrong place. His mom's throat was missing, and as he watched, her head lolled. He remembered feeding Wonder bread to the ducks with her, and the way she used to cut his apples width-wise, so he could see their stars.

Then the worst thing happened. Worse than he could ever have imagined. Her neck was mostly chewed up, and her head was tilted back. It began to loll. Only a little bit of bone was still holding it in place. The rest was gristle. The bone broke. It sounded like a knuckle cracking. Her head made a wet sound as it squashed against the carpet. Then it rolled in his direction. He thought maybe it was alive. It was trying to tell him something. It stopped only a few inches from his feet. Its mouth was open, and for a moment he thought it might speak.

"Hhhh," he wheezed, again and again: "Hhhh . . . Hhhh . . . Hhhh." He covered his mouth with his hand, and hoped his dad wouldn't hear. His dad had done this. His dad was a monster. And then he remembered his brother. James had done this . . . Or was it his dad?

He started for the back door. Careful, so careful, not to trip on the thing on the floor. His heart was in his throat, beating fast.

"Brother," a voice said. The sound was cold, and wet, and wrong.

Danny looked, and there was James, blocking the door. The kid's eyes were completely black. His toes, impossibly, looked like they'd grown back since the other night. The new ones were pale and perfect. Not even crooked, like they used to be. The hair on his scalp, lashes, and eyebrows was gone. His pale skin was sagging, so he looked like James, only aged one hundred years.

Danny hauled ass. He kicked the thing on the ground by accident, and it squashed as it rolled. Her eyes didn't blink from one revolution to the next, and he wondered if it hurt her. His heart was in his mouth now. He was biting it as he ran.

James lunged and grabbed his legs. He clung tight until they both fell. Danny turned onto his side, and suddenly James was on top of him. His skin smelled rotten, like it was falling off his bones, and Danny gagged.

Overhead, he could see his mother's headless body, arms still swinging, baaaack and foooorth, so slowly. "Dad!" Danny tried to shout, only it came out a whisper.

"Dad!" James mimicked. "Daddy! Daddy!" he shouted. When no one answered, Danny understood that their father was dead. Absurdly he thought: *The king is dead. Long live the king.*

James's face contorted into something ugly and full of hate. A crippling, useless, idiot hate that burns so hot it devours itself before its flames can lick the object of its loathing. The kind of hate that spurs a kid to kill his own pet. James bared his teeth, and went for Danny's throat.

Danny kicked up his legs as hard as he could. James went flying. He crashed into the body in the chair. They toppled. Danny winced at the sight of Felice's blue wool socks. There was a hole in one of them, and her big toe peeked through.

He opened the breakfront, and grabbed a steak knife. He didn't want to, but he pointed it at his kid brother. James got out from under Felice's body. They squared off. James smacked his red lips. Danny tried not to make the connection, but his mind moved faster than he wanted. Blood. His little brother was wearing his parents' blood.

He did the worst thing he could imagine (*I'm so sorry Mom and Dad and God and James*). He drove the knife down in a low arc. It connected with James's chest. He tried to pull it back out and stab again, but lost heart, and left it there. James staggered back, but he didn't fall. With a howl, he pulled the knife from his ribcage. It clanged against the floor.

James bared his teeth, but Danny could see now that he was frightened. He hadn't expected this. "I'll show you!" he said, and his voice wasn't flat anymore. It was full of worry. "I'll see you in the woods, Danny. I'll see you there!" He was crying like they were kids again, and Danny had been teasing him too hard.

Weakened, he dropped to his knees and crawled out the back door. His blood trailed him like a shadow on the ground. Danny followed, and watched as James tore at the grass for purchase. He lumbered across the lawn.

Danny leaned in the doorway. He wanted to scratch his nose, but his hands were bloody. He wanted to be inside, but his house was bloody. He watched his brother disappear into the dark, and he wanted to rescue him, to save this last member of his family, but he understood that for this disease, there was only one cure.

TWENTY-THREE
Wheel of Fortune

This is where I live. Under a sign marked empty.
This is where we part ways. When everything
  runs out.
That feeling in your stomach. You do not
  imagine it.
That feeling in your stomach is how you
  murder me.

The thing formerly known as Lois Larkin clutched a piece of pink stationery. Scrawled across its thick grain was a poem she'd written. It was a poignant thing, and she knew it by heart. Had repeated the lines over and over, though she couldn't remember what it meant. All she knew was that she was hungry.

It was late Saturday night. She lay in a bed of her own filth and stink. The itch had returned. It crawled between the folds of her wrinkled skin, under her sagging breasts, and on the inside, too. Her organs, her dying muscles, her thickening bones; they felt like scabs that would never heal. She was changing. Her black hair was falling out in clumps. It wasn't just daylight that made her squint; it was the bulb in the hall whose halo shone under her door, and the headlights of cars that passed on the street. She was becoming *not Lois*. So she squeezed the paper tight, and recited the poem like an incantation, trying to revive the woman she used to be.

But she hated that milksop, didn't she?

The thing that lived inside her blinked. She felt it slither behind her eyes. Its wetness satisfied the itch. *Sweet Lois,* it crooned. *Your father's here with us. He says you can give up now. You tried your best. He's so proud of you.*

Lois looked up at the cracked ceiling, and tried with her mind to make it come crashing down.

Feed me, Lois, it demanded. This time, it didn't croon.

She covered her ears with her hands. Water leaked through her eyes. She didn't know why. Was this crying? Did humans cry? Did that mean, by deduction, that she was still human? She felt a flutter in her chest beneath the itch, and named it hope.

You win, my Lois. You figured it out. You have to eat, or I die inside you. Feed me now.

"Daddy?" she whispered, even though she knew it wasn't her daddy; it was the buried thing. It was reading her mind, and telling her what she wanted to hear.

She squeezed the paper and wished she was dreaming all this. Wished she was back in the woods, only this time, she had run. This time, she'd made a better choice. But she had made so many bad decisions that they had gathered into the fossils of her history, and trapped her in this child's bed—flesh within bone.

"Daddy, please tell me what to do," she whispered, only her voice was flat and unrecognizable, even to herself.

Lollipop, stop fighting, a voice answered. It sounded

so much like her dad that she smiled. His words stumbled over themselves like nervous dominoes, just like they used to. *You know what to do*, her daddy whispered, *It's the only way.* But this couldn't be her father. Her father would never suggest something so . . . hideous.

In the next room, Lois could feel the vibrations of Jodi's breath as she mouthed guesses to the *Wheel of Fortune* puzzle: *Sus . . . soup . . . Susquehannah Hat Company!* The itch was bad now. She scratched her stomach and her last fingernail snapped off. Her fingers didn't look like fingers anymore.

For the first few nights after eating the dirt in the woods, she'd eaten everything in sight. Food in her belly had slaked her itch, like cold water on a burn. The steaks in her mother's freezer had been the first to go. Then worse. Then the animals. She could still remember the shiny eyes of a garbage-fatted raccoon and its wild scream as she'd broken its neck with her teeth. She'd told herself in the morning that the memory was a fever dream, but even then she'd known the truth.

She could guess something about this thing that occupied her body. Like the bright, sweet flowers that attract bees, when it was nearby, it spread its sulfuric scent through the air and infected people's minds. It had tricked her into eating it, and giving it a home. Right now it was taking over her body, cell by cell. It was speeding up her metabolism, and making her hungry. It was making her in its image. Making her *not Lois.*

But why mourn? She hated Lois, didn't she?

If she listened now, she could hear the infected roaming the streets. They liked the night, because the sun hurt their black eyes. Last night they'd banged on the windows, and her mother had screamed. They would come back again tonight. There was something about her that they liked.

Most of the infected changed in seconds. A few lasted long enough to cough their way to the hospital. A lot of them died, or else the virus damaged their brains, and they became simpletons, so that the virus became simple, too. It was only as smart as its host. Because of that the infected had made stupid mistakes. They'd eaten all the animals, and now had no choice but to move on to humans.

Lois wasn't like the others. Her mind was still sharp, if *changed*. Simple body chemistry. One in a million can carry typhoid. That was why it wanted her. To survive, a virus seeks its most perfect host. She'd been trying to starve it out of her, but the hour was growing late, and her hair was falling out in clumps.

Stop fighting, Lois, the voice said. This time it sounded like Dr. Wintrob. *You know the truth; before this, you were nobody. Not even Ronnie Koehler could love you.*

Her cheeks were cool in the places that her tears fell. She squeezed the pink stationery and muttered: *This is how you murder me*, even though she didn't know what that meant. Its words were comforting. They were human, unlike the thing that lived inside her. Unlike *not Lois*.

What was she becoming, anyway?

Feed me.

Her stomach growled. She'd said three rosaries to her father today, hoping that his ghost would send her a sign, but she had no fingernails with which to scratch her itch.

Feed me, Lois.

She licked her lips. Even the baby inside her kicked. Whose baby was it, anyway? *Ronnie! You used to love him. Remember?* a voice pleaded. No, to be honest, she didn't remember. She'd never loved him. She'd never loved anyone, had she?

In the other room, her mother chuckled. Vanna White was riding a unicycle.

They held you down. They kept you meek. They never knew what you could be. The voice sounded like her father, and Dr. Wintrob, and her first boyfriend, and most of all, it sounded like the cold, flat thing that was uncurling like a worm inside her mind. She listened to it, and tried to steel herself against it, and then stopped trying. If it weren't for her mother and Ronnie, she'd be a professor at UVM by now. She'd be married with three kids and a dog. They'd stolen her life from her. How fitting that this inhuman creature was the only thing that understood that.

She deserved to be free from this cage she was trapped inside. This bed, this house, this town, this Lois Larkin. She was hungry, but the steak was gone. So were the animals. She heard her mother mumble, "Buy the vowel you moron."

. . . She was hungry for something human.

The infected crowded against her window. The virus blinked inside her, and she could feel its desperation. Without her, it was only instinct and hunger. Without her, it would eat until nothing was left, and then would die.

She got out of bed and walked over the traps she'd set for herself; the jangling bells that would alert her mother she was ambulatory, the missing floorboard through which the old Lois had hoped the new one would fall. They smiled when they saw she was on her way, and the buried thing inside her giggled. Or maybe it wasn't the buried thing; maybe it was she, giggling.

She thought about Russell Larkin, who she knew

would be disappointed in her. But she was disappointed in him, too. Back on that snowy road, he should have called for help. He should have written her a note. He should have crawled out of that car on his hands and knees, if only to tell her good-bye. She took the pink paper on which a poem was written, pressed it inside her mouth, and began to chew. She devoured the old Lois Larkin, and it tasted like nothing.

She pulled the nails from where she'd hammered them. Her fingers bled, but quickly healed. She opened the window. They reached their pale arms through the aperture and climbed inside. She stood waiting in her white nightgown—(*This is how you murder me*) like a bride.

Up front stood every single child from her fourth-grade class. George Sanford's lips were red, but not, this time, from Crayola. Caroline Fischer. Alex and Michael Fullbright. Donna Dubois. They were lost now that they walked during the night. Sick from the change, they didn't know how to take care of themselves. Their instincts were all wrong. *They need their mother, Lois,* the buried thing whispered, and it was true. Her babies needed her. Poor Caroline was bleeding. She'd gotten so hungry that she'd gnawed the skin from her own thumb.

Lois's eyes watered. Her babies. Yes, she still loved after all. She loved her children.

She saw a pale stranger in the mirror. Joined teeth and dark eyes. Gaunt and lean like a shaved animal. It moved when she moved. She looked down at the children, who weren't children; their eyes were too black, their grins too wide. Her throat tightened: *What were they changing into?* But then she stopped wondering. Whatever it was, she liked it, because it wasn't Lois Larkin.

James Walker hissed. She could read his mind. He

had murdered his parents tonight, but he was still hungry, because he hadn't known to finish them. Poor baby. He climbed inside her arms as if he belonged there (*This is where we part ways*). "Sweet boy," she said. She remembered the way he'd teased her lisp, and squeezed his cheek so hard he squirmed. The buried thing inside her smiled. Or maybe it was she, smiling. "I'll take care of all of you, now," she said.

She felt the buried thing open its eyes when she finally gave in, and then her own eyes turned black. All of their eyes now were black.

She left the room. She followed her hunger, and the children walked behind her. There were more infected outside the house. She could feel them; not just the children, but all of Corpus Christi. The virus had sent them to her, their leader.

As she started down the hall, a shadow walked the other way. It was shaped like her, only its scent was NILLA Wafers and its steps were leaden with sorrow. She knew then what the poem had meant. It had been a message from her soul. *This is where we part ways. Under a sign marked empty.* The shadow passed through her. *This is how you murder me*, the old Lois Larkin whispered to the new one as it sank down below the wood, and into the earth, and below the dirt. If she could have caught it, and devoured it so that even its memory ceased to exist, she would have done so. She hated Lois Larkin that much.

In the kitchen was the woman. Hunched over a glass of milk. Her eyes widened into craters. Lois's hair was gone now, and her skin sagged in flaps. She was unrecognizable, but the woman knew her. They'd lived together almost thirty years. Behind her, the hungry children watched in silence. Only the outlines of their pale faces were visible in the dark.

Jodi jumped up from the table and threw the glass. Lois sidestepped it, and milk splattered along the floor. In unison, the children shrieked: "*Oooohhhhh.*"

"Please," Jodi cried. "Oh, please. God, no."

"He killed himself because of you," Lois said.

Jodi's terror was a stingy thing, like a pinched penny. She saw that she would not win this fight. She saw that she would not survive. "He never loved you. Neither did I," she said.

Lois grinned. She didn't take her time. She wasn't gentle. She tore the meat of her mother's throat with her teeth. As Jodi's body shivered, the thing formerly known as Lois crawled beside it, and taught her children how to free flesh from bone.

PART FOUR

DISEASE

TWENTY-FOUR
Quarantine

Sunday morning in Corpus Christi was lazy. Birds didn't chirp. Possum didn't play dead. Deer didn't peregrinate through the woods, sniffing for garbage and half-eaten apples. Lawns weren't mowed. Even the sun was bashful, and hid behind the clouds.

The U.S. Army arrived during the small hours before the sun began its ascent. Seven Humvees and three jeeps drove in a caravan down Micmac Street. Their numbers were fewer than the residents of Corpus Christi had hoped. They didn't bring answers, salvation, or even food. Although Tim Carroll begged the commanding officer to do so, they didn't fortify the town hall and advise the uninfected to move there, where they could be protected. Instead they patrolled the entrances to I–95. Their guns were pointed, not at the ground or sky, but straight ahead. The town was riddled with virus, they'd been advised, and no one was permitted out alive.

During its short tenure in Corpus Christi, the CDC had gleaned a great deal of information, none of it helpful. They'd staged animal studies and closely monitored the progression of the disease in humans at the hospital.

In the lower species, the viral and sulfur-fixing-bacteria complex spread through scent. It entered their olfactory systems and then crossed their blood-brain barriers. Once inside the nuclear envelope, it lysed the memory and instinct centers of the cerebral cortex, where its DNA replicated. The animals released the contagious virus along with the sulfur bacteria that carried it, during respiration, which accounted for the foul breath of the infected. All tested animals died within hours. They forgot how to eat, fly, care for their young, and occasionally, breathe.

In humans, the spread of the disease was more complicated. Their advanced immune systems and tight cell junctions prevented the virus from penetrating brain cells. Only when humans were bitten, or exposed to the kinds of large concentrations of virus found in infected blood and saliva, did their metabolisms become overwhelmed, and they contracted the disease. Progression varied dramatically. Some got sick within minutes. Others didn't become symptomatic for days. Symptoms included altered brain chemistry, photosensitivity, raised metabolisms, morphological changes to the musculoskeletal system, and varying states of dementia.

Because the virus tended to seek out human hosts that could sustain it, and because it also seemed capable of inter-host communication, there was some speculation that it was sentient, or became sentient when it hijacked host neurological centers.

Upon gathering this information, the CDC made the decision to protect its staff and resume operations in Washington. Publicly they advocated calm, and a vaccine. In a private memo to the Federal Emergency Management Agency, they advocated a quarantine enforced by any means necessary. At the same time the CDC pulled out, the army pulled in.

By Sunday morning in Corpus Christi, the infected outnumbered the healthy. Overnight, the stores along Micmac Street had been looted. Stop & Shop's windows were broken and jagged like glittering teeth. The meat had been emptied from its freezers. Trails of thawed burger beef and legs of lamb shanks that had been dragged down the aisles left bloody streaks. The infected gravitated toward dark, cold places. They died while gnawing frozen meat, their lips upturned in rictus expressions of ecstasy, as if, in their last moments, they'd learned a secret.

The *Corpus Christi Sentinel* didn't release a weekend edition for the first time in over one hundred years. The editor-in-chief was missing, along with more than half the staff. At nine A.M. Sunday morning, KATV began broadcasting static. Soon to follow were the local cable access stations. Only network television remained. Those who'd survived the night were no longer comforted by smiling Linda Lopez, whose top story, as reported from Washington, D.C., was the shocking rise in tween girls willing to perform fellatio. No state of national emergency was announced, and the president did not return from his golf outing to make emergency preparations. Only a small mention was made of the virus, which Linda noted had been isolated to Mid-Maine. For all the people of Corpus Christi knew, the television programs were prerecorded, and the whole country was in ruins. Or worse, the country was just fine, and they'd been forgotten.

They had not been forgotten. But when stymied, a bureaucracy folds upon itself and makes its knowledge secret. Corpus Christi had been quarantined by a nameless board for an indefinite period of time for reasons best not described or made public. By a secret court literally located underground, national writs of habeas corpus had been suspended, and the army had been instructed to shoot the infected on sight. But despite the quarantine and Linda Lopez's Homeland Security–mandated assurances to the contrary, the virus continued to spread.

Phone lines quickly went down in Corpus Christi, followed by the Internet. But it was reported over CB and radio that the fatal illness had spread to Portland, Boston, Amherst, Rochester, and Buffalo. Survivors described family members who'd bitten them during the night so that they now carried the disease, and anonymous military personnel reported that the president was not playing golf but had retreated a mile underground, to the Air Force base in Offutt.

Three people were shot at the I–95 border by special operations army Green Berets. The first two were infected. The soldiers on the south periphery spotted the black-eyed men on infrared and shouted for them to halt. But they did not raise their hands in surrender, and they did not explain why they were loping on four legs toward Hank Johnson, who'd never shot a gun at a living person, and wasn't old enough to order a beer in a bar. Still, Hank might not have fired if he hadn't spotted the still-squirming body of a bird clamped between one of the infected men's teeth. He aimed at the man's shoulder, trying to set the thing free. Instead he hit the man's head, and both bird and man went down. More shots followed. The sound was wrong, and Hank reflected aloud that he'd never expected to fire his weapon on domestic shores.

The third person killed at the Corpus Christi I–95 border was a fifteen-year-old girl. Unmoored by their last encounter, this time Hank and the other men didn't fire a warning or shout on their bullhorns for her to stop. She was not, in fact, infected. She was celebrating. "No demon seed!" she'd whooped into her best friend's cell phone a half hour before she died. Then she did a jig, ate two pieces of chocolate cake, and decided she was too happy to be contained. She went out for a walk, feeling free as a bird.

Tonight her urine had behaved admirably, and refused to make a plus sign. Life was good. Life was spectacular, and she was *never* going to mess it up again. On her walk, she wandered toward the south side of town near the highway. She'd forgotten about the quarantine. She'd forgotten about everything, except that in eight months, she wasn't going to be the girl that everybody pointed at like an After School Special. It was dark, and the grass was wet and cold. She started to run through it, because she felt so good, and happy. The bullet hit her between the eyes. She was still smiling as she lay on the ground. She was killed instantly.

Sunday morning, the survivors opened their eyes to a changed town.

Enrique Vargas's mother sat in the kitchen with her husband. Their eldest son had never come home last night. First the army, now this. If they had known how their lives were going to turn out, they would have stayed in Mexico. Enrique's mother hid her face. "Don't," her husband whispered, and she didn't shed a single tear.

Down the road, Ronnie Koehler slapped the doze button on his alarm for the seventh time, meaning he'd be at least an hour late for breakfast with his parents. Good thing his dad was going to retire soon; he could stop shining him for a raise. Bad thing, too, because the bank might finally fire him. The alarm started ringing again, and he remembered: Brunch was canceled. His parents were sick. Beside him Noreen didn't rouse, not even to hurl the eleven-year-old Sam's Club Timex indigo alarm clock at his head, or to call him a nincompoop. Her body was cold, but she was still breathing. A patient bit her arm last night at the hospital, and she'd gotten the virus. She'd been up coughing half the night, but at least now she was getting some rest.

After smoking a bowl he opened the front door, but the Sunday paper wasn't on the stoop. Instead he found a brown paper bag. He opened it and broke into a sweat. It was a horse's tail. Somebody had gone Don Corleone on his ass! He lifted it from the bag. It was black and thick. He held it for a while before he realized the truth. It was Lois Larkin's hair.

Lila Schiffer lay in a hospital bed with her eyes open at dawn's first light. She was the sole patient locked inside the Corpus Christi Hospital mental ward, and the staff had forgotten about her. She hadn't eaten in more than a day, and though etiquette would have had her feign a lost appetite, she was *starving*. As soon as the sun went down last night, the screams began. From outside her door, she'd heard someone, maybe that nice nurse who'd given her a copy of O Magazine, cry "Jeeze—" And then there was squeaking, like sneakers running along the floor, and then a crash (a gurney? the front desk?) and then worse sounds. They begged for mercy, every one of them. She couldn't guess how many. They all said the same things: *Please, don't, stop it, oh God*. But the words were cut short by screams, and smacking lips, and grinding, like celery breaking. Lila curled herself into her cot and closed her eyes, but even with their voices lower pitched and monotone, she recognized them. Outside the door, Aran and Alice giggled at the nurses as they died.

The people who went to work Sunday morning did

so because in their shock they needed the security of
routine. Bankers turned on their computers and sent
e-mails assuring clients that they were safe. Before
Time-Warner's signal went out Donald Leavitt of
Morgan Stanley wrote: "The stories you're hearing
are exaggerated. I assure you that the current situation
in Corpus Christi will in no way compromise my abil-
ity to serve my clients. Please contact me if you have
any concerns. In an effort to serve you during this
time, I am extending my hours to eight P.M." Then he
logged off, and tried to rouse his slumbering wife,
who'd stopped coughing early in the morning, and
was now cold but still breathing. He rolled her over to
her back. Her short page-boy haircut made her look
like a lesbian, and for years he'd been trying to con-
vince her to grow it out again. He crawled into bed
next to her and whispered, "Don't leave me." Then he
coughed.

Maddie Wintrob watched the sunrise out her window.
The cherry of her cigarette glowed, and though she
hadn't gone to church since her mom had enrolled her in
after-school religious studies when she was twelve, she
said a prayer for Enrique's safe passage home.

Meg Wintrob slept soundly. Her husband did not.

Danny Walker sat in a small, dark room in a house
that quartered his mother's remains. He was alone for
the first time in his life, and he wept.

Albert Sanguine reached under his bed and found the
last of his bread pudding. He drank it down to silence
the virus inside him, and wondered if his suicide would
be courageous, or cowardly.

As the living rose to face the day, the infected took
their rest. They slept under rocks, and in their beds.
They slept in hospital gurneys, in the woods, in piles
stacked and ready for the hospital incinerator, and in

damp cellars. Their skin was cold, but their loved ones didn't dare bury them; they saw small movements of the chest, flexing fingers and toes. They waited in the ominous silence of daylight.

As dawn ascended into day, the thing formerly known as Lois Larkin lay in a clearing in the woods, surrounded by two thousand infected creatures of the night.

TWENTY-FIVE
It's Okay to Eat Fish, 'Cause
They Don't Have Any Feelings

Fenstad pulled into the hospital parking lot. Not a single car was on the road at nine A.M. that morning. Traffic lights, when illuminated at all, blinked a cautious yellow warning. Throughout Corpus Christi, car and burglar alarms resounded, but no police arrived. The leaves of trees were turning red from the autumn chill. They were also dying, along with the lawns, weeds, and late-season tomato vines. He didn't notice any of it. He was thinking about Meg.

He'd spent half his day yesterday cleaning bones from the lawn. There were hollow-boned bird remains, and marrow-chewed fox thighs. The German shepherd had been too big for the trash, so he'd stomped on its spine until it fit into the bag. And then, as he'd dry-heaved into the withering azalea bushes that lined the front of the house, he'd had an epiphany.

There were more bones on his lawn than on any other house on the block, which either meant that his family had been divinely marked for disaster, or that someone—a skinny Italian with a big mouth—was trying to break him. He figured it out right then. She'd heard him moaning about the dog in his sleep Tuesday

morning, and had devised a plan beneath her croco-
dile tears. She'd seduced Graham Nero into killing
Kaufmann, littered the lawn with butcher waste, and
bribed Lois Larkin into playing the tit game, all so she
could declare him insane and have herself a clean
divorce.

He'd stood on the lawn with a Hefty bag full of dry
bones, and peered at her pink skin through the dis-
torted bedroom window on the second floor. His house.
The beautifully steadfast Victorian with its original
moldings and built-in bookcases. Its Persian rug in the
hall worth seven grand. She was tearing it down. She
was setting it on fire. She had to be stopped.

The moans out his window kept him awake all Saturday night. He thought he was imagining them, the way
he'd imagined Sara Wintrob in Lois Larkin's bed. What
else could they be, if not manufactured by his mind?
Surely they weren't screams.

Next to him, Meg had slept in the nude. She rolled
into the crook of his arm and inserted her uninjured leg
between his thighs. He realized then that he had all the
proof of her faithlessness that he needed. Normally
she'd be chewing a hole of nervousness into her cheek
right now. With all that was happening with the virus,
she'd be pacing the carpet off the floors. So why was
she sleeping? Because she knew something he didn't:
There was no virus. She and Graham Nero had *planted*
those bones.

As the sun rose, he reached over her still body and
placed his hand just above her mouth and nose. The
shadow of his fingers made her brows appear furrowed.
He decided that if she woke, he'd smother her. If she
slept, he'd leave her be. He teetered, like balancing on a
long razor blade in bare feet. On which side of the
blade would he fall?

After a while, Meg stirred. She squeezed her eyes tight, as if in her dream she was crying. He knew he should feel sympathy. This was his wife. He knew that he was suffering from post-traumatic stress disorder, because these moans out his window sounded human. Still, he wanted to smother the bitch.

A tear rolled down the side of her face. After a while, she turned toward him, and, still sleeping, kissed his bare chest. Her lips were warm and wet. He rolled away from her, a failure. He could not hurt her. He loved her far too much.

The sun rose, but the day didn't brighten. It was raining out. Still, by 6 a.m., the night sounds (screaming!) resolved into quiet. The calendar on his alarm clock told him it was Sunday. A wave of worry hollowed out his stomach. When had he last been to work? Thursday? Would they fire him for breach of contract? Then he remembered the virus. And then he remembered Lila Schiffer. She'd been in lockup for days. With all this chaos, had anyone bothered to let her out? Had they even *fed* her? If he failed one more patient, he thought he really would lose his mind. He bolted out of bed, grabbed whatever clothes he could find, left Meg a note, and headed to the hospital to find Lila.

The streets were thick with morning fog. As he pulled out of his driveway, he didn't notice the abandoned cop car where, during the night, the Simpson twins had been assigned to survey the Walker house. One brother had been bitten, and had turned on the other. His plea for help had awakened Maddie from a sound sleep, and now his bones lay scattered in the street. Fenstad's Escalade rolled by, and smashed them to dust. It sounded like passing over a pothole, and he saw what looked like chalk in his rearview mirror.

On the national news radio, Corpus Christi got a

scant mention. Instead of the normal news hour, the radio host was taking calls. A woman from Austin reported that she'd called an ambulance for her sick husband, who'd been coughing all day, but instead of an ambulance, an army truck arrived. They locked him in the back with the rest of the infected, some of whom were dead. She didn't know where her husband was now. There were more calls. Fenstad turned off the radio, and rolled down the window so that his face got wet with drizzle. To calm him nerves, he whistled the Beach Boys' "I Just Wasn't Made for These Times" and wasn't sure whether this reaction confirmed or disputed his sanity.

The hospital lot was quiet, and the few cars he recognized looked like they'd been parked there for days. Since Thursday night, the hospital's main entrance had been blocked by CDC staff, but now the CDC was gone and the place looked abandoned. Not even the army was here. The automatic doors near the ICU opened and closed and opened again, as if waiting for a very late guest, while light drizzle fell.

He pulled up to the entrance and let the car idle. The large building was shaped like a rectangular collection of cinder blocks, topped off by a round widow's peak. It was as still as a mausoleum, and he wondered how many of the dead or infected might be inside. "I don't want to go in there," he muttered as his windshield wipers swished. They made shadows like crashing waves against his face. In his mind he saw pretty Lila Schiffer's bridge of freckles, and her crestfallen expression when he'd taken her children away.

He got out of the car and strode through the blinking electronic doors just as they opened for him, as if it was he they'd been waiting to swallow, all along.

The stench was thick, and sulfurous. His eyes watered,

and a wave of nausea passed through him like an electric current. The hallway buzzed with fluorescence, and the generator hummed. There were no orderlies or nurses carrying mops or pills. No phones ringing. No doctors drawing blood, sipping coffee, complaining about HMOs. He didn't even hear anyone coughing. Just the blinking electronic doors, and the wind that rushed through them, and sent papers and charts skittering along the floor like leaves.

He walked past Admitting and toward his office. There was an elevator, but he didn't trust it to work, so he headed for the stairs. At the intersection between the ICU and Admitting, his eyes lingered on the red streaks along the white tiles that had dried like rust. They traveled in the direction of the yellow tape, and toward the basement.

Better run, Fennie, he thought. In his mind, he saw Lois Larkin's unbuttoned nightgown. His hand was on her breast, and she flashed a monstrous grin. Had he hit her the other day? Knocked out her tooth? He didn't want to believe it, but the knuckles on his right fist were black and blue.

The stairway was empty, save for a bloody pair of pink scrubs. He gave it a wide berth as he walked, and he moved daintily, so that his shoes made no sound. He could feel something intelligent within the walls of this building, and it wasn't human.

On the second floor, his office door was open. Papers were strewn across the desk, and files lay open on the floor. His Dali print was smashed against the couch, and the wall where its melted watches had once rested was especially white. Someone had torn the place apart.

"Dr. Wintrob?" a voice asked.

He spun around with clenched fists, and almost punched his secretary Val in the chest. Then he took a breath, felt his mouth to make sure the mask was still there, and pretended to be calm. "Yes, Val," he said.

Instead of a rubber band–clasped ponytail, her hair hung loose around her face. "I wanted to say good-bye. I called your wife. She told me you'd be here," Val said. "You were my boss for seventeen years, you know?"

"I know," he said.

Val held her arms wide as if hoping for a hug, but he didn't come any closer. Instead of khaki trousers, she was sporting skin-tight jeans. When civilizations fell, it was the small social mores that frayed first. Men stopped wearing suits, women started showing their bellies. Walls were tumbling all around him, and in his mind he heard his Victorian groan from within. Val nodded at the mess in his office. "They stole Albert's files Friday night. I couldn't stop them. The CDC people, I mean, though I don't think they were all CDC. A few looked like regular army. My cousin's a sergeant, so I'd know."

"What did they want with Albert?" Fenstad asked.

Val shrugged. "I'm going to sneak across the border to Canada. I have family there," she said. "There's no gas at the Puffin Stop, but I figure I can siphon some if I need it . . . It can't be that hard, right?"

"Is it better in Canada?" he asked.

She looked at him for a few seconds, and then burst into tears. He opened his arms. It was an automatic response. No feelings associated with the gesture. He wasn't ready for feelings just yet. She wept on his chest, and the vibrations tickled his skin. In his mind, a song was playing. The tune was familiar, and it soothed him. His wife, his daughter. They were not against him. They loved him. More importantly, they needed him. But that didn't change the fact that this virus was spreading like poison ivy. It didn't dry all the fucking blood on this carpet that was sucking off his shoes.

"I killed . . . him last night," Val murmured, and at first Fenstad thought she was Meg. Meg had killed him in his sleep, and now he was dead. He was relieved. He could stop worrying now.

Val pulled away from him. "You should know. It's the smell you want to avoid when they're infected. That's how the virus reads your mind. Like . . . a probe. It's trying to figure out if it wants to live inside you, or eat you."

"Made for These Times" played softly in his mind. . . . *They say I got brains but they ain't doin' me no good. I wish they could . . .*

Val was weepy and snotty. Two of his least favorite bodily functions. Her tears were wet against his chest. He was wearing the same clothes as yesterday, and the day before that, and the day before that. The death scent here was different from the Boston County morgue, where he'd done his clinical rotation. It was electric, and full of copper. He suddenly realized the difference. The human body produces adrenaline when it's frightened. Like animals in a slaughterhouse, their adrenaline hits the air when they're cut open. He thought about the dried blood in the hall and something clicked: This place stank of murder.

"Jeremy was such a good kid, you know? I loved him so much," Val said. He patted her back. A tune played in his mind (. . . *Sometimes I feel very sad* . . .), and he pictured the sun setting, and hundreds of infected rising up like an army in this very building, and gutting his colleagues like fish.

"They lie when they're infected. When he came home last night his eyes were black. He told me he hated me but it wasn't him talking. It was the virus. That's why I had to take him out," Val said.

Fenstad blinked, and replayed what she'd just said in

his mind. He thought of Meg, and then Madeline, and finally, David. He said a silent prayer for them: *I'll never do that to you. Never. Be-okay-be-okay-I-love-you-so-much-be-okay.*

"I was right, wasn't I?" Val asked.

He nodded, because from her expression he understood it was what she needed from him. Probably it was why she'd come here looking for him. She wanted absolution from someone in authority. It suddenly occurred to him that she'd murdered her son. He was thinking about that when she said good-bye. He told her *Good luck. Take care. Get to Canada safe.*

When she was gone, he sat on his couch for the first time since he'd bought it. There was a view of his desk, and diplomas, and a Winslow Homer seascape on a calm, cloudless dawn. His heart was pounding in his chest, and his blood felt cold and exposed, as if his skin had peeled away. His organs were turning to liquid, and pooling inside his groin.

He thought about Meg, and the ways he might murder her. Like idle masturbation, the thoughts were comforting. She'd done nothing wrong. He knew that. Meg Wintrob wasn't the problem here. He was suffering from an acute dissociate disorder precipitated by the tide of blood in this hospital that was sucking off his shoes. Still, it felt good to imagine his fingers around Meg's throat. Her skin was thinning with age, and would be soft in his hands.

When he got home he would have to tell her what was happening, not just at the hospital, but inside his mind. For her own safety, she needed to know that he was falling apart. He pictured doing this, and the way she would raise a single eyebrow, like he'd just announced that his real name was Tinker Bell.

It was after ten A.M. when he looked at his watch again. He'd been sitting for so long that his feet were numb. For a second he thought the carpet had sucked them into the floor, along with his shoes. But that was crazy, right? He laughed aloud. The laugh echoed in the empty room, and it sounded like a ghost laughing. This hospital had to be full of them. Was he dead, too?

He thought of a solution, and it seemed like a fine one. He left his office and found the supply room down the hall. He popped open a bottle of the opiate Oxy-Contin, and crushed one of its pills between his teeth. The feeling tingled and then warmed his stomach.

He climbed the stairs, even though it wasn't the way out. "I want to go home now," he whispered as he walked. The room was locked from the outside, and the hall was red with dried blood. He didn't see any bodies. Funny, where were the bodies?

She was sitting up in the bed, fully dressed with her lipstick applied, waiting for him. She didn't turn to face him when he opened the door. "Dr. Wintrob," she said.

"Lila." He smiled widely, like the world was wine and roses. His whole gullet was numb. This stuff was better than cocaine. While he talked, he popped another in his mouth. "How's my favorite patient feeling today?"

"Fine." She looked at him without flinching. The gauze on her bandage was torn, and the wound was bleeding again. She licked the blood, then looked up at him and explained. "I don't want them to catch the scent."

This made sense, so he nodded. He remembered bones on his lawn, and the smell of murder, and his secretary confessing that she'd murdered her own son. (*They get hungry when they're sick, Fennie. They eat cough syrup and bones and fish*.) Best to think about it later, though. He'd go mad if he thought about it now. Already, he wasn't sure if he was crying. Wasn't sure if Lila was being polite, and keeping silent about his leaky eyes. "Shall we try to find your children, now?" he asked.

She shook her head. "They're not mine anymore."

"Now, Lila. They're still yours, whether you have custody or not."

Her voice was flat, like one of the infected. "I told you. They're changed."

He couldn't argue this point, so he didn't. "I'm sorry I wasn't a better psychiatrist. I got cocky. Anyway, I should let you go. There's no one here to feed you, and it's the end of the world. Anybody left here is probably infected, and I'm afraid when it gets dark they'll eat you."

She watched him, but didn't say anything.

He continued. "I never said this because it's against protocol to give opinions, but you should know your ex-husband's a sonofabitch. You're all right when you're not being a phony, though. I'd like to see you work on that."

He turned and left, but made sure the door stayed open, so she could find her way out if she wanted. It's important to give people options.

He decided he should leave, too. He'd didn't like this virus business. Men of reason didn't encounter such things. *What would Freud do?* he wondered, and stifled a giggle: Maybe Jung was the man to ask. He popped another OxyContin and chewed. Three was his max. Any more, and he could go into heart failure. He let it melt on his tongue, and everything got thick and wet. He was swimming deep under water, a fish without feelings.

He took the back exit, which turned out to be a bad idea. He wasn't paying attention, and climbed down one level too far. He opened the door to the basement, and found the bones. They were piled high against the incinerator. At first they looked like elegant bricks. They fit together perfectly, a wall of Tinkertoys. He didn't look again. Once was enough. In the wild, animals do such things to mark their territory, and to keep prey from recognizing where they've been. He thought about the way that dogs and cats keep mementoes of their kills like trophies. He thought of Meg, too. In his mind he put her in a safe place where no one could ever touch her. He wrapped his whole family in blankets, and laid them to rest.

Opposite the wall of bones was a large room, encapsulating what remained of the CDC's operational base. It was sectioned off by mesh netting. The air was pumped along the ceiling through a network of plastic tubes that he guessed were still powered by the hospital generator, because he could hear them hum. Inside the netting were rows of gurneys. About half were occupied by fifty or so sick or dead patients. Something moved, and his heart pounded numbly in his dead chest. White ghosts picked through the rows, stealing souls. They fluttered like honey bees, gathering the breaths of the infected, one man after another.

He gasped, and in tandem, the ghosts jerked their heads in his direction. Their eyes were dilated, and both licked their lips. One was short, the other tall. Their strides were perfectly matched. Their hips and arms swung drunkenly as they approached. He saw that they weren't ghosts; they were women in lab coats white as the afterlife.

They stopped short of the netting. Together they ran their fingers along the plastic, as if its touch was pleasant. The taller woman was holding what looked like a chicken drumstick. She tore the flesh from the bone and chewed noisily. Smack, smack, smack. God, he hoped it was a drumstick.

He looked behind him for a weapon. No scalpels nearby. He wanted to run, but he was afraid to turn his back on them.

They grinned, sparkling white teeth, and he was reminded of Lois. "You two CDC?" he asked, because who knew, maybe if he reminded them, they'd act like the people they used to be.

The tall one kept chewing.

"Lab techs," the short one said.

"I'm army reserve. They sent me to check up on things. What's the status?" he asked. He was shaking.

The tall one's surgical cap slipped off the top of her head to reveal a pale, hairless crown. She sucked on the bone.

"Initial mortality of thirty percent has increased to fifty percent over a period of three days. The rest . . . sleeping," the short one responded. She was in her early twenties, and had a blue daisy tattooed to her forearm. It was pretty, and he wondered briefly what kind of girl she used to be.

"Origin of virus?"

"Bedford woods," the tall one spit. Pieces of chicken sprayed against the plastic net. "Which, if you were army, you would know." He hoped it was chicken; he really did.

The tall woman kicked her bone in his direction. It slid underneath the netting and hit the tip of his sneaker. Then it swiveled a few times, scraping with each revolution against the granite floor. He looked at it, even though he didn't want to. Then he sighed with such relief that he almost cried out. It was a cooked chicken leg, after all.

"Any immune?" he asked.

They shook their heads in tandem, and something sank inside him. It might have been hope. But at least he was calm. At least he was full of medicine, so he could see this through without screaming.

"Why'd they leave you behind?" he asked.

"The experiment." He detected a note of pain in the short, tattooed girl's voice.

"What experiment?"

The tall woman turned back to her wheezing patients. She pressed her ear against an old man's heart. Then she licked her lips like she was hungry, and he suspected that the man's tenure on this earth would be short.

The tattooed woman sneaked up on him. She found the opening and yanked back the netting until they were facing each other. The medicine made him slow. He jumped, but not fast enough. Her hot, stinking breath fanned against his forehead. Her tattoo daisy was gnarled with thick scar tissue near her elbow, where its stem belonged. She'd tried to remove it, he realized. In another life she'd rubbed her skin with sandpaper.

He stepped back, and she stepped forward. Were they dancing? She rattled as she walked, and he saw that her ankle was shackled by a black chain attached to the far wall. He hadn't noticed it before, but now she pulled on it until no slack was left. It gave her enough room to tend to the patients, but not enough to get out. The sinking thing inside him began to drown. What the hell was this?

"Please," she said. Her voice was high-pitched, and

alarmingly human. "Did you talk to Major Dwight? I want to go home."

"I lied," Fenstad said. "I'm not army."

"Please," the woman begged. "Let me go." She might have been a beauty once. Now only a few strands of hair remained on her scalp, and her skin sagged.

He said it like a question, but he knew it was true. "You got sick, so they didn't take you with them. They left you here to monitor the others. Both of you," he said.

The tattooed woman shook her head. She didn't look at him when she said, "We volunteered to stay behind."

"Then we got sick—" the tall one answered from across the room.

"So we made our own chains—" the short one added.

"Because we didn't want to hurt anyone—" the tall one finished.

"We're mostly infected—"

"But not all the way—"

"When we're done we'll walk on all fours. The way man is supposed to begin, not end."

"We'll never be the same."

The women spoke as if they were one person. As if they were the virus. These pitiful monsters.

The short woman twisted her ankle inside the metal cuff until it bled. It took him a moment before he understood that she was trying to tear her foot off in order to break free. "Don't do that," he said, and he meant, *Pick the lock instead. Otherwise, you could lose the whole leg.* He also meant, *Don't do that; it hurts me.*

She dropped her ankle and shouted "I want to go home!" Her voice echoed in the empty hospital, and he was afraid she would wake the infected, or maybe just the ghosts. The air pump hummed. It was reassuring, this mechanical thing. It had no capacity for a soul.

Across the room, the tall woman dropped her chart and charged at him on all fours. Her gait was awkward. Her arms weren't long enough, and her body wasn't lean enough. The effect was a shamble. She fell twice as she strode, and got within a few inches of him when the chain yanked her back.

They stood next to each other again, like oddly sized sisters. He looked into their black eyes. He thought he could feel them inside him. Drowning him. They were eating his soul because they'd lost their own, and they were hungry. The sulfur on their breaths penetrated his mask. "Fennie, do you feel it?" they asked in unison: "Is it a lump?"

He stepped back. One step, two steps. Together they cocked their heads. His legs were numb. His feet, too. He stumbled into the stairs behind him, and then backward, began to crawl: *One step, two steps, three steps, blue!*

The top of the stairway was colored red like blood, but it was only tape. He kept crawling. Red to yellow. He knew he should stand like a man, but he couldn't. He went toward the light. Toward the doors that opened, and closed, and opened, and God they should have warned him. They should have told him that this place was for the damned.

In the hallway right in front of the exit was Lila Schiffer. She'd wheeled a set of gurneys out of one of the sickrooms. At first he couldn't tell what she was doing, but as he got closer, it became clear. Tears streamed down her face, but her jaw was set. Determined. She'd made a real mess. The scalpel isn't a functional tool when it comes to cracking open a two-hundred-pound wrestler's chest.

Aran Junior lay on the table. With her scalpel, Lila was fishing inside his guts. Fenstad stopped short in front of the gurneys, and Lila looked up at him. Blood ran down her hands, all the way to her elbows.

"I'm their mother," she said. "I have to. It's my job." Then she looked at the other gurney, and Fenstad followed her gaze.

Alice Schiffer had been a less fortuitous experiment than her brother. Her head lay on the floor, eyes open, while her body bled on the table. Lila had severed the girl's head with the dull blade of a scalpel. To do something like that, you've got to be determined, and strong. You've got to use plenty of elbow grease.

Fenstad was crying again, but this time he didn't try to hide it. His gut was numb, and he couldn't remember why. He thought maybe Lila was fishing with a scalpel through his stomach. That was he on the gurney, his intestines untwined. He crawled toward the doors that swung open and shut. His knees hurt, because men weren't meant to crawl.

"I have to make sure they stay dead," Lila explained behind him. "They heal too fast to bleed to death."

The door was close. He could smell the fresh air. So close. He crawled through its opening, and into the rain. Then a dog was barking. That fucking dog. No, it was he. He was crying in loud brays. He was outside, oh thank God, he was outside. He was crying from relief.

His car was there. A big, hulking thing. Still on his knees, at first he didn't recognize it. The keys in his pocket jingled. He pulled them out and got into the car. He started the ignition. The smell here was good, and sweet. The smell here was free. He thought if he blew his own head off right now, he'd be happy.

He pulled away. But like Lot's wife, he couldn't help himself. He turned once and looked back through the doors. They opened to reveal Lila Schiffer's manicured hands. Her scalpel was raised high. On its tip was Aran Junior's heart.

TWENTY-SIX
Juliet, the Belly Dancer

Maddie's eyes were sore and swollen. She hadn't slept a wink all night. She was supposed to meet Enrique at the bus, but she didn't know what time it was scheduled to leave Corpus Christi, and he wasn't answering his cell phone. She waited until nine on Sunday morning, and then called his parents' house. No one answered. Why had she let him go last night? She should have talked some sense into him: The army didn't want him now that he'd been exposed to the virus! But what if she was too late, and something bad had happened?

She wanted to go back in time and mess up her anonymous bedroom before he ever saw it, and fill her bedside table with candles and rose petals. If she'd coated every piece of furniture with hot wax like an S&M vixen, he'd never have left. He'd have loved her enough to run away to Canada with her, where he could have written poetry, and she could have . . . plied her trade as an exotic belly dancer.

She took a deep drag off her smoke and looked at her cell phone, where no calls had been missed, and the time read ten A.M. Was he too chicken to say good-bye? She wanted to cry, but she'd done enough of that already. She wanted her life from before he'd enlisted, before David left for college, before her parents' cold war that left her nauseated and dry-heaving at the breakfast table, before this virus that had turned her town into a quiet, lurking place. She wanted her mother.

She found Meg sipping black coffee from a giant green mug at the kitchen table. She was flicking the keys to the new deadbolts between her fingers, and listening to WMHB college radio, which was talking instead of playing music, for a change. Something about bottled water versus tap, and how the eyes of the infected are hypnotic.

Maddie plopped down next to Meg. "I can't find Enrique. I hate my life," she said drolly. Then she saw her mother's face. Mascara streaked dirty lines down her cheeks. "What is it?" she asked.

Meg wiped her eyes. She hadn't plucked her brows in about a week, and they were starting to get hairy. "Don't worry. It's okay."

"No, it's not. What's wrong?"

Meg shook her head. "It's nothing, Maddie."

Maddie stood. "Did somebody do something to you?"

Meg played with the keys. There were four of them, and Fenstad had spent most of Saturday installing their matching locks with a power drill. Then he'd collected the animal bones into the garbage can without even wincing. She'd watched his simmering rage all day, and had wondered twenty years after the fact: *What the hell have I gotten myself into?*

She tried to smile, but failed. "Have you been listening to the news?"

"Not since yesterday afternoon."

Meg squeezed one of the keys and let its shape impress itself into her palm. She usually made a big breakfast Sunday mornings, but today she'd forgotten. Actually, she'd forgotten about dinner the last few nights, too. The whole family was probably starving. "Sit down," she said.

Maddie looked at Meg for a few seconds, but didn't ask any questions. She sat.

"There were some murders last night," Meg said.

"Enrique!" Maddie gasped.

"Not him, that I know of. But on our block, and all over town, too." She'd gotten the calls from friends and volunteers at the library. People were trying to get out of town, but I–95 was blocked, and there were rumors that anyone trying to leave through the main roads or even the woods was shot on sight. She itemized the dead with her fingers while holding Maddie's gaze: "The Simpson twins. Miller and Felice Walker. Carl Fritz. Molly Popek. Plenty of others . . . I need you to be calm," she said. "We have to help each other. You can't get carried away on me."

Maddie nodded, but didn't speak, and Meg wasn't sure whether this was an indication of strong resolve, or shock. "It's the virus. Maybe you didn't notice Dad cleaning the bodies yesterday, but the animals are gone. There aren't any left."

"I noticed. I didn't want to scare you," Maddie said. She'd taken the purple paint off her fingernails, and without it they looked naked.

Meg smiled. Then she frowned, because what she had to say next was ugly. "It's just gossip right now, but I think I should tell you, because . . . Because I believe it's true. During the day, they're supposed to sleep while their bodies adapt to the infection, but at night, they get hungry. They eat anything they can find. The animals . . . Maddie, the people who died . . . It wasn't always because their bodies rejected the virus. A lot of them were bitten to death."

The blood rushed to Maddie's face. "Where's Daddy?"

"One of his patients is trapped in the hospital. He left to get her out. He'll be home soon. When he gets here, I'm going to suggest that we leave town. We'll have to sneak out, if they're still enforcing the quarantine. We'll stay with your dad's parents in Connecticut."

Maddie's eyes were wet like a deer's. She didn't wipe them, and more tears fell, "Enrique's missing," Maddie said. "He came to see me last night, to tell me he'd be shipping out this morning, except they must have sent the letter before the virus started to spread. We had sex."

Meg's eyes widened. "You had sex because he was shipping out? Maddie, that's the oldest trick in the book!"

Maddie shook her head. "No . . . I wanted to. But then he was afraid Dad would find him so he walked home in the dark. I knew I should have stopped him." A tear rolled down her cheek and she scowled. "I *told* you that Albert was eating people!"

A line of worry thickened across Meg's brow. She liked Enrique, she suddenly realized. He'd shown the good sense to love Maddie. "You haven't heard from Enrique since last night?"

Maddie's face froze. "I'm going to look for him, Mom. I have to. I'll ride my bike."

Meg cupped her shoulders in her hands. Her ankle was hurting again, but she'd decided not to take any more codeine. She'd taken too many last night, and instead of sleeping, had passed out. This morning she'd woken to a missing husband, a headache, and the news that life as she knew it was over. "It's not safe for you to go off on your own. His family will look. Besides, maybe the phones aren't working and he's fine."

"But I love him," Maddie said. "If you love someone you have to help them."

Meg thought about that, and then she thought about her husband. "Trust me. I'm telling you the right thing. If he's at the hospital your father will find him, and if he's not there and he's not home . . ." Meg debated saying this, and then decided that protecting Maddie from the truth was tantamount to getting her killed. "He's probably dead."

Maddie hid her face in her hands. "Oooooh," she said as the air literally left her body, and she curled her head into her chest. "What's happening?"

"I don't know." Meg lifted Maddie's ponytail and kissed the back of her neck. Then they hugged, a gaunt pair of women with cold hands and warm hearts. At first it was only Maddie, but then both were crying into each other's shoulders.

After a while Meg asked. "So you had sex with him?"

"Yeah."

"You want to talk about it?"

"Later . . . What if he needs me?"

Meg drew back and looked at Maddie. "I love you," she said. "What I'm telling you is right. Trust me."

Maddie nodded. Her green eyes were so much like Fenstad's: one part alien, one part soul mate. "I trust you," she said.

TWENTY-SEVEN
Going Lou McGuffin

Danny Walker wanted to cry on Sunday morning, but he was afraid he'd wake the dead. So he covered his mouth with his hand and gulped down his tears like he was eating them. He was sitting against the cold, wet wall of his basement. No light shone through the small gutter windows, and the day was a rainy one.

His stomach growled, and he wondered if he was infected. He started sobbing in awkward, muffled jerks, and that made him think of Felice, whose worst blues used to come with the rising sun, like the promise of every new day had terrified her. He understood that now.

Then he lifted the gun in his lap, ran his finger inside its chamber, and wondered: *Was she still sad now that she was dead?*

After he ran from the house last night, he drove to the police station, but no one was behind the desk, or in any of the offices. He found only Lou McGuffin, who lay facedown on the floor of the holding cell. Lou's blue shirt was untucked, and Danny could see the blubbery sides of the pot belly that he'd kept hidden all these years. Tucked into his fist was a green plastic toothbrush whose tip had been filed to a sharp point. A shank. The toilet and sink were white porcelain and the floor was boxed granite tile. Danny tried to focus on these things, instead of the body. Another body. They were stacking up, and for a brief moment he wondered if it was he, not James, who'd done murder.

"Mr. McGuffin?" Danny asked. "Lou?"

Danny didn't want Lou to answer. He was afraid the man would stand up and gurgle, "You ruined my life, kid."

Danny stifled a moan, mostly because he didn't want to hear his own echo in this empty place. A week ago he'd been smiling through a steak dinner with Miller Walker at the golf club, prince of Shit Mountain. The faucet by Lou's cot dripped. Blood was smeared all over the floor, sheets, and toothbrush. It took Danny a while before he pieced together what had happened.

"I'm sorry," Danny said, which was true. He was sorry his dad was gone, and he was sorry that his mom was in pieces. He was sorry his brother was a psycho who, even without the virus, liked to kill things large and small. He was sorry he was a bully, but had never stood up to the people who counted. He was sorry he'd chosen to come to the police station where he'd found only this foolish man, who'd killed himself by impaling his body against a sharpened toothbrush. From the looks of things, he'd done a bad job, and it had taken hours before he'd died.

After he left the police station, he tried the hospital. But the place was a ruin. Doctors and nurses raced in every direction, and even when he grabbed their white aprons stained in blood like butchers, they didn't stop to listen. He wasn't alone. Wild-eyed and hysterical, the waiting room was full of people. They chased every able-bodied doctor they could find, insisting, "My

sister . . . my mother . . . my brother . . . my father . . .
my best friend . . . they're dead . . . they're infected . . .
What's happening?"

Finally, in the cafeteria, which had run out of food
and was serving only coffee, he found the police chief,
Tim Carroll. "My parents are dead," Danny said.

Tim put down his coffee and squeezed the back of
Danny's neck, hard. "That's tough luck, kid."

"Can you help me?"

Tim looked at him for a while, and then he sighed,
deep. "No. There's not enough help to go around."

Danny looked down at his hands, which were still red
from digging the rabbits' grave at the dump. "Lou Mc-
Guffin killed himself. My dad framed him for kiddie
porn because my brother killed his rabbits," he blurted.
When he looked up, Tim held his gaze, and he liked that,
because it wasn't like Miller, who was always trying to
get him to flinch.

"I know how your dad works. It would have blown
over. What Lou did to himself is on him, not you."

"It's my fault, too," Danny said.

Tim shook his head. "Some people got no sense.
They're like those starfish that turn inside out, just to
scare off predators. It hurts them every time, and in the
end they still get eaten. Their instincts are all wrong,
and there's not a thing you can do about it. What you
need is to find a place to hide, and stay there." Then he
picked up his coffee and headed out of the cafeteria.

After that, Danny started walking. He could feel
something coming like an electrical storm about to
blow. This hospital wasn't safe. There were too many
sick people inside it. If this trouble with James had
started because he'd gotten infected, then a lot more
trouble was on its way.

He followed the yellow line, which got him thinking about the yellow brick road, which got him thinking about teaching James to make wintergreen Life Savers sparkle in the dark. Even then, with the lights out, a part of him had been scared of that kid.

The tape went from yellow to blue, blue to green, green to red. The people working tonight didn't look fit for duty; most were coughing, and the rest were so tired they could hardly stand.

He saw a sign that said, "St. Lucy's Chapel" and peered inside. Relatives of the sick clogged the aisles. Some held rosaries. Some coughed. A lot just cried. They were packed tightly in their pews, and painted all over the murals along the walls were renderings of shepherds with their sheep.

Mares eat oats and does eat oats and little lambs eat ivy.

This hospital was full of infected, and the food in the cafeteria was gone. He thought about the rabbits James had eaten, and the bones he'd seen on lawns all over Corpus Christi this morning. An idea occurred to him, but he didn't want to think about it just yet, so instead he thought about a nursery rhyme his mother had taught him during better days.

A kid'll eat ivy too wouldn't you?

He left the chapel and kept walking. Red to black. He was thinking about his mom's beguiling smile, like anyone she shone it on was the most important person in the world. Maybe he'd imagined the shock on her face in the dining room, like at the last minute she'd known what her younger son had become, and it had broken her heart.

But James had done something even worse. As Danny had fled for the police station, he'd spied a body impaled on the spiked cast-iron fence surrounding his house. Its legs had swung a little in the wind, and for a second Danny had thought it was still alive.

Before seeing that thing on the fence, he'd still hoped that there was something in James worth saving. Sure, they hated each other, but he'd always believed that when the shit storm flew, they had each other's backs. In that moment he understood that James was a monster. Impaled on the spike was Miller Walker's lifeless body.

Off one of the rooms in the red-taped hallway, he heard a low-pitched scream. The sound was cut short, and then nothing. He turned and started back. Time to go, he knew, but he forgot why (*They're hungry, remember? Get out of here, Danny, while you still can!*). He walked backward—red to green. The patients off the green tape in ICU weren't coughing anymore, but plenty were squirming out of bed. Some looked strong, but the rest were slow. Their legs were too long, and their backs too short, so they couldn't walk, but they couldn't crawl, either. It was like the virus inside them didn't fit quite right. He blinked and decided to pretend that a part of him was home watching *Elimidate*. A part of him was safe.

He pressed himself against the light blue wall as he walked, trying to make himself small. They were in their rooms still, and none had gotten into the hall. Maybe they wouldn't see him. Maybe they wouldn't do the thing that James had done.

Murder!

It was quiet all of a sudden, like the electricity storm he'd felt coming had finally struck. The halls were empty of people now, and only the sick in their beds were left. No one was complaining about their dead friend, parent, or cat. No one was praying, or even coughing. The nurses, doctors, and even the orderlies were gone. *Where did they go?* a little voice inside him asked. He thought he knew the answer, and it was terrible. Something flopped on the floor behind him and he turned. It was child-sized, and not moving fast enough to catch him. It took him a while before he realized that it used to be human. A baby. Its eyes were black.

He stumbled as he ran.

Green to blue. Blue opened up to the large room where he'd started. Admitting. A few feet ahead was the exit, and behind the counter was a doctor in pink scrubs whose name tag read "ROSSOFF" in black, block letters. He held up his hands, the universal sign of surrender, which was how Danny knew he was still human. His lips moved, and he mouthed what looked like *mercy.*

The emergency room gurneys were all empty, and surrounding Rossoff were the patients who'd recently been sleeping. Danny watched, even though he knew he should run through the automatic doors ahead of him. Something was stuck inside them, so they opened and closed, again and again. But loneliness is a terrible thing. He didn't want this man's last moments to happen without a witness. Or maybe it was Danny who was lonely.

A fat girl, he knew her—Alice Schiffer—took the doctor's hand like she was going to lead him away and save him from the crowd. The doctor let her hold his palm, and Danny could see the relief on his face like someone had splashed him with cold water, and he was suddenly less numb, and a lot closer to breaking down. Danny felt relief, too. *Thank you, God,* he thought. But then Alice lunged. "Wha—?" the doctor shouted. His arms and legs were skinny, but he had a big gut, which made Danny wonder if he'd always shown deference to fat people because they reminded him of his dad. Rossoff jerked his bleeding hand from her mouth. Her lips were red. The others closed in, until Rossoff wasn't standing anymore. Danny couldn't see him; he could only hear the man's screams.

His throat hurt, and he realized it wasn't the doctor screaming, it was he.

At the sound, several of the infected scurried toward him. They crawled, slithered, and even walked. Muscles twitched under their pale, paper-thin skin. They were coats, he decided. White lab coats and blue gowns like pictures from a book. He avoided looking into their black eyes, but he still recognized Aran Schiffer, the orderlies he'd so recently begged for help, and his first kiss Frannie Saulnier, who'd probably been the nicest girl he'd ever dated, which was why he'd dumped her. He'd wanted her to meet somebody better.

Frannie took the first step. "Danny, I've been waiting a long time," she said. She'd been a wet-eyed, emotional kind of girl, who touched her heart when she saw people she loved, like they didn't just live in the world, they lived inside her, too. She touched her heart now, but in her voice, there was no emotion at all.

He ran out the doors, and into the night. They followed him to his mom's Mercedes. Once he got into the car he locked the doors, and then—wham!—he was up on two wheels. He stomach flipped like he was on a

Ferris wheel that breaks free of its base, and he slammed hard into the driver side door. Then the car fell, and he bounced once, twice, and was level again.

What was happening? He looked out and saw their shining black eyes. Five? Ten? Fifty? He couldn't tell how many. The big one, Aran from the wrestling team, was trying to flip the car. The Mercedes was heavy—a German tank, practically, but still. Aran took a few steps back, and started to charge. This time he had re-inforcements. Two others were running with him. Danny reached into the glove compartment and pulled out the keys. He turned the ignition just as three of them slammed against the door. The car ricocheted, then went up on two wheels, and for a dangerous split second, almost flipped. Danny was pressed against the window. "Shit!" Danny screamed. "Shit! Get-me-out-get-me-out!"

He reached down and gunned the gas. The car jerked forward and slammed down. Tires groaned and bounced. He sideswiped somebody's SUV, and thud-thud-thud, hit a few infected, too. "Out-out-out!" he yelled, just as the hysterical kid on the college radio shouted through the Mercedes speakers: "If this disease is out of Maine, this might be the end of the world!"

In the rearview mirrors, those shining eyes got farther away, and he counted backward from ten, so he didn't ease up on the gas and start crying, while on the radio the kid from Colby announced, "Thanks, caller. Another thing I don't want to think about. Now, if anyone knows my mom on 16 Temple Street in Portland, could you stop by and check on her?"

Bump! The car lurched over something solid, and then dragged it from the chassis. A body? Whose body? Any body home? He giggled. The car slowed, even though he was pushing the pedal to the floor. In the rearview mirror, those shining black eyes came closer. "Fuckers!" he cried.

"Her name's Eunice Hilledebrandt and she'll make you dinner if you drop by. Thanks, man. Thanks a lot. You'd be doing me a solid," the kid on the radio said, like he'd forgotten this was a pandemic, and he was still trying to be cool.

"She's dead, you moron," Danny answered. "The second you stand still, you're dead." Then he pumped the gas, and flop-flop-flop! the thing on the chassis finally broke free. He was cruising again, and the eyes got farther away.

The scenery went by, and he remembered that he was driving. It meant he was still alive, and he'd gotten out of the hospital. He hit a few things in the road. He hoped they weren't his mother's head. A mile later he pulled into his parents' driveway. Where else could he go? The thing on the spike (*Never let them see you coming, Danny, boy!*) was gone, and he wondered who the hell had gone and stolen his old man. Then he wondered if he'd gone mad.

From far away, he could see the eyes following him. Still, the eyes were watching.

He raced inside the house and looked for the thing he needed. He couldn't think of its name, but he saw a picture of it in his mind. He found it in the hall closet, behind the squash and tennis rackets, under the skis and poles, the fly-fishing equipment, the golf clubs, the *Playboy* calendars in plastic shrink film like collector's items. It was a heavy thing, stored in a shoebox. He put the bullets in his pocket but some spilled. They rolled, and the sound was too loud. It would wake the dead.

He opened the door to the basement and locked himself inside. He held the gun pointed at the door for about an hour before he remembered to fill its chambers with bullets. Sometime later, he didn't know how much—his cell phone wasn't working right, and he didn't have a watch—a window on the main floor shattered. Then something swished, and the wooden floor creaked.

The sound was slithering, and he imagined bodies pulling themselves across the floor. The sick ones, who didn't move quite right. He followed their path along the ceiling with his eyes. They were in the hall, and then the kitchen, and then in the dining room. He gasped. They were with his mother. He should have buried her. Oh God, he should have laid her to rest.

After a while, it got quiet again. At first he was relieved, and then he wasn't. It was dark in the cellar. He didn't dare turn on the lights. He thought about his mother's eyes. His dad's eyes, too. In his mind he could see the outlines of their faces like photo negatives; pale and without emotion. Now that they were dead, they were changed. They were bad. They blamed him for what James had done.

He should have buried them better. Like the rabbits. He'd never done a decent thing in his whole life, and now the end of the world had come, and all his chances had run out.

His body felt bloated, like his organs were soaked with sorrow, and because of that they were expanding inside him. They were about to burst, and when they did he would die. "Mom and Dad, please stay dead. I don't want to see you anymore," he whispered into the darkness. In his mind, he could see their faces, so disappointed. They watched him all night.

And then, exhausted, he slept.

When he woke Sunday afternoon, he discovered that while a new day had begun, the nightmare persisted. He ate his tears, and imagined Felice and Miller's humorless ghosts watching him in the dark, and, finally, he turned the gun on himself.

TWENTY-EIGHT
Witch

Fenstad didn't go straight to his house after he left the hospital. Instead he parked at the top of the hill, and waited for his heart to stop pounding. Except for WBAI at Colby College, most of the local radio stations had switched to national satellites. These were broadcasting prerecorded sets or else announcing press releases advising citizens across New England to lock their doors because help was on its way.

Fenstad's mind was a jumble of images. He tried not to let them affect him. As if he were visiting a shark tank at the aquarium, he tried to stay on the safe side of the glass. In his mind he saw Alice's severed head, and he remembered his fifth-grade teacher's running joke: *Heads will roll*! He saw the short woman's mutilated daisy tattoo, and the chicken bone spinning against his shoe.

Better run, Fennie. His lips were numb, and he wondered if he might be having a heart attack until he remembered the OxyContin. He felt his breast pocket, to reassure himself that more pills remained.

He got out of the car and looked down at the town. Plumes of dark smoke wafted up from the business district (fires? explosions?), but otherwise, all was still.

Houses were shuttered and doors were closed. He wondered how many people, if any, were left. Nestled within the fertile green lawns were ivory specks: bones. A few feet away from him on the street was a picked-clean human skull. Even its scalp was gone. But the town wasn't completely abandoned. Tim Carroll's cruiser was tooling through the streets. The man had definitely earned his pay.

The morning's drizzling spits intensified, and the rain began to pour from the gray sky. For the first time since this had started, Fenstad had an appropriate emotion. He was terrified.

He didn't like the word "evil." It was an ignorant word. He'd treated enough tortured schizophrenics to understand that. But at this moment, he changed his mind. Evil did exist, and it was here, in Corpus Christi.

He got back into the car and flicked off the radio. *Better run, Fennie. Do you feel that?* He closed his eyes. His heart was beating slowly—he'd taken too many pills. He squeezed his hands until they hurt to get their circulation flowing. *Fennie? Is it a lump?* He looked down at his feet and reassured himself that there was no bloody carpet. Reminded himself that the dog couldn't be barking anymore: The dog was dead. He thought about Meg, who three times this week had told him that she loved him. He thought of his daughter's purple hair, and the smiley-face doodles she left on notepads (*Maddie Bonelli Wintrob Vargas, Extrordinaire!*). They were his world. It was time to take stock. It was time to stop falling apart. His family needed him.

He counted to three, and then ten, and then fifty. He did what he was best at. He removed himself from the problem, like looking at a slide under glass, and tried to find its solution.

The virus created a hostile, schizophrenic state within

its hosts. Maybe it read minds, maybe it only engendered unpleasant hallucinations that rendered its hosts vulnerable. Regardless, he was a shrink; if anyone knew how to treat altered psychological states, it was he. Would massive doses of lithium pacify the infected? He wondered if anyone at the CDC had tried it. Then he shook his head. No, this virus turned people into monsters.

Still, what if there was a cure? Was there a way of protecting the brain from infection, or metabolizing the virus once it got there? Most people didn't know this, but human DNA was composed of viruses. Every human with an ancestor who'd survived infection, from smallpox to flu, had the code for those same viruses imprinted in his genetic material. If this virus was old, maybe some people had an acquired immunity, and they carried the vaccine in their genes. Better yet, what if the infected had particular aversions to things like fire, the smell of methane, or chlorinated water, that kept them from attacking? If this thing was going national or even global, such knowledge could come in handy.

The women in the hospital basement said that the infection had originated from Bedford. Just a few weeks ago people had been living in trailers near the river there, which meant that the virus had only recently become hot, or it would have wiped them out long ago. If anyone still lived there, he might have answers.

He nodded to himself. Okay. Good. Okay. Then he felt his pocket and ran his tongue along his gums. He popped another OxyContin. *Okay.*

He chewed on his lip, and because it was numb he didn't notice that it was bleeding. The rain was falling hard. Messing around in Corpus Christi didn't make a lot of sense. He'd rather get Meg and Maddie to safety.

Even if all the borders were guarded, he was pretty sure he could talk his way across them, and into New Hampshire. It would get dark in another three or four hours, which meant he had some daylight left. Like his secretary, he could siphon gas from other cars when he ran out. But Meg couldn't walk more than a few feet on her broken ankle. That would be a problem if stalled cars on the highway forced them to get out and walk the 150 miles to the state border. He could carry her for a while, but not forever.

No, he decided. Right now they had a house whose doors they could barricade. On the road, he didn't know what they'd find. He pulled the car out of park and began driving. As long as they were staying in town, he might as well use the daylight, and see what answers he could find in Bedford.

He pulled back on the road and headed north. When he reached the back entrance near the woods, a pair of MPs holding what looked like automatic weapons blocked the road that joined the two towns. He slowed to show them his license, but they waved him through. They were older men, both with gray hair and plenty of stars pinned to their collars. High-ranking lieutenants, at least. So what were they doing on grunt duty? An idea occurred to him, and he didn't like it one bit. They were on grunt duty because the grunts had either abandoned their posts, or were dead.

Bedford was just as quiet as Corpus Christi. The houses, as far as he could tell, were abandoned. But along the valley he found the trailer park, where the last holdouts were rumored to still live. It was built inside a muddy valley that had recently been flooded. Some of the RVs were caked in dirt all the way to their roofs.

He pulled in front of the fence surrounding the park

and got out. Rain splashed against his face and his sneakers squished. He was surprised to see a sturdy-looking woman with a shock of gray hair along her temple walking toward him. She looked about forty years old, maybe fifty. She was tall, and her shoulders were broad. She wore a yellow slicker over corduroy trousers and a blue wool sweater. She could have been the president of the Corpus Christi PTA.

He waved as he approached. "You live here?" he asked. He expected her to say she was visiting from Bangor, and looking for clues just like him.

"Yeah," she said. Once she spoke, he knew she was a local. Her voice was flat and without animation, like most of the people from Bedford. "Twenty years. Used to live in a house but it collapsed in the fire."

"Does anyone else live here?"

She shook her head. "Used to. But they're gone now. They got the consumption disease. They still come around at night, though." When she smiled at him, he saw that no PTA in their right mind would have her. Her teeth were black. Not brown, like she didn't brush them, but black, like all she ate was Hostess cupcakes and raw sugar, so that layers upon layers of crud now coated her rotting teeth.

"There are infected here, too?" Fenstad asked.

She raised her hand over her head to protect her hair from the rain. "You can call them that, but they're tough as oxen." Then she wiggled her front tooth with her index finger, and he had a vague recollection of punching Lois Larkin senseless. His pulse soared at the very notion, but like flotsam in a river, the memory quickly sank.

"Where do you sleep?" He raised his voice so that she could hear him over the rain.

She smiled, and spoke while wiggling her tooth so

that her words were hard to discern. "Used to have two girls but they both left. A husband, too."

He wanted to turn around, but he was here already and maybe she knew something. After wasting half a day, he wanted to at least to have news to bring home to Meg. "May I ask you a few questions?"

She nodded. "Inside. Even before the flood, I always hated the rain." Then she headed for the trailers. The RV where she stopped was the shoddiest in the lot. It didn't even have wheels. More worrisome were the life-sized dolls fashioned from children's clothing and nylon stuffed with cotton that hung from nooses along its wood-paneled side. Each effigy held a metal street sign with a word spray painted across it in childish scrawl. When read together it said: "She is always hungry. She is never satisfied."

The woman pointed at the effigies. "Not my place, but I tried to decorate as best I could." Then she looked at him and smiled. "*Ha*!" she shouted.

He jumped.

"Gotcha!" she said, and began to cackle. "It was like this when I got here." The she climbed the three steps to her stinkhole RV, and slammed the door behind her.

After a few seconds and a lot of noise, she was back. She waved him inside, and he assumed that her disappearance signified either tidying up the place, or hiding what she didn't want him to see. She was panting, and he realized that she was sick. Not with the virus, but simply ill. She'd gotten winded too easily for someone her age and size. He wasn't sorry for her. On the contrary, her frailty made her less dangerous.

He put his hand in his pocket and felt the bottle of OxyContin for reassurance. Then he entered the trailer. The room was small. A folded Murphy bed and kitchen table were pressed to one side to make room to walk.

The floor was waxed and bright. In the garbage by the door, empty boxes of Mallomars, Hershey's Kisses, and Twinkies crackled, as if they'd recently been tossed there, and then pushed down with a booted foot. She followed his gaze and nodded. "The power's out most places, and there aren't any stores, so I just take the stuff that isn't rotten and the night people don't want. That way I figure they'll leave me alone. Sugar, mostly."

On the table was a photo of two girls; one slight and blond, the other a rosy brunette. Neither smiled at the photographer.

"Tea?" she asked. "I've just got the Lipton. Woman on my own, I can't afford much else. My living daughter has a chemistry scholarship, but I never see a dime. Lives in sin with her boyfriend . . . Yeah. So, tea?"

He didn't want tea, but the shrink in him wondered whether she knew how to brew it. "Yes, please."

To his surprise, she had a pot ready, and poured its contents into a cup accompanied by a chipped saucer. "I was expecting company. I keep my ear to the ground . . . actually, the mill. I keep my ear to the old mill. If you do that for long enough, you hear everything." She winked.

As he brought the cup to his mouth, a green pea floated to the surface (Cup-a-Soup?). He hoped it was a pea. He brought it to his lips and pretended to drink, then placed the cup on the table next to the photo of young Susan and Elizabeth Marley.

"When did people here start getting sick?" he asked.

She smiled. Then she spit. His stomach turned. A tooth came out in her hand. She hid it in her fist like a piece of gristle that she didn't know how to politely dispose of. He thought about Lois. He'd struck a woman. But maybe that wasn't so bad. Maybe he was just an ordinary man, and these were extraordinary times.

"Started long before the fire, but the people and animals that got it died before they passed it on, so it didn't spread. Then the sulfur came and fed it, so it got stronger." Then she leaned forward. "Why don't you ask your real question?" she asked, only now she had a very slight lisp: *quethion.*

His mind was on the hospital, and the tidal wave of blood that must have crashed against it during the night, so he gave her the shrink answer: "What's my real question?"

"So clever, aren't you?" she said. "You don't care how it started. You want to know how to stop it," she said. "But you can't stop it."

He felt his cheek with his tongue and it was numb. He was glad. He wished the rest of him was numb, too.

"The boy came along. James Walker. He found the bones of the last man to carry it, and he sucked them dry. In him, it spread," she said.

"How do you know this?" he asked.

She grinned. Her mouth wasn't bleeding from the lost tooth, which made him think it had already fallen out, and like the methamphetamine addicts in Midwest who got rot-mouth, she'd tried to glue it in place with a little Polident. "This place is haunted."

"I'm not sure I follow," he told her.

"Of course you don't," she hissed. The she picked up a Twinkie and tore the foil with her teeth. Miraculously, her incisors stayed in place.

"What happened here in Bedford?"

She leaned across the table. "Go home and beat your wife, or whatever it is you men do."

He startled. Did she know about Lois? About Kaufmann?

A smile slowly spread across her face. "Hit a nerve, did I?"

He got up to leave but she grabbed his arm. Her fingers were sticky. "I'll tell you."

He waited even though he wanted to leave. He had to know. She grinned widely, like she couldn't wait to drop this bomb. "A girl came and saved this place. She swallowed our nightmares like candy." Then the woman stopped, and with her free hand scooped a Twinkie down her throat. She talked while wet crumbs spilled from the sides of her mouth. "I swallow candy, too . . . I swallow it for her, so she knows I'll never forget. I swallow it to be closer to her." Then the woman took the tooth, and crammed it back into her gum so that her lisp was gone.

Fenstad had seen enough. He tore his wrist free and headed for the door. She called after him. "But you can't swallow all the nightmares. Not in a haunted place like this. Stupid cunt. This place *makes* nightmares."

Fenstad opened the back door. The rain out there looked good, like it would wash this woman's stink from his clothes. She smelled like sulfur.

"It's been alive before, but this time it's different. This time it's smart. It started out like James Walker; stupid and mean. But now it has a new leader. Can you guess who that is? Your life depends on it."

Fenstad looked back at her. He wanted to believe she was insane, but he knew she wasn't. The woman smiled. "Do you know why they won't eat me?" She pointed at her temple with her index finger, in a gesture that looked a lot like a cocked gun. Then she pulled the trigger. "Pow!" she said. "Cancer. They don't like the taste."

He was halfway out the door. He noticed, then, what she'd hidden from him. A white sheet was draped over a small lump underneath her kitchen table.

She saw where he was looking. "I cook them real civilized. Burn out all the virus," she said.

Poking out from the sheet was a child-sized finger. Fenstad swallowed, but his bile didn't stay down. He opened the door and vomited.

"I only eat the dead ones, Mr. High and Mighty!"

He staggered down the steps. The sun had set. The rain felt good. He wanted to cry, the rain felt so good. Even the dark was better than the monster behind him. Even the virus was better. He jogged, and then ran for his car.

"You'll see! You'll do it too!" she shouted as he pulled away.

TWENTY-NINE
Brother's Keeper

Danny pulled back the safety. At least he hoped it was the safety. The metal was warm because he'd been holding it all night. He bit down. He was shaking, so his teeth chattered against metal. Already he was thinking this might be a bad idea. Still, he counted. On three he'd pull the trigger. This time he wouldn't wuss out. He should have buried those rabbits right. He should have been a better brother. He shouldn't have buried those rabbits at all.

"Un," he said with a mouth full of well-greased steel: one.

His parents' ghosts were watching him from the corner of the room. Photo negatives without color, they were dark where they should have been light. Neither smiled. The veins in Miller's neck were swollen, like his rage was about to burst them wide open. Felice held his hand like a little girl clinging to her dad. They were dressed for a night at the golf club. Her fur coat was made from rabbit husks.

He took the gun from his mouth. He didn't want them here to witness this. He wasn't trying to protect them, he realized; he just didn't like them. "Get out of here," he said. "You're dead."

He and his old man locked eyes. Miller glowered, like he wanted Danny to flinch. Danny pulled the trigger. The recoil pushed him into the stairway wall where he'd been sitting all night, guarding the door. "Oooph!" he said. He looked up at the wall, and his parents' ghosts were gone. All that was left was a badly aimed bullet hole about three feet off the ground, and Danny smiled for the first time in days, so glad that the hole was in a wall, and not his head.

He got up, lifted the lock, and opened the door to the soft light of the midmorning clouds, like a mole rising up to the sun.

An hour later he'd combined what ingredients he could find left in the kitchen, and made pancakes cut with Rose's Lime juice to quiet the rumbling in his belly. Then he summoned the courage, and went into the dining room to find and bury his mother's remains.

But the room was empty, and all that was left was some blood on the floor. His face crumpled. They'd taken her during the night. He was outraged. He was also re-lived.

He looked out the window. His yard was still, and so were the neighbor's yards to either side. Then he walked down his driveway to the front yard. Miller's body was gone, too. The man had probably expected to live to one hundred. At his funeral, he'd probably thought he'd get a twenty-six-gun salute, a college named after him, and an open-bar cocktail party at the club. And then, after all the bad shit he'd done, all the deals he'd made with the wrong kinds of people, in the end he still died, just like everybody else. The taste of disgust was bitter on Danny's tongue, like ashes, and he wept a couple of angry tears.

From the town below, small fires burned. It looked

like most had started last night, and were now on their last embers. The valley smoldered in the afternoon mist. He walked back up the drive. It was time to go.

Except for the dent in the passenger side door that Aran had left there, his mother's car was in good shape. He got inside and turned the engine. It hummed smoothly. Gas was low. He'd need to find some. His stomach was still growling. He'd need food, too.

He drove slowly, looking for signs of life. He didn't see any. The stores on Micmac Street were empty. Windows were broken, and stupid things like air conditioners and Persian rugs bled from their holes. At the supermarket, all the food was gone. The meat, the produce. Even the ice cream had been emptied from the freezers. Danny grabbed some Bubble Yum. They could bill him. Last month he'd grown more than an inch, and half the time his knees hurt so much from this year's growth spurt that it hurt to walk. He knew he should be grieving, but he was also thinking about bacon and eggs.

No fuel was left at any of the three gas stations. Even the diesel had been broken into, and what remained from the tanks lay evaporating against blacktop. He decided to take his chances, and tried to enter I–95. A Humvee blocked the ramp. As he neared it, the soldier in the passenger seat rolled down his window. "Turn around or we'll shoot!" he shouted through a bullhorn. Danny slowed but didn't stop. The town was in ruins; where did this guy expect him to go?

Then the back window rolled down and Danny stopped. An automatic was pointed in his direction. "Turn around immediately!" the soldier shouted.

Danny put the car in reverse, but apparently, that wasn't good enough. "Pop-pop-pop!" The sound rang in his ears. He pushed down on the gas and drove backward until he spun off the ramp, and was back on Mic-mac Street. His rearview mirror was gone, and it took his a second before he realized that it had been shot off. They hadn't been shooting into the air; they'd been shooting at him!

The only other way out was through Bedford. He turned onto the road, unnamed, that had bridged the two towns since they'd been built. There were soldiers here, too. He stopped near where their truck was parked and rolled down his window. Two men in green slickers holding machine guns walked toward him, and in his mind he said a silent prayer that consisted of two words: *Don't shoot*. The man looked into his eyes and then, without speaking, waved him along.

He sped down the road. Thick trees surrounded him on the left and the right. *I'll see you in the woods,* James had said. Was he still out there? Was that where the rest of them were hiding, too? He entered the empty town of Bedford. In his mind's eye, he saw his parents' ghosts, too. They stood on the corners, shaking their heads at all the things he'd done wrong.

Bedford's Main Street was empty. Shop windows were broken. It looked a lot like Corpus Christi, and he suddenly got the idea that from now on no matter where he went, everything would look like Corpus Christi. The whole world was haunted now. The dead, the infected, the living, they all shared the same real estate.

Danny wiped his eyes and sniffled. His parents' ghosts were watching him. His innocent brother (but had he ever really been innocent?) was dead, too. In his place a monster had risen.

There was only one way to make the ghosts quiet, and there was only one cure for his little brother.

I'll see you in the woods.

He pulled off Main Street, and parked at the picnic area near the woods. It was getting late. Four o'clock. The days were shorter, and sunset wasn't far off. He took a deep breath, touched the gun in his pocket, and went hunting.

The deeper he walked, the more the cord of adrenaline inside him unwound. He was tired, not from walking, but from shaking, from being ready to run for so long now that the blood rushing through his veins at twice its normal speed felt natural.

The sun got lower in the sky. Everywhere were fallen trees. His instincts told him to turn around, but he couldn't leave his brother. Not again. The boy was all alone, and for once Danny would do right by him.

After a bit, the trail opened up into a clearing. Dead animals surrounded the periphery. He could make out the empty pelts of rabbits, deer, and even the mammoth antlers of a moose. He dry-heaved only once before stepping over their bodies and heading for the center. He was high with his own adrenaline. He'd been mainlining it for so long that he could have run a marathon.

He bent down and touched the ground. It was black and cold and wet. He got to the center of the clearing. From a distance they looked like a single clump, and as he closed in he saw that there were hundreds, maybe thousands, of them heaped atop one another. They stank like garbage.

It hit him suddenly, and the cord of terror sprang upright in his belly and twisted. It filled the empty spaces inside him. He was shaking. Not just his hands: his whole body. His mother, Miller, Lou McGuffin, the doctor in the hospital; they were dead. Hundreds. Thousands. Maybe millions. Dead.

Some of the bodies faced the dirt, as if even in dreams they were trying to lick the blood from the soil. He made a fist and squeezed three knuckles into his mouth. He pushed his hand in so hard his teeth hurt, and that helped a little. It gave him the strength to come closer.

He walked on tiptoe. He had to piss all of a sudden but he didn't want to unzip his pants in front of these things. He didn't have control anyway. He let loose and his jeans got hot: This was the nest.

In the center of the bodies lay his old teacher Lois Larkin. Her hair was gone now, and she didn't look the same. All her soft edges had become angles. The rest of the bodies were pointed toward her, like they were protecting her. She was the leader, of course. As Miller Walker's son, he knew a leader when he saw one.

He was drawn to her. He wanted to protect her, too. An eye opened in his mind, and he felt it watching him. He walked toward the Lois thing. He thought maybe he'd lie down next to her and wait for dark.

That's right, Danny, she whispered sweetly. *I'll take care of you.*

As he climbed the pile of bodies, he tripped over someone's waist. It was Ryan Simpson, the cop who'd once tried to bust him for driving underage. The gun in his belt fired and he jumped. The bullet shot straight down through the edge of his shoe and into Ryan's head. He was bleeding (his little toe, maybe?), but only a little. He was afraid the scent of blood would wake them up. It would make them hungry. The gun was so hot it burned his hip, but he didn't bother to move it. Instead he stuck his hand into his mouth. All four knuckles. He bit down as hard as he could. That helped a little, but not much.

His mom, his dad, Lou McGuffin, Dr. Rossoff at the hospital who had begged for mercy. They were all dead. But maybe they were lucky.

OPEN YOUR MOUTH WIDE, DANNY, she commanded, only her voice wasn't feminine anymore. *PULL THE TRIGGER.*

Danny backed away. "No," he mumbled through his knuckle sandwich. He sucked on his fingers in there, and that felt good. He wanted to swallow himself a little. That way he could hide inside his own stomach.

PULL THE TRIGGER! she hollered, and her voice was hoarse wheezing, loud and legion.

"No," he said, even though he knew it would win if he talked to it, just like Miller. Never argue with a madman.

The thing's eye blinked in his mind, and then everything started to itch. His ears, his skin, his blood. He itched in the places he couldn't reach. He tried to reach them anyway. He took his hand out of his mouth and scratched inside his ears so hard they hurt. He was crying again, but this time he didn't talk. He backed away.

That's when he spotted the boy. A hairless cherub folded inside Lois Larkin's arms. He looked peaceful. He looked innocent, like all the problems inside his broken brain had been cured. He looked happy.

Danny felt the gun on his hip. He crouched down on top of bodies. He reminded himself of Miller's head on a post (*The king is dead—long live the king!*), and Felice's open-eyed terror, and the rabbits that had once been white. He *had* to do this. He owed it to the memory of the boy James had once been to do this. His parents' spirits would never rest unless he did this. He crawled across the bodies. He lifted the gun. The insides of his ears itched so bad he wanted to tear them off.

PUT THE BULLET IN YOUR CHEST, DANNY BOY. YOU DESERVE A LONG REST. The thing shouted so loud that his head swelled.

Breathing through his mouth so he wouldn't have to

smell them, he climbed over their arms, legs, and swollen necks. The half-formed ones made cracking sounds as their brittle bones broke. They were like snakes, shedding their skin. Changing . . . into what?

He stopped only once to vomit. But even vomiting here, on these things, made him feel vulnerable. They're wood, he told himself. Soft kindling. The thing interrupted him: *WHEN THEY TOOK HER TO THE LOONY BIN SHE SAW YOU WAVING. SHE KNEW IT WAS YOU, BUT SHE DIDN'T WANT TO BE YOUR MOTHER ANYMORE.*

"Stop," Danny whispered as he bent over his brother's body. He didn't want to look at it, but he had to. He pulled James's ice cold hand free from Lois's flat breast, and rolled him on his back. The bodies (wood!) he was kneeling on weren't stable, and he tumbled a little, and scrambled to regain his balance.

James's brows were gone. In their place was transparent skin and thickened bones. His wounded shoulder had healed now, good as new.

"You're not my brother," Danny whispered as he pointed the gun against James's temple, so this time he didn't miss. Yes, he decided, his real brother was a sweet kid. Misunderstood, but sweet. The kind of kid who'd turn out fine, once somebody bothered to give him a little attention. The trigger was half-cocked when the thing screamed at him: *TRY IT BOY, AND I'LL STRING YOUR ENTRAILS ACROSS YOUR CAR LIKE CHRISTMAS LIGHTS. I'LL LET YOUR BROTHER EAT YOUR SWEET MEATS.*

Danny was leaning on top of Lois Larkin's shoulder. It cracked. Broke maybe. Then he giggled, which he knew meant he was losing his wits.

I'LL WRITE THE CORPUS CHRISTI WELCOME SIGN WITH YOUR BLOOD.

Danny stopped. He didn't notice the itching. He didn't care about the pile of bodies he'd scrambled atop. He was pissed off. Pissed off enough to wonder: If you kill the leader, do the rest get set free?

Danny redirected the gun, and aimed it at Lois Larkin's face.

His chest convulsed. He was crying and giggling at the same time. The thing's eyes opened inside him, and showed him all it had done. The civilizations it had toppled. The hunger it engendered, that fed on itself without end, until the infected were engorged like fatted ticks, and the survivors watched their skin turn to bones. In the end they all died, because there was nothing left to consume.

Danny was laughing. He couldn't help it. He turned the gun on himself. Lou McGuffin. He was tougher than Lou McGuffin. He'd show his mom how tough he could be. Fuck the toothbrush to the heart. He'd shoot himself in the head! He was still laughing. He couldn't stop. He laughed so hard he forgot to breathe through his mouth. He smelled the rot. After a while, he stopped laughing.

He backed away. One knee after the next, over soft wood, until he was with James again. He didn't think about it this time. He pointed and pulled the trigger once, twice, three times. It happened so fast he didn't see the bullets slash through his brother's chest. Only saw the boy ricochet, like he'd been punched.

Mom and Dad and God and James forgive me, he prayed silently as his bowels let go with a long gasp of air. James opened his eyes and snarled, and Danny knew the lie he'd told himself. Virus or no virus, his brother hated him. He'd always hated him. Danny's heart broke a little bit, knowing that.

"It said I would be your king, and you would be the

fool. It would make you a half-wit, like I used to be," James whispered, and Danny shook his head. As Miller's son, shouldn't he have guessed that such a promise was a lie?

Then James closed his eyes. Danny felt his wrist. His pulse slowed, and then stopped. They didn't open again. Danny lifted him up and carried him away from the rest of the bodies. The wet ground was just soft enough. With his hands he dug a shallow grave. He buried his brother inside it.

By the time he was done, the sun was low, and he knew he'd have to go back to Corpus Christi tonight. He'd find shelter, and leave tomorrow with a full day of sunlight behind him. He looked once more at Lois Larkin. His gun had two bullets left. He could tell the army people what he'd found, but he didn't think they'd listen. He was alone out here.

He pointed the gun and aimed it at her head. He shot once. Missed. Again. Missed. Again, only this time, the chamber was empty. In his mind, Lois Larkin let out a deafening scream, just as the sun fell down below the horizon, and the bodies began to shiver.

He ran. Like a track star, feet pumping high as his ass, he raced to his car. If he survived the night, he would leave Corpus Christi. There was nothing left for him here. There never had been.

THIRTY
From Death, Life

The last rays of the sun crawled across the horizon. They were yellow, then red, then brown, then gone. Lois didn't see colors anymore. Only shadows and shapes. The world was shades of gray. Her thoughts weren't the same, either. She wanted only to survive, to feed, to find a dark place in which to sleep. It was an easier life, and she didn't regret it, or miss what she'd once been. Didn't regret her mother, whose heart, surprisingly, had not been bitter.

On Sunday night, she woke in a clearing. The sun didn't hurt her kind, but it put them to rest like dolls laid flat, their eyelids closed. The others did not dream, or remember the day. Their sleep was deep, and during it their bodies changed. But she was different. She could feel the things around her even when the sun was bright.

There had been a moment there when she'd been frightened. Danny Walker had cracked her bones. But he was gone now, and so was his threat. From now on she would sleep in a covered place.

Her body had changed. She was longer in the torso, and her knees and elbows had thickened. It hurt her to stand; she preferred to crawl. She was becoming the same as the virus that lived inside her. Already her hair and eyelashes had fallen out: a hundred wishes on her finger, but she wanted just one thing—Ronnie and Noreen's blood.

Around her were bodies. One thousand, two thousand. Five thousand. More than she could count. When she woke Sunday night, her bones were whole again. All cuts and wounds healed in this place. All things were eternally temporary.

In her dreams her soul lived underground. She'd been separated from it. Instead of feeding on her body, the worms ate her soul. In her dreams it wasn't the virus that gave her hunger; it was her body, longing for its mate. It was the ashes in her mouth from this deal she had made with a lover not even human.

But those were dreams, of course.

She had no regrets, of course.

She stood, and around her the children knelt. The virus was instinct, and she was direction. Together they were better than their parts. She had a plan. They were feeding too fast, and unwisely. They were making too many of their own kind. They would be more selective in spreading the virus, and they would harvest what they ate. In her way, she would be a scientist, after all.

She touched her belly. In this she was not gentle, either. The thing in her stomach had not adjusted to the change, and while she slept, it had died. There was no pain. There were no cramps. Its corpse remained fixed inside her, a fossil of skin.

The old Lois Larkin screamed at her from under the ground, and she was glad she'd buried it there. She hated that woman almost as much as she hated herself.

As Danny Walker fled the Bedford woods, she and the children woke, and then slithered through the rainy night.

THIRTY-ONE
The Lump in the Bed

Sunday night, Graham Nero sat up with a start. He felt better than he'd felt in years. Strong, vital, a fucking he-man. The room was dark, but he could still see the floral bedspread and yellow wallpaper. Could see the fibers and specks of dust that hovered in a thin layer over the thick blue carpet. Could hear the weak mewing of his brood.

A lump lay in the bed next to him. She'd always been a lump. Useless dead weight. Got knocked up a week after their wedding. Told him the pill wasn't fail-safe, but he was no fool. He called the pharmacy. She hadn't refilled her prescription in months!

She quit her job as an executive assistant at his office to raise the kid, so suddenly he'd been stuck making payments on the house that they'd bought at the height of the market all by his lonesome. Eight hundred thousand dollars is a lot of steak dinners, especially when your partner in crime can't gather enough scratch to cover the country club fee. When he met her, she'd seemed like somebody who could take care of herself. Efficient on the phone, typed forty words per minute, dressed in discount suits that weren't all that stylish, but had fit her curves just right. He'd never guessed what lurked underneath.

Now she worked part-time in circulation at the *Corpus Christi Sentinel*. Every couple of months they threw her a bone and let her write a bleeding heart human interest piece about halfway houses or crystal meth–addicted kids. She'd wanted to be a writer her whole life. At least once a week she thanked him for supporting her in doing it, as if he'd had a choice. After she got knocked up, the bank told her that unless she came back full-time, to clean out her desk.

That's what he liked about Meg Wintrob. She worked for a living. She didn't sulk to get her way; she yelled. He wished she'd come with him to room 69 the other day. Instead he'd had to settle for an underage girl from the bar. She'd tasted young, and now his favorite hotel room was a mess.

Graham could smell his own breath, and it wasn't good. He pulled a tin of Altoids from his suit pocket (he'd stolen a whole carton of them from Puffin Stop), and crunched on about twenty at once. Smarted, but he kept chewing. Then he wondered: *Why did I wear my suit to bed?*

Down the hall his brood wailed. Maybe she was hungry. Or scared, or stupid. Isabelle reminded him of Caitlin. The women in his life were the rocks tied to his ankles in a ten-foot pond.

He looked at the bed. The brood didn't stop crying, and predictably, his lump didn't get up. He put his feet on the cold floor. He was late for work, wasn't he? The bitch had forgotten to wake him and make his coffee . . . But wait, it was night, and Sunday, at that. Did he usually sleep during the day?

In the mirror he didn't see his face. Only a silhouette. The rashes on his neck and chest were gone. His cough was gone, too. How had he gotten the virus? Oh, right, the high school girl he'd met at the bar a few nights ago had leaned in to kiss him, and instead she'd bitten him! He couldn't remember, now, what had happened next. Only that he'd been hungry.

None of that mattered, though. All that mattered was his clean-shaven face and the dimple in his chin that the ladies liked to trace with their slender fingers. Even the girl from room 69. What was her name? *Sheila, Laura, Dora, Flora?* He couldn't remember. She'd been his first fatty.

He swished a mouthful of Listerine and spit. Smelled his breath, rancid, and cracked open another tin of Altoids.

Out the window, the streets were empty. Not even street lamps were lit, which was nice, because he hated the light. The radio played softly, Stravinsky. His wife's music. He changed the station. The news was a special bulletin. Keep your doors and windows locked. Do not go out at night, the announcer exclaimed.

Graham smiled at the mirror. The toupee was on the sink, and he decided to leave it there. He liked his new look. Sleek. He used to spend hours in the bathroom. Even when Caitlin knocked because she had to pee, he'd never opened the door until he was ready. Once he'd caught the ninny squatting into a jar in the kitchen because the downstairs toilet was broken and she couldn't hold it in. He smiled at the memory. Then he opened the door. He was hungry.

The lump under the covers reminded him of Meg Wintrob. That she'd turned him down was a splinter in his foot. Insignificant until you notice it, and then relentless. If she had come with him, he wouldn't have suffered through the nervous giggles of the virgin. If she'd come with him, maybe they could have fed together.

She'd called him about six months ago and told him it was over. Like he hadn't already moved on to the stripper at Lucifer's Delight Men's Club. Meg had a good body and he liked her, but she was long in the tooth. In a year or two, her eggs would be old, and her crotch would stink. He'd seen it before in the women who waited to marry at his office. They became moody vice-presidents who went on Internet dates, and by the time they were forty-five they smelled.

Yeah, so she dumped him, and he'd smiled and said, *Sure, babe*, even though he'd wanted to cut her into little pieces. Didn't the skinny bitch know he'd been doing her a favor? He'd pretended she was sexy, even though he had a wife at home with a double-D cup size and a dimpled smile.

He'd been thinking about her for a long time now. After he got the infection, he'd thought about her even more. It was like a switch had been turned inside him, and he couldn't let her go. When he closed his eyes she was waiting with folded arms, like nothing he could buy for her, no tricks with his tongue, would ever be good enough.

A few days ago, holding Isabelle with one hand and eating an apple in the other, Caitlin offered him a back rub, and he'd snapped. He'd been sick then, but not completely infected. It had only been a cough, a rash, a few clumps of hair here and there. His hand had been in the air, and then against her skin. Again and again. Until he was tired. Until his hands and teeth ached. Then he'd washed his hands and mouth with scented soap until the water stopped running pink. His next stop was the library. He'd pulled back every stop on the Graham Nero charm-o-meter. It hit irresistible. Meg Wintrob had still said no.

Graham started down the hall. The lump under the sheets had begun to smell, so he left it there. It was red and still a little wet. Lazy bitch hadn't even cleaned it.

He passed Isabelle's room. She sat in her crib, her lips blue, her face white as snow, her eyes black. She was hungry, but she didn't know how to feed. The kid was useless, just like her mother.

He went down the stairs and opened the front door. Looked out into the night. In the darkness, there were others. Their bodies long and lean; graceful. They shone in the moonlight. They sniffed from house to house, looking for the scraps that remained. Meg Wintrob on his mind, Graham stepped out into the night on two legs, and then ran on four.

THIRTY-TWO
Mostly It Was Just Plain Sad

Ronnie woke up from his nap. It was Sunday night, and he and Noreen were sitting on the couch. His cough was gone, and so was Noreen's. He felt good, sort of. He felt the strongest he'd been since high school, when he was Corpus Christi High's longest-armed shortstop. But he felt mean, too. Something inside him was tearing things up. He blamed Noreen. She'd done this to him, the bitch. He wanted to rip out her throat, just a little bit.

It was business as usual at the Ronnie and Noreen chateau of domestic bliss. He was watching *Gilmore Girls* in rerun because Noreen had the remote. There wasn't any food in the fridge. Nothing worth eating, at least. All the meat was gone, so right now he and Noreen were passing a rat between them. It was bleeding all over his chin.

It made him sick, the sight of that rat. He hated it, and still he kept eating.

He was hungry all the time now. Didn't matter how often he ate. He was tired when the daylight came, too. His pot stash was gone, which was the only thing he'd valued in his shitty life. Worse, his dealers were dead, which meant he wasn't getting more.

The change happened this morning. His eyes turned black. He remembered gasping, and praying for something, but he couldn't remember what. Something to do with peace. He'd been asking for peace. And then he didn't remember anything at all, except for waking up tonight in front of the television with Noreen, watching the *Gilmore Girls*.

Noreen was laughing. The older Gilmore girl was saying something smart and witty. "You're a couple of dogfaces," Ronnie said to the television screen, which wasn't like him. Before he got sick he never would have said something mean like that.

Noreen turned and spit in his face. It landed on his lip and rolled slowly down. He didn't think about it; he just acted. He throttled her. She fought at first. Thrashed against the Jennifer Convertible stain-resistant plaid couch, but then her face turned from white to blue. Her whole body jerked, like she was dying, and he knew he hated her. Hated himself. Hated what they'd become. But he was so goddamn hungry.

He let go. As soon as she caught her breath she tried to strike him. Plump baby hand all curled into a fist. He grabbed her arm and squeezed until it broke. But that was fine. She healed fast. He couldn't hurt Noreen unless he killed her, no matter how hard he tried.

"I'm hungry. I don't want rat," he said.

She nodded. "We'll go to the Dew Drop Inn."

They left the apartment. He headed for the car, but she didn't. "We don't need that," she said, and it was true. He was walking on four legs. His body was low to the ground, which was nice. Made it easier to catch the things that crawled. Spiders, mostly. He preferred insects over the things for which Noreen had an appetite.

He followed her pale body down the street, fast as a

deer. The air felt good. His eyes saw best in the dark. From the top of the hill, he could see all the way to the highway clogged with cars. They weren't moving. Pulled over, or out of gas. The people driving them had been killed where they sat during the night. He could smell their bodies. Somebody had gotten lazy and left plenty of gristle.

He wondered, briefly, if he was damned.

They got to the Dew Drop Inn. Wooden planks boarded its doors, but he could see light through the cracks. Ronnie pried the nails with his fingers. The boards came off, along with some of his skin. But even before it started bleeding, the wound was already healing. He opened the door. TJ Wainright was sitting all by himself at the bar. He smelled sweet as a suckling pig, and he was high, too. When Ronnie saw the chemical red in his eyes, he moaned. He wanted that pot so bad. He started to charge, but TJ lifted a gun from the bar and pointed it between Ronnie's eyes.

Ronnie kept coming. He wanted TJ to shoot him. He was sick of being hungry all the time. He wanted this to end, while there was a part of him that was still human.

Noreen held him back. "TJ, let me in, won't you?" Her voice echoed, and Ronnie could hear it not just in his ears, but in his mind.

TJ looked up, only his eyes were different. Noreen had gotten inside them. He looked at the gun for a couple of seconds, like he knew he was doing something stupid but couldn't help himself. Then he placed the gun on the bar. "That's right, TJ. Noreen knows best," she said. Ronnie got dizzy just listening to her. The virus was stronger in her than in him, he suddenly realized, which wasn't good news. Noreen looked at him and smiled, like she'd just figured that out, too.

"We'll all have a drink. I'm sorry about your boy-friend, TJ. But you had to do it. We understand," she said, and TJ nodded: "He woulda bit me otherwise."

Noreen lunged. Ronnie could smell TJ's fear. TJ didn't fight, or even scream. Noreen moved a little bit, so that there was space for Ronnie to nibble, too. He closed his eyes like it was just more spiders, or a squirrel, and began. When they were done, it was like TJ Wainwright had never been. All that was left was his scalp, and few hunks of bone.

Soon, Ronnie would be like Noreen. His fingernails would fall out, and his skin would thicken. He wouldn't be Ronnie Koehler anymore. Maybe even now, he wasn't Ronnie Koehler. He thought about that, and wished, once again, that he was dead. But he was so fucking hungry.

That's when she came into the bar. The gap between her teeth was gone, and so was her hair. He remembered the present he'd found on his welcome mat. He'd left it there because he'd been afraid that if he took it inside, she'd come looking for it.

He could see the blue veins under her skin. She'd grown a few inches taller, even though she didn't walk on two feet anymore. She stood above all the rest. The virus was strongest in her, which was funny in a way, but mostly sad. He didn't want to see her like this. He liked her, he realized. And that was sad, too.

Behind Lois were more of them. At least a hundred. Probably more.

"Lois," Noreen said like they were best buddies, still. She crawled across the floor on all fours, and kissed Lois's hands.

Lois, Ronnie thought in his mind, *I'm sorry*. He looked around at the crowd, hoping to find a friendly face, but there was a mean thing inside them, and it had changed the way they looked. It was inside him, too, and he wanted to weep.

Lois came to him. Her ring finger was missing, and he wondered how many times a night she had to eat the stump to keep it from growing back.

He took a chance. He kissed the stump of her ring finger.

Lois stepped back and opened her arms. The others became still, and listened. "There's too many of us. The animals are gone. The people are gone. There won't be enough food left. These two have fed unwisely, and we must make an example of them."

It happened fast. He and Noreen were holding hands. He tried to run, but Noreen wouldn't let go. They converged on him. He wished Lois had killed him before now. Before he'd become this thing, and murdered a man. The floor of the bar groaned and split under their weight as the infected attacked.

Ronnie and Noreen fell into the cellar. Up above a sky of pale faces peered down at them. One by one they jumped down and began to feed. He felt his life leaving him, and wished that she'd killed him before now, when he had no soul to free him from this body. But at least, finally, as he took his last breath, Noreen finally let go of his hand.

THIRTY-THREE
The Victorian

The women were waiting when Fenstad got home.

Maddie ran to him, and he held her stiffly. "Daddy, I'm so glad you're safe. Did you see Enrique?" she asked. Her green eyes peered up at him like a kitten's.

"No. I didn't see him."

Meg limped across the kitchen. He noticed that she was walking worse now than when she'd first gotten the cast. It was healing wrong because she wasn't using her crutches. She needed it broken and reset if she ever wanted to walk without a limp, but there wasn't anybody around to do that, except him. He winced at the thought of such a thing, or having to go back to the hospital for more plaster.

"I can't get in touch with David to let him know, but we've got to get out of here," Meg said.

Fenstad didn't answer. Maddie let go and stood back so that the three of them formed a circle. It was dark out, and already Meg had heard sounds she didn't like. The animals were gone, so who was moaning out the window? "I packed our clothes in a bag on the bed. We'll stay with your parents in Connecticut."

"We don't have the gas," Fenstad said.

Meg was leafing through the kitchen cabinets. She hadn't taken a codeine all day, and her ankle was swollen and hurting. Fiery sparks of pain radiated through her leg, all the way up to her groin. She filled a few jugs with water, and then started pulling cans from the pantry. Creamed corn, pineapple slices, tuna. In a pinch, they'd make a meal. "Go now," she said to Maddie. "Get the bag you packed, and mine and Daddy's, too."

Maddie nodded solemnly and started out of the room. She looked like she'd aged ten years since flopping down the stairs this morning. Meg felt for her. All day she'd wanted to give in and look for Enrique. But what if they found him, and like the rest he was infected?

Fenstad didn't help her with the supplies. He looked like he'd been crying again, which she knew was a bad sign. "The deadbolts were a good idea," she said. He didn't even nod. "What is it? What happened? Did you get Lila out of the hospital? Does she need to come with us?"

"Nothing out of the ordinary. Business as usual," he said.

She cocked her head. "I doubt that . . . Anyway, we've got to get going."

Fenstad didn't move. "We can't leave."

"Christ, Fenstad! Look around. We've got to get out of here!" she shouted. Then something caught in her throat, and she tried not to cry. She lowered her voice. "I *can't* stay here."

"It's a virus. It's everywhere, Meg. By now it's probably global. Leaving won't make a difference."

She laid her hand flat on the marble counter so she could hold herself more erect. "This is the center. Everything started here. We'll be safer once we're outside of it."

He shook his head. "You're hysterical. You need to calm down. The worst thing we can do now is get Maddie upset, too. The worst thing we can do is travel like this, without a plan." His diction, she noticed, was especially stiff. He pronounced every word fully, and with equal emphasis.

"What's wrong with you?" she asked.

He looked at her for a while, and set his jaw in disdain. "You're the one with the problem. We can't run from them. The second we step outside, especially at night. They . . . Don't you understand? They *feed*." His eyes got far away, and she could tell he was remembering something. She'd hoped all the rumors were false. She'd hoped he would tell her that all of this could be rationally explained. She knew for sure now that wasn't going to happen.

Then he was smiling. It was a blank smile, like the real Fenstad had decided to take a nap behind those green eyes. "There's no gas—you think you're going to walk to Connecticut on that ankle? Hey, I know! We'll pick a couple of guns up at the police department. They won't need them—they're all dead. Then we'll walk to Connecticut in the dark. If it turns out my parents are infected, we'll shoot 'em! It'll be great. You're a genius, Meg."

Meg closed the pantry door. *What a jerk* was her first thought. Her second was: *He's right*. Her plan would get them killed, or worse, infected. When she'd told Maddie they were leaving this morning, she'd assumed that Fenstad would take care of everything. She'd give the order, and he'd carry it out. He'd plop them into the car, and they'd arrive at his parents' house by the sheer strength of her will and his wits. She could rest for a while. Snooze in the backseat, because he'd drive. But none of that was going to happen.

She limped toward him. Her left leg slid across the floor. She hadn't cleaned the kitchen since Monday, and her cast was black with dirt. This place was turning into a sty. "So what do we do?"

He gritted his teeth. "For the last time, would you use your goddamn crutches?"

"Okay," she said, and kept walking toward him. The musky scent of his sweat was strong. She liked that smell; it was specifically *Fenstad*. He'd been wearing the same jeans and shirt for four days now. It was strange, she'd made a point of leaving fresh shirts on top of his dresser.

"I'm not kidding. And take a codeine. It hurts just looking at you sweat like that."

"I know," she said, and now she was close enough. She leaned her head on his shoulder. He stiffened. She waited. He put his arms around her. To her own surprise, her eyes teared up. She held him tight. "I'm scared," she said.

He rested his chin on the top of her head and took a ragged breath. They stood there for a long while. She felt her muscles loosen. He wasn't acting like the man she'd married. The man she married never said a word in anger. Never, for that matter, said an angry word. Still, it felt good to be in his arms. It felt good to rest.

Finally she pulled away from him. "I don't know what I'd do without you," she said.

His eyes were red. He nodded, like he felt the same way, and she wondered how, over the last few years, they'd managed to drift so far apart, when between them there was so much love. "Tell me what happened to you at the hospital. Tell me what you saw," she said.

He looked out the window for a while, and she thought maybe she'd gotten to him. She'd cracked him. It was scary, because she wasn't sure she wanted to see him crack. She wasn't sure she wanted to know what he looked like, when all his walls came down. "Tell me," she said.

A tear rolled down the side of his face, and more than anything else, it was the tear that sent her pulse soaring fast enough to make her whole body throb. This had to be very bad. "The virus turns your mind. It knows the things that make you weak. Like about your dad. About me. I hit a woman, Meg. I hit my patient. I think . . . I'm suffering from a nervous br—" He was interrupted by a loud crash in the front hall.

They looked at each other, and Meg couldn't help it. She sobbed. She'd heard there were looters who roamed at night. Worse things than looters . . . The bones on the lawn.

In the front hall, the stained-glass bay window had been shattered. A huge hunk of slate from their roof lay on the Persian rug. Fenstad bent down and examined it for a long time.

"What happened?" Maddie hollered as she came pounding down the stairs.

"We don't know. Go back to your room. Lock the windows. Draw the curtains," Meg said.

"Can I help?" Maddie asked.

"You can help by going to your room."

Maddie frowned but didn't resist. "I'll be here if you need me," she said, and started back up the stairs.

Lost in his thoughts, Fenstad didn't look up from the slate. "How did they know about the German shepherd? Did you tell them?" he asked.

German shepherd? Meg swallowed. He held the slate loosely, like he might drop it, and she suddenly knew what he'd been about to say: *I'm suffering from a nervous breakdown.*

Before she had the chance to finish that thought, the

doorbell rang. Like a robot, Fenstad turned the lock. "No!" she shouted, but he didn't heed her. He opened the door. Graham Nero's smile was wide, and his eyes were black. Even from far away, she could see her reflection inside them.

"May I come in?" he asked. His tone was refined, but he stood on all fours, like a wolf.

"Holy God," Meg whispered.

Fenstad looked from her to Graham Nero, and whatever he was thinking, she didn't like it. Then he did something foolish. Slate in hand, he stepped outside.

"What do you want?" Fenstad asked.

Graham grinned. He was drooling, and only his face was recognizable. The rest of him was pale and hairless. "She invited me here. Told me to kill that dog, too. We're running away together."

Fenstad charged. Something flashed so quickly that she could hardly see it. Her mind put together the pieces and guessed what it was. The hunk of slate. He caught Graham off guard and plunged it through his chest. Graham screamed. The sound was a high-pitched, wheezing bray of pain. Fenstad wiggled the slate and forced it in further. His face was sweating. She wanted to close her eyes, but she knew she had to watch. Fenstad was grinning. His smile was wide. He pulled out the slate. Graham crawled across the lawn like a dizzy drunk. Fenstad brought the slate down again, this time in Graham's neck. He pulled it out and brought it down again. And again. And again.

The sound was thumping, but not wet. You'd never know. You'd never guess. Meg wanted to close her eyes but she didn't. This was her husband. She had to watch. "Stop," she mouthed, because she didn't care anymore about Graham, or even about their safety. She only wanted Fenstad to stop. She only wanted that smile to go away. He was panting. Even after Graham's face was gone, he kept stabbing, until the corpse didn't look like a body anymore. It was a mess of gore.

"Stop," Meg whispered. "Stop. Please stop. Oh, God, stop."

Meg felt someone's hand take her own. The hand was familiar, and automatically she squeezed. Maddie. She kept crying, even though she wanted to be strong for her daughter. She'd never been so sad in her whole life. She'd never imagined that her husband had this kind of violence inside him, or that he could commit it with such glee.

After what seemed like hours, but was maybe only five more minutes, Fenstad stopped pounding. The slate had broken to pieces by then, and he was using his fists. His shirt and face were red with blood. When he turned toward the house Meg instinctively pushed Maddie behind her.

He came at them. Meg flinched. He shoved her. Hard. She spun and fell to the Persian rug on the floor. Something snapped. Her ankle. The pain was so bad that she lost consciousness for a second or two. When she came to, he was standing at her feet while Maddie grabbed her arms from the other end. She pulled Meg's body away from him and toward the stairs.

He nodded at them both, and then went to the door. He slammed it shut and turned the deadbolt, locking them all inside.

THIRTY-FOUR
Room 69

Maddie pulled Meg by the arms, but with each tug Meg cried out in pain. Her ankle hurt too much. "Stop, Maddie!" she called. Maddie let go and crouched by her side.

Fenstad pulled a bottle from his pocket and opened it. He shook a few pills into his mouth and chewed while Meg watched. "Okay," he muttered, "okay." Then he left the room. Meg looked up at Maddie. "Run!" she whispered, but Maddie shook her head. "No, Mom. I won't leave you."

When he came back he was holding a gallon of Grey Goose vodka. He poured its contents on his hands and face, and then doused her and Maddie with the rest. "Daddy! Stop it," Maddie cried, but Meg didn't think he heard. Sweet Jesus, was he going to set them on fire?

He put down the bottle and pulled a chunk of slate from his pocket. He got closer and Meg thought: *This is it.*

"Go to your room, Madeline. Now!" Meg shouted.

Maddie threw herself across Meg's body. "No, Daddy. No! He's dead. It's over. No!"

The slate dangled from Fenstad's hand. His face was red with blood, and his green eyes blinked. "*Daddy!*" Maddie shouted.

He lifted the slate and looked at Maddie for a long while. Throbbing pain coursed through the place where Maddie had lived for nine months: her womb. *Run, Maddie. Run!* she thought, but she didn't want to say it. Didn't want to provoke him with the sound of her voice.

Something changed, and his posture relaxed a little. He dropped the slate. "Alcohol probably kills it," he said. Then he headed back into the kitchen.

Maddie was crying softly, and Meg petted her curly hair. "Quick. Help me up the stairs, honey," she whispered.

Maddie nodded. Together, step by arduous step, they reached the second story. Meg didn't just lean. Maddie practically carried her. "My room," Meg said. She wasn't sure why she was doing this, but it seemed as good an idea as any. "The first aid kit in the bathroom," she said. "Second drawer, behind the towels." Maddie started walking. Meg opened the bag she'd packed and emptied the contents of the side pocket. Earrings. A few necklaces. Diamond studs. Good thing they'd never bothered with a safety deposit box: It added up to about twenty grand. She swiped all of it into one of Fenstad's striped tube socks. When Maddie came back with the kit she said, "Come here."

Maddie complied. "Are you hurt bad?" she asked.

"It's nothing," Meg said, even though she got the feeling that the bone in her foot was no longer connected to the rest of her leg. It felt heavy, like dead weight. She tugged the neck of Maddie's T-shirt, and stuffed the jewelry-filled sock down her cotton bra. "No!" Maddie whispered. Her eyes filled with tears and she started shaking, while downstairs Fenstad began pounding the walls. *What the hell was he doing?*

"Yes," Meg said. "Tomorrow morning I want you to—oh shit, you can't drive. Okay. I want you to ride your bike to the highway, and hitch a ride to your grandparents' house in Wilton. I'll stay with your father, and when he can travel we'll join you."

Maddie squared her shoulders like the sock Meg had put there was plague. "I don't want this!" she whispered. "It's *yours*!"

Meg held her by the shoulders. "You might need it to sell. Don't worry. I don't need any of it. Anybody stupid enough to trade a pearl for food or gas can have it."

Maddie was sobbing. The sobs were quiet, and hopeless. Meg lifted her chin and got very close. "You have one job, do you hear me? Say you hear me."

Maddie nodded.

"Say it."

"I hear you," Maddie whispered.

"You have to stay alive, no matter what. That's your job. No matter what happens to me or Daddy, that's your job. You have to stay alive. Do you hear me?"

Maddie nodded.

"Say it," Meg said.

Maddie hitched her breath. "Mom," she begged.

"Say it," Meg said.

"I have to stay alive."

Meg kissed her forehead. "Good girl. Now make sure you've got everything you need. Don't pack too much. A good coat and spare walking shoes. And don't talk to strangers. I know how you like doing that. Even if they look nice, don't trust them. And if they try to have sex with you, don't be afraid to hit below the belt. That's why they've got those things, so we at least have a fighting chance." Maddie didn't move.

"Go on," Meg said. "Now."

Maddie bent down and pressed her forehead into Meg's chest.

"Don't be scared," Meg crooned. She tried not to

think about smiling Maddie all alone on a dark road full
of bones. She tried not to think about the sweet, shel-
tered girl who'd never been anywhere on her own except
once, on a summer camp trip to Paris with a bunch of
rich kids. "You'll be fine. I know it. Now go pack."

Maddie sniffled. She looked like she wanted to say
something, but when she saw Meg's exhaustion, she
nodded. "Okay . . . I love you, Mom."

Meg kissed the corner of her eye. "I know. Me, too.
Now hurry."

As soon as she was gone, Meg leaned on the bed.
Fenstad had rebroken her ankle. She was sweating
again. The back of her shirt was wet. She closed her
eyes and tried not to cry. She wasn't sad. She hurt too
much to be sad.

That's when she heard the scream. It was Maddie,
and the sound was bloodcurdling. She hopped as fast as
she could. Each slam on her good leg shook the bum
one, and sent sparks through her skin like biting live
cable wire. From the bureau she swiped a pair of sew-
ing scissors, in case she needed to use them against an
intruder or her husband.

What she saw when she got down the hall confused
her. Maddie was struggling on her bed, and Fenstad
was holding her down. Then Meg got closer. Maddie's
wrists were tied with pillowcases to either bedpost, and
Meg suddenly became so angry that she saw red.

"For her own good," Fenstad said.

Meg was shaking with fury, but she tried to sound
calm. "Fenstad . . ." she said. "You just tied your
eighteen-year-old daughter to a bed."

His face was a blank. Worse than the coldest fish expression she'd ever seen. He almost looked dead. "If we
stay here we'll be safe . . . And I know her. She wants to
run off and see her boyfriend."

He pushed past her and started down the hall. She squeezed Maddie's foot to reassure her, and then followed him to their bedroom. "You're out of your goddamn mind," she said.

He grabbed her waist. She didn't struggle. Her ankle hurt too much for that. She let the scissors drop. Even now, she wasn't ready to use them. He pushed her onto the bed. Her head hit the frame with a thunk. By rights, she should have fainted from the pain. But she was too pissed off. He pinned her to the mattress, and tied each hand to the bedpost using sections of their finely woven Egyptian cotton sheets. Then he secured the knots so tightly that she couldn't make a fist.

"Fenstad. Stop this. We have to get out of here," she said.

Fenstad didn't answer. He checked the sturdiness of the knots, and then tied her right ankle to the bedpost, too. He didn't tie her broken one, at least. She knew she should be scared, but mostly she was mad. "You jackass! Let me go!"

He cocked his head. The blood on his face and in his hair was beginning to dry. "Room 69. I'll bet you thought that was funny," he said, and her heart fluttered. "You know how I found out, don't you? I followed you. I watched." He closed the door when he left, and everything went dark.

THIRTY-FIVE
The Cellar

The night was howling. Danny drove down the road from Bedford, toward Corpus Christi. It was too late to leave town, and he needed to find shelter. He could hear screaming, and it wasn't the wind. The rain was so thick that he could hardly see ten feet in front of his mom's car, and he made sure all the doors were locked.

He pulled in front of his house. They would try to catch him, now that he had found their lair. They were coming, he could feel them. Their smell, once you know it, was unforgettable. He was getting snot-nosed with all his crying, but he didn't try to stop. There wasn't anyone alive left to see.

But then the headlights of his car shone on Fenstad Wintrob across the street. He was drilling a wooden kitchen table over the bay window in front of his house. Danny cried out in delight. No need for civility—he pulled the car onto the Wintrob lawn and cracked open the window. Driving rain flew in.

"Hey," he shouted. A witness! Someone else left alive.

Fenstad turned. His face was bloody, which Danny didn't find nearly so alarming as he might have just a week ago. He was holding several long nails between his teeth, and he pointed the drill toward the sky like an unaimed gun. He didn't seem at all startled, or even surprised. Lightning lit up the yard for a moment, and then was gone. Animal bones were everywhere. More than on any other lawn in town. But then maybe it was because he knew Lois Larkin, and she'd marked him for something, the same way, he suddenly realized, that James had marked the Walkers.

"You're okay?" Danny asked.

Fenstad shrugged. He wasn't wearing shoes. Danny looked more closely, but the guy wasn't sick, and he wasn't changed. Danny could still see the whites of his eyes. "I'm leaving town tomorrow," he called through the rain, hoping that Fenstad would spit out the nails and say, "Great. Me, too. Come on over. Hang out with my nut-job daughter and eat some homemade lasagna. I'll adopt you. We'll all leave together in the morning."

He didn't say that. He came to the car's open window, and smiled, like today was an ordinary day. "No thanks, kiddo," he said. "My wife and kid are sick, so looks like I've got to play doctor. Maybe next time!"

Danny looked at him for a long while until he was certain. Fenstad Wintrob was insane.

He didn't bother saying good-bye. He pulled the car in reverse and parked in his garage. He didn't want to, but no other place was safe. He went inside. He locked the door behind him, even though the house was a tomb.

He got the rest of the bullets and loaded his gun, then locked himself in his basement again, and guarded the door. There, he waited for the inevitable. He waited for the infected to come.

THIRTY-SIX
Quickening

The thing formerly known as Lois Larkin stood over the hole in the floor of the Dew Drop Inn, where Ronnie and·Noreen's remains lay. She'd taught the virus something new tonight.

Civilizations had collapsed in its presence; New Guinea, Sumer, Akkad, where the last men left had flailed themselves in hunger, and in the end eaten the bodies of the dead, and drunk water from the ocean. But it did not understand that with the death of man, her kind died, too. They had to maintain a balance. They would build strongholds on the coasts, and leave the middle of the country for the humans, like animals fatted in cages. Those who trespassed or ate more than their share would be hanged in the sunlight, and left to waste away.

Towns across the country were falling. She could see them in her mind: New York, Boston, Austin, Sioux City, Salt Lake. She could see every thought, every final gasp, every hysterical giggle, every sunset from ten thousand eyes. Soon she would do the thing she'd dreamed about her whole life. She would leave Corpus Christi and march west. But first she would hunt down the people of this town until none were left. Until anyone who'd ever known the old Lois Larkin was dead, and even her memory ceased to exist.

Lois pointed at Ronnie and Noreen's bones at the bottom of the hole. "Them, too," she said, and the infected complied, until even their scalps were gone.

THIRTY-SEVEN
Mad-e-line!

Maddie lay in the bed Sunday night. It had been hours since her dad had put her here. At first she'd cried her eyes out, and then she'd just been scared, and now, finally, she was pissed. Bound to a bed! How was she supposed to defend herself, or her mom, or find Enrique, if she was tied to this stupid bed? Where had he gotten this idea, the porn channel?

Most people, even her brother, David, would probably be surprised by what her dad had done, but she wasn't. She'd always known her dad was kind of nuts.

She didn't yell, like she heard her mom doing (*Fenstad! Come back! Let me explain! What are you DOING down there?*), while down the stairs, he pounded nails into the walls. Yelling only made him nervous, and when he got nervous he got weird. Funny. After all these years, her mom had never figured that out.

Maddie struggled. Maybe she'd break her thumbs like Houdini. She pulled hard on her left side, and tried to force her hand through the knot, but it was tight. Even if she managed to break her bones she still wouldn't be able to wriggle her way out.

That was when she saw his face in her window. Her dad had hammered shut every entrance on the ground floor, but he'd forgotten that if somebody wanted to get in, he could climb the porch and break into the bedrooms. It was dark, and all she saw were his changed black eyes. He swept his hand down the glass pane like he was trying to touch her. Her eyes welled up with tears. Enrique. He looked nothing like the boy she loved, because when he saw her, he didn't smile.

"Mad-e-line," he whispered, like it was a game they were playing, and he didn't want her parents to hear. Romeo and Juliet.

He lifted the glass and climbed in. She wanted to scream, but she was afraid for him. She'd seen what her dad had done to Graham Nero. Or worse, if she yelled, her dad would get nervous. He'd hurt the wrong person, like her mom.

"Mad-e-line, I missed you," he said, but she didn't think that was true. His brows were knotted like he was angry. He walked like a spider, graceful but ugly.

She tried to roll from the bed, but she was trapped. "Go away," she said. "You're not the same." It was true; just looking at him, she knew that the boy she loved was gone. This thing that had taken his place was an insult to his memory, and she hated it.

"Shhh," he said. His black eyes shone, and she saw herself inside them. Tears were falling down her cheeks like she was drowning in them, even though out here, her eyes were dry. She'd been about to scream, but now her voice was gone. It was trapped in the dark, wet place. It was trapped in his eyes.

"Mad-e-line," he said. She could feel him in her mind. He smiled like he loved her, but she knew it wasn't true. Maybe it never had been. That made her sad, too.

She tried to look away, but she couldn't. From his eyes, there was no way out. She saw him in her bed, holding her tight. That was all he wanted. He wanted to hold her one last time. She could let him have that. She wanted it, too.

"Stop," she whispered. "Puh-please." But her voice was a croak. She could hardly hear it.

"Now I'll never leave you," Enrique told her as he put his pale hand over her mouth, so she could not scream. His fingers were cold, and he pushed so hard that her teeth cut the insides of her lips. "We can be together. You can live inside me and I'll carry you with me."

Behind him was Rockwell's framed *Freedom from Fear*. Two parents were kissing two children good-night. She was drowning now, and she wanted a good-night kiss, too. She wanted it from Enrique.

He'd come all this way to find her, even though he was changed. He'd done it because he couldn't let her go. He loved her too much. She wanted to believe that. He was telling her that with his mind, but she knew the truth. Now that he was infected, he didn't love anybody, and this thing that bound them to each other had nothing to do with affection. It was instinct, and hunger.

From the window, another body slithered inside and down to the floor. It was his little brother Thomas, and the virus didn't fit inside him quite right. He moved like a worm.

Her reflection sank inside Enrique's eyes. Instead of endless worry, there was calm. Instead of hurt, there was still water. Instead of love, there was hunger. It was a beautiful thing.

He licked her lips with his cold tongue, and nothing mattered. She didn't care about her parents, who without her, she knew, would tear each other apart. She didn't care about David, whose first boyfriend at school

had been so mean, but he hadn't been able to tell anyone except Maddie, because he'd been ashamed that the
people he loved weren't women. She didn't care about
the end of the world. She didn't even care about herself.

Enrique placed his hand on her breast. It was cold,
and he didn't warm it for her. It seemed wrong that this
rank-smelling thing was wearing Enrique's face, though
she couldn't remember, now, why. "Mad-e-line," he
said, "there's a balance. There are too many of us, and
for now we can't make any more."

What he said sank deep. She was drowning in it. He
was going to kill her. He didn't even like her enough to
change her. Suddenly she was mad. Her image fought in
his eyes and reached the surface again. She pulled her
leg back and kicked him as hard as she could.

"Dad!" she screamed. "Help!"

Enrique reeled. "You spoiled bitch," he said. Then he
bent down, and for a short instant she thought he would
kiss her. But his teeth pierced her shoulder. It felt awful,
and cold. Something black and ancient as tar crawled
inside the wound. It threaded through her blood. She
felt it move into her chest, her heart, her lungs, her liver.
She felt it in her legs, her arms, her ears, until all that
was left of Maddie Wintrob was a tiny spark, looking
out behind the prison of the monster's eyes.

Enrique smacked his lips, and for the first time since
she'd known him, he looked satisfied.

Her bedroom door swung open. Her father charged
while the warmth ran out of her. Thomas went down
first. He was crawling on the floor, and Fenstad hit him
in the back of the head with one swift stroke. Then he
held up the bloody hammer and went after Enrique. She
smiled, because a tiny piece of her was screaming. It was

trapped inside this lump of hungry flesh, and that was funny, too.

Her father chased Enrique to the window. Then he was gone. She could read his mind now, and she knew that he'd be back. He'd marked his territory. Now that his brother had died, she could live.

Her father pressed hard against her sticky shoulder. The sheets were pink. He poured something that fizzed all over her wounds, and filled the hole in her arm with gauze and tape. Pushed so tightly that the blood stopped flowing. She wanted him to stop pushing, so that the blood would flow from her body. She wanted the virus out, too.

She imagined jumping out her bedroom window. By some miracle she'd fly, or else fall. She tried to rise, but her father held her down. "Dead," she said, and by that she meant, "The person I am is dying."

"He will be," her father answered. "I won't let him hurt you."

The things she cared about slipped away. The people she loved, the world she inhabited, the possibilities to come. They slipped through her fingers and into a deep lake. They took Maddie Wintrob with them, and she drowned. She watched from the prison of her eyes, while a mean thing inside her yawned, and blinked, and finally surfaced.

She smiled at him, this man who'd tied her to a bed. "Honey?" he asked. "Sweetheart, answer me. Can you hear me?" He was holding her in his arms now, and she could feel his heart beat.

"I'm hungry," she said.

Her shoulder had stopped bleeding, and he was holding the bandage in place against the wound. It felt good, the healing. She was doing it so fast. "You might need a blood transfusion," he said. "I'll give you my blood, and we'll see if that helps."

She looked out from the cage and was very sad, but the rest of her didn't know why. "Feel that, Fennie?" she asked. "Is it a lump, or are you just happy to see me?"

THIRTY-EIGHT

My Heart Stopped Beating,
But Still I Go On

Fenstad sawed the nightstand's legs from its base and hammered it against Maddie's window.

"You wouldn't hurt your dear, sick mother, would you, Fennie boy?" she asked.

He grabbed the wad of cotton on the floor, which happened to be a pair of Maddie's white underpants, and shoved it in her mouth. He secured it there by gagging her with a red bandana. Blissfully, she became quiet.

He pulled up a chair and sat. The hammer's face was smooth, and he slapped it against his palm while Maddie watched. His daughter was infected. So was his wife. He was the last man on earth.

Sure, the rest said they were uninfected, but he knew better. Take Danny Walker. As soon as the sun had set tonight, the boy had come speeding onto his nice green lawn, feigning the wide-eyed grief of a lost puppy. Fenstad had almost fallen for it. He'd felt bad for the kid, younger than Maddie and all by his lonesome. For a second he'd imagined that the boy was the best luck he could have hoped for, because together the rest of them could carry Meg through the blocked roads they might find, and escape. But then he'd remembered: No brood of Miller Walker's could possibly cry real tears.

Fenstad had smiled, while in his hands he'd spun the power drill to the ready. The boy was infected. He wanted to tear down the Victorian, and Fenstad was the last man holding it erect. He lifted the drill just as the kid pulled his car into reverse.

On the floor, Thomas Vargas's blood smelled rank. Fenstad scratched his scalp because it itched, just looking at this mess.

He popped an OxyContin and crushed it between his teeth. At this rate he'd run out by sunrise, and have to hit the hospital again. He was vaguely aware of the fact that OxyContin affects the central nervous system, and because of that he wasn't thinking clearly. If he'd been sober, he would have remembered to block these windows. But he felt okay. Under the circumstances, he felt just fine.

On the bed, Maddie writhed. The dead boy on the floor was leaking blood like a squashed bug. What if he wasn't dead? What if, right now, his bleeding brain was healing and when Fenstad turned his back, the boy rose up and attacked his daughter?

"Fenstad?" Meg called from down the hall. She'd given up screaming, and now sounded meek.

He wished he had a cup of coffee, but he didn't know how to make it. His gums were numb anyway. So was his tongue, and his throat. He started to hum "God Only Knows," because it was the only song right now that he remembered.

"What's happening? Maddie, are you okay? Fenstad, please answer me," Meg called. Like a baby, she was hollering herself hoarse, and would soon fall asleep. That was best, he decided. He didn't want to worry her with the news that Maddie had been bitten. She always carried too much on her shoulders, and then, when she couldn't support it, all of them fell.

Besides, he knew she'd betrayed him. When she'd suggested abandoning Corpus Christi, she must have known what he'd do. He'd never sleep under Sara Wintrob's roof. A plot, probably, to elope with Graham Nero. Why else had the man arrived on their doorstep tonight, if not to take her away?

But even now, he would stand by her. Even now, he would protect her. She'd made a mistake. That was understandable. He'd made some mistakes, too.

Fenstad peeked out the three-inch aperture in the window where no wood had been hammered. His breath caught in his throat. Pale bodies raced down the block. They leaped gracefully, like gazelles. They were beautiful. He wished he could be one of them. Instead he was his women's beast of burden. Maybe David had had the right idea all along.

Fenstad looked from the Vargas boy's body, to his daughter, to the window. He'd killed a kid tonight. But that was understandable. Sometimes extraordinary things happened to ordinary men.

Fennie, I'm so lonely. You left me all alone, someone whispered in his ear. He looked out the hole in the window, and instead of racing infected, he saw Sara Wintrob's reflection. She was wearing a white cotton nightgown. The first three buttons were undone. He could see her navel, which was deep. He looked down at his shoes, and blushed. He'd killed a boy tonight. Murdered him. His eyes were leaking all over the floor.

Let me in, Fenstad, the voice said. *It's so cold out here.*

He kicked the boy's body. Hard. Again. And again. Not his daughter—he'd never do that. No, he kicked the boy on the floor. It sounded wet. And then, after a moment, it moved. He looked at it closely, and saw that it was still breathing. The gash on its skull was beginning to heal.

He looked at the hammer. It was a crude instrument, but it was also all he had. He couldn't leave this room. He couldn't leave his daughter alone. Then he remembered the saw in the corner that he'd used to break apart the night stand. He worked fast, just in case the boy still had feelings. Just in case this hurt. His instrument was a savage thing. He sawed and sawed. What had been one became two, and the bedroom floor was covered in gore. Thomas Vargas's severed head looked up at him, unblinking.

His eyes might have been leaking. He didn't know. This was excessive. He wished he had a mop. What a mess he'd made! But he didn't know where Meg kept the mops, and he couldn't leave Maddie alone.

Fennie, my heart stopped beating, but still I go on, someone whispered. It sounded like Sara Wintrob, but he knew it was Thomas Vargas. Who else could it be?

He pulled a white sheet from the bed and covered the boy's parts with it. His hand peeked out from underneath.

Fennie, it's lonely out here. Open the door downstairs. We're so hungry, and you know this is the way it has to end. If you love something, set it free.

He thought maybe he was back home in Wilton, Connecticut. The carpet was thick with blood. His mouth was numb, lips to gums to tongue. He thought maybe he was dead, only he was the last to know.

A chainsaw would have worked better. The saw was crude. After a while the hand came off, but then a bare foot poked out from the sheets, so he sawed that off too.

And then something flopped, like maybe it was still alive, so he separated the legs from the trunk, just like in good old medical school. By the time he was done the saw's teeth were dull.

There wasn't enough sheeting to cover all the gore, so he used Maddie's sweaters. She wasn't moaning anymore. Her eyes were cold. She watched. He wished she hadn't just witnessed this. He wished he could have protected her from such a terrible thing. But it was good in a way, too. He was so tired of the way she clung to his every word. It's not easy being a hero when your feet are made of clay. At least now she knew: He was a messy boy.

His clothes were sticky. They were dirty, just like they used to be in Wilton, when his mother was mad at him, and she let his hamper fill until it overflowed, but he wasn't permitted to use the washing machine, so if he'd wanted to wear something clean he'd had to rinse it out in his bathroom sink.

He tucked the sheet around the gore like a bedtime story. He hoped his mother wouldn't find out about the mess. She lay in the bed. She'd seen what he'd done, even though he'd wanted to protect her. He couldn't stop crying now, because he wasn't imagining it. He'd never imagined it. All these years, the carpet really had been thick with blood.

Feel that, Fennie?

He leaned over the bed. The woman was watching him. He picked up the saw. He wanted to shut her up. He wanted her to stop looking. But then he saw her purple hair. Did Sara have purple hair?

A trick!

He charged down the hall. Threw open the door. Her eyes were wide, and guilty. The sneak. She'd do anything to tear down his house. "Fen," she started, but she didn't have time to finish. He pinched her nose and shoved a tube sock down her throat. "Stop your games," he said, and then slammed the door shut.

He went back to Maddie's room, and sat in his chair. He kept vigilant, and protected his women, as the last man on earth.

THIRTY-NINE
The Persistence of Silence

The sun was one of the few things that rose Monday morning in Corpus Christi. No cars patrolled. No televisions emitted a spectrum of color as Regis and Kelly traded insults. No toasters popped. No pans sizzled. No eggs fried. No children coughed, cried, laughed, or even screamed.

The infected slept. Graham Nero's daughter, Isabelle, would never learn to walk. During the night she'd crawled from her crib, and now lay next to her mother, where she'd found sustenance. They slept in their homes, they slept underground, they slept on gurneys in the hospital near the doctors upon whom they'd fed, they slept in their cars that clogged the highway.

The thing formerly known as Lois Larkin lay in her childhood bed, where snooping eyes would never find her. While the others rested, she began her search. She scanned the minds of the slumbering infected. It was easier to read them when they slept. Their thoughts were not guarded. She accounted for the sick, the devoured, and the missing. She found their friends, their newspaper boys, their carpool buddies, until finally she had a list of those who remained, and remembered the name Lois Larkin.

On Micmac Street, car alarms resounded for hours, until batteries drained, and silence persisted like a new form of entropy. There were seven healthy people left in Corpus Christi, and none of them dared make a sound.

FORTY
Cyanide

As soon as daylight filtered across her forehead, Lila Schiffer pulled her son's bike from the garage and headed for the hospital. She didn't bother with a car. They slept during the day, but who knew for sure? She didn't want to attract their attention. The infected had gotten into her house last night, but she'd hidden in her basement, and they hadn't looked for her there. It was then that she'd noticed that her wrist was beginning to pus. Blue-red streaks spun out from the wound like bicycle spokes. Dr. Wintrob's antibiotic ointment wasn't working; she needed penicillin. It had dawned on her then that there wasn't anyone nearby to take care of her. She had to take care of herself.

The town was empty, but she guessed that a few people were still alive, only hiding. If the infection had started here, then she needed to get out. An island off the coast was probably her best bet, but she didn't have a boat.

Alice, Aran, a little voice said. Their names were a mantra repeated over and over in her mind. She couldn't picture their faces, or her memories of them over the last fifteen years. She wasn't thinking about their first steps or toothy grins. Just their names. The order of their loss was wrong. She should have gone first. Good mothers always find a way to die before their children, don't they? The tape was coming off the handle bars of Aran's bike, and its brakes squeaked. It shamed her that his bike had not been better cared for. It meant no one had taught him respect.

At the hospital there weren't any coughers left. The halls were empty. Here and there, she spied the slumped body of a goiter-necked corpse, or sleeping infected. They lay on the floors and in gurneys. She'd avoided the front entrance and come in through the emergency room. She hadn't wanted to see her children's remains. She hardly remembered doing what she'd done. Only that she'd had to do it, to let their spirits rest.

Growing up, her mother had made her work part-time and cook dinner twice a week. But in Corpus Christi, Aran Senior had explained, if you wanted your kids to be *Ivy League material*, you drove them to soccer practice, and piano lessons, and made sure their clothes were never wrinkled, or even frayed. You sent them to Europe in the summer, and let them explore their inner emotions. Instead of setting rules for them, you *negotiated*. It had sounded sensible until she woke up one morning and realized that she'd left the trailer park, only to become a rich man's cleaning lady.

The generator wasn't humming anymore, and except near windows, the hospital corridors were dark. She wandered, looking for the pharmacy, but she didn't see any signs. Suddenly she heard a bird whistle—but the birds were all dead, weren't they? She couldn't help herself, she broke into a smile. Here, of all places, a bird still lived. Its whistle got louder, and her smile faded. It wasn't a bird. The sound echoed, and she wondered if her children's spirits had returned. They would never forgive her, but that was fine. She would never forgive herself.

She peered into the darkness, and a figure walked toward her. The tune was familiar, an old Beach Boys song that she remembered hearing Dr. Wintrob hum. Was that he, down the hall? The figure was tall, and it walked on two legs. She ducked into the first doorway she could find. The office was a mess of broken glass and scattered papers. When she saw the Dali painting of melting watches on the floor she let out a breath of air like a sagging sail: Oh, no. She'd walked into his office.

Too late to turn around. She spun in a circle, headed for the closet—but there wasn't time! He was right outside the door. She squatted behind the leather couch. He walked inside. She cowered behind the armrest. She couldn't see his face, but it was daylight and he wasn't coughing, so he probably wasn't sick. Still, his clothes were covered in blood. Then again, so were hers. Her heart thumped in her chest, and she reminded herself that unlike many, it was at least still beating.

Aran! Alice! her mind screamed, because it would always scream those names, for the rest of her life.

As he reached into the desk drawer, she bumped her knee against the coffee table. He spun around, fast, and pulled something from his belt loop. A hammer. She held her breath. He looked under the broken glass coffee table and she almost shouted, "Don't swing!" But he didn't see her. He turned back around, opened a drawer from his desk, pulled out a set of jangling keys, and left the office. He was whistling the same tune, and now she remembered it: "Feel Flows." It had an eerie quality amid the silence, like a hospitalwide requiem.

She got up and started out of the office. He was headed for Admitting. She knew she should walk in the opposite direction. He'd gone mad—she could tell by the way he moved too carefully, like he hadn't figured

out that that the whole world was already broken. But
then again, he wasn't infected. He was a rich doctor,
too. He might have a boat. She followed him. The halls
were so dark that she slid her feet instead of lifting them
in order to keep from tripping over the soft objects
(*Aran! Alice!*) that lay on the floor.

Funny, the people who died from infection didn't get
eaten. The only bodies left were the ones with swollen
necks and bloody rashes. Maybe they didn't have a taste
for their own kind. He was standing near the window. It
was raining a little, so the light that came through the
windows looked wet. On the ground was Dr. Wintrob's
secretary, Val. Lila recognized her rubber band ponytail. She wasn't dead, just infected. Her chest was moving and her lips were red. Strange that she'd come here,
of all places, to sleep. Maybe it was where she felt most
safe. Or, like Lila, a small part of her had been looking
for Dr. Wintrob, hoping he'd tell her what to do, and
forgive her what she'd already done.

Aran! Alice! a voice inside her screamed, and she
wished she could reach inside herself and flip a switch,
because she was beginning to remember their faces.

Dr. Wintrob stopped whistling. He shoved Val's body
with his sneaker. Then he pressed his hammer against
Val's forehead. He tapped once, lightly. Flesh against
metal; it sounded like a slap. "Just kidding, Val. You
know I'd never hurt you," he said. "Guess Canada
wasn't such a good idea after all." Then he walked
ahead, still with a bounce in his step.

At Admitting, he used the key from his desk to open
the cabinet. Took out a few bottles of something, then
locked it shut again. It alarmed her that he'd done this,
instead of breaking the glass and taking what he needed.
It meant that unlike everyone else, he was still following the rules.

Dr. Wintrob turned and saw her. She stopped. The hall was dark, and it was just the two of them. She swallowed and thought about running, but he might have a boat. Better yet, he might hold her hand and tell her that she was having a bad dream. *Alice! Aran!* When she left them yesterday, she'd forgotten to close their eyes.

"I'm sorry," she said to Dr. Wintrob, because it was all she could think to say.

"How are you, Ms. Schiffer?" he asked. She was wearing a sweat suit, but suddenly it wasn't warm enough. She nodded at him, because she was too frightened to speak.

"Lovely to hear it." He pulled the hammer from his pocket again. A chunk of hairy scalp was embedded in its sharp end. "It's dark in here. You like the sun, do you?" he asked.

She nodded. He came closer, hammer in hand. He held it tightly in his fist, like he meant to do harm. "I came here for penicillin." She rolled up her sleeve and shoved her arm out, like evidence.

He tried to touch it with his free hand, but jammed inside his fingernails was dried blood. Without thinking about it, she drew back. He acknowledged the slight by cocking his head, but for now at least, he didn't strike her. "Lovely body on you, Ms. Schiffer."

"I know," she answered.

The two of them stood, while around them at least twenty corpses lay sprawled on the floor. Pieces of bones littered the hospital like dust. They littered her lawn, too. And Micmac Street. The infected were playing knick-knack paddy-wack.

"Do you want something?" Dr. Wintrob asked.

Normally she might have grinned at him and told

him he must have seen some awful things. *My, Dr. Wintrob, aren't you brave!* she would have said with a come-hither grin. Instead she motioned at the orderly slumped in his chair, and then at Val, and the rest of the infected. "You know most of these people, I guess," she said.

He stopped smiling. He ran his hands over his face, and when he finished, he looked more familiar. He went back to the cabinet, opened it, grabbed another couple of bottles, and gave them to her. She put them in her purse without looking at them. "Lock yourself up somewhere," he told her, "until this passes."

"It will pass?" she asked.

He shrugged and nodded at her purse. "One way or another." Then he popped a pill into his mouth. As he crunched on it, he moaned, like it tasted better than a Milky Way, and she realized that the guy was an addict.

He reached out like he was going to pat her shoulder, but then pulled back, and patted the hammer in his jacket pocket instead. "I'm sorry about your kids . . ."

It took her a moment. She didn't remember. *Aran! Alice!* And then she knew why her wrist was infected. Sawing Alice's head with that scalpel had reopened the wound.

His voice got gruff. "My kid is sick, too."

"Sorry," she said, even though she wasn't. She didn't care about his kid, or even him. She only cared about Aran and Alice, who were dead, weren't they? Yes, she'd murdered them.

Dr. Wintrob began walking. She watched as he left the building. She wanted to follow him, but he'd gone mad, so instead she walked in the opposite direction.

The air was still and rank. She followed the red tape

to the blue, and then to the yellow. She got to the front door, and then remembered: Alice and Aran were here, too. She forced herself to look. They weren't her children anymore. Just messy shells. She took some sheets and laid them across the mess. The sound of the sheets opening was like flapping wings, and she hoped it was their souls, set free.

Then she backed out of the hospital, and into the day.

She left Aran's bike and walked to Micmac Street. Store-front windows were broken, and wooden doors splintered wide. She walked inside them, and took what she needed: rubbing alcohol, Tic Tacs and shaving cream. A brass knocker shaped like a lion for the front door, and gold wrapping paper and bows, because it was always *some*one's birthday. A pretty necklace for Alice. She dropped them as she walked, like a trail of breadcrumbs, because her arms were so full.

She cried as she walked.

Aran! Alice! If it weren't for her, they'd still be alive. They'd be living with their father, who surely had gotten out by now. Who surely was on the island where they used to spend their summers, eating fresh blueberries and combing the beach for shells.

But if he loved them so much, why hadn't he come for them? Because he was dead, or worse: He'd abandoned them. So maybe he wasn't such a good father, either.

Her wrist was hurting so she opened her purse. She opened one of the bottles and swallowed a pill, then remembered to look at the label: penicillin. Then she took out the second bottle and gasped: cyanide.

It will pass?

One way or another.

She tossed the bottle on the ground and kicked it.

Then followed where it landed, and kicked it again. And again, until the plastic split open, and with her feet she crushed the pills into dust. It was only then that she realized that even though her children were gone, she wanted to live.

FORTY-ONE
Choke

Where did I go wrong?

Meg heard Fenstad's car pull out of the drive Monday morning. Maddie had been quiet for hours, which was a bad sign. She didn't want to think the worst. If Maddie was hurt, her intuition would tell her so. Problem was, her intuition *was* telling her something. She was afraid that Maddie was dead.

She'd been lying in the same position for hours. Her arms were numb, she couldn't wiggle her fingers, and long ago she'd given up fighting her way out of these bindings. The knots were impossibly tight. Still, something was wrong with Maddie. She could feel it. And there was the other thing she didn't want to think about. This might be her last chance to get away before Fenstad came home and killed them both.

He'd stuck a wad of something in her mouth before tying the gag, and though she hadn't seen it, she was fairly certain that it was one of his dirty tube socks. It tasted . . . *bad*. The cotton had expanded with her saliva and was now working its way down her throat. She was beginning to have trouble breathing. She'd lost feeling in her arms and couldn't move them, so she leaned forward, hoping the extra weight might eventually rip the sheets and set her free.

She thought about her dad on her wedding day, and the thing he'd said. He'd summoned her to the formal dining room, and even though it was a rainy day, he'd sat with the lights out, in the dark. He was supposed to be her official witness, but at the last minute he'd refused to drive her to the justice of the peace. The rest of her family, afraid to defy him, hadn't come, either.

They'll never accept you, he told her the day she'd announced her engagement. *They might be polite, but behind your back they'll call you the shiksa. I'll pay for your wedding, but only a proper one, in a church. Trust me, Meg. I love you more than anyone else. I know what's best. Break it off.*

But she hadn't trusted him. Her first act of rebellion against Frank Bonelli had been the only one. Wearing a smart white suit, she drove herself to the justice of the peace that day, and he never spoke to her again. Now, twenty years later, here she was tied to a bed, trying to decide whether she had the strength to attack her husband, and if so which weapon—a pair of fabric scissors or a blunt object—she should use.

Where did I go wrong? her father's memory asked, and she shrugged, and wondered that, too.

That's when she saw Albert Sanguine. He smashed the window with his fist and crawled inside. His gown was open to reveal skin so pale it was blue. He was a large man, and with each step he took toward her, he got bigger. By the time he got to her bedside, he was towering over her.

She tried to scream. Cotton slid further down her throat. She gasped but couldn't get any air. Suddenly she was choking on a dirty sock. He leaned over her, and she remembered the way he'd sent her flying into the plastic wall. She remembered the sound it had made, and the crack of her ankle. She would have struggled more if she hadn't been trying so hard to breathe.

His hands were gentle, but not deft. She didn't know what he'd done until she saw the necktie that had held the sock in place in his hand. Still, she wasn't quite sure. She was gasping, but nothing was happening, and the harder she tried to breathe, the farther the sock slid. There was a weight on her hips suddenly, but she didn't know why. Her eyes were closed, but even if they'd been open, she would have been too panicked to realize that he was sitting on her to hold her still.

He squeezed her jaw until it opened. Then his hand was in her mouth. She tried to bite him. She couldn't breathe! He held her chin with one hand, and with the other stuck his meaty fingers down her throat. She tasted salt. Sweat. She dry-heaved, and out came something long and wet. Cold air burned her throat. She gasped, and this time was greeted by air. It rushed her lungs and filled them.

Albert dropped the sock in front of her so she could see it. Her saliva over the long night had expanded it into a foot-long snake.

"Stop fighting!" he hissed. Then he coughed a full, watery cough, and began untying the knot at her left wrist. His fingers worked slowly. He was different now. His Tourette's was gone, and his eyes were black. He was infected, clearly. But it was daytime. Why wasn't he sensitive to light like the rest of them?

"They're sleeping, but she knows I'm here. She's watching through my eyes. I can feel it," he said. He turned his head and coughed. A ream of phlegm splatted against her sheet.

"She's after the survivors. She'll come for you tonight."

Meg's right wrist came loose. Numb, it fell from the bedpost. She tried to pick it up and place it in her lap, but she couldn't even rotate her shoulder. Her hand was purple and swollen, like something that has been under water for days.

Like a gentleman, he gestured at her other wrist. She nodded her permission, and he began loosening the knot. He smelled like the others, like rot. "What are you?" she asked. Her voice was hoarse.

He didn't answer for a second, and stopped work on her wrist. She wondered if she'd made a mistake. If, like Fenstad, she'd said the wrong word and flicked a switch inside him, and now he would pounce. She flinched, in expectation. It occurred to her that among her laundry list of problems, she was officially a battered woman.

"When I was little I heard it in the woods," he said. "My brain, the way it works, and the way the virus works, they match. More than Lois, or anyone else. So it called to me. I could hear it, even though nobody else could. It got stronger when the sulfur fed it after the mill fire. It wanted me to dig it up but I wouldn't. But then a little boy found it, and brought it back."

He looked at her, and she nodded. Her throat was too raw to speak.

"I drank it away. I filled the spaces in my mind that it wanted to live with bread pudding so it couldn't have me, not completely. It healed me," he said, pointing at his wound, which was open, but not bleeding, "but only a little. I drink too much to let it change me. I'm always hungry. It waits for me to get tired of fighting." He smiled at her like the sweet Albert she used to know. "It's strongest inside Lois Larkin now. She's using it to hurt everyone, because she's so angry. I help her, even though I don't want to. I can't get free."

Meg's wrist finally dropped. He picked it up and began to rub her forearm between his massive hands. She couldn't feel it, only saw him do it. "I never eat the kills. Only rats," he said. She nodded, like this was a huge distinction, and maybe it was.

"Are there others like you? Partially immune?" she asked. The feeling slowly returned to her hands. At first it was pins and needles, and then burning pain, and then, finally, she could wiggle her fingers. She smiled. Thank God for small favors.

He shook his head. "Maybe. But who would want to be? My mind and my body, they live together, and they hate each other."

"Oh, Albert . . ." she said. She wanted to tell him she was sorry for him, but she didn't know where to start. He'd been dealt a far worse hand than she had ever imagined, and yet he'd managed. It gave her hope that her family might manage, too.

He seemed to understand, and he nodded. "You have to leave town before dark. I came here to tell you that."

Meg tried to lift her arms, but they were still too weak, so she sat back in the bed, and waited for her strength to return. "Why are you doing this?"

He smiled, like the answer was obvious. "Because you were nice to me."

"Thank . . ." she started, and then stopped, because she didn't want to cry in front of him, and she knew that if she thanked him she would weep. "What will happen when she finds out you came here?"

He smiled bitterly, and she caught a glimpse of the man he could have been. "She'll kill me. But I want that."

"You'll come with us. We'll leave together."

Albert shook his head. "I have to go now, Ms. Wintrob," he said. Then his voice got husky. "The hunger is never quiet. If I stay I'll hurt you."

She knew it didn't make sense, but she felt ashamed suddenly, that there was something so hard inside her, that from the men in her life she inspired violence.

He spread his bloody arms, and his gown opened farther. Perhaps he did not remember that he was naked underneath. "Get out. Go far away. It'll make my life worth something, if you get out," he said, and even as he spoke she could see a mean thing inside him. His upper lip was curled, and his black eyes showed her reflection, the way she imagined a spider might look, when it gets close to its prey.

"Yes," she promised. How could she not?

He backed out of the room and gave her one final nod. The porch creaked as he descended. She understood then, what it might feel like, to straddle the mouth of hell.

FORTY-TWO
Escape

The inevitable didn't happen. The infected didn't come. As soon as the sun rose, Danny Walker packed a bag. Later he would remember packing, and wish he'd chosen better shoes or a warm coat. But instead he stacked chewing tobacco and a pile of socks into a red duffel bag. He didn't bring any photos, or food, but he wanted some kind of memory of them, so he pulled the to-do list off the refrigerator and crinkled it into his back pocket. On it was written, "Buy ice cream."

He got into Felice's car. His car, now. A quarter tank left of gas. It might carry him as far as Portland. He turned the engine and searched for a radio station. Not even the emergency broadcast system was beeping. The entire spectrum was dead air.

He leaned against the wheel and took as deep a breath as he knew how. Yes, okay. Maybe they were all dead. Maybe the whole world was gone, and he was the last kid left, but he still had to leave this place. He still had to try. He just wished someone was with him. He wished he wasn't alone, and that in the backseat of the car, Felice, Miller, and James weren't watching him with dead eyes.

He pulled from the driveway. Across the street he saw

movement behind the curtains. Alive! Someone was still alive! Screaming Maddie Wintrob. He'd kiss her feet if she got in this car with him. But then his stomach sank. He didn't want to ring Dr. Wintrob's bell. The guy had gone nuts. Besides, he'd said that his wife and daughter were infected, and that part might have been true.

Danny put the car in drive and started toward Bedford, where he would enter I-95 at a place that he hoped wasn't guarded. His windows were rolled up, so he didn't hear Meg Wintrob's hoarse voice shouting, "Stop!"

FORTY-THREE
Hunger Pangs

"Stop!" Meg shouted out her bedroom window, but Danny Walker's dust red Mercedes chugged to the corner, and then up the hill. She leaned against the sill, and even though she knew he couldn't hear, she kept shouting. "Come back! Please! Come back!"

She hadn't eaten in a long while. She was weak, and so hungry that her stomach had stopped growling long ago. Her hands were better, but the deep skin ached, and the outer layers of her wrists were still numb. She was balanced on one leg while she stood at the window, because the other one couldn't bear any weight.

She tried to walk to the hall, but her leg hurt too much, so she got down on her knees. As she headed for Maddie's room, she came up with a half-baked idea, and decided it would have to do. She would untie Maddie before Fenstad got home, and hide her in the Escalade. Then she'd slug Fenstad over the back of the head, tie him up, and take him with them out of town.

She tried not to disturb her ankle, and instead put her weight on her hips, which made her bursitis flare. If she and her husband survived this, would they laugh?

Remember that time you had to crawl to your daughter's rescue? Remember that time that stinky sock in your throat almost killed you? Remember when you found out everything you'd ever believed about your marriage was a lie? Wasn't that funny?

One leg after the other. She crawled. Just a few more feet. Soon she'd be with Maddie. Maddie would be her legs, and together they'd build a splint. Maddie would help her fix dinner, so this pain in her stomach would go away.

She reached up and turned the knob. The smell of infection was overwhelming. She let out a shriek of relief when she saw Maddie sleeping like a cherub in her bed, and the body draped in a bloodstained sheet and pile of wool sweaters on the floor. There'd been a scuffle here last night. Fenstad, God bless him, had fought something off.

The light shone across Maddie's pale face. Her snores were loud, and wet with fluid. Meg didn't say anything for a long time. Didn't touch Maddie's cheek. She didn't want to know for sure. Instead she looked at her sleeping, purple-haired angel. She imagined climbing into the bed with her, and holding her. Curing her by force of will and strength of love.

"Maddie?" she whispered.

Maddie opened her pretty green eyes. Her mouth was gagged with a red bandana. Meg hoisted herself up to the bed. Maddie didn't lift her head or move her legs to help her sit. Instead she watched, and because of that, Meg knew for sure. But still, she hoped.

She untied the gag. It was double knotted, and nearly covered not just her mouth, but her nose. She cursed Fenstad for that. Yes, he was allowed a breakdown, but accidentally suffocating his wife and daughter was just plain stupid. Wedged in her mouth was a pair of wet white underpants. Clean, at least. Maddie nodded and she waited. She was too frightened to speak.

A large strip of gauze covered Maddie's shoulder. The skin along its edges looked burned, as if Fenstad had tried to cauterize it. At first she was furious, but then she understood; he'd been trying to burn out the infection. Maddie was infected.

Meg's eyes filled with tears. She felt Maddie's forehead. She wanted this to be a temperature. A fever that would break. "Who did this to you?" she asked.

"Can't you guess?" Maddie smiled.

"Enrique," Meg moaned.

"He'll be back for me, Mom. They'll all be back. And then we'll leave here. They're taking me with them. Can't you feel them?"

Meg touched Maddie's foot, ten little toes all perfectly formed, and Maddie grinned.

"Where is he?" Meg asked. She was crying, and Maddie seemed to be enjoying that.

"Everywhere. We live everywhere. I'm so hungry, Mom. You wouldn't believe how hungry."

"Do they live in the woods, mostly?" she asked. She and Fenstad would go into the woods before it got dark. They'd set the whole place on fire. They'd find every one of the infected, and cut them to pieces to keep Maddie safe.

"Some," Maddie said. "But they also sleep where they lived. They like their old beds." Then she cocked her head. A flicker of comprehension passed over her brow. Underneath it all, Maddie was a practical girl. "Dad!" she screamed. "*Daddy she's loose!*"

"He's not here," Meg said.

Maddie grinned, but the grin was frightened and Meg

understood that she'd hit a nerve. They were still vulnerable. If she got to Enrique, or even Lois, before dark, it might change the course of the infection.

"I know what you did in room 69, you whore," Maddie whispered.

Meg tried to get up, but her ankle hurt bad, and she didn't want Maddie to see her crawling on her hands and knees. "Stop it," she said.

"You went wrong the day you were born!" Maddie shouted. Meg tried to hobble off the bed. She fell with a thump, and began to crawl, while behind her, Maddie hissed, "You married a psycho, and you pretended not to notice because you like your pretty house."

Meg kept crawling. She was crying now. "Shh, shh," she said as she moved, one knee after the next, and she wasn't sure whether she was speaking to her child or her own frayed nerves. "Hush," she said. "Please. Oh, please hush."

Down the stairs, the front door slammed shut. Fenstad was home. She tried to crawl faster, but she didn't make it in time. Fenstad was standing in Maddie's doorway.

Meg looked at his snarling face, and gave up. She was done. Her leg hurt too much. She was all alone. If only David was here to help her. She kept crying.

Fenstad bent down, and Meg didn't bother, this time, to fight. He lifted her into his arms. His face was still as wax. She was bawling. She didn't try to explain: *You tied us up, and I was just trying to get away. You see now how I needed to do that, don't you?*

He carried her to their bedroom. She was inconsolable. When he lay her down, her ankle twisted. She yelped in pain, and then continued crying. "Please," she said. "Oh, please. Just stop."

He left the room, and she kept bawling. She could hardly catch her breath. When he returned he was carrying the Ginsu knife she'd ordered by phone as a practical joke. *You can cut cans with it!*

"Don't!" she cried as he brought it down against her skin and began to cut. The cast came apart. Her leg was swollen and red. She couldn't see her ankle. Only puffy, purple skin. His hand was on her shoulder, and she cried a little less. Then he pulled hard on her leg. One swift motion. It cracked. She saw stars swimming across the room. Then she fainted.

When she woke up, her leg was in a splint made from furniture legs, he'd somehow found the plaster to set a new cast, and he was now dabbing her face with cold water. She started crying again. The feeling of loss preceded recollection. Then she remembered. "Maddie's sick," she said.

He didn't answer. He bent down on the nightstand, and snorted white power. "OxyContin, crushed. Takes the edge off," he said. "Maddie says I'm not her father. She told me Graham Nero."

Meg swallowed. "Fenstad. It's not possible."

He nodded, but she could tell he wasn't convinced. At this point she wasn't sure she cared.

"They're in the woods, I think. Enrique and all the others. That's what Maddie says. We could start a fire. Start with the woods then go from house to house and burn them."

He shook his head. "We need to wait this out. We'll keep her tied to the bed until there's a cure. You, too."

"I'm not infected."

He shrugged. There was white shit all over his nose. In less than a week he'd gone from perfect husband with a cold streak to wife-beating-drug-addicted lunatic. Either way, her stomach rumbled, and could no longer be ignored. "Could you take me downstairs? I haven't eaten in more than a day."

He eyed her suspiciously. "I think you've got the advantage, here, Fen." He picked her up and walked her through the hall. His movements were stiff, and without emotion, but she thought she might still be able to get through to him. He'd fixed her ankle, after all.

When they got down the stairs, she saw what he'd done to the house. It was torn to bits. The furniture was in splinters. The legs were ripped from all the tables and chairs. He'd hammered boards against all the first-floor windows, so that it was dark even on this fine, sunny day.

"You had a real party," she said.

He didn't say anything, but since there were no chairs on which to sit, he placed her on the kitchen counter. "If you heat up the stuffed peppers in the Tupperware we can eat," she said. He thought about it for a second or two, and then dutifully stuck the leftovers in the microwave.

"So what do you think? That I'm trying to kill you? Is that it? That my secret lover is that asshole Graham Nero?"

He didn't answer.

"I'm not trying to kill you. For starters, you're our only way out of here. Also, before you broke my ankle, I was pretty sure I loved you."

"Somebody broke in while I was gone. Was it Nero?"

The microwave beeped. His eyes were glazed, and he looked at it for a while like he'd forgotten what he was doing. "Get two forks. We'll share." He got the forks, and carried the peppers to the counter.

They both began eating, ravenously. There were four peppers, and neither stopped until the first two were gone. The food felt good in her stomach. It threaded through her blood like a drug. Everything was easier now. Everything was slightly more possible.

"Thank you," she said.

He nodded. "Needed something. Salt."

She looked at him for a few seconds. Then she started laughing. She wasn't sure where it came from, and it certainly wasn't happy laughing. "You're kidding me," she said.

He smiled. Then he held her hips. A tear ran down his cheek. She rubbed it away, still laughing, and then he chuckled, too. "It did need salt," he said. That made her laugh harder. He lifted her hands to kiss them, and saw that her fingers were still engorged to twice their size from where he'd bound her. He turned them in his hands and sighed. She wasn't laughing anymore.

"I'm not well," he said.

She nodded. "Yeah."

His voice was sandy. "I love you so much, Meg." He hadn't told her this for more than ten years, so she was surprised that it came now.

"Well. If you don't hit me, I love you, too."

"I can't go into the woods. I can't kill another one. Maybe you're right, and it'll help Maddie, but I can't do it. The things I saw in the hospital . . . a man shouldn't have to see that."

She nodded, and decided not to tell him about Albert. He couldn't handle it. "But they're coming for us. What should we do?"

He shook his head. "Meg, I can't."

"We'll sleep on it. We'll eat something. If we get through the night, we'll talk about it in the morning."

His eyes were watery. "I'm afraid for you. You should go. I'll stay with Maddie. You'll get help for us when you can."

She sighed. "You're forgetting something. If we have to walk I'll need you. Besides, I'll never leave either of you. You know that."

He looked down at his feet. "Yes," he said. "We'll stay together." He held her hands in the empty, broken room. It was mid-afternoon. They had the luck of light for a few more hours, but with the boards over the windows they couldn't see the sun. "They'll come soon," he said.

"We'll be ready," she answered, while up the stairs Maddie began to laugh.

FORTY-FOUR
Separation

By the time the sun had fallen below the horizon, they'd doubled in number, and her emissaries were on their way to taking over both coasts. Lois Larkin stood. They surrounded her. They were one now. A single mind. They'd grown stronger inside her, and now she knew everything. She looked for the one who'd betrayed them. In their mind's eye they saw him cowering in his apartment, drinking fermented yeast.

They raced there on four legs so fast that the wind slashed her skin like a whip. She burst through his door. "Please," he begged. It was a word she'd heard a million times in a thousand languages before.

He thought they would kill him, but the thing formerly known as Lois Larkin had a better idea. It would pain him more, though he didn't know it. There is no punishment greater than being separated from the one you love. She released him.

The virus inside him withered. It emptied out from his eyes like tears. Ended the battle inside him. Instantly his teeth fell out one by one. The scar along his stomach opened and began to bleed. He wept, and then cowered, too weak to speak. They left him there, to slurp his bread pudding, and die a slow death all alone.

Then they went in search of the last survivors of Corpus Christi's plague.

FORTY-FIVE
King Solomon's Dilemma

Enrique Vargas shoved his hands through the opening in Madeline Wintrob's window and broke off the nightstand holding it shut. He stepped inside. His boots were muddy from the woods, and his long hair was beginning to fall out. He stalked from the window to the bed, where Maddie had been bound and gagged. A red bandana stretched across her face like a smile. He touched her neck with his fingers, in a gesture that to Meg seemed almost delicate. Maddie was kicking and jerking, which he probably mistook for fear. It was a warning. Fenstad came out from behind him and stabbed the boy in the back with the Ginsu knife.

The sound was wet. Meg flinched. She wasn't strong enough to use a knife, so he'd given her a hammer that still had the remnants of someone else's gore. Her chair was set up behind the bed because she could not stand. She was a liability here, more likely to hurt than help, but Fenstad needed her. Without her, he'd lose his direction.

Enrique didn't fall. The knife was a few inches off the mark, and hadn't gotten his heart. He bent down and tore the sheets that bound Maddie's arms.

Meg got up. She didn't move fast. She limped. Maddie's

bandana came loose. She sat up and took Enrique's hand. They didn't leave. They remained in the room, and they looked hungry. That's when Meg knew for sure that her daughter was gone. She tried to scream, but nothing came out. The children approached.

They went after Fenstad first, and Meg could do nothing to stop them. Enrique wrestled Fenstad to the floor. Fenstad stabbed him again in the chest. The boy was still for a moment. He looked like a boy again. Meg didn't like to see that. She didn't like to see his pretty brown eyes. Weren't they all just lovely, the way their skin shone like the moon? She was going a little mad, too.

Then Fenstad went after Maddie. Held her down while she snapped her teeth at his fingers. "Stop. Let her go!" Meg said, but he didn't.

She limped closer. "*Stop!*" she called again, while at the window, even more of them began to climb up the trellis. Fenstad's face was as still as wax. He was gone again, and there wasn't time to get him back. If this thing had happened slowly, if they'd had a month, or even a week to digest the end of the world, she knew he would have returned to her, stronger than ever. He was a better man than even he realized, and she loved him more than she'd ever guessed.

But there was no time.

Meg limped closer, hammer in hand. Fenstad's knife inched closer to Maddie's neck. Meg bent down between them and looked from one love to the next. She did her duty, even though she didn't want to. She swung the hammer into his head. He reeled, and spasmed. The blood didn't flow at first. He smiled drunkenly at her, like he'd forgotten everything that had happened, and they were back at that bar on Boylston Street, where he was about to confess that he'd always been a sucker for brunettes. But then his foot gave, and he spun in a half circle. She saw the blood gushing down his back, and knew that the blow she'd dealt him was fatal.

He was still smiling when he fell, and even before he hit the ground, she knew she'd made a mistake.

She inched back, and Maddie got up from the floor. The bodies of the men lay on the ground. More pale hands reached through the window. The infected, looking for a meal. She dropped the hammer. She didn't want it anymore. Didn't care anymore. Maddie flew at her. She closed her eyes. *Okay*, she thought. *Get it over with*. And then, *At least I'll always be a part of her this way*.

Maddie ran her hand down the length of Meg's arm, and then her injured leg. Her green eyes had turned black. Then she leaned in close, and licked Meg's cheek.

"This one is mine," Maddie called out.

The thing formerly known as Lois Larkin watched from the Victorian's broken window. She didn't answer; her mouth was no longer shaped so that it could make words. Something transpired between then. Meg could feel it in the air, like static during an electrical storm. "This one is mine," Maddie repeated.

Lois climbed down the trellis. The rest, including Maddie, followed. They raced through the street, and the town, and across Maine, and New England, all the way to the Pacific Ocean, and beyond. They went howling into the night.

And there Meg Wintrob stood, the last living woman in Corpus Christi.

FORTY-SIX
Luck and Divinity

On his way to Bedford, Danny saw a woman walking slowly, with her shoulders slumped. If he wasn't so lonely, he probably would have been more cautious. Instead he stopped and rolled down his window. The woman looked at him. She didn't say anything. She didn't smile. He could tell she wasn't sick.

"I'm leaving right now. Do you want to come?" he asked.

She hesitated and looked in the backseat, and then in the front. Then at him. She held his gaze for a long while. "Where?"

"I don't know. Just out."

"My kids are dead," she told him. Then she held up her slender hands like they were killing things. Her long fingernails were painted red.

"I murdered my brother," he said, and once he said it, he started crying. "I'm alone now. I have no one."

The passenger side was dented, so she walked over to the driver's side and opened the door. He scooted over. "I'm not old enough to drive," he said.

She sat down. Then she reached over and turned off the radio, which had been set to static on high volume.

Ahead of them were the woods, and then the highway. Behind them was Corpus Christi.

She was so quiet that he thought she might be a ghost. He wiped his eyes and looked at her. *Please touch me*, he wanted to say, but he was afraid.

She put her foot on the gas and they began to drive. He felt her eyes on him. Hard things, without much compassion. But thank God they were blue. "We'll take care of each other," she said.

He was so grateful that he was struck mute.

Together they drove to the highway ramp in Bedford, which the border guards had abandoned. When they hit New Hampshire, they saw the stopped traffic and empty cars, so they pulled onto the shoulder, and off-roaded through small towns until they picked up Route 88, and headed west. By luck or divinity, they drove through the day, and long into the night, and no one stopped them.

EPILOGUE

It's been two months now, and I wait for news. The
streets are empty during the day, save for Tim Carroll, who has gone mad, and still wanders Corpus
Christi, searching for all those who have gone missing.

My candles are almost run out. I've had time to think
about the week that ended the world. More time than
anyone should. I miss my husband. I miss my daughter,
too. My leg is nearly healed, but the bone knit wrong,
and I walk with a limp. To keep the savages from de-
vouring his remains, I stored my husband in the cold
cellar. It awaits a proper funeral.

I've got a radio that receives frequencies from all over
the country, and there are still some cities standing in
the Midwest. But with this leg I am trapped. There is no
food left, not even sacks of flour or sugar on the shelves
of grocery stores. I've bound all the second-story windows with wooden planks. At night I hear them, but
they never come in. The ones who survived the change
don't look human anymore. Perhaps Maddie is protecting me. She does not travel with the rest at night, and I
often see her alone, at the door. I want to let her in.

I think about Canada. This virus can't last forever.
But there is David in California, and I imagine that he

is driving cross-country to find us. He is on his way home. I wait for him.

Brothers, sisters, mothers, fathers. We lose more with each passing day. It cannot last forever. This thing that has plagued this country, this bloody civil war, must end.

But for now I wait, and light my candles, and use the days to scavenge food. I am so hungry that my fingernails are full of holes, and my hair is falling out. My husband's body is preserved in the cellar. I think about that, too.